Thin Line

Between

Book One of the Wandjina Quartet

Thin Line

Between

Book One of the Wandjina Quartet

M.A.C. Petty

Cold Spring Press

Cold Spring Press

P.O. Box 284, Cold Spring Harbor, NY 11724
E-mail: Jopenroad@aol.com

ACKNOWLEDGMENTS

Many thanks to my editor, Jonathan Stein of Cold Spring Press, for continuing encouragement and guidance, peppered with common sense and a dash of good humor when needed most.

Thanks also to Laura Young and Lynn Holschuh for editorial advice and copyediting expertise, and to Sandra Coffey for meticulously proofreading the final manuscript. Special thanks to April Petty, Lissa Griffin, and Cathy Ekblad for their valuable comments and suggestions as the manuscript went through its varying incarnations.

And last, but of course not least, thanks to my husband Bill for putting up with yet another manuscript in the works. Without him I could never have gotten those fungi sorted properly.

As a work of fiction, the characters and events of this story are my invention, so obviously any similarity to persons living or dead is coincidental.

For Bill and April
Who served as inspiration for most of the characters in this book in one
way or another, even the weird ones. Okay, especially those.

NOVEMBER

CHAPTER 1

THE CREATURE licked its thin lips. The brat was lagging behind, not keeping up with the tour group. Its parents were ignoring it, hanging on every word the guide fed them and trying to take their tourist photos of the shadowy figures painted across the rock face. In moments they would be into the deeper fissure that formed the cave shelter and out of sight.

The boy was poking around the rocks, looking for whatever. Just poking. The creature flattened its flaccid bag of a belly against a shallow overhang and watched its prey. It hadn't eaten in so long, and it was famished. Vaguely man-shaped and twice as tall, but reed-thin, it was a darker smear among the shadows that dappled the escarpment. The child came closer, reaching for a cave-roach with a fat hand that made the creature drool; long strings of its saliva dropped with a hiss and bit into the eons-old sandstone. A shiver rippled over its coarse black hide as it shifted into a frilled desert lizard no bigger than a hamster.

It popped its head up over the ledge and looked the boy full in the face. Cocking its head, it transfixed him with its eyes, red pinpoints in the half-dark.

"Lizard!" the boy yelped and made a lunge for it.

The shape-shifter hopped just out of reach behind a dip in the ledge, and the boy clambered after it. Its tongue darted out, tasted the dry air mixed with the scent of human sweat, and slid back between needle-sharp teeth. It was so hungry.

The boy scrambled up onto the ledge, where dark stick figures danced on the wall just beyond his head. Sitting still as death, except for the trembling tip of its tail, the lizard waited. The boy reached out to grab, and in a flash the kid was on his back with the creature's horny taloned foot across his gullet to stifle any screaming and its long fingers groping for his midsection.

In one swift stroke a talon slit him from neck to navel as his startled eyes went milky. The creature was just about to hook its claws into the soft blubbery belly and draw out the entrails when it felt a thump inside its chest – a pull and a reverberation like a bowstring stretched and released.

"NO!" it squealed, drool hissing onto the boy's blood-soaked T-shirt. It could feel the pull, relentless, unavoidable. The black one was trying again, trying to make the crossing, and the creature had no choice but to go with him. Resisting, it hissed and bared its teeth. It was famished, just one taste before it was yanked away from its meal ... the cave walls dimmed and it felt the pull like a fist clamped around its heart.

"Nononono ...." It dropped the body and winked out of the landscape.

The dark was musty, with hidden spiders and tiny brown roaches lurking in crannies of the toy box. The creature spat at them and they vanished in a hurry. It sat in the closet for some time, shivering in rage at its interrupted meal. Nothing to do now but torment the girl in the bedroom because it wasn't allowed to eat her. Blast the black one for linking them in the first place. That kind of thing wasn't supposed to happen, and no one, not even the big shots, understood fully how it had happened. But there it was – they were both trapped. The black one was still scheming, trying to find a solution, for all the good it would do him. But something was up, the bristles along the shape-shifter's back told it. The air around this wretched child was charged lately, something was coming, eyes were watching, noses were sniffing. It could be sensed around the mother too, but the scent trail was not as pungent. Strange that the child should be a closer link than the mother. The creature could see that the air around the girl fairly crackled when she was sleeping, which only made it slobber onto the carpet of the closet. She would taste so good once it was allowed to have her. Shivering with pleasure, it assumed the shape of a small dog and tiptoed out into the darkened bedroom.

Sitting down in the middle of the carpet, it scratched absently at its fleas. The girl moaned in her sleep and rolled over, but did not wake up. The creature waited, sniffing the air in the room and looking around at the human-girl things that littered the floor of the bedroom. Books, stuffed animals, stacks of CDs, discarded clothes. Inhaling the scent of her socks and underwear, it felt saliva pool around its tongue. It toyed with the idea of leaning over her and whispering into her ear with her mother's voice, telling her to wake up. The potential image of her terrified sleep-fogged face when she opened her eyes was enough to send it into a shuddering, salivating ripple of delight and need.

9

It shrugged off the dog shape and straightened up to its full height, just grazing the ceiling. A paper-thin shadow, it slipped out of the room and down the hall to the mother's room. She was the one it should have been more concerned with, since it was she on whom the banished one's hopes were pinned. Entering her room, it crept up onto the edge of the bed and hovered, a darker smudge against the gloom. The woman slept deeply, dreamfree, a solitary figure in the large bed. She would have been easy to take if it'd wanted to, but she was not its prey. Humans were only good for eating, but it much preferred children. It would take an occasional adult if one strayed across its path, but that was not its preference. And there was that matter of the black one's prohibition against eating either of them, yet. It thought about calling to her in her daughter's voice, but the torment value was not as good. It went back down the hall.

Margaret jerked in her sleep and then sat up.

"I know you're there," she whispered.

The dog-thing bared its teeth in an amiable grin and generated a small luminescence around its body, just enough to let her see it. It could hear her intake of breath, and its own hungry heart beat faster.

"What do you want?" she whispered again.

"Just checking on you," it said in her mother's voice. It was good at mimicry, which was how it usually lured its prey. The boy in the cave had been almost too easy ... it hadn't even had to call him. Growling deep in its throat, it fumed at the memory of the wasted food.

"Stop using my mother's voice. Can anybody else see you besides me?" the girl was asking.

"Depends. Why don't you call your mother and find out?" They'd played this cat and mouse, or dog 'n rat, game countless times, and both knew that if she called, the creature would just disappear.

"I tried, but she didn't wake up. Why can I see you?"

"Hmm. Because I want you to?" Round button eyes blinked, bright against the shadows. The creature darted a red tongue over its lips.

"Am I still asleep? I know you're not a real dog. Maybe you're an astral."

"An *astral*," it said, mimicking her voice. "Foolish human. I should bite you for such stupidity." Its tail swished against the carpet, petulant, impatient.

The creature became a small red lizard, caked in mud. It skittered over to the edge of the bed, and the girl pulled her feet away, rubbing her eyes and staring into the dark.

"That's right," it said. "You're still asleep and I'm just a repeating nightmare." It chuckled wetly.

The spot where it crouched became marginally brighter as it took a step forward, eyes glittering and head cocked. Its thin tongue darted out, tasting the sweet scent of fear rolling off the girl like perfume from a night-blooming datura.

"This is intolerable," it growled from the back of its throat. "I could be anywhere, doing something useful like finding a real meal, but instead I'm stuck here."

Suddenly it was on her bed, pointy teeth clamped onto her ankle. Margaret shrieked. And woke up.

Alice lifted her head. Her daughter's cry lingered on the edge of waking ... there, but not there. She waited, tense and listening, as her eyes adjusted to the darkness. The house was quiet and still.

"Mom?"

This time she heard it clearly and got out of bed.

"Coming," she called, fumbling for her bathrobe. Alice rubbed her hands over her face and yawned. Pulling the robe tightly over her chest against the pre-dawn chill, she went down to her daughter's room at the end of the hall. Margaret was hunched up in bed with the covers pulled to her chin. Alice sat down beside her.

"Another bad dream?"

The girl nodded. "Can I come get in your bed?"

"How about if I just sit with you awhile, until it gets light?"

Alice leaned against the headboard, settling herself into the pillows and cradling Margaret's head in her lap. She yawned again, but knew she probably wouldn't go back to sleep. Even as a toddler, Margaret had endured cycles of frightening dreams, but now that she was approaching her teens, they seemed worse and more frequent. Alice wondered if it was the hormone shift.

She couldn't remember if she'd been like that herself at that age. She decided not, and wondered why Margaret seemed so susceptible to nightmares. They'd talked about it, and she'd tried to assure her daughter that she would grow out of it, but tonight's recurrence was making that hard to believe.

In the dark, red eyes watched, and waited.

CHAPTER 2

THUNDERING RAIN and men's voices filled the parking bay in a multilevel frog chorus set against low throbbings of diesel engines at idle. The open maws of two semis were backed up to the edge of the loading dock, their ramps like steel tongues reaching down to the concrete floor. Inside the trucks, monumental rectangular forms swathed in padded covers were tied with heavy cord to hooks along the sides of the trailers, waiting to be moved out of the trucks and upstairs into the pillared main gallery of the Hardison Museum's arts wing.

Even in the ground floor hallway, Alice could feel the subsonic rumble of the trucks. She pushed open one side of the double steel doors leading to the dock and was assaulted by the noise of the trucks and the rain.

She had driven to work under the lowering cloudbank, and now it had turned nimbus, with waterfalls cascading off the roof onto the noses of the trucks.

"Alice!" Shelton waved to her from the far end of the dock, tall among the shorter, stouter men who clustered around him with paper-stuffed clipboards and other transfer-of-goods paraphernalia. Cigarette smoke hung around their heads in a baleful cloud. Gulping her last breath of fresh air, she joined them in the smokers' corner of the dock. Museum security guards waited by the entrance and in the street below, hunched in their rain slickers.

"Tom, this is—"

"Stand clear!"

Shelton's attempted introduction hung fire as they backed away at the mover's shout, and the first panel crate, its outer padding removed, rumbled toward the downward ramp. The loading crew hauled at an overhead iron hook and crane and positioned them over the crate. Sitting on top of the trailer, another mover grabbed the hook and slipped it through rings clamped to the top of the crate. For heartstopping moments, the container swung out of the truck and hung, swaying, over the museum crew scuttling to maneuver a large four-wheeled dolly into place beneath it.

"How many panels per crate?" she heard Shelton ask one of the shippers.

The man consulted his clipboard. "One to a box. We were gonna roll 'em down the ramp, but decided not to ... safer this way."

Alice watched as the plywood packing crate, easily ten feet high and nearly twice as long, was lowered onto the dolly with precision and the hook and cables removed. Steadying the unwieldy crate from both sides, the museum's receiving crew pushed and pulled the load into the freight elevator that would take them up to the gallery's receiving area. The exhibit design technicians had already installed the necessary apparatus for hanging the panels along the walls, and as soon as Vera, the museum's registrar, verified the catalog IDs and recorded the condition of the murals, they would be ready to put in place.

Loud scrapings and grindings began afresh as the truckers jostled another crate to the trailer's edge to be ready when the dolly crew returned. From where Alice was standing, there looked to be five more in the truck.

Alice's pulse quickened at the sight of the crates concealing larger-than-life photographic images of Australia's Aboriginal cultural heritage. She tried to imagine what those paintings and carvings must have looked like to the explorers and archaeologists who first discovered them on cliff faces in the narrow gorges and shallow caves that hadn't seen torchlight for hundreds or even thousands of years. These pictures told of a mythological event known as the Dreamtime, long before earth with its animals and people existed, in which supernatural beings roved through the formless landscape, sculpting matter from their whims and desires. After these ancestral beings completed their Dreamtime activities, some entered a sky home in the Milky Way, and others became the very bones of the earth, their powers made accessible to human men and women, the ancient Aborigines of Australia, through images incised and painted on rock or bark. Wandjinas, the spirit caretakers of life through the cycles of weather, figured prominently in the exhibit design.

Shelton touched Alice's arm. "Let's go upstairs. I want to be sure it gets delivered to the gallery floor with no problems."

She hurried to catch up with him, his long strides already taking him across the cargo bay and through the steel double doors. No, she wouldn't want to miss the sight of the first one out of the crate. She'd seen the slides and small prints of each panel supplied by the exhibit sponsors as well as the previous museum housing the show, but that knowledge would be nothing compared to the real thing. Even knowing the dimensions beforehand, she hadn't fully appreciated the size of the photomural panels. Stepping out of the elevator onto the museum's main floor, Alice followed Shelton through a side door to the freight entrance and watched, overwhelmed, as the immense crate rumbled at the speed of a space shuttle flatbed out of the service elevator, barely clearing the entryway at the back of the gallery receiving room. The exhibit's construction lab was two floors down in the basement where carpentry, welding, sanding, painting, framing, and modeling took place, but each of the four large gallery rooms had its own antechamber for final assembly work as well as repair and temporary storage.

She stood quietly in a corner, ignoring the lab photographer bouncing around in front of her, clicking away, documenting the arrival of the famous show from New York, Chicago, London, and Sydney.

"Excited?" Vera approached, clipboard in hand. No taller than five feet, Vera was a mannish woman who dressed consistently in oxford-cloth shirts, tailored blazers, dark slacks, and penny loafers. She wore her graying brown hair in a tight cap of curls that made Alice think of the fur on a poodle. Vera had been with the museum since its beginning, working her way up from volunteer to registrar, and now she reigned supreme over the inventory process.

Alice smiled and nodded. "A little nervous." She had supervised exhibit installations before, but never on an international scale such as this, so that every step in the process had to be approached with flexibility and an unsettling sense of adventure. It was also her first exhibit under her new title of Curator of Fine and Decorative Arts.

"Once we get this business in place, we'll never want to take it down," Shelton said, joining them.

She smiled, she hoped, with confidence and nodded again. A back wheel of the dolly appeared to be stuck at a right angle from the others, and she watched with concern as one of the lab guys helping the movers reached down to straighten it out.

She let her breath out and tried to relax, although her pulse was racing. "I can't wait to see them all in place and properly lighted. It'll be incredible, won't it?"

"Possibly the biggest draw we've ever—" Shelton's sentence hung fire, cut short by an agonized shriek.

Time stopped for the length of a heartbeat; then suddenly people were shouting and the room seethed to life as movers and museum staff, released from the paralysis of the scream, swarmed around the panel crate.

"Holy shit!" Alice heard someone shout as she looked in astonishment at the edge of the dolly – its rear wheel had collapsed beneath the weight of the plywood crate and crushed the hand of Lewis, a part-time lab assistant. He lay on his back, pale and moaning, his face slick with tears and sweat. Alice realized, too, that a dark stain was slowly spreading around the corner of the panel where it met the floor; terrible, but she couldn't stop looking.

Even as she stared, shocked, the crate came unbolted and one side fell out past the steel rails of the dolly, crashing with a splintering sound to the floor. Revealed in all its high-resolution panoramic detail was a ten-foot-high image with the most intimidating face she'd ever seen. The ghastly white head was shaped somewhat like a light bulb, with long bulbous rods or spikes emanating in a corona around the skull. The eyes were wide and elongated, ringed with fringes and slashed down the middle by a nose not unlike that of a proboscis monkey. There was no mouth. Ranging behind the figure, smaller ghostly white forms leaned to the right and left, as if peering around its shoulders at the foolish mortals who had just allowed this creature to see the light of day. It was as if the figure had suddenly acquired mass and weight, and had kicked itself free of its wooden encasement. Her hand went to her lips in cold panic.

The hollow round centers of its eyes were staring right at her, through her, if that were possible, making a cold little knotted-up place just about chest level ... where ... her breath was coming in shallow gulps, her lungs refusing to expand. Her chest was frozen, her ribs made of ice, as if she had suddenly been ejected into deep space far beyond any sun. This couldn't be real, but it *felt* real.

Everyone was shouting at once. Vera's clipboard fell to the floor, and Shelton had his cell phone out, barking orders to the dock crew.

"Hold the rest downstairs – no! Don't send anything else up!" He shook her roughly by the elbow. "Call 911. Get the life-flight over here, now!"

He pushed her toward the gallery entrance. Where was security? Blinking, she raced for the nearest phone – Faye's, in the museum shop just outside the door – as the widening red pool inched its way toward the marble floor of the gallery. An oddly disconnected part of her brain was methodically wondering what cleaning solution would remove bloodstains from matched Georgian marble tiles bought at great cost from some quarry in Italy. The other thought that bounced around in her mind was this: the panels were huge and unwieldy, but should not have been heavy enough to blow out the wheels of the dolly and nearly sever a man's hand. She also realized that her teeth were chattering.

Trembling, Alice managed the call with Faye's help and then sat shivering on the stool behind the cash register. Faye stared in silence out the shop's glass doors toward the gallery entrance, and then cleared her throat.

"Want me to go look?"

Alice shook her head and tried to take a normal breath, but her chest was still too tight. A high keening, wailing sound began to wind its way through the open doors and into the museum lobby, assaulting her ears and her mind with white waves of noise. What inhuman beast made such a sound?

"There's the siren," said Faye, recognizing the city hospital's helicopter Klaxon. "Didn't take 'em long. That's lucky."

Alice was rubbing her temples. "You won't believe this . . . I actually thought some creature was making that noise."

Faye pursed her lips and made a sound somewhere between curiosity and disbelief. "You're spooked. I can understand. But blood is just blood, they'll fix him up."

"I don't know, you didn't see ... I thought—" She shut her mouth. There was no way to describe what she had seen and felt. A bad omen for certain. The exhibit was starting out under the pall of a freak accident, possibly a fatal one if too much blood had been lost – and it had all been captured on film. Alice was thankful they hadn't invited the press and media people in to witness the arrival. But of course it was going to be in the news anyway. Too many witnesses, plus the hospital emergency reports. Her head was swimming.

"You look like you need a barf bag," said Faye. "Maybe you should go home." Alice was instantly reminded that she had a sick child at home recovering from the previous night's migraine. She was tempted.

"I wish I could, but I can't, not with all hell breaking loose in there," she said, standing up. "I'm the curator and I'm responsible for that exhibit, whether it tries to kill somebody or not. I'm okay now." It was a lie, but saying so almost made it true, and she felt better. A bit.

"Well, come back if you need a break."

"You know I will."

Faye half-smiled and sat down behind the counter, propping her elbows on its glass surface and cradling her face in her long hands. A graceful, poetic gesture without even trying. Envying Faye's effortless beauty was an old pastime, but Alice couldn't afford it at the moment. No amount of visualizing and wishful thinking was going to undo the unbelievable turn this morning had taken. Shaken, she walked back to the gallery.

By now Lewis and the paramedics were gone, and one of the lab janitors was swabbing pinkish soapy water around where the dolly had stood. The photomural panel hung suspended from the vaulted ceiling, its blind stare two-dimensional and photographic. Alice looked it over cautiously, but felt nothing unusual; it was just an oversized picture like any other hanging mundanely under its diffused track lighting.

She saw Shelton, Vera, and Jessie, the conservation lab director, with several other museum staffers conferring beside the entrance to the loading corridor. Their lowered heads and hands-in-pockets slouches gave no clues that she could read, so she approached, deliberately neutral. The heads came up.

"Is Lewis all right?" she asked.

"He's alive," said Jessie.

"Probably going to lose the hand," said Shelton evenly.

"That's horrible. But what happened? It looked like the wheel axle broke or something. Was it that heavy?"

The older man frowned. "It couldn't have been. We had the weights from the shipping invoice. This shouldn't have happened." His voice was flat, unreadable. "It's going to be bad press."

"Maybe not," said Jessie. "You know how morbid curiosity works – people will be repulsed and yet want to see the very spot where it happened. We could have overflow crowds for the opening."

"I hope not." Shelton was tight-lipped. Alice had seen him look like that only on very rare occasions, like the time the Rudiger Foundation reneged on its promise of a million and a half to refurbish the observatory in the museum's cupola. "Well, I'm sure we all have work to do. I'll see you in the planning meeting tomorrow morning." He touched Alice on the shoulder. "I'm counting on you – do what you can in here, and let's get this installation back on track."

In four strides he passed the spot where Lewis had been pinned beneath the staring image of the Wandjina and headed in long purposeful lopes across the gallery and out to the elevators in the lobby. Even in distress he seemed calm and knowledgeable, the way heads of state ought to look.

It was no wonder Shelton MacBeth had been museum director for over fifteen years.

Alice turned back to the others, but couldn't think of anything to say. Jessie smiled and shrugged. The situation was tense, but they would all weather it.

An hour later, sitting at her desk with its wide orderly expanse of neatly stacked things to do, things to file, things to put off until later, Alice tried to get her thoughts back in gear. She needed to call the curator in Tucson about shipping the Karl Bodmer collection of Old West paintings. It was a small but popular exhibit loaned to the museum, and she intended to do it right. A couple of private patrons had expressed interest in adding one or more of the pieces to the Hardison's permanent fine arts collection. All those things people typically said of her – creative, organized, diplomatic – Alice now found herself needing in full measure, but her concentration had flown away in the chopper with Lewis and his nearly severed hand. Jesus H. Buddha. She shut her eyes.

Sitting silently, she banished the image of Lewis from her mind. Then she tried to see as clearly as possible the Dreamtime exhibit properly presented, with crowds of appreciative visitors flowing past the photomurals on the walls and the displays of modern Aboriginal art scattered about the center of the room. Alice realized she was holding her breath again – she deliberately leaned back in the chair and let her muscles go slack. She was giving a lot to the museum and making progress in her job, but it was hard. Only now was she beginning to appreciate what it could take out of her. She took a deep breath and thought about giving Margaret a call.

The phone on her desk rang, its intrusion sending tiny shock waves over her skin. She caught it before the next ring.

"We need to talk about the exhibit." Shelton's anxious voice over the receiver sent another adrenalin surge.

"I'll be right there," she said.

"No, tomorrow. I've got commitments for the rest of today, but how early can you get here in the morning? I know it's a long drive for you, but I'd like to talk over the situation as soon as possible."

"I can be here by seven."

"Seven it is. Thanks, Alice, I appreciate it."

Hanging up, Alice let her breath out. What was supposed to be her moment of glory was stacking up to be the exhibit from hell.

The exhibit itself was a marvelous thing, this morning's shock notwithstanding. It came in two parts – half a dozen ceiling-high photomurals of high-resolution images, valued at thousands of dollars each, reproducing in life-sized detail the photographer's record of rock paintings from Australia's Aboriginal past, plus a large collection of modern paintings on board and canvas, wood sculptures, and elaborately decorated boomerangs, didjeridus, and ceremonial shields from nearly a dozen of the country's most important Aboriginal artists. The whole thing represented a significant investment for the museum. She knew Shelton had taken a risk in convincing the museum board of directors to go after it, and they couldn't afford bad press to ruin its run. It was an important part of Shelton's mission to establish the Hardison as a small but highly prestigious natural history museum and art gallery. She was starting to sweat.

The exhibit covered a number of major rock art sites from across the northern part of the Australian continent and on down to the south. From the Kimberleys, Kakadu National Park in Arnhem Land, Cape York sites, to Carnarvon Gorge in south-central Queensland and more, it covered an astonishing gallery of animals and ancestor spirits. Examples of several distinctive styles of rock painting were included, in particular the graceful Bradshaws and ghostly Wandjinas, stick figure Mimis, and startling x-ray-style images both old and new. The discoveries had been written about and photographed for a number of years, and now it was an eye-popping museum exhibit, especially when combined with the vibrant work of modern Aboriginal artists.

As arts curator, Alice had read all about it. She knew that the source for one of the best panels in the exhibit was a site on the Gibb River in the Kimberly District. It was these very Wandjina images that had made their untimely and frightening exit from their packing crate barely an hour ago. Their vivid alien presence was disturbing to modern eyes, their mythology largely unknown and incomprehensible to all but those who remained connected to it. Modern Aboriginal peoples believed the images to have been produced by beings who wandered the earth during the mythical Dreamtime before men and women were created. If the scholarly interpretations she'd read were accurate, the images represented momentous events and sites sacred to those once-powerful spirits. Many sites were considered taboo and highly dangerous to the uninitiated, and access to them was restricted or forbidden. But of the public sites, many astonishing friezes and groupings were there for all to see.

One detail of the rock art discoveries intrigued her especially: many of the paintings had been maintained and periodically retouched over the centuries, leading archaeologists to understand that historical Aborigines kept a ritualistic, cultural connection with the ancient mythographers. Unlike the Western concept of art as artifact, Aboriginals approached their carvings, drawings, and paintings as an important process rather than an end in itself. In fact, there was evidence that new rock art continued to be produced long after those older Stone Age images had sunk into their sandstone canvases. These artifacts had been the dream finds of archaeologists and explorers like Joseph Bradshaw in the late 1800s; more were still being discovered in remote caves and canyons, but who knew how many hidden fissures in the cliffs and outcrops across the sunburned land held mysteries yet to be revealed?

Modern Aboriginal artists benefited from the art world's interest, now that images of the ancient Dreamtime mythology had become highly collectible. Some artists were stunningly successful, and several of those names were represented in the exhibit. She wondered if her father, a white man who'd done paintings in the Aboriginal style and had died in Australia before she was born, would have become famous if he'd lived long enough. It was common knowledge at the museum that she'd been looking forward to this exhibit for more than just professional reasons.

She picked up the phone and punched in her home number. Margaret had turned twelve a few months ago and insisted she didn't need babysitters anymore, but Alice still felt nervous when she was home alone. After a dozen rings, she heard Margaret's sleep-drugged voice.

"Yeah ... ?"

"Sorry, Munch, I didn't mean to wake you up."

"Mm. 's okay."

"Is everything all right? How're you feeling now?" She knew from experience that Margaret was groggy and somewhat disoriented the day after a migraine.

"Not bad. What are we having for supper? We're starving, me and Figaro."

Alice relaxed. That was what she wanted to hear.

"Whatever you want; I'll stop by the grocery store on the way home."

Maybe she would treat herself as well with a carton of ice cream ... chocolate mint or something equally sinful. The way her day had gone, she'd earned it.

CHAPTER 3

SOMEWHERE A gong, or a bell the size of a dumpster, was cracking the air with its brass voice. Its repeated clang was insistent, demanding attention, impossible to ignore or resist. Was she being summoned?

The lizard-dog sat on a rock, flicking its tongue at nothing she could see. It was just tasting the dry air. For fun, or because it knew she found it irritating.

"Maybe I'll feed you to the reef sharks. They're quite large and always hungry." It made a rasping noise that might have been an attempt at laughter.

"Why do you keep hassling me? I don't want this ... I want you to go away." Margaret stood in rust-red sand up to her ankles; it was all she could see straight out to the horizon in any direction, except for the rock outcropping where the pig-lizard sat flicking and flicking. Its tongue made a snapping sound.

"That's really gross. I *hate* that."

"I know." It smiled down at her. It had turned a deep orange with liver-colored spots across its humped back. "Well, what shall we talk about since I'm not allowed to eat you yet?" The spots merged to a darkened crimson flush that turned chocolate brown near its head and down its chest. It looked like it was trying to sprout feathers. A bird-dog, thought Margaret, and laughed out loud.

"I can't stand it when you laugh," it whined. "Such a horrible human sound."

"Good. Maybe you'll leave, then."

"You know, I shouldn't even be bothering with you yet. I have other business that needs doing. But you leave such a wide open scent trail, who could resist?" It was starting to drool. "By all accounts, I should be attached to your mother, but she doesn't see me. Her dreams are just all about humans humping and doing disgusting things to each other – she likes it when that pale one does just what she wants, but it's not always the same male, mind you. I should like to rip them both, when they're joined up like that. But I can't ...." Its voice narrowed to a scratching whine. "And anyway, my specialty is children."

A flush pulsed over its quivering skin, tinting it dark as dried blood.

Margaret turned her back to it and began walking. Behind her, the shape-shifter stood for a moment in its true form, a tall thin man-shape that cast no real shadow on the ruddy sand. Its red-rimmed eyes stared unblinking into the sun.

Margaret was slogging away from it through the drifts of sand. She was suddenly aware that off in the heat haze a structure of some sort was shimmering... a giant sandcastle, with columns maybe, if she could just see it more clearly. Which made no sense at all, but nothing else did either, so she was less disturbed by its presence than by the pig-dog that trotted at her heels. Somehow its webbed feet didn't sink in the sand. Webbed? Was it a dog or a lizard?

The sand began to swirl around Margaret's ankles in eddies and whirlpools, and abruptly became rushing water. She sank like a stone, gulping and retching as her lungs filled with liquid. The gong noise was splitting her head open.

Margaret forced her eyes open and sat up, as the sound resolved itself into the telephone ringing. Dazed and coughing up phlegm, she rolled off the couch, got tangled in the comforter, and tripped over Figaro, who'd been asleep beside her. She made it to the phone in another couple of rings and was relieved to hear her mother's voice. She didn't feel capable of intelligent response, but moved her mouth and hoped the words came out okay.

She was still groggy when she hung up the receiver, but believed that some discussion about food had taken place. Her stomach was growling at the suggestion. She shuffled to the refrigerator and pulled out a bottle of juice that was pushed to the back behind her mother's cans of diet cola. Carbonated sodas were just plain nasty, and she sneered at their very existence.

"Well, cat, I don't know what in shit that dream was all about. I think you put a sleeping spell on me. Every time I lie down and you get on me, I fall asleep. It's all your fault." She nudged Figaro with her toe. He gave her a silent meow, which was part toothy yawn. "Sorry, no smelly wet food you can suck up. We got nothing but dry crunchies. Gotta wait till Mom gets home with the good stuff." Figaro continued to circle her feet, looking hopeful. Margaret filled a glass with juice, cut it with a little tap water, and chugged the whole thing almost in one breath. Revived, she went back to the couch and sat down.

Where could she find out what this creature from her dreamland reminded her of, other than a dog that sometimes was the shape of a pig or sometimes had scales and skink feet? She knew firsthand about skink feet; skinks were everywhere around her house – on the deck, on the porch swing, in the garden. For certain this thing sometimes had skink feet. There were plenty of books of the encyclopedia type around the house, but she didn't think she was likely to find it in any of them. It wasn't a real dog, anyway, and she had no idea what to call it in order to look it up. Then she got an idea.

"C'mon, Fig," she said, getting up and bundling the comforter around her. It wasn't that cold in the house; in fact, the thermometer in the hallway read 71, but she just liked the feeling of having the comforter wrapped around her shoulders and back. She went into the spare bedroom halfway down the hall; it served as Alice's study and on rare occasions a guest room because it contained a day bed. Nik had spent the night in there once, before he'd officially moved into Alice's room. Margaret thought it was funny the way he'd made a show of saying good night and going into the spare room with his backpack. She knew that as soon as all the lights were out he would go in to be with her mom. Which she didn't mind too much; it gave her really good stuff to relay to Judy, her best friend who lived in the same subdivision, several roads to the south. At least Nik and her mom were quiet and spared her the embarrassment of having to listen to them. He was okay. Actually, he was better than okay. He could draw.

Margaret sat down at the computer and logged onto the Internet. First she checked her e-mail messages and saw half a dozen from Judy. It was mainly stuff about CD swapping, spending the night this weekend or the next, and Judy's ongoing struggle with a toxic boy who rode their bus and tormented them both beyond endurance. The last message detailed her trip to the mall with her older sister to buy her first bra. Margaret frowned. Her own chest was so flat she couldn't fill out a bra with the help of all the toilet paper in the state of Florida.

"Time to Google," she said to Figaro, who jumped onto her lap. He head-butted her a few times, and then settled down to lick his fur. She pulled the keyboard close and typed "red dog pig lizard" into the search field, which produced a lot of garbage that she didn't have the energy to sift through. Clearing the search, she sat with her fingers on the keys, thinking.

What would such a creature be called? It never referred to itself as anything, but those blue lizard-faced guys who showed up in her dreams once in a while had called it something. What was it? She racked her brains to remember. The bad thing about the phenobarb tabs was that they turned your brain to mush while they were zapping your migraine pain centers, which meant whole chunks of time were flat-out gone when the effect finally wore off.

Finally she typed "legends lizards dogs desert" and was rewarded with a search result that veered off in a surprisingly new direction. The first entry, sitting there at the top of the list, sent prickles through her scalp. It was quite unexpected, a link that just had not ever crossed her mind, but now that she stared at it, the question was why it hadn't occurred to her before. The entry was labeled "Australian Dreamtime." She clicked on the link, and began to read:

> "**Legends** of the 'Dreamtime' are handed down by word of mouth and by totem from generation to generation ... In the creation period, Tatji, the small Red **Lizard**, who lived on the mulgi flats, came to Uluru ...Two blue-tongued **lizard** men, Mita and Lungkata, killed an emu, and butchered it with a stone axe ... The Sun Mother gave each creature the power to change their form to whatever they chose. The rats she had made had changed into bats; there were giant **lizards** and fish with blue tongues and feet ... Each clan group has its individual dreamtime stories although some of the **legends** overlap. Dreamtime originates with the Giant **Dog** or the Giant Snake ... their stories tell of great geological changes – the rising of the seas, the change from lush vegetation to the great red **desert** that is the center of the continent – its so-called Red Centre. The **legends** present a story of the origins of men and animals in Australia, from dingo-**dogs** to crocodiles to the Aborigines who lived off the bare land."

Well, now. Margaret sat back in the chair, hugging her sides. So the shape-changing lizard thing really did exist in somebody's mythology. Bizarre as it seemed, this was a comforting idea because it meant basically that she wasn't psycho and that school psychologists were full of crap. It also meant there really could be a connection of some kind with her mother, like the creature said ... maybe through the Australian art exhibit stuff or even her mom's father who died in Australia.

Margaret sat for a long time without moving while the gears in her brain worked over this new information. Was the creature really a Dreamtime spirit? Which one? Figuring that out would tell her if its repeated threats were just bluff or a reason for her to be really afraid. And more pressing at the moment, how was she going to explain all this to her mother in a way that would convince her?

Margaret clicked back to the first image that had appeared on the site and stared at it for a long time. The fact that it was a pretty crude piece of art didn't matter. She'd seen that lumpy piggish shape, all right, just not on a painted slab of rock like that.

"Maybe she'd believe it if we just showed her," she said to Figaro. Giving him a quick smooch on the nose, she bookmarked the site. That was the best way; just bring up the image and let her mother see it. Then she could make her own connections.

CHAPTER 4

FIFTEEN MILES away from Citrus Park where the Hardison Museum was located, and seven hours away from the morning's disaster with the Wandjina panel, Alice was driving too fast along rural State Road 87, past the tree-lined entrance to Camp Apalachee, a summer camp for kids that featured horseback riding, and down to the crossroads at St. Christopher's United Christian Church. She hoped the Thanksgiving weekend coming up would be sunny. A few friends were coming out to the house on Thursday for the obligatory turkey consumption, and she'd planned to allow oyster shucking out on the deck. She also hoped her sister-in-law's unruly children would play outside.

Turning onto Old Sawgrass Road, a local name for the county road whose official number none of the locals ever used or could remember, she squinted into the setting sun. Its yellow heat soaked into her skin in slanting rays of diffused light. November in Florida could be paradise: robin's egg sky clear of clouds and temperatures in the 60s, just cool enough to make the sun feel good. There was no riotous color change in the trees, but the woods gave off a damp leaf-mould tang that had signified fall to her ever since childhood, and she savored it now as wooded tracts rolled by. Tall stands of goldenrod and daisy flea-bane filled the roadside ditches with autumn color as the road curved its way toward Snake Bite, a townlet several miles from her house, which was built on a wooded ten-acre plot in the sparsely settled Black Creek area.

Alice welcomed the seductive warmth of Gulf Coast autumn, convinced that anyone who willingly chose snow flurries over beach sand had a serious character flaw. Whit's face edged into her mental landscape, and she banished him to the basement of her mind where ex-husbands and failed dreams belonged. Instead, she turned her attention to an old wooden church off the road to her left, about a mile past St. Christopher's, and watched it shrinking in her rear-view mirror. It reminded her of a story Margaret had told her several months ago when they had driven past the modern gray fieldstone and stained-glass house of worship that was St. Christopher's United.

"When we were at Camp Apalachee last summer, Brandon went in that old church," Margaret had said, pointing up ahead. The St. Christopher congregation's original plank building, half-hidden by a stand of pine and scrub oak thick with blackberry brambles, was from another time. It hadn't been used in nearly sixty years and was rotting to pieces in quiet solitude.

"And you know what? Brandon found this dangling piece of rope that he said went up to the bell at the top and that a man was hung on it years ago."

"Where'd he hear such stuff?" Alice had asked.

"Brandon said he saw the skeleton still hanging on to the rope."

"Umm. And I'm a stegosaurus."

"Well, that's what he *said*. The rope really *is* there." Alice remembered the sound of Margaret's voice, escalating in pitch and volume.

"And how would you know that?"

"Everybody knows. Anybody who goes to camp there knows the story."

It was a camper's legend, told and retold to each generation of gullible newbies. Alice had smiled and given her opinion.

"I'm sure there's no such thing – it's just an empty shell. To be honest, I kind of like the looks of the old wooden church better than the newer one. More organic. But I *don't* like the idea of the camp counselors letting a bunch of campers go exploring in a dangerous old building like that."

"Then it really is dangerous?" It was Margaret's "gotcha" tone of voice.

"Only because the wood's so rotten it might fall down on your hard head." They both had laughed.

She thought about that now as the crossroads receded from view. The newer church building was a largish chunk of masonry that seemed out of place on the sandy lot where nothing but sandspurs and crowfoot grass thrived. By rural Massalina County standards, it was impressive, and it was clear that a lot of money had gone into its construction. Alice slowed at the intersection of Old Sawgrass and Magnolia Parkway and, seeing nothing coming, didn't actually stop. She turned onto the parkway, with its rows of dogwoods and crepe myrtles that made the highway a showstopper in spring and summer.

Just a mile or two down the road was the Black Creek subdivision, a mostly wooded tract of forty acres where Alice and Whit had built a house nearly eight years ago. Another five miles down the parkway led you to the outskirts of Magnolia proper, which had been more a village than a town when they'd first moved out here. Today, the town was expanding in leaps and bounds, and she had more neighbors, but one less husband.

"Want me to tell you the story they told us about the church when I was at camp? It's called the Camper's Legend."

Alice recalled how Margaret's voice had dropped to a graveyard whisper as they'd driven past the old church. She imagined her daughter and her friends squashed together on a cabin bunk, listening to one of the older kids tell the story, flashlight pressed under chin.

"Long ago, maybe hundreds of years," Margaret had intoned, "there was an evil medicine man, an Indian named Old Joe, who lived in those woods behind the church. The medicine man put a spell on the preacher's daughter and made her kill herself. Then the townspeople who lived nearby attacked him with hatchets and rakes and whatever they could find."

"That's disgusting."

"Yeah, and it gets better. They dragged him inside the church and used the bell rope to hang him. But after that the people had to move out of the church because it got haunted, so they built the new church way down the road at the corner."

"Your time scheme's a little off. The new church was built in 1945, right after the end of the war. That's 60 years ago, not several hundred."

"So? Maybe the guy was two hundred years old. I don't know exactly."

"I imagine the story changes every year. Different kids, different edition. When you go back there next summer you'll probably tell the new campers your own version."

Margaret had frowned. "I don't think I want to go there again."

"What's wrong with going back to camp? You never mentioned this last summer."

"Just don't want to."

Alice remembered the exact tone of voice Margaret had used: a statement of absolute fact phrased in the conditional. Margaret had then changed the subject from camp to boys, and the issue had gone out of Alice's mind until just now, while she was thinking about the camp legend again. She turned onto Black Creek Ferry Road, the dirt track that ran past her property.

A mile down the road, Alice braked and entered a narrow leaf-covered track marked by a ten-foot palmetto palm. It was the only landmark indicating the driveway to her hideaway in the woods. On Thanksgiving Thursday she intended to tie balloons to it so the townies (her sister-in-law's family and Dr. Eisner from the university) could find the driveway. Ahead she could see the peaked hip roof of the house through the beeches and magnolias that grew thick along the winding drive. It was growing dark under the canopy of trees. She wasn't happy about the idea of kids from camp snooping around the old church, and she'd said as much to Margaret back then.

"That was a really stupid, dangerous thing to do - you must have left your brains in the suitcase under your bunk."

"Do you think there could be evil spirits in there?"

"I was referring to real dangers, like *tramps* who might be sleeping in the building."

Margaret had persisted. "But what if there was something there? We all felt something."

That was, of course, the slip Alice had been expecting, which confirmed that Margaret had actually been in the abandoned building herself and hadn't been relating an adventure second-hand.

Alice decided that after supper she would ask for a retelling of the camp adventure, to get an honest first-hand account rather than a fabricated one. It occurred to her that the tale had the kernel of a great short story. She hadn't felt the creative urge to write in months, but now an idea was flickering in her brain, a tiny beacon in the dark. Alice pressed the accelerator a smidge, the urge to be home intruding into her daydreams.

An image of the Wandjina appeared in her mind, and she pondered her aborted attempt to tell Faye what she had felt and heard as she'd looked into its hollow eyes - it seemed now that she might have imagined those sensations, especially since no one else seemed to have experienced anything of the sort. She drove the remaining length of the driveway immersed in her thoughts, coming out from under the canopy of trees into the sunlight when she reached the clearing where the house rose on stilts. Long shadows were stretching across the western edge of the sandy yard. Alice pulled up under the house in the nearest of two parking bays.

She got out and flipped a switch on one of the house pilings. As the bulb flashed and then burned out, Alice sagged against the stair railing. "Well, hell, what's next." It was merely a statement, an acknowledgment of the obvious, but she immediately said, "Not," just to clarify that this was not an invitation to the fates. She didn't consider herself superstitious, but there was no harm in being careful.

She clumped up the dozen steps to the deck landing, carrying provisions and belongings in her arms as an orange and white cat tiptoed down to meet her.

"Figaro, come here, kitty-bear!" Alice plopped her grocery bag down in front of the door and scooped up the cat with one hand. "Did you miss me? I know you hate being alone here all day, but at least today you had somebody home with a lap. Did Margaret remember to feed you?"

Alice did her balancing act again and maneuvered the house key into its slot without dropping purse, briefcase, and cat down the stairs. "Jesus, what a hassle," she muttered.

She pushed the door open and Figaro squirmed to get down, heading at a run for his food dish.

"You *could* just put everything down and unlock the door first, like a normal person," Margaret observed from the couch, the room darkened in the fading twilight.

"That would be too easy."

Margaret raised an eyebrow. "Parentals."

Alice felt around the wall for the switch with her free hand and flipped it on, flooding the room with yellow-white light. Margaret shaded her eyes, but didn't complain out loud. Alice retrieved the groceries and took them to the kitchen counter. Finally comfortable in her little island of security, she kicked off her shoes and hoped she could unwind, and maybe not think about Lewis's nearly severed hand for the rest of the evening.

It was well after dinner when she remembered the Camper's Legend. She was stretched out on the couch, trying to read the newspaper, but images of the morning's accident and the horrific face of the Wandjina kept intruding. The mental leap from disembodied rock spirits giving the museum staff a fright to campers being scared silly in an abandoned building wasn't all that difficult; in fact, Alice's sudden sense of panic in the gallery might have been close to what the kids had experienced as they spooked each other with images of grisly death. She put down the paper, shoved Figaro off her stomach, and went to Margaret's room at the end of the hall.

Her daughter was sitting on the floor surrounded by paint tray, cups of pastel-colored water, a roll of paper towels, and a coffee-table book of photographs of the Lascaux cave paintings in France. She was meticulously creating her own spidery images of bison-type creatures galloping across heavy grade art paper. Hannah, Alice's research assistant, had given Margaret an entire the tablet of the stuff last time Alice had brought her to the office. The tablet was archival quality 100 percent acid-free paper used for line drawings and technical illustrations in the conservation lab. Margaret was deftly creating a charcoal wash over the colored pencil outlines that looked remarkably like the image in the book.

"Don't you have a test to study for?"

"Yeah," Margaret answered without looking up, "but it's only baby math. I'll do okay." Margaret's disdain for the tedious word problems her pre-algebra teacher was so fond of could barely be stifled.

"Can I see?" Alice leaned over.

Margaret held up the watercolor painting.

"That's really quite good."

Margaret squinted. "Mmm. I don't like the reddish-brown I put on there, but the rest is okay."

Alice wished she could do something even half as good; she couldn't draw squat. Her father was the only artist in the family that she knew of, but his skill hadn't come to her. It was becoming obvious that Margaret had gotten it instead; she might have benefited from his knowledge or encouragement, but that was a lost opportunity since Ned Waterston had died years before Margaret was born.

Alice stepped over the art project and sat down on Margaret's single bed. The mattress and box spring rested directly on the floor, at Margaret's request, as reassurance that nothing unwelcome could be living underneath.

"Remember the Camper's Legend you told me about? And how you didn't want to go back to camp next year?"

"Oh, yeah... " she responded, eyes focused on the artwork in front of her.

"So, what was that all about?"

Margaret stopped what she was doing and looked directly at Alice. Her ginger-colored eyes had gone dark. In moments of stress or intense emotion, her pupils dilated widely, giving the impression that her eyes were black. It was a disconcerting trait that took getting used to, especially with her halo of flame-red hair. The hair was her grandmother's, on Alice's side, but the eyes... God only knew whose long-lost genes were responsible.

"I never had such terrible nightmares in my life," she said. "Not here, not at Grandma's, not anywhere. I was afraid to go to sleep the whole time."

"Aw, Munch, you should have told me." Alice slid down onto the floor beside her.

"Well, I sort of did, but I don't think you paid much attention."

Alice was flooded with guilt. Was this what the child psychology books meant when they talked about the separation anxiety experienced by children of divorce? Margaret had been nine when Whit moved out, taking all his belongings with him. Maybe she was more affected by his absence than she let on.

"What types of dreams?"

"Oh, you know. Being underwater and finding out just before I drown to death that I can really breathe the water. Or being chased."

"By what?"

Margaret shrugged slightly. "Sometimes it's big machinery, like bull-dozers or tanks—"

"Sounds like too much anime watching to me," said Alice.

"No, I don't mean mechas or transformers." Margaret was annoyed. "These things weren't like that."

"Okay, what else?" Alice was trying to inject parental calm and understanding into her voice, but it was hard to do, knowing that whatever hid in the child's psyche was probably nothing she could reach easily.

"That little pig-dog thing kept telling me stuff. Like it really would break your back if I stepped on the cracks in the sidewalk. I sort of believed it for awhile when I was young."

Alice was truly unnerved.

"It comes out of the closet and stands where you're sitting." Alice's rump suddenly felt prickly. "It talks to me in this kind of whiny voice. At camp it told me that we'd be sorry if we went to the old church, and it was right."

Margaret took a deep breath and sat quiet for a moment, as if she'd told more than she intended and now couldn't avoid letting the rest of the squirming worms out of the can.

"Who is we, exactly?" Alice asked.

"Me, Brandon, Jeff, and Thomas."

"You were the only girl?"

"Well, yeah, nobody else had the guts to go do it."

"So it was like a dare, huh? Pretty stupid, for a supposedly smart kid like yourself." Margaret sat unmoving, her eyes on the Lascaux bison.

"Well, I think you're right about one thing – no more Camp Apalachee. I don't know what we'll do next summer, but that's clearly out."

They sat in silence for a few moments, Margaret's eyes fixed on the hooves that had emerged from her brush tip.

Alice couldn't decide if she should feel pissed, worried, or totally spooked. "You know, you worry me when you say things like some creature comes out of your closet and talks to you."

"Well, that's why I didn't say anything about it." Margaret dipped her brush in the water, pinching the tip to a thin edge. She laid an expertly controlled line along the shaded antelope shadow she'd sketched in.

"What did you mean when you said you 'saw' it? Not a flesh and blood creature, like Figaro?"

Margaret put down the brush. "I don't know ... I see stuff in my head ... sometimes it's really clear and sharp, like watching a movie. That dog-thing is mostly about the same size as Figaro. Sometimes it's not even that big, like when it's a lizard. Once I thought it was a dragon, but without any wings. Really gross and ugly. It slobbered." Margaret curled her lip.

Alice was thinking. There were images of dingoes and crocodilians in the rock art samples she'd been poring over these past couple of months. Twelve was an impressionable age. Too much exhibit research done at home? It was worth considering. "Tell me if it happens again, okay?"

"What happened today at work?"

Alice was caught short. She had been about to get up, but not now. She readjusted her train of thought. "And that question has to do with ... what?"

Margaret stared at her completed painting. "You just sounded funny on the phone is all."

"Did I." It wasn't a question. She settled her butt back down onto the pig-dog's spot. "Well, there was an accident unloading the Wandjina panels into the gallery. An assistant from the lab got hurt and had to be taken to the hospital."

"Hurt bad?"

"Bad enough. I have to go in early in the morning to talk about it ... to be sure it doesn't hex the show." She half-smiled.

"You could put up a light shield," said Margaret. "Like you do in traffic and stuff like that."

Alice blinked. The trouble with having a smart kid was constantly having to explain yourself over things you assumed they didn't notice, like muttered supplications to whomever for safe passage on the roadway during a blinding rainstorm.

"The light shield is just a figure of speech. A rhetorical statement." Alice's mind hiccupped; she'd nearly said *ritual* instead of *rhetorical*. But to be honest, it *was* a small ritual. She'd been doing it for several years, basically ever since Whit moved out and left them alone in the house together. At first it had been a bonding exercise to make them both feel more secure, but now that Margaret was a little older and much more her own person, it had become mostly a mental exercise. It wasn't an act of superstition, exactly; it was just putting yourself into a mindset that closed the door to random acts of chaos.

Margaret was looking at her with wide black eyes again. "Could we do it now, like we did when we protected the house from the hurricane?"

"If it'll make you feel better."

Alice didn't literally believe in magic or disembodied spirits, but she couldn't deny that she always felt better after they had cleansed the air and visualized a great wall of shimmering white light surrounding the property. She took Margaret's hands and they leaned foreheads together, breathing each other's exhaled breath.

"See the white light of the universe, pure and unspoiled, surrounding this house, and this property, like an unbreakable shield. Nothing we don't want can penetrate or come near it. Any darkness that touches the wall will instantly be turned to light."

"And so it is," said Margaret softly. Alice squeezed her hands and stood up.

"Well, since you aren't going to study, you might as well get ready for bed. Like I said, I need to leave early in the morning, so you'll have to get right up when I call you."

Margaret began gathering up the paints and brushes. "Thanks, Mom."

"You, too."

Alice went back to the living room with a tight knot in her throat. A controlled person who rarely let her emotions out in the open, she sometimes loved her daughter to the point of tears.

Too bad, perhaps, that she had never felt that strongly toward Margaret's father. Or any of her lovers, if truth be told. She was a loner, just like Whit had said, and spent entirely too much time in her own head. That wasn't necessarily a bad thing, if you thought about it, which she often did. She also wondered how much else there was about Margaret that she didn't know.

CHAPTER 5

ALICE EASED into the early morning caravan of traffic heading down the truck route toward Citrus Park, a city written up in the new state atlas as one of the fastest-growing urban areas in Florida, due in part to its proximity to the state capital and several mega-vacation theme parks. Yawning, she punched up the volume on the car radio. She'd been listening half-heartedly, but no mention of the museum accident had showed up in the local news. It was anybody's guess how Shelton planned to deal with the event if it did.

She settled back in the seat, lulled by the car's steady hum. Sleek, black, and too expensive for her budget, she cherished every moment of its velvet glide along the highway. That didn't stop her, however, from wishing she'd spent the extra money to buy a model with all the amenities, like power windows and a CD player. But money had been more of an issue on the day of purchase than it was now, and she had settled for basic black. It pleased her that every cent of her divorce settlement had gone into it.

This car was her statement of independence, her alter ego, making its way through the world with self-confidence and not intimidated by anyone's traffic. She remembered with amusement that sublime moment of terror and exhilaration driving away from the dealership in a vehicle whose seat required a semi-reclining position and whose hood was so low and raked that you couldn't even see the top of it from the driver's seat. It took her weeks to develop a sense of how close the nose of the car was to objects in front of it. But now the symbiosis was complete, and she and the black beast navigated the road as a single entity.

Nearing the downtown block dominated by the Hardison Museum, she nudged the volume up again. Eventually she would get around to buying a museum parking lot permit, but the $500 annual price tag still seemed too steep. More to the point, she was usually good at manifesting parking spaces along the one-way street that ran behind the museum. It was personal magic on a small scale, if you believed in such things. But not today, it seemed. She scanned the line of parked cars, irritation creasing her mouth into a tight line. Even this early, all the spots were taken.

Hell, what good were the damned deities if they wouldn't answer when you needed them? She swung around the block for another pass, her attention drifting. In terms of both prestige and economics, the exhibit, trucked south at considerable cost aboard two eighteen-wheelers all the way from Chicago's Field Museum, was possibly the most important show the Hardison had brought in within the last five years. Shelton, the exhibit design coordinator, the budget staff, and herself had spent months of correspondence with the Australian Rock Art Heritage Cooperative in Sydney and hours on the phone with the people in Chicago to set things up.

And now that the show was finally happening, it was not behaving as planned. She stomped the brakes and honked as a truck cut in front of her. Must pay attention. The turn onto the back street was coming into view.

She'd ordered large title boards printed for the museum foyer and entrance to the main hall where the exhibit was being housed: *Land of Legends: the Dreamtime Art of Australia*, white and ochre-yellow lettering on a rust-red background with a black border. The entire Hardison staff from Shelton down to the nighttime janitors had expressed some degree of awe at the significance of this exhibit with its international exposure – it was prime time. By facilitating this show and several peripheral acquisitions, Alice felt that she had finally, beyond question, begun to earn her promotion to curator. After several years of lower-level jobs for which she was hopelessly over-qualified ("What can you do with a B.A. in Art History and a Masters degree in Archaeology besides dig and teach?" her mother had asked on graduation day), this was her long-overdue and long-deserved reward.

She stomped the brakes again as a car blatted its horn and pulled out of the company lot just inches in front of her. Still no spaces. She circled the block one more time and thought with determination, all right now, let's have it. Total concentration, picturing what was wanted in detail and infusing it with desire was what made the charm work. She had been doing it, the visualizing, long enough to expect a certain hit rate (since childhood, to be honest), succeeding not as often or as consistently as she would like, but enough to keep her trying.

Mostly it was small everyday things, like conjuring up parking places and making green traffic lights hold long enough for her to get under. Or finding lost objects – she was pretty good at that. There were occasional large-scale successes, like last year's hurricane, during which she'd willed a falling tree to miss the house, although Nik later decided its trajectory would have taken it past the deck in any case. But when she tried too hard, it seemed to make things worse and sometimes even brought about the opposite of her intentions. Her best successes came when she could see the thing clearly and directly, then put whatever it was out of her mind. That was the hardest part, letting go once you'd done all you could.

There it was, an opening between a van and Jessie's mud-splattered Jeep. Angling her car into the space, she worked its sloping nose past the Jeep's rear bumper, carefully avoiding the rear-bolted racing bike, which was not much more than wheels, spokes, and a narrow seat that could only be regarded as a torture device. The shadow of a smirk loosened her mouth and quickly vanished, as did the image of Jessie perched on said seat. Whit had thought her sense of humor was morbid. She could also be amused by that.

Alice locked her car door and looked up at the back of the museum. It was built on the slope of a hill, so that the main front doors facing the busy street on the other side actually opened onto the second floor of the building. The back doors gave access directly to the ground floor, where the exhibit construction area, loading dock, and conservation laboratory were located. Jessie Birch, the museum's high-profile laboratory conservator, knew a lot about everything, or so he said. There was a bit of Indiana Jones to him as well, which he didn't mind cultivating. He'd been interviewed by *National Geographic* and was considered an expert on Spanish shipwrecks. He was also a former Rhodes Scholar and published prolifically. Alice nursed a closet attraction to him that she knew wasn't worth contemplating, because she'd have to get in line behind everyone else attracted to Jessie. And, of course, now there was Nik to consider.

She pushed open the back door and headed down the narrow hall to the elevator. The ground floor hallways always reminded her of a fallout shelter: tan vinyl floors, lighter tan concrete block walls, and rectangular fluorescent fixtures set at ten-foot intervals in the ceiling. She paused a moment outside the heavy double doors opening into the lab, then kept going.

The building became more civilized the closer one got to the exhibits and the public areas upstairs – lights were brighter, potted ferns were strategically positioned in the hallway beside the receptionist's office, spongy carpeting replaced scuffed floor tiles. The Hardison was privately established, but received a good deal of state funding as well, which explained both the elegance of the gallery areas and the Florida-centric nature of many of its exhibits and educational programs. She rode the elevator up to the third floor and stepped onto a carpeted hallway that ran the length of the building.

Heading north, the long hall dead-ended at Alice's own door. Hands full of briefcase, purse, newspaper, car keys, bills to be mailed, and sheathed umbrella, she maneuvered the knob and pushed the door open with her toe, then elbowed the light switch on. With relief, she dropped everything onto the wing chair by the door and went to look out her one window before heading to Shelton's office suite at the opposite end of the hall. She caught a glimpse of Hannah hurrying across the street below, carrying what looked like a large pizza box. Somebody else coming in early. The phone on her desk rang too loudly and Alice jumped.

"Alice Waterston," she answered in her business voice.

The voice on the other end was low-pitched and smooth, like honey. "Look on your desk, will you?"

It was Faye. Alice pictured her leaning over the glass counter in the museum souvenir shop. Faye had no real competition in the looks department: mahogany skin, long swan's neck, high cheekbones, wide-set luminous eyes. If Alice didn't like her so much she'd never be seen in her company.

"Look on your desk. See the card?"

Alice picked it up: a birthday card with a warning about people over 30. "Who's this for?"

"Jessie," Faye's voice was sly. "Surprise party for him in the lab. Hannah's put everything together."

Alice allowed herself a frown. "Maybe it's just me, but it seems a little crass to be having a party down in the lab." Lewis's contorted face was fighting for attention in her mind's eye. "Lewis is on his staff, remember?"

"Too late, the cake's been bought. Unless you think we should just leave it on his desk and let him figure it out."

"I'm the wrong person to ask. You know how I am about surprise parties." She intended to personally come back to haunt anyone who sprang one on her.

"Well, at least sign the card and pass it on."

"Will do."

Faye clicked off the line. Alice looked at the card again. Thirty. She'd always assumed he was older than she was because he just acted that way.

Did she look thirty-four? Not that anyone besides herself even cared, but it was an issue, all the same.

She tended to think of herself as ordinary. Regular small-featured face, hazel eyes, thick horse's mane of hair that was sometimes reddish and sometimes blondish, depending on the light, sometimes wavy, sometimes frizzy, depending on the humidity. She kept it cut at shoulder length; when it got past her shoulder blades the weight of it pulling on her neck was headache inducing. Alice's best asset, in her estimation, was not her looks but her brain. She was a smart cookie, thank you very much, and proud of it. That said, she looked at all the clever things people had written on the card and tried to think of something suitably wry. No puns, no catchy turns of phrase would come. The two eighteen-wheelers and their horrific cargo were still churning through her brain and being clever wasn't an option at the moment.

She finally just signed her name, small, on the front. Alice disliked office parties, especially surprise ones. In fact, she disliked surprises in general.

"Whatcha frowning about?" Gene Quaig's question slid into her office; he was lounging against the doorframe.

"Was I?" Alice smiled, not too encouragingly. She didn't like him very much, with his fat middle-aged stomach, short-winded lungs, and toupee too brown for his eyebrows. Worse, he was a toucher, with fleshy, clammy hands. She usually kept someone between them at meetings.

"So what's Accounting up to this morning?" she chatted. "Any news worth sharing? Are we being sued by anybody this week?"

He grinned. "Got any coffee?"

"No, I haven't had time to make any yet. Try again in an hour." While I'm meeting with Shelton, she thought. And if you so much as get on the elevator with me ...

"Any news about that guy from the lab?"

"You mean Lewis? No." Alice glared at him.

"Everybody in Admin is having a cow over this thing." He waited, hovering on the threshold. Alice was prepared to wait him out. "Somebody said you were from Australia. That's kinda cool, huh? You being Australian and doing the rock art show."

Alice gawked at him. "My father died there, but I wasn't born there. I never met him. Sorry, but I'm a Floridian, not an Aussie ... that's why I do shipwreck exhibits." That was wasted on him, but it had popped out anyway.

Gene shrugged. "Hmm, don't know who told me that. Guess they were wrong. Yeah, well ... later, then." He shoved off the doorway and ambled out of her line of sight, his empty coffee cup hanging from his index finger as if on a hook.

Alice carefully folded the brown and blue Chained Square quilt along its stitch lines and returned it to its tissue-filled storage box. It was a hundred and six years old, and as she handled it with dentist's gloves, her meeting with Shelton was still fresh in her mind.

"I've spoken with the reporter from the *Herald*. Just to make sure they have their facts straight. No front-page story." He hadn't smiled, although his voice had sounded pleasant enough.

"Well, that's something," she had agreed.

She moved down the display racks: New York Beauty, Double Wedding Ring, Churn Dasher, Old Maid's Ramble. The patterns unfolded in faded ginghams and calicos of pink, gold, indigo, and moss green. Mixed in were a few newer quilts in polished chintzes.

She removed them with care from the rods and packed them away, to be picked up that afternoon by the Antique Quilters Society people. A good, solid show; not pretentious or flashy, but a steady draw for the month it had been up. The newly opened side showroom had proved to be perfect for smaller, intimate displays such as this one. Just the opposite of what now occupied the main gallery.

She checked her watch: nine forty-five. By now, the birthday surprise would have been sprung, the initial embarrassment gotten over, and the obligatory coffee cake sliced. She had squirmed at the idea of Jessie being put in an awkward situation like that, although she was sure he'd handled it much better than she would have. For certain he wouldn't have worried about the potential loss of dignity. That was her job.

Alice pushed open the lab door in time to catch the tail end of one of Hannah's monologues. She liked Hannah, a funny, bawdy young woman who took everything in stride, even her husband running off last year with another man who was younger than both of them. She had wished them well.

"There she is," Jessie said as Alice approached the circle of people clustered around several marbelite-topped lab tables that temporarily held edibles rather than specimens. The well-wishers were mostly denizens of the lower levels, lab staff, exhibit technicians, and temps from the university with a couple of administrative types sprinkled among them. She stepped over the iron grating that criss-crossed the lab floor in a network of shallow drainage trenches that divided the area into large quadrangles. The birthday boy stood on the grate nearest the door.

Jessie Birch carried himself with a slightly raffish attitude. His dark but early-graying hair curled just below the collar line, and the clothes he wore, though ordinary and often rumpled as if he'd slept in them, seemed to hang just right on his body. Of medium height, he had the sinewy shape of a runner and cyclist. Alice knew, though, that as a divorced woman with a school-aged child, looking was about all she could expect to do with him. She looked away.

"We thought you wasn't coming." Cheryl, Jessie's receptionist, returned her nail-bitten fingers to her mouth. Her desk sat halfway between the wide double doors and Jessie's small office located inside the lab, offering her a panoramic view of the lab table maze and cavernous artifact submersion tank area beyond. With her dyed black hair and heavy eyeliner, Cheryl looked like she had lived a lifetime already even though she probably wasn't old enough to vote unlike her current male companion who was, she'd informed them, twenty-five years her senior.

Alice smiled kindly at her. The term "trailer trash" tried to surface in her mind but was soundly whipped back to the uncivilized corner of her brain that held such opinions. She disapproved of Cheryl in numerous ways, some specific and some vague, including the girl's daily proximity – with its implied intimacy – to Jessie.

She remembered the time Cheryl had interrupted them in his cramped office during an intense debate over whether his shipwreck cannons would fit into the space provided for them on the Florida room's exhibit floor. Hannah, of course, had made a running joke for weeks afterward about his cannon being too big. In a flash of controlled aggression, Alice had imagined a door slamming in Cheryl's pouty face when she'd presumed to ask what all the arguing was about. Not long after, as they were leaving for the day by the back exit, the door blew shut just as Cheryl stepped across the threshold. Made her nose bleed, but no permanent damage was done. That small moment in time served to remind Alice that you should be very careful what you wished for.

Abruptly, she felt just the faintest brush of a presence against her arm, an intrusion into her personal space that made her skin go goosebumpy.

"Hey. I'm a little late." Gene stood just behind her, within breathing, touching distance. Alice felt that rip-an-eyelid-off caged-animal panic she sometimes got when things felt slippery, just a whisper away from the ice breaking under your feet. Not today, she thought, please no psychic hot flashes today. That moment in the gallery with the Wandjina had been enough to last her for the rest of the year, and then some.

Faye was perched on a high lab stool, her long slender legs folded underneath it, and Alice went to join her, avoiding Gene and whatever invisible bad karma he'd brought with him. Not that she believed in the concept itself, but the terminology was useful.

The group was quiet, Lewis's absence an unstated pall over the gathering.

"Piece of cake?" Faye asked. She was carving it quickly with practiced skill. If you wanted a party organized or hosted, Faye was your connection.

Alice was tempted, but didn't cave in. "I never touch the stuff."

"It's really good, you ought to try it. One little piece won't hurt. You aren't overweight ... not even close."

"Easy for you to say."

Faye put the offered plate back on the table. "Alice, you look great. I don't know why you get so paranoid about yourself. You got curves, woman ... much better than being a stick."

"How's your little boy?" Alice asked, changing the subject.

"Fine. New babysitter, things'll be better now."

Alice nodded. "I went through the same thing, trying to work full-time when you have a preschooler. Not fun, for you or the kid."

"That's about it." Faye stretched and slipped off the stool, abandoning her cake duties to others. "I don't get to wind down till I hit the bed. Then I'm too wired to sleep!"

Alice nodded some more; she'd been there and was still, to some extent, doing that. It had been really hard adjusting her image of herself from married to single parent – Margaret had been eight when the initial split came, which spawned problems at school (issues of insecurity and abandonment, according to the school psychologist). But now that Margaret was a bit older, they were settling into a workable routine with after-school activities and summer camp, so the need for babysitters was minimal. She watched as Faye headed toward Jessie and whispered something in his ear that made him laugh. He kept his eyes glued on her retreating back until she was well out of the door.

Damp fingers touched Alice's forearm.

"You make any coffee yet?"

She sagged. "Yes, Gene, I did. Help yourself to all of it."

"Hey, thanks. Just can't seem to get revved up this morning. God, what a place to work." His eyes roved over the windowless cavern of the conservation lab. "Like being underground."

"Gene, it *is* underground. I guess you upstairs people have a whole different perspective on things."

"You're an upstairs person."

"Yeah, but I do like to visit the underworld occasionally."

She needed a way to terminate this conversation. She knew he'd hang on forever, only needing the most miniscule response from his victim. Others were gradually leaving, heading back to whatever they'd laid aside to come pay homage to the man of the hour, who lingered near the cannon tank, mulling something over with a few guys from the restoration dive team. She thought of joining them, then decided against it. Instead, she stepped carefully over the grate and headed for the door.

"Hey, I'll walk with you, get that cup filled up."

Alice's mouth settled into a thin line. She would have loved to be able to spit out one of Whit's dry one-liners with the sting of a paper cut. After nine years of marriage to Walt Whitman Sullivan, a man whose brain was hardwired toward puns and satire, one would think some of his style should have rubbed off on her, but it hadn't, and now he was gone. And so was his name. She'd reclaimed her father's family name, because it was respectable-sounding and all she had left of him. She waved to Jessie and pushed open the lab door.

"Have a happy," she called.

She headed reluctantly back to her office, with Gene lumbering along behind her. If she was distant enough, maybe he wouldn't stay. The hall clock registered 10:15. Nervous and edgy already, she opened the door to her office and motioned to the coffee pot. While Gene filled his fat cup – 10 ounces at least – to the very lip, she waited by the door and wondered how long it would take for the oily blackness to slop over the top and scald his fingers.

"Oww!" he squeaked and grabbed the cup with his free hand.

"Did it getcha?" she asked.

"Damn, that's hot," he said. He waved heat-reddened fingers in the air like a bear that had just stuck its paw into a beehive. "Guess I better be more careful, huh?"

She nodded and escorted him out with his steaming cup, then shut the door. She sat down in the wing chair and rubbed her temples. If she could be that good at manifesting her whims, she needed to be damn careful when the Wandjinas were revealed to the public. No surprises allowed.

43

She picked up the phone and dialed Vera's extension. Getting her perfunctory voicemail greeting, Alice hung up and dialed her cell phone. She answered almost immediately.

"How's it going?" Alice queried. Although most of the photomurals had been secured in place this morning, there was still much work left to do unpacking, cataloging, and displaying the work of the individual artists in the show.

Vera informed her that all the smaller packing crates were off the trucks and accounted for, and the first one had been opened and its contents successfully verified and put in place in the display island designed for that particular artist.

"Wonderful. I'll be down in a few minutes."

Alice gulped the rest of her coffee, stuck a note on her door, and caught the elevator just as the door was closing. Hannah held it open for her to slip in.

"I was going outside for a smoke, but if you need something I can put it off." Hannah had a cigarette case in her hand, but put it back in the pocket of her voluminous cargo pants as they rode down to the main gallery floor.

"No, go ahead. I'm just going to help unpack the artwork."

"It's a really big deal, isn't it?"

"*Land of Legends?* Yeah, it is." She laughed. "It lets me prove to my mother what one can do with a couple of useless art and archaeology degrees."

"Hey, I got one of those, too." More laughter.

Alice thought about how everything she had hoped for when she'd applied at the museum seven years ago was now coming to fruition. Her marriage had gone south, but her career was rising steadily. She hoped the *Land of Legends* exhibit would confirm for everyone that their trust in her abilities was not misplaced.

For the next several hours, working through lunch, she helped unpack boxes and supervised placement of the pieces as the exhibit designer and his technicians worked to bring the central part of the show to life. From the Cape York area came an astonishing array of wood and resin sculptures of animals, including highly stylized echidnas, sharks, birds, snakes, and wallabies. Other pieces from Arnhem Land included larger paintings depicting episodes from Dreamtime myths told in terms of two-dimensional landscape features. Smaller pieces presented locations where a significant Dreamtime event took place or portrayed figures who took part in those events. A clear favorite was the Lightning Ancestor, painted on both bark and canvas. It was fascinating to Alice how each different artist had taken the stories of Namarrkun and given them his or her own variation, like and yet unlike the image of him on the Nourlangie Rock panel. If she'd had any artistic talent, she might have been inspired to try her own version. She wondered how Margaret might paint him.

One piece in particular, a totemic dog about a foot high with painted patches of black, red, white, and mustard yellow, caught her attention. As she carefully lifted it from its packing nest and placed it on its display pedestal, there was a tingling in her hands so distinct that she kept her fingers well away from its open mouth and painted carved teeth. Two feet in length, the sculpture was simplistic, yet there something about that mouth and those little beady eyes that made her wonder what it would be like to have the ancestor that it represented as a clan totem. No thanks, she'd rather have a nice songbird or butterfly any day.

But the piece that resonated with her the most was a fabulously detailed acrylic on tent canvas done in the Central Australian dotted-motif style. One of the larger paintings – four feet by five and a half, according to Vera's notation – it depicted an event labeled "Storm Dreaming," and the more Alice looked at its impossibly complicated design of connected spirals, flowing wave patterns, and rich array of pinkish reds, browns, greens, and blacks with accents of white, the more it resembled some vast Aboriginal fractal freakout. It was made by a highly regarded new artist, and the label text told how it had taken her and several assistants many hours of labor to produce it. It sent Alice's mind reeling whenever she looked at it.

"Did they send any prints?" Vera was staring at it herself. "I'd pay any amount to have one."

"No. Wouldn't you know it, the one I want the most doesn't have any prints."

"One of a kind," said Vera.

"Absolutely."

Alice had even rashly considered emptying her bank account to buy it until she'd seen the asking price listed on the catalog page proofs. No matter. If she couldn't own the original, at least for the length of the show she could bask in its swirling energies that spoke to her of storms and flooding rivers and secret singing that filled her heart and mind with a longing for something she couldn't put into words.

CHAPTER 6

THANKSGIVING DAY crept in gray and damp, but unseasonably warm. Moisture-heavy greenhouse air permeated the upholstery in Alice's living room and brought out all the wet-dog smells buried and long-forgotten during the spring dry season. It was sad how the ghost of their old dog lingered on in the couch cushions. Alice joked that he must have gone looking for a house with better food, but she and Margaret both believed he'd died out in the woods somewhere, snake bitten or something. She'd avoided getting a new dog because losing them once they'd become family members was too painful.

Alice leaned over the deck railing, watching Margaret and her sister-in-law's twin sons kick a soccer ball around on the patch of grass below. Nik's dog played dodge ball with them, plunging between their feet and chasing the ball as if his life depended on it. An occasional loud yark punctuated the game when he connected.

This high up, the tip of the nearest neighbor's roof was visible through the trees. In summer you couldn't see two feet into the canopy, but now the tangle was thinning and the sightline into the trees was deeper. Beech leaves were beginning to hang brown and shriveled; basswoods and hickories were shedding their foliage, turning skeletal against the gray sky. It fit her mood. Margaret saw her looking and waved. Alice smiled and waved back, wishing she could banish the image of Lewis pinned under the loading dolly. It was making a knot in her stomach and had killed her appetite for Thanksgiving dinner.

Laughter and animated conversation tumbled out of the open glass door behind her. Inside, the wide single room that served as dining room, living room, den, and foyer was populated with half a dozen close friends. At one end of the room a breakfast bar holding covered dishes and a turkey carcass served as a barrier to the cramped kitchen area behind it. The opposite wall was mostly glass with the sliding doors that opened onto the deck. For Alice, the house was a haven of solitude that she and Margaret kept to themselves except for occasional sleepovers, but today it was transformed by ritual feasting and communing. She would have preferred a quiet day off, especially after the shock of the accident, but these were good friends and it was worth making the effort, as long as the party broke up early enough.

Alice could hear the kids mucking about down below and only occasionally getting in trouble. Inside, the adults conversed about food, weather, and world events, occasionally making sorties among the picked-over remains. Aromas of food were mingled with the damp-dog smells in a way that was not wholly unpleasant.

Shoving her hands into the pockets of her jeans, Alice dismissed the sour note of the museum accident that ran like an undercurrent of discord, a faint basso continuo of unease beneath the day's surface harmony. A quick scan of the morning's newspaper had revealed the article she was dreading, but it was small and the headline innocuous: "Museum Worker Injured in Accident." It wouldn't draw much attention, in spite of what Shelton MacBeth had said.

She felt someone leaning against her side.

"Hello, Munch." Alice put her arm around Margaret.

"Were you watching? I beat both of them."

"I saw." She could see something of Whit in Margaret's upturned face, framed in hair fine as spider's webwork. She had his cheekbones, but not his eyes. Whit's eyes were gray, like the surf on an overcast day. Odd that she felt nothing at all at the memory of them. Margaret's eyes were dark, flecked with yellow. Not like anyone else in the family. Maybe Neddy Waterston had those eyes. No way to know, though, since there were no photos of him and Alice's mother claimed she couldn't remember what color they were.

"What're you looking at, Mom?"

"Just you." Alice gave her a squeeze. Margaret leaned against her and then pulled away.

"Is there any food left?"

"Go see. Maybe they'll leave us enough for snacks tonight." Alice watched her slim body squeeze through the adults hanging out in the doorway. Hard to believe that her best friend was her twelve-year-old child. It was true, though; Margaret was more adult than some grownups she knew. Come to think of it, Margaret had never been childish by ordinary standards, although she could produce some supremely bratty moments. She'd been treated like another adult in the house, and they'd never baby-talked to her. Although she had been a late talker by Dr. Spock standards, once she'd begun to communicate in language, it had been in whole sentences, not babbled half-words. Alice could only assume her thinking processes had followed the same line of development. Margaret was an independent thinker whose inclination to challenge classroom teachers when they said something she thought was wrong had gotten her in hot water more than once. Alice was reluctant to reprimand her for it as long as she could do the research to prove her points sufficiently.

"Alice!" Raine, the neighbor whose roof she'd identified through the beech branches, shouted over the party chatter and music filtering out from the living room. She sat cross-legged on the far end of the deck where a raw oyster bar was temporarily set up. Her husband shelled oysters with the practiced ease of a surgeon, which he was. "Do we have more crackers? Tim's running low."

"I'll get them."

She flashed a look at Nik, her off-again on-again lover, crouched on a stool beside the oyster bag, his long legs and arms partially folded, mantis-like. He smiled back, self-contained. He wasn't much of a party person, but seemed comfortable enough with the situation. His major professor from the Zoology Department had showed up, so he wasn't completely isolated among Alice's friends. Dr. Stuart Eisner was a mycologist of some repute, consulted by toxicologists and quoted by journalists. Nik had been studying with him long enough that they now seemed more like colleagues than student and master.

She and Nik had been an item for a little over a year now, with occasional separations fueled mostly by mutual misunderstandings over commitment and what a more permanent relationship might mean to each of them. Lately, though, he'd been more permanent than absent. Intellec-tually they were a comfortable match, which had led them to gradually become more than colleagues at the museum, which was where she'd met him.

Inside, Eve Lee, Alice's ex-sister-in-law who'd remained her friend even after the breakup, was getting an earful from Eisner about the field guide to Florida mushrooms he and Nik were working on as part of Nik's doctoral program. Alice wondered if Eve needed rescuing, then decided not. Alice was flattered that Stuart had made the long drive from town out to her little gathering. He was affable, talkative, knowledgeable on a great many topics, and enlivened the group with no deliberate intention to dominate the conversation. She was only slightly embarrassed to be dating his doctoral student, who was eight years her junior. It wasn't an issue for Nik, but Alice felt defensive about it, depending on who knew.

"—he's extremely gifted, both as a field photographer and an illustrator. It's very difficult to take good field-guide-quality slides, but many of his are publishable. Nikolas Thorens will become a well-known mycologist one of these days, and I will have had a hand in it." Eisner leaned back in his chair, smiling; Eve was nodding, her interest genuine.

"I'm the one responsible," he continued, "for loaning him to the Hardison Museum. Whenever they need to contract a technical illustrator, Nik's their first choice. He's a man of many talents." Alice caught his eye on her way to the kitchen. Had he winked? Surely not.

"Was the seafood dressing your invention or some recipe from Nik's Swedish grandmother?" he called to her.

Alice retrieved an unopened box of crackers and went back to the living room. "Nothing exotic – just oysters, scallops, sun dried tomatoes, sage, a bit of fresh dill. Something Margaret and I put together."

"Excellent combination," he said.

The small moment of flattery had its effect, and Alice smiled. The gray cloud of dread was beginning to lift.

"Hey, what was all that about a museum guard at the Hardison getting hurt unloading some out-of-town show? At least three versions of the story were all over the Upper Chamber yesterday."

Alice felt the smile fading from her lips. Eve's husband Dan Lee was a lawyer and lobbyist with one of the state's oldest law firms. Among its clients were soft drink, health care, and snack food corporate giants, as well as less commercial entities such as the Hardison Museum. He spent a lot of time patrolling the halls of the state capitol brokering support for this bill or that amendment. Dan Lee thrived on rumor and innuendo. She suspected that he knew precisely the details of the story, but wanted to hear her take on it. Eve gave him a sharp look.

"Don't put Alice on the spot. It wasn't the museum's fault."

"No, it's all right," Alice said, sitting down on the hardwood floor in front of them. "It wasn't a guard, it was one of the conservation lab assistants. I guess technically he shouldn't have been helping push the dolly, but hell, the guys from the lab help us set up all the time. Nothing like that's ever happened before." Alice saw recognition in Stuart Eisner's face. "This is the Australian art exhibit, isn't it?" She nodded. There was nothing for it now – they were all looking at her. "We unloaded it Monday morning," said Alice. "The first crate off the truck, the Wandjina panel, was too heavy for the dolly. Somehow the wheel collapsed just as Lewis— the lab guy—put his hand down near one of the dolly wheels to guide it onto the main gallery floor. It pinned his wrist under the edge of the cart. He lost a lot of blood." She could hear the hiss of their breath as each imagined the unimaginable.

Raine, with Nik behind her, came into the room. "Hey, where are those crackers? Um, what's this, a tribunal?"

Alice imagined how the scene must look: three somber-faced listeners intent on her testimony as she sat at their feet.

"Alice was telling us about the museum accident," Dan Lee said. "So," he turned to her, "how badly was the fellow hurt?"

Alice took a breath. This was really not what she wanted to be describing as an after-dinner tale. "Doctors reattached his hand, but who knows how much use of it he'll get back, or even if it'll be a good graft." She could feel her skin prickle. There was a silence in the room. Nik sat down beside her, just close enough for their knees to touch. He made no other move and said nothing, but she was glad of his support. That was his style: reticent, Scandinavian self-effacement that you had to be attuned to in order to read him correctly.

"Ewww! Somebody's hand was cut off! WOW!!" The twins bolted through the open door and descended on their parents in a flurry of oversized athletic shoes and spilled sodas. Eve grabbed the closest and yanked him down onto the couch beside her.

"Ethan!" She glared at him. The boys continued to gawk at Alice, her grisly tale eclipsing whatever they'd been doing out on the deck. Figaro darted in, a flash of yellow fur against the baseboards, and disappeared into the kitchen.

"So this is where the party disappeared to," said Tim. He had followed the twins inside and hovered, looking for a place to sit. He finally wedged himself next to his wife in Whit's old easy chair. Margaret reappeared from behind the breakfast bar, Figaro draped over her shoulder.

Alice was now aware that she had nine people staring at her, completely fixated on the one thing she had resolved not to think about today.

"So, Doc," said Dan Lee, "anybody talking about this at the hospital? How bad was it?"

"Well, that's not really my area—"

Raine cut in. "Tim's an orthopedic surgeon in private practice. He works on football players. He would hardly be on call at the hospital emergency ward." She gave Dan a look.

Alice knew that Dan was probing, and she could see the ideas forming in his mind, all revolving around the words *lawsuit* and *Worker's Comp.*

There was an awkward silence. "I assume the exhibit goes on as planned," said Eisner.

Alice nodded. "In a perverse way, it might draw more people in to see it. Bad news can sometimes serve the same purpose as good news. Shelton doesn't think there should be any serious negative fallout."

"Was there a picture in the paper?" "Can we see it? "Was it gory?" The twins were insatiable.

The image of Lewis's blood being swabbed off the marble floor swam into Alice's mind. And that sound, a keening in the background blur of the scene that she'd thought was a human scream, even now replayed itself in her ears, a riff with gigantic hooks.

"Evan! No, there wasn't any photo. You two are awful." Eve's expression was full of apologies. "Alice, I'm—"

Alice felt a knot tightening between her shoulder blades. The newspaper story wasn't as invisible as she'd hoped. She shrugged. "It'll blow over. Don't worry about it. The exhibit is wonderful, and I hope you'll all come see it."

Dan leaned back and crossed one leg over the other. "So basically, we have the stodgy old Hardison under siege from evil spirits."

Eve turned on him. "Who said it was spirits? Alice said it was an equipment failure."

"Who said the Wandjina were evil?" Raine chimed in.

Alice could feel her face heating up.

"What's a Windjammer?" asked Ethan. Eve glared him silent.

"*Wand*jina, like magic *wand*," said Margaret.

Alice took a breath and launched into her spiel. "*Wandjina* can mean either a group of Dreamtime spirits or a single Creator Ancestor called Wandjina, depending on which clan's mythology you use. Our exhibit uses the name in the group sense. The Wandjina are creation and weather deities, revered ancestors, not evil monsters. But that's not the main point of the exhibit. It's intended to show the beauty of ancient and modern myth-based art, and all the marketing and educational materials that were done for the show emphasize the reverence the Aboriginal clans have for these deities. In their eyes, these beings are mysterious and majestic, they made earth and all its animals and humans and then ascended into the heavens as Sky Gods with homes in the Milky Way, and as horrific as some of those images may seem to the likes of us," Alice paused for breath, "it's because we don't understand their origins."

"Can they see us from the Milky Way?" Ethan's eyes were round.

"Are they watchin' us?" asked his brother in the same breath.

"They're watchin' *you*, snot-face." The two began to tussle.

"That does it — out to the car! Now! I'll deal with you two in a minute." Eve corralled the boys and herded them through the glass doors and toward the stairs.

Dan crossed his arms over his ample stomach. "So a group of angry ancestors from Australia has invaded the Hardison Museum. Do you suppose Shelton will be adding an exorcist to the budget?" He barked a laugh.

Flushed with sudden fury, Alice opened her mouth to skewer him, but Raine intervened.

"Why do you keep assuming they were evil?"

Dan turned to her. "Well, if they aren't Christian, they're pagan, so you might assume—"

"Just stop, okay?" Eve scowled at her husband and sat back down on the couch. "Could we just skip the religious arguments? I don't think this is how Alice wanted to be spending her Thanksgiving holiday. Could we talk about something else, like how beautiful the woods are this time of year?"

Dan settled further into the couch cushions, an expression on his face that suggested this was old ground for them. "No problem. Inquiring minds just want to know, as they say."

"The Dreamtime spirits aren't evil per se – that's an uninformed assumption," said Alice.

"And I've just been informed," Dan said, laughing. "Relax, I wasn't trying to disrespect anybody."

Alice knew her face was flushed, but she couldn't stop. "We can't say precisely what's meant by the Aboriginal art at many of these sites. In some tales, the ancestor spirits did frightening things, to show people how not to behave. Some rock paintings have messages about sorcery, love, and magic, or hunting and fertility; some are records of celebrations and times of war or hardship. The exhibit is intended to foster respect for the culture of the Australian Aboriginal people and their long tradition of art, and I don't want what happened to Lewis to ruin that!"

There it was – the truth spat out like a toad in front of them all. She had finally articulated what upset her the most about the whole blasted event. The toad blinked as another silence descended. Alice wondered what each of them imagined they would see at the gallery, and if they did show up, how they would react.

Nik said softly, "Strictly from an artist's point of view, Aboriginal art is complex. It shows a surprisingly sophisticated level of design. You could almost mistake some of the images for stylized figures from the twentieth century. The ability to stylize shows true art rather than just mechanical reproduction of the subject, whether it's people or animals or landscapes." His English was only faintly accented, with just enough Nordic lilt to mark him as foreign. "I understand the exhibit has some excellent modern paintings as well as the photomurals?"

Alice pressed his knee in silent thanks. Now she was back on solid ground and launched into a small rehearsal of the patter she intended to give while circulating among the reception patrons.

"There are half a dozen panoramic photo reproductions of the art from rock overhangs and cliff faces," she said. "And then we have pieces made by modern Aboriginal artists, who could easily be direct descendents of those people who painted and carved the images in the caves and shelters. The pictures were tended and touched up by clans elders, at least until the white settlers came and screwed everything up. All the lore, all the mythology, that surrounds each image has been handed down through the generations in story and art, as well as dance and song. We're only now beginning to appreciate the depth of that heritage and allow them to reclaim some of it."

She didn't know if she was preaching to the choir or boring them to death, but she was impassioned about the larger issues and missed no chance to emphasize them.

"What do the paintings look like?" Raine asked.

"Some of the modern work is highly traditional, bark paintings and such, and some is done in materials like acrylic paint on canvas. It has beautiful patterns and colors, ancient content blended with modern designs. Some of the showiest pieces are of Wandjinas, ancestral spirits of the Northern Territory clans, and Namarrkun the Lightning Man. But my favorites are the landscape maps or abstractions of Dreaming events and where they took place. The level of artistry is quite astonishing. Some of these pieces sell for thousands in the galleries that represent them. We'll be selling prints of some of them."

"For how much?"

Alice suspected Raine could already see a grouping on her walls, and of anyone there she was the most likely to buy a print or two.

"We're going to offer two levels: limited edition, signed prints will go for around five to eight hundred, depending on the artist and size of the print, and then we'll have a group of numbered but not signed prints that'll cost less. All are reproduced in archival quality inks and papers, so with the right matting and framing they'll last for years. The show covers a wide range of styles – pointillism, x-ray style, stenciled hands –" Alice stopped. There was that forbidden image again.

"Well, I know nothing about Australian art, but I'm intrigued. I'll definitely come, just because it's your baby."

Raine pushed herself up out of Whit's chair. She went to Alice and leaned down, giving her a quick hug, her long dark braid falling over her shoulder. "Bye, all," she said, straightening up. Taller than her husband, her frame was angular, yet she moved with a surprising fluid grace. Those who knew could recognize her dancer's training. She gathered up her casserole dish, and Tim followed her out, waving goodbye.

Dr. Eisner stood and stretched, making motions of heading toward the door. It served as a cue, and the Lees got up as well.

"We should go," said Eve. "It's a long drive back to town."

Alice followed them out, leaving Nik and Margaret picking over the turkey remains.

Out in the driveway, Dan and the kids got into the biggest sport utility vehicle she had ever seen. Eve lingered at the bottom of the steps,

"It was good seeing you again," she said, looking up. "I always did like this house."

Alice loved it, too. It was a beach-house design built on nine-foot pilings with open decking along two sides, and a Tahiti hip roof that gave it a bit of an island look. The house was well anchored, its pilings sunk in concrete slabs that provided parking berths for two vehicles as well as an enclosed laundry room and small tiled patio where the stairs to the upper level began.

"I've missed coming out here ... getting away from town. But I worry about you and Margaret being alone in the woods."

"It's not that remote. Raine and Tim are on the next road over, and Margaret's best friend lives on the one after that. We can actually cut straight through the woods to Raine's back yard. I like the peace and quiet, but I know what you mean. The house has good locks and I'm thinking of putting in a security system. And Nik has a dog..." She let that last statement hang in the air.

"He's cute. Nik, not the dog." They both laughed.

"He and Margaret are great pals. She likes his morose Scandinavian humor."

"Well, stay safe," Eve said, heading toward the car. "And don't be a stranger. Come by anytime or call if you need anything."

"I will." She sat down on the steps and watched them drive out toward the dirt road.

The sun was slipping below the tree line, and a chill damp breeze swept through the upper branches of the surrounding woods. Although the property was ten miles inland, breezes blowing from the Gulf sometimes had a salt tinge that brought the sea indoors. This evening it was clammy.

Alice ran her hand over the weathered stair railing. She loved the house and property, with its stands of beech and oak, probably more than she had loved Whit near the end, which said something about them both – that he would so easily give the place up and she was so determined to stay.

They had built their pole house nearly a decade ago when their marriage was young and money scarce. They'd done all the finishing work themselves, including pasting and plastering the sheetrock walls into place and running their own wiring with a friend of Whit's who claimed to be a master electrician, although Alice had her doubts. Anticipating repairs, she'd meticulously photographed every wall for future reference while the wiring and studs were still exposed. Where those packs of photos were now was anybody's guess, so their usefulness was moot. But it was the act of documenting that had been important, not so much the end result. That was, in fact, her strong suit – documenting, researching, cataloging, making lists and looking for connections, obsessing over the details that she remembered better that anyone. It drove Whit nuts, and probably, if she was honest, was part of what had driven him away.

Alice waited until the Lees' taillights disappeared, then she turned at last and headed back up the stairs. Nik and Margaret were sitting beside the oyster bag. They'd finished off most of the oysters and were surrounded by empty shells. Like the walrus and the carpenter, Alice thought, remembering her favorite poem from *Through the Looking Glass*.

"Eaten every one?" she asked, stepping over the litter of shells and cracker crumbs. Nik grinned and winked at her.

She flopped down onto the wooden porch swing and pushed off with her foot. Her thoughts ranged past the pots of aloe and bluebells on the railing to the fringe of trees. It stood like a tonsure around the clearing where the house was built. Half a mile beyond it was a pond, shrunk to a squelching bog in time of drought or swollen, like now, and quick with mosquito larvae. Her own ten acres, she thought, unmortgaged and mostly undeveloped, with the central two and a half acres donated to the house and its sandy yard where spiny blackberry canes insinuated themselves into the struggling grass plots. A wild turkey gobbled from the cover of a massive water oak. Alice closed her eyes and pushed the swing. She could smell the trees – magnolia, ironwood, red cedar, pine, sweet gum. The place was paradise. What idiot wouldn't want to live out here?

She imagined a life in which she could just stay out here in the woods and write stories, never having to make the drive into town unless she wanted to just for the hell of it. No getting up at the crack of dawn to rush to the museum on time. Instantly her dread surrounding the museum flooded back with an adrenaline wash. Damn Lewis for getting hurt like that, ruining her joy over the impending show, and damn herself for thinking that way about him because now the workplace she admired so much was tainted. Such a shame, she thought. It was a beautiful piece of architecture; the support pillars of the largest gallery were like trees, a canopied arch of plaster and steel. And under that canopy ... Wandjina spirits and blood.

Alice opened her eyes. It was nearly dark now, but she made out the figures of Margaret and Nik walking across the yard with the bag of shells, headed toward the compost heap. An incongruous pair they made – Nik, tall and lean as a lodge pole, and Margaret a will-o'-the-wisp beside him. Dawg followed wagging at their heels. She remembered the first time she'd laid eyes on Nik. He'd been researching shipwreck cannons in the museum's archives library, preparing to do the technical illustrations for the Florida Shipwrecks pamphlet series published by the Hardison year before last. She had allowed herself to check him out, something she was not accustomed to doing because she was still adjusting to her newly unmarried status, which Jessie had jokingly referred to as her "singularity," a state she found both liberating and unnerving.

"Who's that?" she remembered asking Vera.

"Some guy from the university, contract illustrator for the shipwreck books," Vera had told her with a certain disinterest, men not being her particular cup of tea. Alice had looked at him more closely, since she was part of the writing team for the books. She could see him now, balancing an open book on his forearm, pushing wire-rimmed glasses up on his sharp nose, corn-silk hair pulled back at the nape of his neck into a ponytail bound with a rubber band. A dark blue T-shirt and worn jeans revealed a wiry frame that was a bit slender for her taste, but she'd come to appreciate both his shape and his brains as they'd worked together on the manuscripts and then met for art films on campus with coffee afterwards. Eventually, they'd reached that night in his apartment where their pleasant intellectual relationship had turned physical. She had been both embarrassed and exhilarated, and had not been able to read him at all. But she was getting better at it, and they were still a work in progress.

On a whim, Alice closed her eyes again and imagined a wall of white light surrounding the house, sealing in warmth and security, and protecting it from – what? Feeling foolish, she got up and walked to the rail, and watched Nik and Margaret coming back toward her in the half-light.

It occurred to her that things had worked out rather better than she'd hoped with those two. She wasn't asking Nik to be a father substitute, and Margaret didn't seem to want one, yet they were accepting of each other in a way that allowed Alice to have a life with them both. She could almost feel smug about her current good fortune, if it hadn't been for ... She stopped the unwelcome image before it could come into focus.

Alice shivered, the warmth of the day replaced by a damp chill. Thanksgiving Day faded and the fog rolled in, shrouding the trees. She was glad to have a dog in the yard again.

DECEMBER

CHAPTER 7

"IT'S ALL over . . . they're too strong. Fall back! I don't want to see Goku get hurt!"

"Your time has come! The battle that decides the fate of the universe is about to commence! Aaaaiiiiiiyyyaaaa!!"

The shriek was followed by roars and explosions. Alice jerked awake, disoriented, and then fell back on the pillows. It was Saturday morning, *Dragonball Z* was on the Cartoon Network, and she was safe in her own bed.

"Margaret, could you turn it down," she called. She buried her ears in the covers next to Nik's bony shoulder.

"Sorry." Margaret's voice was dutiful, but not contrite.

Alice stretched and sat up. She was still somewhat unused to having her bed shared once again and found it difficult to fully fall asleep with him there, as if some part of her kept guard lest she do something embarrassing in her sleep. Nik had spent the night occasionally over the past year of their relationship, but for the last month he'd been a live-in member of the household. The fact that he still paid rent on his apartment in town proved that he also regarded their arrangement as tentative. At least now there was a dog patrolling the property. A motley mix of who knew what, Dawg had an unpleasant fondness for rolling in carrion, which sealed his fate as an outside dog. No way he was getting a chance to add his smell to the couch cushions.

She nudged Nik between the shoulder blades.

"Do you want breakfast?"

His muffled "no thanks" was a welcome response since cooking breakfast didn't fit into her plans for the morning. The urge to write was strong, and last night she lay awake for close to an hour mulling over story ideas. Alice was itching to get started turning the Camper's Legend into a piece of saleable fiction as soon as her brain unfogged; she intended to stay in the kitchen just long enough to nuke a cup of water in the microwave for coffee.

She pulled on sweat pants and a heavy sweater, but couldn't find her slippers. Padding barefoot out into the main room, she blinked in the light. Morning sun warmed the December chill out of the breakfast nook, but the rest of the house was cold. Margaret was bundled in her comforter on the long couch, an empty cereal bowl on the floor beside her. She was breathing steam from a cup of hot chocolate cradled between her hands.

As soon as her coffee was made, Alice sat down on the other end of the couch and slid her icy feet up under the comforter.

"Yiii!" squealed Margaret.

"Sorry. Couldn't find my slippers."

"Damn, Mom, you got the coldest feet." Figaro emerged from under the comforter and made a dash for the cat door. "See, he can't take it, either."

"Don't curse," said Alice.

"Why not? You do."

"Yeah, well, I've lived long enough to earn the right – you haven't."

"Everybody I know talks that way. It's no big deal."

Alice folded her legs with her feet up under her butt. "Well, I think it's a big deal, so indulge me." She sipped her coffee. "About that Camper's Legend tale ..."

"Yeah?"

"I'm wondering what the inside of the church looks like..."

"Why?"

"I might want to write about it. I'd have to jazz it up a bit, make it truly weird for it to sell as a short story. But the potential's there."

"Are you gonna put me in it?"

"Depends. Do you want to be?"

Margaret slurped her hot chocolate. "Maybe not."

"I wouldn't use your real name or anybody else's."

Margaret was silent. She had a look Alice knew all too well – something wasn't sitting right with her.

"What're you thinking?"

Margaret shrugged. " It's just ...."

"Just what?"

"It's like, when you write something down ... and it gets printed, it might, you know, kind of make it happen."

Alice laughed. "Well, it that were true, I'd be in a hell of a mess by now, given the stories I've published."

"No joke." Margaret was wheeze-laughing now.

"You don't sound too good, kiddo. Are you catching a cold or something?"

"My head's stopped up. I didn't sleep much."

Alice got up. "I'll turn the heat up, it really is too cold in here."

She toyed with the idea of starting a fire in the small brick fireplace set into the room's west wall, but gas would be quicker. She crossed the room to the hallway heater and turned the knob. Small blue flames flickered into larger spouts of blue and yellow-orange. She heard Nik stirring in the bedroom and felt a momentary twinge at the male invasion of her space, then a warm flush in the pit of her stomach at having him there. She stood for a moment, soaking up the heat, then returned to the couch.

"What on earth gave you the idea that writing a story *you* told me in the first place would somehow make it real? By that logic, I assume there are little versions of all the fiction that's ever been written swirling around out in the cosmos somewhere."

"Parallel worlds – yeah."

"It's an old theme and it's been done to death."

Margaret frowned. "But when it's about yourself, it's different ... it's like somebody's telling another version of your life, or something."

"It's called biography – writing one never changed the events of anybody's life that I know of."

"That's not what I mean. Oh, forget it. It's a cool idea. You should do it."

"Thank you. I intend to." Now they were both in a sulk, a pattern, Alice noted, they fell into whenever one of them was sick or feeling off kilter.

"I think we could use a fire out here – this room's pretty icy." Alice looked around; she hadn't heard Nik come into the kitchen, but that was typical. His presence in their house was as quiet and unobtrusive as he could make it.

"I'll just get a fire built up and then go check on Dawg."

Instantly the tension was dispelled; even if it hadn't been intentional, his instinct was true. He was an observer who missed little. It was a necessary trait for his line of study, but it was useful with people as well. Alice appreciated that it was not the first time he'd rescued her.

"Do you think Dawg was warm enough down there?" Margaret was concerned. "Maybe we should have let him sleep inside."

Alice shook her head. "No way. I'm sure he was plenty warm in the laundry room, sleeping next to the hot water tank. But yeah, somebody should check on him."

Alice watched as Nik expertly stacked a few large logs, smaller sticks, and kindling into the firebox, then lit it with a long kitchen match. The pile obediently caught flame and within moments sparks were swirling up the flue. Nik grabbed his jacket and pushed open the glass door. Cold air rushed in through the gap.

"Back in a minute."

Alice nodded, then turned to Margaret.

"So. Did you actually go in the old church, or just look around outside?"

"Brandon went in, like I told you."

"Did you?"

"Am I gonna get in trouble over this?"

"No, no. I just need some details to get ideas going. What did it look like inside?"

"Scary as shit, um ... sorry."

"Forgiven. Anything inside? Like a choir stall with an organ, or a preacher's pulpit?"

"Uh uh." Margaret shook her red frizz. "A few old benches is all."

"Okay, so tell me what made it so scary, other than the fact that it's rotten enough to have fallen down around you. Or that some homeless person could have been using it for a shelter."

"Well, Brandon said he saw a body hanging from the bell rope and started screaming, and then we ran all the way back to camp. Then he said he just made it up. But I thought I saw something in a corner, but when I looked closer nothing was there, but then Jeff said later he thought he saw an animal in there too, so who knows?"

"What did it look like?"

Margaret hesitated. "Can't remember. Jeff said he thought it was a coyote but that's dumb because coyotes are out West, not in Florida. Maybe it was a fox or a raccoon."

They could hear Nik's boots clomping up the steps to the deck, accompanied by the tik-tikking of Dawg's paws on the planking.

"Now that *does* worry me. A rabid cornered animal could have been really dangerous. One bite from an infected animal and you're toast – there's no cure, so you die."

"What rabid animal?" Nik came in and pulled the door closed before his dog could wedge its way in between his legs. Foiled, Dawg began licking a damp patch where his warm breath condensed against the glass. Alice could see his scruff of a tail thumping. Mindless happy licking – that was Dawg.

Margaret shrugged. "Maybe I imagined it."

"Something in the woods?" Nik's tone was more curious than worried.

"No, no. This is just story research. An escapade some campers got into last summer ..."

"Margaret being one of them." Nik smiled at her. "What's the plot, then?"

"My basic idea is that a campfire story told to a bunch of adolescent campers turns out to be true, revealed in a way that gives the reader a good scare."

Nik filled the teakettle with water and lit the gas burner underneath it. Alice watched him rummaging around in the pantry for something he could brew instead of coffee.

"Sorry. I forgot to get green tea when I bought groceries– it's just not in my consciousness. I'll remember next time."

"There's hot chocolate packs in the cabinet over the stove," said Margaret.

"Just the thing, *tack så mycket*."

"You're welcome," said Margaret. "That's Swedish. Nik taught me that. It means 'thanks a bunch,' right?"

Alice smiled at them. Accommodating – that was what Alice most liked about Nik and why after three weeks he seemed to have settled in. She had worried that his continued presence could be a disruption in the life she and Margaret had made for themselves, but so far, so good.

She thought about the camper story. Images of Old Joe swinging from the bell rope, scaring hell out of a bunch of children, began to materialize in her idling brain. Maybe it would work as a juvenile adventure story. There was a decent magazine market for that kind of stuff.

She went to the study and turned on the computer. Opening a new file, she typed in the title, "The Camper's Legend" and stared at the screen. What next? She chewed a paper clip and rocked back in her chair, trying out words in her head, cutting and pasting them and mentally listening to the altered versions. Then she began to type.

The Camper's Legend

Flames contorted the storyteller's face into a mask. His eyes were black pools of shadow that sparked red from the campfire light. His young listeners stared at him, rapt.

"And they hauled Old Joe into the church and strung him up with the bell rope." The storyteller's eyes squinted and seemed to disappear. The boys and girls huddled together around the glowing logs, and, although the summer air was warm and humid, they shivered as with one body.

"And Old Joe kicked and hollered and wouldn't die. He looked 'em all in the eyes and called down a terrible curse on their heads." The speaker paused and let his words hang in the air. A chunk of pine log burned through and fell away from the pile, showering sparks.

"What did he say, Screaming Eagle?" one of the boys whispered.

"He said, 'I'm comin' back to HAUNT YOU ALL!'" The campers from the Tocobaga boy's cabin and the Chowkowbin girls' lodge screamed in terrified delight as Screaming Eagle shouted and rose up in the firelight to tower over them. He was a senior group leader, and they believed whatever he said. Then he started to laugh.

"That's it, kids. Put the fire out and let's head back to the cabins." A chorus of protests followed.

"Awww, tell some more. Please?"

"Don't stop, it was just gettin' good."

But eighteen-year-old Screaming Eagle, known outside the campgrounds by the ordinary name of Buddy Foster, was already kicking sand into the smoldering pine coals.

"Sorry, kids. Wakeup bell's at seven-thirty. I shoulda had you guys in bed a long time ago. So move it!" He scooped up Nathan, who was smallest and lightest, and plunked him over his shoulder, then trudged chuckling up the bank away from the springs where the Massalina River went underground. Nathan pounded Buddy's back helplessly. The rest of the campers followed, chattering and whispering over the lurid tale of Old Joe and his grim fate.

Later that night, Nathan lay still as stone on his bottom-level bunk, trying to fall asleep. He hadn't really been scared down at the campfire, but just the same, he wasn't going to make any noise. If Old Joe's ghost wanted to make a house call, the church where Screaming Eagle had set his story was only a short walk through the trees and over the fence on the other side of the camp property.

Every camper who ever spent the night there had heard the Camper's Legend about the haunted church and its hanged Indian. It was part of camp tradition. In fact, the very bell that woke them up in the morning once belonged to the old church. And there were plenty of grisly stories about how the camp had acquired the bell, but Nathan knew it had really been salvaged from the unused church by a camp administrator with an interest in local history.

But now, alone in the dark, he didn't want to think about the bell or the church. He was just starting to doze when a hand clapped over his mouth. He just about died of fright, then recognized who it was.

"Shhh. It's only me." Andy's voice was beside his ear and the hand slipped away. "Me and Keith and Ted are gonna go look at the old church. Everybody else is sleeping. You wanna come?"

Nathan sat up, wide awake. He weighed alternatives, like being left out of the group or having heart failure again. He decided the latter wasn't necessarily a given, while the former definitely was if he stayed behind.

"Yeah, I'm comin'." They were the Gang of Four at school and did everything together. Camp was no exception.

"Then get dressed. The others're outside."

Moments later, four figures slipped like shadows across the clearing around which the cabins were clustered, past the swimming pool gleaming silver in the moonlight, along the dark walls of the recreation building, over the footbridge crossing the springs, and into the sheltering trees on the far side. The eight campers' cabins, each named for southern Indian tribes, seemed a hundred miles away.

They struggled through Florida creeper and sharp-thorned blackberry tendrils, tripped over saw palmettos and rotted fallen trees. Twigs snapped and leaves crunched under their feet. The strip of woods between the camp and the old church wasn't wide, but it was dense and Nathan was glad he'd taken the time to pull on heavy socks along with his running shoes. He felt sorry for Ted, whose ankles were already ripped to shreds by the brambles. It was hard going, but at last they reached the rail fence separating camp property from the church clearing.

"Who's goin' in first?" asked Andy. Nathan supposed that, as organizer of the expedition, Andy would see to it that someone other than himself would get that honor.

"Why can't we all just go in together?" That was Keith, the voice of reason. Nathan respected his opinion above all others.

"No, all of us'll make too much noise and wake Old Joe. One person needs to sneak up to the door and look in. If there's nothin' there, then the rest of us'll come on." The group stood in tense silence, watching the back of the wooden church where it sat in a cleared area surrounded by pines. In front, the county two-lane blacktop ran just a few yards past its sagging steps.

Andy cleared his throat. "Well?"

Still they stared. The church was only just beyond the fence, but no one moved to climb over.

"Well," said Andy again. "It needs to be somebody who can slip up there and not be noticed." Nathan knew what was coming. "Like Nathan. He's little, Old Joe'll never notice him."

"I'm not doin' it."

"Sure you are. Look, just sneak up to the back door and peek in. Then wave to us if it's okay."

"And if it's not?"

"Nothin's gonna happen. Just go on."

"Only if Ted goes with me."

Ted backed away a couple of steps. "I'm not goin' unless everybody does." He planted his feet firmly in the weeds and jammed his hands down in his shorts pockets.

"I'll go." Keith shrugged and swung a leg up over the fence rail. "Come on, Nathan. Let's do it before somebody comes lookin' for us."

Nathan breathed deeply and let the air out. He hoisted himself up onto the fence and dropped to the other side, scrunching dry leaves and oak twigs. They ran across the moonlit clearing to the back of the church. It was a rectangular wooden structure built up about three feet off the ground on brick pilings. The back steps had rotted away, and the back door was gone. They could see straight through to the front entrance, which was also open.

Nathan felt better with Keith there. Maybe even a little bit daring. He leaned his head through the back entryway and strained to see into the gloom. Moonlight frosted the grime on the windowpanes and dusted the empty floor inside. There was nothing to see. The church was a hollow shell—even the pews were gone.

"There's nothin' here," whispered Nathan.

"Let me see." Keith leaned in next to him. "Right. Looks good." He turned back to the encircling trees and waved in a wide arc to the other boys. Soon they were all standing in the back churchyard.

"So who's goin' inside?" Andy asked.

"Hey," Nathan protested. "You said we would just look in the door. Well, there's nothing inside. So let's get out of here."

"Only after you go inside and tell us if the bell rope's still there."

Nathan knew he was trapped. He could refuse and be ridiculed as a coward for the rest of the two weeks camp was in session. Or he could be a hero.

He faced the group. "I get all the money you got on deposit at the camp store." If he was going to die, at least he would leave something to his mother.

"Done," said Andy. The others nodded.

"Then help me up."

Keith bent down and formed a stirrup with his hands. Nathan put his foot in and pushed up onto the floorboards of the church. They were filthy with dirt and dust from the road. He stood up and walked deliberately forward into the center of the large room. It wouldn't have looked so big with the right church furniture in it, but right now all he could think of was being in a cave. He couldn't even see the ceiling; it was too high up in the shadows. His footsteps sounded muffled and intimate, tiny sounds close in his ears. He decided to walk straight across the room and right out the front door. Then he would sneak around the side of the building and scare the pee out of the others. And then he stopped. Something had brushed across the top of his hair. He stopped breathing and looked up. He saw the frayed end of a dangling rope.

Outside, the three boys fidgeted in the deep grass and weeds behind the church. They scratched and twitched as ticks and redbugs crawled up their legs in legions. Their furtive glances at each other revealed that they were all thinking the same thing: what was taking Nathan so long? Suddenly his high shriek shattered the silence of the pine grove and he came tumbling out the back doorway, oblivious of the three-foot drop. He lay in the grass as the others crowded around.

"Man, what'd you see?" Andy demanded.

Nathan scrambled to his feet and ran for the fence. Like panicked rabbits, the others tore after him. He didn't slow down when he hit the woods, but kept on running.

"Nathan!" called Andy, his breath coming in ragged gasps as they sprinted across the footbridge. "WHAT DID YOU SEE?"

"Great," Margaret said, putting the pages down. "You turned me into a guy, with a dorky name." Dressed in her standard uniform of jeans, oversized T-shirt, and China flats, she was sprawled on the daybed beside the computer table.

"Well, you said not to put you in it."

Margaret grinned and handed the printout back. "Just kidding. We really were scared, just like you wrote. Is that where the story ends?"

Alice got up from the computer and stretched. "I don't know. It seems like there should be more, but I don't know what."

"The way you told it was just like the real thing. I was so scared, I would've believed anything was after us."

Alice looked at her carefully. "No wonder you had such nightmares."

"No, the bad dreams started before we did that."

"Then I'm surprised they could talk you into going with them."

"Yeah, me too. Sometimes I just decide to do things, scared or not. Dunno why."

"I still wish you—" Alice shut her mouth. The look on Margaret's face as she headed back to her junkpiled bedroom was protest enough.

Alice turned back to the story. She read it again, vaguely dissatisfied. Thinking about it, there were other things she could do with what she'd written. She could research the plot from a couple of angles, maybe take a more historical approach to the material. Already she was starting to get more ideas than could fit into a single short story of limited page count. Maybe it wasn't a short story at all.

She could interview the current church's pastor, talk to the camp personnel, take a look through the old newspapers in the county library. She loved to go there anyway, just to appreciate the building. Erected in 1823, it was a towering monster of white-washed clapboards with a peaked roof and steep musty stairwells. It had done time as a settlement church and later on as the first county courthouse. Alice had recently served on the Save Our Library committee that had raised enough money to put a new roof on the building, saving the third floor books and Massalina County archives from rainwater damage. It was a fun place to poke around in, whether you found anything useful or not.

Alice stared at the computer screen, thinking over the possibilities. There were problems, though, with turning it into a book. Could it still be told from the children's point of view, and, if so, would it remain a juvenile adventure or need to be reworked into something else?

"Margaret," she called down the hall. "Who's the activities director at Camp Apalachee?"

"Big Buffalo."

"No, nutbrain, his real name."

Margaret looked in through the doorway. "I don't know. Nobody goes by their real names at camp. Are you gonna ask him about the Camper's Legend?"

"I was thinking about it."

Margaret had a conflicted expression. "Don't tell him ... you know, that we sneaked out."

Alice smiled. " I should, but I won't."

"You can just tell him you're doing research or something."

"Well, that would be true."

Margaret nodded. "He'll go for that. He tells everybody he's the camp loremaster – such a dork."

"Dorkiness I can handle, but does he really know anything?"

Margaret shrugged. "I guess."

Alice felt a little nip of excitement experienced only when she was in research mode. She was on the trail of something. She was also amused at the way Margaret had quickly shifted from informant to truant.

"Thanks, I'll definitely go talk to your camp loremaster about the legend. And if there isn't a history to it, I'll just invent one and go from there. Your grandmother thinks I can make up anything – maybe she's right."

"Grandma likes me best," Margaret lounged in the doorway, smiling crookedly. Snarky. That was the exact expression. Alice stared her down.

"And she lets you get away with murder, which I try not to do when I can help it. Sorry to keep nagging you about the dangers of sneaking around abandoned buildings in the dark – any normal parent would have grounded you for the rest of the year for doing such a thing."

Margaret continued to smirk. "But you're not a normal parent."

Alice saved the file and leaned back in her chair. "For which you should be eternally grateful."

"Does that mean I can spend the night at Judy's house again?"

"You aren't making a nuisance of yourself over there, are you?"

"Yeah, but they don't care."

"Don't make assumptions. Ask her mom to call me and we'll see."

"Can't I just ride my bike over there and find out?"

"Did Judy invite you over? They might not appreciate you just dropping in on them. And I thought your bike had a flat tire."

Margaret made a displeased face. "You know what, you're starting to act normal and it's creeping me out."

Alice laughed out loud. The fact that Margaret tended to act older than her age most of the time encouraged Alice to treat her with a fair amount of leniency, and it always brought her up short when she butted heads with the pouting preteen instead of the more mature kid she was used to.

Trying to be a normal parent was something she'd become much more conscious of, especially since she'd introduced an abnormal element – a live-in lover – into their home environment. She didn't know how it would affect their family dynamics, but it would bear watching.

As if on cue, Nik came up behind Margaret and stood watching them with an air of mild curiosity.

"What was so funny?"

"Mom's being *difficult*." She said it with just enough sneer to make her point but avoid outright cheekiness.

"Hey, I only said–" But Margaret had already sidled around Nik and disappeared down the hall. They heard her door close with a little more force than usual.

"Well, hell. I wasn't trying to fight with her ... I was just trying to be a concerned parent, for once."

Nik came in and sat down on the carpet beside her chair.

"You should count yourself lucky. If that's what you consider a fight, it's pale beside the tantrums my little sister could throw." He took one of her feet into his lap and gently began to massage her instep.

Alice was smiling in spite of her frustration. "I didn't know Swedes could throw temper tantrums. I thought you were genetically incapable."

"Where'd you hear any such of a thing?" He was grinning, crinkles forming at the corners of his eyes, which were ice blue, like glaciers.

"I don't know," she said, putting her other foot in his lap. "Doesn't matter. Ooh, that feels nice." She shut her eyes. "How old is your sister, anyway?"

"Twenty-one now, but I remember what she was like at Margaret's age. Not as even-tempered by a long way. I probably contributed to some of it."

"You don't mean you tormented your younger sister?" Alice was looking at him. "You don't seem the type."

"Why not?"

"You just seem ... more subtle."

Now it was Nik who laughed. "Does it please you, Alice, to have a 'subtle' lover?"

He pulled her down onto the floor beside him.

"It pleases me to have *you*," she said, "subtle or otherwise."

"Otherwise could be arranged, if you like."

She buried her face in his hair and brushed her lips against his neck. "Well, I wouldn't want to go so far as having to 'arrange' anything, but whatever happens spontaneously is good."

"I can learn that ... to be spontaneously 'otherwise'." They were both laughing.

This was a part of Nik that Alice loved – his sly, teasing wordplay that she had come to realize was a form of foreplay. Listening to his accent was a turn-on; it slurred certain consonants and accentuated others in ways that did strange things to her animal brain.

"Spontaneously otherwise," she said in his ear. She softy closed the door, and then there was no more need for words.

CHAPTER 8

ALICE SAT alone in the museum's upstairs conference room, fifteen minutes early, by choice. She wanted to think about what she intended to say when it was her turn to report. These marathon administrative sessions came once a month, like bills. All division directors and mid-level administrators were required to attend, and Alice had been a participant for several years now. Shelton would appear punctually at 9:00, and departmental heads would start showing up soon after.

Typically they'd be dealing with interdepartmental shit like where to reposition the Spanish cannons once they'd been moved out of the Florida shipwreck room or why Jessie refused to conduct the Inuit culture workshop in the temporary classroom suite – Inuit culture was his specialty and some of the demonstration pieces were from his personal collection; he'd rather kill than have any of it damaged by unfinished construction. But for the last week there had been only two serious topics of discussion: mounting the Australian exhibit and planning the Museum Patrons' reception for it, held the night before the exhibit officially opened to the public. It was rumored the Governor might attend.

Which meant added security for the show. The contract required it, and with the opening coming this Friday, all the details had to be in place. Several state senators who were museum patrons had already confirmed their presence at the reception, which guaranteed a higher than normal level of security paranoia, and now there was the additional matter of the publicity spin needed to smooth over the accident. Alice felt fatigued, and the meeting hadn't even started.

She'd come to work nearly an hour early, which was becoming too much of a habit recently. Her coffee pot was already gurgling when she arrived, by which she knew Gene was on the premises as well. He was definitely a pain. As budget director, he never missed these meetings, which was a pity. Given the roomful of egos, herself included, things could sometimes get tense, depending on whose toes got trampled, and Gene was sure to egg on the perpetrator in some inane way. Shelton MacBeth, on the other hand, was typically pleasant and cultured, although he too had his moments.

Alice had poured herself a cup of Gene's too-strong brew and contemplated the piles on her desk. The stack in front was paperwork on the shipping and insurance of the Dreamtime artwork with a note in Cheryl's handwriting clipped to it. Alice almost laughed out loud – Cheryl had written "Dreamland exhibit." It was anything but Dreamland. Maybe the Aboriginal inhabitants of pre-invasion Australia (her basic sympathy for the displaced natives prevented her from thinking of the colonization in any other terms) regarded these creation deities with reverence instead of dread, but she was damned nervous around their greater-than-life-sized images. She wondered how the dignitary-filled reception milling around underneath their hollow gaze and outstretched hands was going to react.

Going to the conference room ahead of time had allowed her to snag a seat furthest away from the one Gene usually occupied, and now, comfortably seated at a corner of the long table, she leafed through the documents and mail she'd grabbed off her desk. Most of it was exhibit related: insurance coverage statements, bills of receipt, the contract with Gulfland Security, and an envelope bearing the Field Museum's elephant logo in the corner, which she assumed was the curator's report she'd been promised with clippings from the exhibit's run in Chicago.

Mixed in the pile was Nik's brochure for the Southeastern Mycological Association's Tenth Annual Norwegian Foray. The photos were gorgeous (two were his) – hikers peering over cliffs into fjords, shots from a hot air balloon high over Copenhagen, red sunset on Lake Lucerne, quaint winding streets in Trondheim, pink spring flowers around the Arctic tourist station in Abisko. Nik had been there before and come back with voluminous documentation on the fungi available for study. He wanted to go back again this year if his department could spring for some research travel funds. His doctoral work puttered along in fits and starts, going on hiatus whenever a foray beckoned or a travel opportunity presented itself. He typically made just enough money to keep his apartment, register for classes, and head out on the road to the next foray. As Alice already knew, Nik was a low maintenance type of guy and didn't mind sleeping on the floor of a park ranger's station if need be.

Alice checked the Norwegian foray dates. Sixteen-day tour, departing for Oslo in late February. The cost was steep, but it included everything a foraging mycologist could want. If she took money out of her savings, she could afford to go along. But the Dreamtime exhibit took precedence over everything, straining the museum's resources and skills to capacity, and she couldn't in good conscience take an extended leave from the museum until its run was over.

It was going to be, as she'd told her friends at Thanksgiving, an incredible show. She could imagine with a certain glee the museum's elite politely jostling each other in their cocktail finery beneath the rampant genitalia of the Aboriginal creation deities.

She also couldn't ignore the feeling that something about the exhibit itself, not just the visual imagery, was disturbing. Not counting the thing with Lewis, all this week the exhibit assembly staff had encountered more than their usual share of minor accidents and difficulties. It was as if the exhibit resisted being put together – like a cat refusing to get up from your lap, it was making itself heavy. The show was not cooperating. It was just a gut-level feeling, and she knew it was ridiculous to anthropomorphize objects of ordinary wood, canvas, and stone, but the painted figures, old and new, were unnerving to be around, even though she rationally knew better. It wasn't as if the clan elders had cursed the proceedings – quite the opposite. The exhibit had full cooperation and encouragement from the numerous Aboriginal consultants and artists involved.

She checked her watch; a few minutes till nine. Alice despised being late and would rather be half an hour early than five minutes late, a trait that ground its teeth over Nik's methodical dawdling. At least she and Jessie had punctuality in common. He was always on the mark, ready to get on with it, and ahead of everyone else, if possible.

As if summoned, he came in and sat down next to her. That was a plus. Alice leaned toward him. "Any news about Lewis?"

He shook his head. "I'm going to call the hospital after we get out of here. I'll let you know what I find out." He fidgeted with a sheaf of photocopied pages he'd brought. Alice glanced at them –long columns of tiny print she couldn't read without her glasses.

Gene slouched past her chair and took his regular seat next to Shelton's at the head of the table. He always sat to the director's right, maybe to give the impression he was Shelton's second in command. Nobody was buying it, though. Anybody with a clue knew that Pilar, Shelton's executive assistant, was the real power behind the throne. But today she was absent. As was Fjodor Kamensky, who was off on sabbatical in Iceland researching wooly mammoths. The museum's resident paleozoologist, he was referred to simply as the Professor by most of the staff. Technically, as Natural Sciences Curator, he was Alice's peer in the staff hierarchy, but everyone deferred to him as senior curator because he had enough gravitas to silence you with a tilt of his bald head. He'd occupied his chair on the director's left almost as many years as Shelton had his at the head of the table. He would doggedly argue a point with you long after your eyes had rolled back in your head and your mind had stopped from information overload, and many people found him pedantic and intimidating. Alice found him merely insufferable. She was cordial to him only because he was an old friend of Steuart Eisner and because it could be career suicide to make an adversary of him. No one would dream of sitting in his chair while he was on leave; even in his absence, his presence lurked, scowling.

The door opened again, admitting the Exhibits Designer, Education Coordinator, and Public Relations/Membership manager in a wad. Others followed behind them, and soon the table was nearly full. Shelton entered and shut the door. Alice admired his distinguished good looks; graying hair streaked with white, full black eyebrows spreading like wings outward from a finely shaped brow, prominent Roman nose, and oddly expressive mouth added to the authority he wore well and manipulated with skill. Now in his fifties, Shelton MacBeth would be a handsome man to his grave.

"Hello, all," he said and sat down at the head of the table. He adjusted his tie and looked around at them. "If you don't mind, I'd like to dispense with the usual departmental reports this morning, except for Alice. Are we on track for the reception and opening this weekend?"

Alice cleared her throat. "I think everything's in place, but you'll need to approve this expenditure for extra security," she said, pushing the contract toward him. He reached for it and placed it on top of his other papers without looking at it.

"That's fine. Any problems I need to know about?" The silence was palpable.

Alice thought for a moment of all the things she could mention, then decided against it. "No. I expect everything to come off without a hitch." That was bold. Maybe saying such a thing would make it so. She chewed her lip, but stopped when she realized Jessie was looking at her with a half-smile.

"Well, that's that," said Shelton. He paused, clearly savoring something;

she wondered if it had anything to do with her precious exhibit. "I have an announcement of considerable interest to the museum and to all of us here—"

He paused as the door opened. With muttered apologies, Victor, the Graphic Arts Coordinator, a small rodent of a man in enormous glasses, slipped into the nearest chair. "Sorry, I couldn't get away any sooner. Trying to get your labels corrected." He looked at Alice. She flushed, that little problem of having to return most of the title boards and artist labels to the printer because someone couldn't spell Aboriginal was one of the issues she'd elected not to bring up. She glared at Victor, knowing he couldn't make out her expression from that far away. Apprehension tightened her stomach.

Shelton regarded Alice and Victor for a moment, his moment of revelation evaporating, then began again. "Well, now that we're all here — except Pilar, who already knows what you're about to discover, and the Professor, who has his hands full in the tundra — perhaps our esteemed Mr. Birch would like to enlighten everyone."

"They've found the Marquesa," Jessie said bluntly and rubbed his hands together like a modern-day pirate.

Alice caught her breath.

"The what?" Gene was clueless, as usual.

"The *Marquesa*," Jessie repeated, "of the 1724 Spanish Plate Fleet. To be specific, the *Nuestra Senora de la Marquesa y Santismo Rosario*. She was the fleet leader, the capitana." The Spanish syllables rolled off his tongue.

Alice's research brain was clicking into gear. The so-called plate fleets were known to historians as the ships that sailed between Spain and the New World during the 1600s and 1700s, ballasted with Mexican and South American treasure—most of it gold and silver that fueled the monarchies of Europe.

"The 1724 fleet sank off the Florida Keys in a hurricane," Jessie continued, his hands drawing storm clouds in the air. "Too bad for the Spaniards, though, when word got back to Cádiz. The water was too deep for them to salvage anything. No deep sea dredges and sand movers in those days." Now he smiled around the table, his excitement spilling over them like a shower of confetti. Alice thought he would have been jumping up and down if Shelton hadn't been there. He patted the bundle of papers in front of him. "These, my friends, are photocopies of the ship's manifest, sent at our request from the library in Seville."

Alice was familiar with the library known as the Archives of the Indies.

Any treasure hunters worth their doubloons knew the great trading voyages of the seventeenth and eighteenth centuries had been scrupulously documented and the records preserved in the Seville Archives. She'd had to send them a few inquiries herself in recent years.

"Deep Six Enterprises found it in sixteen fathoms of water south of Key Largo," Shelton added. "That's rather surprising, since they aren't a major salvage outfit."

"Probably jumped somebody else's claim," said Alice. Gene laughed.

"Quite possibly. However, that's the state's headache, not ours. They'll be shipping over four dozen silver bars for verification against the lot numbers on those manifests. I also understand there is much more to come. We're negotiating a cleaning and preservation contract with state officials now, and then I suspect the conservation lab will be very busy." Jessie was smiling, but Alice was thinking hard. She wasn't far off target.

"This is going to be a major event for the museum and the state of Florida," said Shelton. "We can expect heavy press coverage, high-level security—"

"Sounds like the Aussie show all over again, only with treasures from the deep instead of prehistoric cave sites," said Vera. As registrar, her hands were already full documenting the *Land of Legends* show.

"It'll mean a lot of work for all of us, and I don't want us to make any mistakes, whatever the others involved may do."

Alice raised her hand. "By 'others,' you mean the treasure salvors?"

Shelton nodded. "We've never worked with Deep Six, but I wouldn't expect much archaeological expertise from them."

"Probably blew the priceless ship's timbers to smithereens to get at the silver bars underneath," Jessie growled. "We, however, will keep scrupulous records, double-tag each piece, and verify the manifest verbally and on paper against the pieces in the vault, when they come in."

Alice raised her hand again. "Just to play devil's advocate here, how are we going to juggle these two things together? What I mean is, we're already looking at hiring outside security and extra staff for the run of the Wandjina exhibit. What's it going to be like when shipwreck gold and silver starts showing up?"

"All hell will break loose," said Jessie, beaming.

"And we will handle it with our usual professionalism," Shelton added. "Won't we?"

On her way downstairs after the meeting, Alice stopped outside the main gallery entrance. The temporary "Gallery Closed" signs were in place, funneling visitors into the smaller side gallery rooms until the *Land of Legends* exhibit went public. The museum was fairly empty this early in the morning, with just a few people in the gift shop. She could see Faye, slim as a tulip, talking to a young couple with a baby in a stroller. Alice stepped over the chain blocking the ramp that led down into the Dreamtime exhibit.

She would just have a quick look around and make note of anything that needed doing, not that there was much left to take care of at this point. The gallery staff had devised a corridor of velvet rope dividers to guide spectators through the display islands and past the wall photomurals but not allow anyone close enough to touch. All of the contemporary artwork was hung or set up on their proper display pedestals, and Victor's half-time assistant was there installing the new labels, humming tunelessly to himself. Alice took a deep breath. It felt like the calm before the storm. She stared up at Namarrkun, the storm god potent with his encircling band of lightning, and her chest began tightening again, her breath coming in shallow gasps.

"Awesome, huh?"

Alice's heart leaped at the sound of the voice behind her.

"Good God, Faye, you almost gave me a cardiac!"

Faye smiled with perfect white teeth. "Did those artists' prints come in yet? I'll need to set up the store display for the reception."

"The package is in my office – came by FedEx this morning. I'll bring them down to you before lunch. I wish I could afford one or two for myself – they're beautiful. Nothing like the real thing, of course, which is way out of my price range."

"Yeah, mine too. Everybody cool upstairs?"

"I guess." Alice wasn't sure if she should mention the Marquesa. "A lot going on. I got to sit next to Jessie, so the meeting wasn't a total waste."

Faye's eyebrows went up. "Looking to replace Nik already, are you?"

"No, of course not." Flirtation was one of the things Jessie did as naturally as breathing, and there wasn't a woman working at the museum who was immune, except maybe Pilar. Any of them would have been glad to snag him even for a one-nighter, but he seemed uncatchable.

"Just asking." Faye smoothed the skirt over her thighs. "So, is Nik as tasty as he looks?"

Alice blushed to the roots of her hair and couldn't think of a comeback.

Faye shaped her ample lips into a smile, an image of ripe cherries in cream. "He's got a nice butt, better than Jessie's, but that's just my opinion, of course." She winked an almond-shaped eye, and turned to go.

"Let me go get those prints for you." Feeling frumpy beyond belief, Alice escaped to the elevator, which she rode in a funk up to her office. Suddenly she couldn't wait to get out of there.

By 5:30, Alice was speeding across the DeFlores county line into the rural landscape that made the twenty-mile drive home more tolerable. She had called Margaret, explaining her intention to stop by the county library to look up anything on either the *Marquesa* shipwreck or the old church near Camp Apalachee. Nik was still at the university, but Margaret seemed okay with being alone for a while longer. She was busy surfing the Internet and had Dawg and Figaro for company.

Away from the carbon monoxide of Citrus Park rush hour, Alice relaxed. Driving down tree-lined back roads into rural Massalina County, she sometimes took the route through the small community of Whiteoak, but not this time. Instead, she took the highway that connected to Magnolia Parkway, which ran straight through the county seat. Magnolia was, until recently, maybe three houses and two trailers bigger than Whiteoak, but to its credit, it had the Massalina County library.

The library was open till six in the evening. Although by librarian standards it was a rank amateur (rank mostly referring to its persistent aroma of Southern mildew and the pig farm half a block away), it had one of the best caches of original Florida-related material around, a lot of it donated by descendants of settlers in the area. Just the place to find somebody's long-lost account of hurricanes and shipwrecks as well as a lot of local and state history.

The tallest structure in Magnolia, the library was a three-story white whale of a building, trimmed and gabled in peeling gingerbread tracery. At the turn of the century, it had been the grand courthouse of the newly established county seat, but it was burned to the ground a decade later by a man who couldn't think of a better way to erase his criminal record. It was immediately rebuilt using the same floor plans and served its purpose until a new, larger courthouse was erected a block away in the ugly, rounded style of the 1930s, facilitating removal of all the court rooms and legal machinery of county life from the old frame structure. It sat as an empty shell for a few years, until its new life as the county library had taken shape.

Alice pulled into the sand lot near the back entrance and parked beside a shiny red pickup sitting high on oversized tires and loaded with chrome. A vanity plate screwed to the front bumper read GOD, GUNS, AND GUTS. This marvel of redneck high tech belonged to Sandra Potts, the librarian. Alice hurried up the narrow wrought-iron steps to the long central hallway that cut the structure completely in two with entrances (or exits) at both ends of the building. A row of doors down both sides of the hall indicated various divisions of the library. Tiny signs stuck out from the wall, designating a children's reading room, adult fiction, inspirational literature, and the Florida room. A single bulb lit in the dust-encrusted chandelier overhead threw shadows into all the nooks and corners of the hall and stairwell. It would be a good place to get mugged, except nobody in Magnolia was much interested in that kind of behavior. About the worst you might expect would be to step in a pile of horseshit getting out of your car.

She opened the door to the Florida collection and stifled a sneeze. Dust bunnies lurked in all the corners, shifting only when the ceiling fan was in operation during the summer. In winter, the air rarely stirred. Following the narrow aisles between the bookracks, she came to the corner where the local Civil War and Reconstruction-era materials were more or less lumped together. No attempt had ever been made to display them in any order beyond their general subject category, and she was sure none ever would.

Two old men, one in overalls and the other in horrendous green polyester slacks, were holding forth near the end of the stacks.

"Pardon me," Alice said. She squeezed past them and sneezed loudly from the reek of cigar smoke that hung around them. No smoking ordinance be damned, she supposed. Or maybe the offending cigar was outside in the dirt, but its smoke molecules still clung to their clothing.

"God bless," said one of them as she sneezed again.

"Thanks." Alice pinched her nose and resolved to breathe through her mouth until she could get out of there. She went on to the next aisle of shelves, but could hear them plainly.

"The tornaydee that come with that storm just before Thanksgivin' done a mess a damage down to the church."

"Which one you mean?"

"Assembly of God." It sounded to Alice as if he'd said "a simile of god," which was an interesting slant. She stifled a laugh and began thumbing one by one over the spines of the books in front of her. Looking through the card catalog in the checkout office would be time wasted, she well knew, since nothing on these shelves would resemble its organization anyway.

"Made a hole in the roof?" queried Green Pants.

"Noo, god-dog. Hit blowed it slam away."

"Yessup, that cloud that blowed up was black enuf to be one a old Cadjer's spells."

"Shet yer mouth," Overalls snapped.

Alice put down the stack of Florida Annuals she was balancing on her forearm and listened. She couldn't help it.

"You know ain't none a them stories real, else the congurgation wouldn't of built 'em a new church and kept on a-goin' to it."

"You jes keep spoutin' such-like about spells and such. See whut happens to ya. Pastor says never to take the name of the Lord in vain nor blaspheme by naming his enemies if ye want to have life more abundantly." It sounded like "moribund-antly." Alice was getting tickled.

"Awww, Hurley, that's jest a lotta—"

"Shet it. Ah know whut ah'm talkin' about." There was a silence and then feet shuffling on the bare board floor.

"They ain't no proof that none a thet ever happened. But ah wouldn't mind findin' some a that gold, if 'n there really was some."

"Devil's money. Ain't never gonna be found. Took it to Hell with 'im, fer sure."

Green Pants cleared his throat, and then offered, "Say, ah got a bushel-bag a parched peanuts in the truck. Want some ta take home?"

Alice frowned. Pants was about to squelch some of the best eavesdropping she'd done in years. He clomped toward the door, Hurley following.

"You get that book on bees I tole you about?"

"That's whut I'm a-readin' now. Thought about callin' somebody out at the county extension office ta come lookit the hives."

"Shoot. If you waitin' on them, you backin' up."

"Ah know that ..."

Their voices faded out the door and down the hall. Alice stood quietly, both amused and bemused. The locals were always slightly incomprehensible to her, but listening to their piecemeal superstitions had also given her goose bumps. There was some taboo Hurley wouldn't let the other talk about. She wished she'd heard more.

They had been standing at the end of the county history stacks, where she needed to look next. She walked across the room and stood in front of the shelves. On the phone this afternoon Sandra had told her she was pretty sure there was some land grant information somewhere in the Florida room, plus a number of church records from around the county, but there was nothing in the card catalog to indicate what titles these papers might be filed under.

Alice wondered what part of the collection the old men had been looking at. At eye level, there were bound volumes of Massalina County Court records, which she'd used before, and surveyor's documents dating from the early 1900s. The next shelf held pamphlets and books by local government entities like the farm bureau. What else? She'd never taken the time to look at the rest of the holdings because the upper shelves held the documents she was usually looking for.

On the bottom shelf she read a title that seemed more like it belonged to a novel: *Frontier Survival, A Girl's Own Story*. She knelt down on the floor for a better look, sneezed explosively, and discovered that all the bottom shelf items were personal records of one sort or another. *Frontier Survival* seemed to be a typical turn-of-the-century diary. There were also a couple of books by local writers detailing such things as the lives of Florida heroes from the Indian wars or the early timber trade around the county. Then she pulled out a filing carton bound with a flat woven cord that was old enough to fall apart when she tried to untie it. There was no name or title on the carton. If she were really lucky, it might be the file Sandra had been thinking of, but it didn't seem to have been touched in years, maybe even since it was first filed away. Her fingers were heavily coated with dust from handling it, and she felt a monumental sneezure building up inside her nose.

"Aaaahhh ... chooo!" Alice gasped and felt for a Kleenex inside her slacks pocket. Her eyes were watering, but she was too curious to put the folder back. She opened the flap and saw a jumble of papers and envelopes crammed inside, along with a thin, flat book. She pulled out the top sheet, a folded piece of heavy paper yellowed and brittle. Handling it with a curator's skill, she unfolded it and read in the poor light:

First Church of the Heavenly Powers
Agenda for Lord's Day, third week after Christmas, 1889.
1. Invocation and bell ringing
2. Hymn (led by Sisters of the Blood)
3. Exhortation: the Serpent speaks
4. Calling of the Body
5. Oath of the chosen
6. Thanks be given to the Custodian

Signed, this day,
Cadjer Harrow, Minister of the Body, F.C.H.P.

Surprised, she looked at the tiny, crabbed signature and read the name again. Was that the funny name she'd just heard the old men tiptoeing around? Meticulously, she refolded the paper and slipped it back into the file folder. She checked to see if there was anything else on the shelf, then got up at once and headed for the checkout office, all thoughts of shipwrecks left with the Florida Annuals on the library floor.

By the time she'd gotten the folder checked out and another sneezing fit under control, it was dark outside. Sandra followed her out, locking the door. Alice realized that Margaret would probably be having a cat by now, but her cell phone battery was dead so she'd just have to hurry home. She drove carefully, as there was dense fog out on the highway, especially where the road dipped through lowland swampy areas coming up on the Apalachee campgrounds. Creeks from the Massalina River threaded all through the camp's acreage, dappling the ground with low boggy places that were collection points for mosquito larvae. As she approached the twin totem poles marking the camp entrance on her left, the roadway was white with mist all the way to the intersection with Old Sawgrass Road. Vaguely she could make out the hulking shape of St. Christopher's, near the turn.

Alice slowed down and turned on her windshield wipers. A stupid move, because it only smeared the dampened dust into a brown film across her line of vision. She slowed to a crawl, unable to make out the lines painted on the asphalt, and crept toward the turn onto the county road. The church had installed a spotlight in its yard last year that served as a handy beacon, but in the fog it simply made a small pool of diffused light around the base of the pole. Truck headlights zoomed up behind her in the gloom, and a horn blasted as the semi barreled around and past her. Goddamn, she thought, shaking.

The pale rectangle of the stone church emerged from the fog, and she made the turn carefully. She was just beginning to accelerate again when a figure, or so she thought, unexpectedly flashed in front of her headlights. A loud crack, like a tree being split by lightning, sounded outside the car. She pulled hard on the wheel, careening off onto the narrow sandy shoulder of the road and into a shallow ditch. For heart-stopping seconds the car coasted madly on its two passenger-side wheels before skidding to a stop with a bone-jarring whump. The engine cut off.

She sat stunned, barely aware of her aching left wrist and the blood pumping like crazy through her body. Gradually, she decided that she must

83

be all right, but what was back there in the road? Had she hit something? She listened intently, but the only sound was her panicked breathing.

She turned the key and said a silent thank-you to the cosmos as the engine cranked. Wary of oncoming headlights, she backed out onto the road and continued to cruise slowly backwards, but the dark strip of road was empty all the way to the churchyard. It had happened so fast, she couldn't remember clearly now what she had seen, if anything, or what that shock of sound could have been. Accelerating slowly and heading forward again, Alice pondered what she should tell Nik and Margaret when she got home.

Maybe she wouldn't tell them anything.

Trying to explain that she'd nearly wrecked her car avoiding something in the fog would send them into needless debate over her safety and driving abilities, and at the moment she didn't feel like trying to relive the experience in order to tell them about it. In the end, she told them nothing.

CHAPTER 9

ON FRIDAY morning, sunrise crept over the tree line like one of Margaret's watercolor washes. Lavender, lemon, periwinkle, and blue-gray spread across the sky – cool colors warming up with the sun as if it were spring instead of early December. The cold snap had sputtered out, and it was clearly going to be a beautiful day. It shouldn't be, this far into December, but all the signs were there.

Alice drove into town with her window down, appreciating the twenty-plus miles of fresh, dew-sweetened tree smells that would stop not far past the city limits where trees gave way to parking lots. Irritable and out of phase, she dreaded the Patron's Reception set for that evening. Because she'd kept quiet about her near-wreck of the night before, she had no one's input into what might have happened, and her inability to satisfy her own questions about the scare was chewing away at her. If there had been any way to skip the reception, she would have done it. Instead, she was going to have to mingle with the state's nobility in her blue velveteen dress, which should have been in season but would probably be too hot now. She would give her rehearsed mini-lecture at least several dozen times as the guests came and went. And they were bound to have questions when they saw the exhibit – who wouldn't?

She wondered what Margaret and Nik or any of her friends would think. She was anxious for an objective opinion, not only of the show's presentation, but of the subject as well. She thought the museum assembly crew had done an extraordinary job, arranging and hanging the huge photomural panels along three walls of the gallery; each panel was accompanied by explanatory text on label stands and brief recorded narratives that were activated when anyone stepped in front of them. This last feature had been her own bright idea, but now she wasn't so thrilled at having those names invoked out loud every couple of minutes. It almost felt taboo to do so now, but it was too late to change it.

The arrangement of panels and artist islands was carefully orchestrated. To view the entire set, one began the route of exploration with the two murals from Western Australia with their Kimberley region Bradshaw and Wandjina images, moved on to Arnhem Land in the north and its famous Ubirr and Nourlangie rock shelter sites, reached the Cape York region in northern Queensland with the Split Rock site, and ended up with the ceremonial artwork found in the Yourambulla Caves of the Flinders Ranges in South Australia. From there, you were routed into the Red Centre section of the exhibit where the works of individual modern Aboriginal artists were displayed, playing off the concept the "red centre" of the Australian continent. A couple of art critics from the media had already seen the setup and were suitably impressed.

She had considered asking Margaret to stay with Raine or Cathy while she and Nik did their duty at the museum, worrying that a few of the stark, menacing images – Namarrkun and his companions, in particular – might trigger more bad dreams, but Margaret protested so vehemently at the mere mention of being left behind that Alice dropped the idea. In a strictly educational sense, it would be great for Margaret to see the exhibit—no argument there.

She found a parking spot without much trouble near the front of the museum, which made her suspicious that things were going too well; darting through the front door, she hurried to her office before anybody could corner her. Inside with the door shut and her coffee brewing, she sank down into the wing chair. The reception brochures with their Support Your Local Museum donation inserts were stacked neatly on her desk in bundles of fifty. Beside them was the Hardison's standard reception guest book —oxblood leather cover, parchment pages, green satin ribbon marker—ready for the tonight's signatures of the rich and famous, and later of the curious and ordinary.

Closing her eyes, she imagined people threading their way in and out of the exhibit, then discussing what they'd seen out in the foyer while balancing champagne glasses and paper napkins embossed with the green and bronze Hardison logo wrapped around cream cheese and cucumber sandwiches. She genuinely wanted everyone to come see this magnificent display they'd all worked so hard to bring about and just hoped it would all come off without a hitch, as she'd promised. Alice opened her eyes and put down her cup. She knew everything was as ready as it would ever be, but taking another last look around couldn't hurt, just for mental reassurance.

Carrying the brochures and guest book, she went down to the main gallery and stood just inside the entryway beyond the AUTHORIZED PERSONNEL ONLY sign where a wide carpeted ramp sloped gently down to the floor of the cavernous room at the point where the marble tiles began. The ceiling was high and dark, swathed in shadows except for soft pools of light illuminating focal points in the exhibit. She set the brochures and book on a lectern next to the reprinted title board (with its striking red handprints made to emulate the spatter stencils found throughout Australia, guarding sacred sites and warning trespassers) and went down where the real show began. She had to admit, it was an artfully conceived design of contrasts, of light and shadow, of miniature and monumental, that had begun on the designer's drafting table and put by painstaking bolt become the real thing that thousands of people would stare at in open-mouthed surprise.

She decided to put herself in the shoes of one of these visitors and follow the route from the beginning to its climax. Standing in the entryway, the first thing you saw directly ahead on the opposite wall was the main Nourlangie rock panel from Kakadu National Park. The largest of the murals, it contained the most expressive example of a style archaeologists had dubbed the "x-ray" technique. Aboriginal artists had depicted the bodies of the painted figures with exposed internal organs and skeletal features as well as external trappings: heart, lungs, stomach, genitals, backbone vied with weapons and headdresses or scales and skin for attention. Especially fearsome was Namarrkun, the Lightning Man, with stone axes emerging from his head, knees, and elbows, encircled by a band of lightning. Tradition told how he struck the clouds with his axes to produce lightning in showering bright sparks. Tradition also told that he sometimes took on other duties, like punishing those who defied the laws of the people. What that punishment might be she didn't know but figured it couldn't be pleasant. Several of the modern artists in the show had painted their own interpretations of this creation ancestor, in imagery no less intimidating.

The hall was empty, and her footsteps on the marble tiles made the only sound as she moved among the still, silent pieces of the exhibit. The narrative audio system hadn't been activated yet. Alice noted with satisfaction that the panels were roped off just sufficiently out of arm's reach. The last thing they needed was for some tired, antsy kids to grab one and bring the whole business crashing down on their heads.

The first panel on the right-hand wall was a mural of a Bradshaw site, so named for the discoverer of the rock art shelters, from Western Australia in the Kimberleys. She passed in front of sinuous figures waving their long, flexible arms and legs, mostly in profile with protruding muzzles and exaggerated phalluses – seaweed with a hard-on. Goya-esque elongated figures in tall conical headdresses, these figures were judged by some scholars to be as old as the Lascaux bison. In contrast, out in the center of the room was the display of a well-known Aboriginal artist working in the Bradshaw style. His central painting, a bold display of hand prints and kangaroos in bright magenta tones, was possibly the most breathtaking smaller piece in the show, in Alice's opinion.

Continuing, she passed the Bradshaw figures and came to the panorama from the Gibb River Sacred Site containing the Wandjina images that had given her such a fright only a few weeks ago. For brief suspicious moments she lingered before the Wandjinas, forcing herself to stare into those red-fringed sightless eyes. She had the most compelling urge to put her hands on the nearest panel's smooth surface, to trace the sweeping vertical lines flowing away from the ghostly faces, and she suddenly knew, with a cold certainty, that if she did, her fingers would feel not smooth polymer but the weathered surface of a rock outcropping. Alice swallowed. Her fingers were trembling.

It was only a short reach over the ropes. She took one mesmerized step, then halted. Hellfire, what was she thinking? She shoved both hands into the pockets of her slacks and took a deep breath; better keep walking. She went down to the end of the mural where motifs of ibis, catfish, snakes, and hand stencils were superimposed over horizontal and inverted human figures, the symbols of sorcery, according to one of her art books. Recent debates suggested that this was a simplistic interpretation, but she hadn't studied it far enough to find out what the Aboriginals themselves had to say about it. Her general understanding was that they wouldn't tell you the whole story anyway; that was reserved for the initiated and the wise. Reaching the next wall of the gallery, Alice stood before the x-ray figures of the malevolent spirit Namandjoik, Namarrkun the Lightning Man, and a female fertility figure some sources called Barrginj, Namarrkun's wife. The panel stretched horizontally over twenty feet wide, to show the full spread of their anatomy with legs splayed and arms akimbo.

"Show your stuff, fellas," she breathed, her challenge whispered in the still air. The Lightning Man hovered on the panel before her, a crouching creature somewhat like a giant insect with antennae. She was holding her breath again, waiting for the hammers to fall or sparks to ignite the constructions of foam and plastic. Suddenly, she could see flames leaping in her imagination, flashing down from great boiling cloudbanks and brushing the tops of trees with fiery strokes in details so sharp she forgot for a moment where she was. Dazed, Alice pressed her fingers over her eyes; when she opened them again, she saw just an ordinary room with ordinary photographs. Shaking her head, she turned to leave.

At once her ears sensed rather than heard a high keening, or a whine maybe, like a subconscious scraping of talons along a chalkboard in her mind that made her sinuses ache. Startled, she looked around the room, trying to track the sound and hoping it was the air conditioning or a malfunction of the intercom system. She clamped her hands over her ears to shut out the screech, but it made no difference because the sound was inside her head. Panicked, Alice stepped over the rope and ran back across the room, realizing that the keening had acquired a swooshing along with it, somewhat like the skirl of a hurricane plowing its way through cracking branches.

Breathless, she ran back up the ramp, then stopped, and waited. The sound was gone. Turning around to face the silent gallery, she heard nothing at all. The shrieking and whooshing must indeed have been in her mind and nowhere else. And what did that make her – crazy?

"I heard *something*, damn it," she said aloud, as if stating the fact would make it so.

"So did I," said Jessie. He was staring at her with the most perplexed expression, his elbows propped on the lectern as he watched her. "It was your feet thudding the hell out of the ramp. What's the matter, those beauties finally get to you?"

"Something like that," she said. He smiled, and she forgot for an instant her all-encompassing fright. His face was so humanly warm and real, she could have kissed him.

"Will I see you at the reception tonight?" she asked instead. That would make the evening worthwhile, no matter what else went on. She might even get him talking to Nik, which could indeed be interesting.

"You know I never go to those things."

"I know. Just wishful thinking." She headed for her office, more confused than ever.

"You look beautiful," said Shelton, taking her hand in both of his. "Blue *is* your color, that's certain. Nikolas, good to see you again." He squeezed her fingers and took Nik's offered hand in a single smooth motion that was both practiced and elegant. MacBeth was wearing his gold-plated charm tonight.

"Did the Governor show up?" Alice asked.

"No, he sent his regrets, but Randal came in his place." Alice nodded. Randal was the Governor's college-age son, who in his spare time between law classes courted the Secretary of State's daughter, Kelsey, a freshman. They both attended the state university in Citrus Park, which made Randal a convenient stand-in for his father. Alice supposed the bodyguard expense was less as well.

"That's fine," she said. "He's a lot more photogenic. The camera crew from WCPN will be happy."

Shelton smiled. "More good publicity."

"The best kind. How about any senators?"

"Two in attendance, and quite a lot of university faculty. I'm really quite pleased with the group we have here. Now you and everyone else can feel that all your hard work wasn't wasted."

"I never felt that it was, but it's good to hear encouragement, all the same. Thanks."

Shelton squeezed her arm at the elbow and, smiling, smoothly detached himself and segued into a nearby group, the master host ministering to his chosen ones. The foyer was filling steadily with patrons and their guests, and MacBeth was just warming up to the role he enjoyed most.

Alice gave Nik a look. He seemed all sharp angles and inclined planes, a study in self-conscious discomfort in spite of his acceptable jacket and dark pants. If he'd been at a podium addressing moss-covered mycologists with loupes hanging from string around their necks he'd have been perfectly at ease, but this was her gig, not his, and he was making do the best he could.

"The show's really cool, want to come see?" Margaret appeared at his side, her bright flame of hair offset by a dark green silk shirt of Alice's. They'd debated over whether it was too old for her, but when Nik remarked how it agreed with her coloring – strictly from an artist's standpoint – that had settled it.

"Nik? Come on, I'll show it to you. I just cruised the whole thing—it's a trip."

"Would you mind?" Alice asked. "I sort of need to make the rounds and see who's here. I'll catch up with you later."

Nik shrugged. "Sure. That's what I'm here for." He followed Margaret down into the gallery.

Alice watched them for a moment. What would Margaret be like in ten years? Or Nik, or herself, for that matter? A wave of sadness suddenly swept over her for no good reason, and sweat trickled down inside her long sleeves. The damn dress *was* too hot. Blinking away the film of tears that threatened to ruin her makeup and feeling stupidly sentimental, she went in search of the champagne.

The refreshments were laid out in the foyer along two banquet tables adorned with appropriate linen, silver, and crystal provided by the catering service, which had also produced the swan ice sculpture listing in the center of an enormous punchbowl. It was too ostentatious for her taste, but she admired the skill of the sculptor. Anyway, it would soon be melting and forgotten once the guests got an eyeful of the exhibit.

For another twenty minutes Alice mingled with patrons as they found their way to the food and drinks (which were verboten in the gallery proper). She also made sure to point out the guestbook, which Shelton could gloat over later in the privacy of his office. Finally she headed down the ramp. The gallery was comfortably filled but not so crowded that the visitors couldn't make their way around it slowly, lingering and staring. She estimated that well over half of the three hundred invitations sent out had been honored.

Alice moved among the groups, giving her little talk and pointing out details about the images overhead. "The paintings were done mostly with pulverized red and yellow ochre, white pipe clay, and black manganese, with charcoal and clay compounds," she explained to a group of art majors from the university. "They probably mixed the colors with some kind of binder like tree resin or animal blood and made it into a paste that could be applied with their fingers or twigs, or mixed as a liquid to blow over their hands and feet to make stencil prints. Many images have been repainted and maintained by clan elders through the centuries as well. That's why a number of them are still vibrant and unfaded." Too vibrant, she was thinking.

"Aboriginal myths tell that the paintings are actual embodiments of the Dreamtime spirits. Once their work of creating the world was done, their spirits became one with their creations and sank into the rock surface. It was extremely important that the paintings be maintained and the areas where they appear be protected. Usually, each rock art site had its own clan group responsible for the images. Probably a particular shamanic guardian would be assigned to look after the paintings," she told them.

The students listened closely and a few were taking notes. "They actually painted over the old pictures?" asked a thin young woman. "Wouldn't that be taboo?"

"Not at all," Alice answered. "The custodian held a sacred position, like a ritual-master, we think, and was expected to retouch them as part of sacred ceremonies. But for anyone else, touching the paintings was strictly forbidden. To touch without the proper permissions and initiations was to open yourself up to great danger or death," she added, wondering why she had said that; it wasn't part of her prepared spiel. She moved away from Namarrkun and led her group toward the game animals, where kangaroo, ibis, emu, and fish leapt in the air above horizontal human figures. "They also believed that creating or retouching one of these paintings could release the spirit of the subject... it was a necessary part of their kinship group ritual, a way of establishing and renewing the clan's power and direct relationship to that particular ancestor spirit."

"I don't think I'd want a direct relationship with any of these gentlemen," said an elderly man whom Alice recognized as a city commissioner. The group laughed with him and moved on, threading their way through others still gawking along the circuit. So it went for the rest of the hour. Alice didn't see Nik or Margaret anywhere, so she assumed they'd gone out to the buffet.

Back in the foyer, she spotted Randal Crittendon surrounded by a laughing, admiring audience. He was a charmer, but not of the Shelton MacBeth variety. Randal was handsome in a tough, linebacker sort of way, with intense dark blue eyes that pinned you when you spoke to him but sparkled around the edges with hidden amusement. He could laugh in a way that made you believe you had just made him the happiest person on earth. All this at twenty years old. He would make a formidable lawyer if he didn't end up in politics first.

Alice assumed the prom-queen beauty hovering near his elbow was Kelsey Marks, the Secretary of State's daughter. Her curling brown hair just brushed her shoulders, and her fresh, clear face with minimal makeup was straight off the pages of *Seventeen* magazine. Her dress, however, was pure Vogue, a sheath of shell pink watered silk shirred over her hips and up her bosom into a cloud of dyed marabou feathers that wreathed her white shoulders. She wore no jewelry and didn't need any—she was a long-stemmed rose in first flower. Alice watched as Shelton MacBeth emerged from the crowd and whispered something to the couple. Randal nodded, and Shelton raised his champagne glass over his head.

"Your attention, please!" His voice cut through the din of chatter and mock-serious academic discussion filling the entrance to the gallery. He motioned for everyone to move in toward his position near the ramp. Alice jumped when she felt Nik's arm slide around her waist.

"Is it about over?" whispered Margaret, at her other side. "I'm like, dead." Alice nodded and mouthed "almost," then turned back to Shelton's pronouncement.

"I want to thank every one of you for joining us tonight. This is a significant event in the Hardison's history and represents an important step forward in its ability to draw world-class exhibits to Florida and to this area of the state in particular." He smiled generously at the senator to his left.

"And I especially want to thank Randal Crittendon for attending this evening. He has just told me, and I'm sure you'll be happy to learn, that the Governor intends to make a sizeable donation to the Museum Support Fund." He paused while applause sprinkled around the crowd, and then continued. "This endorsement ushers in a new era of prosperity for the Hardison Museum, and I want you to know we intend to continue the standard of excellence established by Virgil Hardison over seventy years ago when he founded this repository of artifacts and art from our state, our nation, and around the world. And now, I'd like to ask Randal to say a few words."

Shelton gestured toward the Governor's son. Randal Crittendon stepped away from his circle of admirers and bodyguards, drawing Kelsey with him. Shutters clicked and video cameras zoomed in as she flashed a cheerleader smile in their direction. He held her close to him with his arm around her waist and said, "I'd like to propose a toast to the Hardison Museum for bringing this exhibit to Florida and for providing its citizens with a valuable resource unduplicated anywhere else in the state." Alice cut her eyes up at Nik; this kid was making campaign speeches already.

"A toast: To the museum," said Randal. At that same moment, a shrill keening sliced through Alice's head, making her eyes water with pain. She clutched at Nik.

"Do you hear that?"

He bent down to her. "Hear what?"

"That *noise*, can't you hear it?"

The look on his face told her he did not. She put her fingers in her ears, as if to keep the rising shriek from leaking out into the assembled bankers and benefactors. Her hands felt numb; something dreadful was about to happen.

She watched in fascination as Randal Crittendon raised his champagne glass in a toast. In slow motion, it seemed, the lip of his glass tipped toward that of his lady, and met, impossibly, in a tinkling crash of shattered crystal that sent an explosion of diamond sparks over the heads of bystanders. Stunned, no one moved as Kelsey still held the splintered stem of her glass aloft and dark blood welled from the slice between her forefinger and thumb, pooling to drop in heavy plops on the pink silk, one after another. In paralyzed horror, Alice watched wine-colored stains seeping into the cloth, spreading in wider circles as each drop joined another. Some managed to reach the fine gray wool carpet Shelton had paid some British dealer a fortune and a half to lay down during last year's renovations. She watched unblinking as Kelsey's eyes rolled back and she fainted into the arms of her speechless fiancée.

Alice stumbled like a blind person against Nik, moving out of the way as Shelton, senators, patrons, and security guards scrambled around like ants stirred with a stick. Margaret was saying something to her in a frightened voice, but all she could hear was the high, faraway screech that rose and fell like gusts of a typhoon trapped inside her skull.

Later that evening, long after Margaret had gone to bed, Nik and Alice continued to sit huddled together on the couch as the fire in the grate burned down to ashes. The three of them had talked over the second museum accident until there was nothing left to say. Alice had tried to describe for them the sound she'd heard just before the glass broke, but it was an exercise in futility because neither of them had heard any such thing. The glasses shattering was a freak accident by all accounts, and no one connected with the museum would be blamed for anything. But still. It was another unexpected injury in proximity to the exhibit, and Alice's synthesizing brain wanted to make connections and look for patterns in spite of her emotional resistance.

Nik's eyes were closed and by his regular breathing Alice could tell he was dozing off. She should have felt cozy and secure, but all she felt was cold dread. She wondered if anything peculiar had been reported from the previous installations of the exhibit. It was worth checking out, but not right now. She had the whole weekend ahead of her, with nothing to do before she had to face going back to the museum. Alice yawned. Finally she was winding down. Her head fell heavily against Nik's chest; she closed her eyes and hoped she could sleep without dreaming.

CHAPTER 10

ALICE SAT at the kitchen table with the Saturday paper in front of her. This time the story had made the front page. Poor Shelton. She felt sorry for him, considering the massive spin job this was going to require. And as she'd feared, the reporter was using phrases like "haunted museum" and "cursed exhibit." She sighed and turned to the comics.

The house was quiet, Margaret and Nik still not up. Alice sat thinking. How to put the past several weeks of her life in perspective? Out the kitchen window she could see the wall of treetops gilded by early morning sunlight; shafts of pale yellow lanced through ironwood and oak, a promise of some warmth to come. This past summer there had been a family of raccoons, a mother and three kits, in a partially rotted giant beech just beyond the margin where yard and woods met. She could see its wintertime framework with massive gray arms stretching up into the sky, its brown and yellow leaves hanging in shriveled tags. She remembered one hot morning in August, lurking at its base with her camera while the kits descended, tiny claws digging into the smooth bark. The smallest one nearly fell on top of her, but managed to land unscathed in the soft rubble of ferns and twigs among the tree roots. She had taken an entire roll of film during the episode, but the prints were disappointing, washed out by the whitened backlighting of the sun. The coons were all gone now, grown up and moved away.

Her thoughts pulled back inside, leaving the trees to their winter meditations. The living room near one of the glass doors was littered with boxes of decorations, pilfered through mostly by Margaret, and waiting for her final attempt at trimming the Christmas tree. This year Nik had found and cut for them a three-foot pine from the woods, which was a relief from Whit's insistence each year on dragging a ceiling-high cedar home from one of the tree lots in town. The sight of those trees lashed across the roof of his struggling Fiat and nearly dragging the ground behind the car was burned into her memory. But no more. She might actually get interested in trimming and lighting a small tree this year.

Alice sipped her cup of green tea carefully so as not to burn her tongue. Nik told her it was an invigorating blend that became a welcome morning ritual once you got used to it. Much better than coffee, he'd said. Well, the jury was out on that so far. She turned back to the reporter's story – luckily she wasn't included in the snapshot of shocked faces. Not too flattering of Shelton, which in itself was a bit of a shock.

"I see last night's excitement made the front page," Nik said, reading over her shoulder. Startled, Alice looked up at his face. She hadn't heard him get up and come into the kitchen.

"That's because the accident happened to an important somebody this time instead of a nobody. It's depressing; people will crowd through the doors to see the exhibit, but for all the wrong reasons. I hate that."

Nik made a sympathetic noise. "Are you going to check with a doctor about that headache?"

"It wasn't a headache. My ears just started ringing for no reason."

"Maybe you have an ear infection. Have you felt dizzy or unbalanced?"

Alice laughed out loud. That was exactly how she felt, but not from any headache. If she described to anyone at the museum what had been going on in her head just before the two accidents, they would definitely say she was unbalanced.

"How would I get an ear infection? I haven't been sick in weeks."

Nik shrugged and sat down at the table. "Just trying to offer suggestions."

"I know." If she had been the mushy type she'd have hugged him or given him some other sign of affectionate encouragement, but she wasn't, and the moment passed. "If it happens again I'll make an appointment."

The fact that it had happened twice in one day did have her a little worried, but this morning she felt all right. Easy enough to write it off as culminating symptoms of stress. Now that the exhibit was open, she could move on to other things. Like the Camper's Legend story, which had been simmering on the back burner for days.

The library folder lay on the table in front of her, cleaned of its dust and emptied of it contents. Nik poked at a few pieces. "Looks interesting. What is all this?"

"I'm not sure. I'm hoping it'll have some church records I can use for ideas."

"Your story?"

"You remembered." She smiled for the first time that morning, and looked at Nik more closely. Must be careful not to underestimate him.

"I liked what I read," he said, "but of course I'm no judge. I know that Margaret likes it."

He took a sip of her tea and quickly put it down – contaminated by artificial sweetener. It was true, though, that Margaret was her best critic. She could be counted on to say honestly if she thought something was crap, and she had read enough good stuff to know the difference.

This set her thinking again. The local legend was a good concept – whether it could be told as a compelling story depended on her own skills. She was adept at plot structure and weaving storyline patterns, but she was relying on the library to come through with the historical specifics she wasn't sure about inventing on her own.

A quick shuffle through the folder had given her some hope. A lot of it was too obscure and made no sense, but there were some documents she could use: records of the land grant for the parcel where the original church had been built (signed X, *His Mark*, by landowner J. Hornbeam), a 1945 article with photo about the ground-breaking ceremony for the stone and stained glass edifice on the corner, copies of sermons penned in longhand on unlined paper by someone named Father Antoine, but best of all, a newspaper clipping of the real Old Joe incident. The newsprint was so yellowed and brittle, Alice was almost afraid to touch it. The item told in some detail how an Indian had been hanged (lynched, actually) for raping a young girl in 1899, in spite of heated controversy over his possible innocence. A local preacher, one Cadjer Harrow according to the story, was quoted as saying he'd "meet the degenerate soul in Hell one day" to assure justice had been meted out.

This struck Alice as a bizarre thing for a minister to say—had he planned to end up there himself? What a concept; the storytelling part of her brain lurched into gear.

Harrow, she'd also discovered, was founder of the original wooden church (then named the First Church of the Heavenly Powers), gathering a congregation and choosing a building site in 1894. She assumed the church had been Christian, but there was no mention of what sect they might have been. There were hints that Harrow was of mixed blood – some said he was part Indian himself, others thought his mother had been African. She'd learned this from his obituary notice, which was near the bottom of a page torn from the *Massalina Countian Weekly*, dated February 21, 1900. No cause of death was given.

Equally tantalizing was a handwritten order for two gravestones, with specific instructions regarding inscriptions and design. One was designated for Harrow himself (paid in cash, it was duly noted), but the other recipient was unnamed, and whoever had made the order was also not listed. Strangest of all, the date was July 15, 1945, nearly fifty years after Harrow's death.

Sipping her tea, Alice began to feel more than mildly curious. The material in the folder was much better than expected as far as fueling her imagination. But it was also becoming clear that a lot of it wasn't appropriate for the kind of book she'd originally planned to write. It was too adult, grisly even. A good example was that Sunday agenda she'd first read in the library – the one with the so-called Body and hymn-singing Sisters of the Blood and that business with serpents. Had they been a congregation of snake handlers? And there was a letter from somebody's grandmother, sweet on the surface but alluding to darker things. She found and read it again:

> Dear grandbaby,
> Happy 4 birthday. Have your precher daddy read this and tell you how much I wish I coud see your beatiful face. My bline old eyes dont see much anymore. I know your being good and Praise God who makes all things rite in the end.
> Love,
> Granny Yoo

It was a genealogical challenge, if nothing else, just to figure out how many different people were alluded to in the folder papers, and what their relationships might be. Alice already had a few ideas. It was pretty clear from the birthday note that the "daddy" mentioned must be a clergyman of some sort and therefore possibly the author of the handwritten sermons. But not everything matched up, because the sermons were mostly about counting one's blessings and were uplifting, loving dialogues from a shepherd to his flock – not the kind of pastoral leader that would set down an agenda of serpents and blood. It occurred to her that she might have the records of several different churches and pastors. She quickly wrote down a list of all the items and labeled them by date where possible. Then she sat staring at the list, trying to see a larger pattern of relationships and events, if indeed there was one.

Next, she made a brief outline of how to start the first chapter, riffing on the historical material in order to create a fictional setting that would have the feel of authenticity. She didn't intend to write a historical account of the church and its founder or of actual events that might have happened in the county – but there was plenty here to fuel her imagination to create her own convincing story. Then she suddenly realized that Nik had been speaking to her, his low voice saying something about mushrooms.

"What? Sorry, I wasn't paying attention," she confessed.

"I was just asking if you wanted to go woods walking with me later on, maybe this afternoon. There's a patch of *pleurotus* on some fallen trees down near the swamp that I want to get slides of before they shrivel up or the squirrels eat them. Since it's rained so hard the last couple of weeks, the dead trees are waterlogged and a sunny day like this should be good for fungi."

Alice had mental pictures to go with most of Nik's fungal taxonomy, but it was also vaguely funny to hear their names used like old friends in ordinary conversation. So, should we pay a call on the *Polypores* today? She was smiling to herself, and Nik grinned back. "Is that a yes?"

"Sure. In fact, I could take some scenery pictures to help with background descriptions that I might need later."

"Is the story set in the woods?"

"Just what's common around the camp area, but good local color details help locate a story in time and place, or set a specific atmosphere."

"Like these," he said, indicating the pile of letters and clippings.

"Mm," Alice nodded. "Although what I've looked at so far is pretty damn strange."

Margaret wandered into the living room, her eyes squinting against the sunlight. "What's strange?"

"All this stuff I found at the county library. At least some of it's related to that old church down the road. And guess what, the origin of the Camper's Legend tale about an Indian named Old Joe is explained in one of these clippings."

"No sh- ... uh, can I see?"

"Let me handle it – some of this stuff is pretty old."

Margaret leaned against her and read as Alice opened up the clipping. "Are you gonna put this in the story?"

"I'll probably use it in some way, but I don't think it's exactly the story we started out with."

"Why not?"

"Well, it's just not ... appropriate. I'm not sure yet where any of this is going, I just need to sit down at the computer and see what I can do with it."

Margaret flopped down on the couch. "I wanna go with you guys. When you go walking."

Nik stood up. "Looks like somebody else wants breakfast."

Alice looked behind her and saw there was a dog nose pressed against the glass door. As she brushed past Nik to head back to the study, he reached out and caught her around the waist. He kissed her quickly, then released her.

"What was that for?" she asked, pleased.

"A spontaneous 'otherwise, yes?'" His face held the barest hint of a smile.

Alice glanced at the couch, but Margaret was studiously ignoring them.

Still smiling, she gathered up the folder and the church papers and carried them to the study. Sitting down at the computer, she saw it was already on. Margaret must have been online. Alice opened her Camper's Legend file and reread what she'd written so far. She could see that it just wasn't going to work with the direction her thoughts were now trending. She closed it untouched, and opened a new file, labeling it Chapter One, figuring a better title for the book would come later. Closing her eyes, she sat very still and cleared the screen in her mind, then waited for pictures to come. She wanted to visualize the old pine church as it must have looked when new; she also wanted to form a strong mental image of Cadjer Harrow, its founder. Her imagination would have to invent one, since there were no drawings or photos of him and no clear descriptions to draw from except for a few sideways clues like the speculations regarding his parentage.

So, Rev. Harrow, she thought, where are you? At once a face materialized in her mind's eye, surprisingly cunning and completely unique with broad features and dark mahogany skin crinkled with hundreds of tiny lines like an old hide that hadn't been properly tanned and was now starting to crack and craze. But the man's face wasn't old – his hair was dark, his teeth evenly spaced in a thin straight mouth that didn't fit the wide nose or jutting brow and prominent cheekbones. Black eyes glistened like polished jet, but they didn't look quite right – she suddenly realized there were no irises, just solid dark orbs centered on the stark white field of the eyeballs. He wore a dark gray parson's hat anchored squarely on the crown of his head, and seemed to stare out from under the brim directly at her, as if spying through a window into the bedroom study where she sat, comfortable and secure.

He held a leather strap in one hand, several coils of it wrapped around his thick brown fingers, and then it became a leash held close against his leg, pulled taut by some animal she couldn't bring into focus. At first he seemed to be just standing outdoors in a wooded area and then suddenly he was pacing in high black boots, worn at the insteps from stirrups, across a rough clearing where pine trees had been felled by axes. Truncated stumps oozed resin from the recent chops and cuts.

Alice opened her eyes and took a deep breath. The image was unnervingly strong in her mind, more like the memory of an experience than the product of her imagination. If the real Rev. Harrow had been anything like this, his congregation must have been cowering in submissive fear from the first sermon onward. She put her vision of Harrow on hold for a moment and pulled the library folder open. One last look at the obituary info on the founding of the church and she would be ready to start typing.

The obit account described an event when the Rev. C. Harrow, "newly arrived in the area from heathen lands," had determined the proper spot for his new church by using a dowsing rod, claiming several significant power lines running through the earth all met in that one place. Alice licked her lips; truth really was stranger than fiction. Now she knew where to start. She typed in the heading and the first paragraph began to unfold:

Chapter One – Foundations

On September 22, 1894, 21 men, 13 women, and 8 children stood in a semicircle at the edge of a clearing and watched their newly acquired minister pace back and forth across the muddy ground. Rain had fallen all morning and still drizzled on the watchers, but the tall figure of the minister held a forked dowsing stick in front of him and ignored the weather.

He crossed the clearing for the fifth time, holding the stick out level with his chest. Then suddenly it began to quiver and dropped sharply to point at a pool of water where a stump had been extracted.

"Here," he said in a loud voice and turned to face the congregation. "Dig the foundations here." The men came forward and marked the spot with stakes, orienting the church layout westward to face the setting sun. After the minister said a brief prayer of dedication over the spot, the families and other church members got into their wagons, mounted their horses, and returned to their homes in and around Little Shiloh, a community of dwellings scattered widely though the wooded countryside.

One woman lingered behind, waiting for the minister to finish his silent meditation over the four stakes, which would mark the entrance to the new church building. She held her 2-year-old son on her hip, and her adolescent daughter hid behind her skirts. The children were dressed in white, a sharp contrast with their black skin.

"Reverend Harrow?" asked the woman, stepping forward. "Would you spare a minute?"

Cadjer Harrow came away from the building site and stood in front of her. He was much taller and looked down at them as from a great height, or so it seemed to the woman's daughter Belinda.

"Yula Rider," he said. It was more a statement than a greeting. "Is there a problem?"

"When you said that, uh ... there should be no ..." she paused, fearful of what she wanted to say.

"No what?" He stared at her unblinking.

"No ... ah, working of the roots and—"

"No heathen magic," he said sternly.

"Not even for healing? And helping folks out with their problems, like peanuts drying up in the fields and—"

"Don't blaspheme, Mrs. Rider," Harrow replied. His voice was cold, the words spoken slowly.

"I didn't mean to say anything wrongful, I just thought—"

"Don't think. I tell you that you should not dilute the power of the new church with your own spells and conjure. I forbid it."

"Yes, Reverend." Yula Rider hung her head and backed away. Her son began to cry.

"Hush, Antoine," she whispered.

"It could go hard for those who do not give up their old, ignorant ways. I came to build a church of unwavering strength in the name of the powers. Would you be a part of that church?" He took a step forward.

"Yes," she said, frightened.

"Would you join with your neighbors in forging the greatest conduit for heavenly power known in this century?"

"Yes," she answered. Though many of his words were confusing to her, their general meaning was not. It would be a severe mistake to go against the community's new spiritual leader.

"I'm glad you agree," he said and splashed past her to his waiting horse.

"Come on, Belinda," she said, taking the girl's hand. "Don't you tell any of this to a living soul, understand?" she whispered.

"Yes, mama." Belinda watched the strange black-suited man ride away, whipping his horse's flanks as it galloped across the clearing and into the trees.

Her mother was gripping her hand too tightly and it hurt, but she didn't try to make her let go. Her baby brother was quiet now, sucking on a corner of his mother's kerchief. She knew her mother was worried, and she wondered if the strange man was angry at them.

"Lift up your skits, girl. Don't let them drag in the mud – only good dress you got."

"Yes, mama."

Belinda followed as Yula Rider entered the wooded trail that led to their shack a mile past the springs on the river. She didn't know why the Little Shiloh people had invited that man to be their new preacher. Maybe he invited himself. She didn't like him, but she had already concluded it would be very unwise if she told anyone.

Alice stopped typing and sat quietly for a few moments, surprised at how easily those opening paragraphs had materialized. It was a good beginning, but she was a little surprised at some of the turns it had taken. Like naming the little boy Antoine. The name, of course, had been in her mind from the sermons in the folder, but it added an interesting twist for the founding preacher to encounter a child of that name. She didn't know how the story would get from Harrow to the real Father Antoine fifty years later, but it would be interesting to find out.

"Mom, you wanna go with us now?" Margaret stuck her head in the door. She was now dressed for the outdoors and had a paper bag with, Alice assumed, some kind of snack food for the trail. She'd been so involved in writing that their preparations for the walk had slipped past her completely.

"I'm coming. Just give me a minute."

She saved the file, and then stood up and stretched, her head still full of Harrow, the church, and the troubled Rider family. She thought about the outline of the chapter she'd sketched before starting to write. Already things had diverged from the plan and there were people she hadn't imagined beforehand, but that was part of the thrill of writing – to see the characters and situations developing out of thin air.

"Mom!" Margaret called from the deck.

"Alice!" Nik chimed in, setting Dawg into a frenzy of barking. Their laughter drifted in through the door.

"Coming, you guys."

She pulled on her shoes and hurried out the door after them, then ran back for her camera. Coming down the stairs again, she only half attended to Margaret's dispute with Nik over which direction they should take through the trees. She was more curious about what life would be like for the people of Little Shiloh once they had finished building their church and had begun using it.

CHAPTER 11

BY ONE o'clock, Alice, Margaret, Nik, and Dawg were following one of the well-worn trails into the woods behind the house. Nik had loaded himself down with mushroom collecting basket, a smallish backpack that doubled as a camera bag, collapsible tripod, and pocket tape cassette for recording field notes. Margaret had stuffed an extra bag of peanuts into the paper sack and hung a whistle "for scaring off critters" around her neck. The expedition was underway.

The woods were beautiful, aromatic in the crisp air, with yaupon and American holly peppering the woods, their glossy branches loaded with bright red berries. Beech, magnolia, and several varieties of oak were common, with an occasional stand of longleaf and loblolly pine. A few red cedars spread their wings in sun-filled clearings made by fallen trees, their blue berry-like cones weighting the limbs at this time of year. There was one near the pond, on the path they were following today. Alice didn't need a guide to Florida trees; she had Nik, who'd identified most of what grew on the property. Catbrier was everywhere underfoot and entangled among lower shrubs and vegetation; it made walking a chore along the less-traveled portions of the trail, its prickly thorns snagging ankles and biting through socks.

"*Helsfyr!*" said Nik, stooping to remove the vine from his pants leg.

"Nik's cursing in Swedish again," observed Margaret.

Alice glanced at her daughter. Snarky. Nik stopped every few feet to inspect the terrain or fiddle with his equipment or dig around in the leaf mould, but Alice felt like running, as if her blood had become carbonated. At this plodding rate it could be dark before they even got to the pond.

When they reached a clear stretch among old-growth beech and oak, she punched Margaret's shoulder. "Race ya," she whispered and sprang forward over the fallen twigs and tree litter, hugging her camera tightly against her ribs. Margaret bolted after her, a fawn at her heels.

105

"Have a care for snakes," Nik called after them. "Could be out sunning in the path ..."

I know, I know, Alice thought, running full tilt until an immense toppled beech across the path forced her to pull up. It was too long and its crown too tangled in the underbrush for her to get around, so she flopped down on it instead. Margaret nearly crashed into her.

"Oof! Sorry—" they were laughing and stumbling over each other. Alice felt giddy – too much fun. She sat on the beech trunk, panting.

Nik was not far down the path, taking his time, his hair white-blonde in the bright sun. Normally he wore it pulled back in a tight ponytail, but today it fell loose around his shoulders. Just slightly longer than her own, it formed a shining nimbus around his face for an instant. Alice blinked. The light transformed everything she saw. From where she sat, yellow rays angled down through the network of branches, the bare bones of oak, hickory, and hornbeam casting a shadowed lattice over the ground. She was already framing the shots in her head. The contrast in color and dappled highlights from Southern magnolia and wax myrtle, the few evergreens she recognized, was provocative, the shifting light hypnotic.

She felt an urge to shoot from every angle, to enhance the descriptive process of memory with the precision of the photographic record. Alice found writing descriptions tedious, sometimes impossible, and preferred to focus on what happened in dialogue and action, keeping physical descriptions to a quick brush stroke. Sometimes she couldn't even see what her characters looked like, an indication that maybe she didn't really know who they were or what was going on underneath the surface. Which made the pages she'd just written about the Rev. Harrow a uniquely unsettling experience. She already knew him better than she wanted to.

In the short story format, she was used to dealing with characters as enigmas, where a tantalizing slice of life was all you got. But a novel was different – she'd have to really understand the people she was inventing and take a close look at their surroundings. There was certainly a lot to draw from all around her, and a stack of good photographs wouldn't hurt to jog her memory for details.

Nik climbed over the fallen beech. "Doing okay?" he asked.

"Yeah, just catching my breath. You guys go ahead, I'll be there in a minute." He nodded, and headed after Margaret who had already set off down the trail.

She took three quick shots, bracketing the settings, and then hurried after Margaret and Nik, who'd trudged on in the direction of the pond. She crunched through leaf drifts ankle-deep, keeping a sharp lookout for rattlers or moccasins, and felt sweat trickling down her side and into the waistband of her running suit, its fleece lining now too warm for the exertion. A wood tick larger than a pinhead made its slow, deliberate way up her shirtfront. Alice curled her lip, and picked it off with care, then squeezed it between thumbnail and index finger. The nasty buggers were all over the woods, even in winter. A good solid freeze would have killed off most of them, but they hadn't had one yet this year.

She caught up with the other two at the pond's edge where the ground became spongy and stuck to her shoes, like walking on melted marshmallows. Skimmers and water beetles skated over the sun-dappled surface of the shallow water. Monoliths of fallen trees leaned precariously on the arms of their neighbors or buried their heads in the muck, exposing roots higher than Alice's head. The woodland floor around the pond showed bare black dirt under the leaf cover except for a patchwork of emerald green lichens and mosses. Somewhere further beyond the ring of trees and up the slope was Raine and Tim Crandell's house.

Nik was lying on his belly, stretched out full length in the moss and dirt with Dawg beside him, angling the lens of his camera over a tiny mushroom about the size and color of a periwinkle. She felt itchy just looking at him, a free feast to the crawling subculture, among which ticks were only the most obvious. He adjusted the tripod, its legs only a foot long, suitable for macro work. When he pressed the shutter release on his remote it took a full eight seconds for the shutter to click and register an image of the tiny mushroom half-hidden by ferns in deep shade. Dawg yawned and sniffed the bottom of his master's shoes.

"*Helvete!*"

"What's the matter?" She knew Nik was careless in the areas of his life having to do with social externals like dress and punctuality, but where his documentation of fungi was concerned he was a perfectionist. He'd shoot the same subject from the same angle half a dozen times before he was satisfied.

"Tripod slipped when the shutter closed."

"I didn't see anything move." She squatted down on her heels.

"It'll be blurred," he said, not looking up. He looked through the eyepiece, adjusted it slightly, and made another shot. "Well, that'll do." He pushed to a sitting position and brushed leaves off his chest.

Alice looked around. "Where's Margaret?"

Nik stood up and scanned the line of trees around the pond. "It's not that far back to the house," he said. "Maybe she went home."

"Well, she shouldn't just walk off without telling us."

Alice was pissed and uneasy. She tried to spot the Crandell's roofline through the trees. It wasn't as far away as it looked; you could almost see the swamp and pond from the deck of their house when the trees were bare. It was conceivable that Margaret might have decided to just keep going till she reached their back fence, but still ... she should have said something.

"Margaret!" Her shout echoed around the woods. They stood listening for a minute or so, but there was no other sound.

"Should we go look for her?" Alice headed around the periphery of the pond.

Nik gathered up his camera gear and stowed it in his bag. "It would make more sense to wait here. She'll probably come back to the place where she left us, don't you think?" His voice was even, reasonable.

"Margaret!" Again, there was no answer. Alice bit her lip. "Well, if she doesn't show up in a few minutes, Dawg and I are going looking."

Margaret had stood around watching Nik with his camera, and then got distracted by a hawk flying low through the trees. Mushroom photography was pretty boring when you weren't the one doing the shooting. Birds were much more interesting, and she might get a good look at it if it lit somewhere. She brushed a gossamer spider's web away from her face and climbed over a couple of tree trunks. It was warming up rapidly, so she pulled off her sweater and tied the arms around her waist, leaving her arms bare in her T-shirt. She popped the last of the peanuts into her mouth and rolled up the empty paper bag, stuffing it into the back pocket of her jeans. Still hungry, she wondered how long it would take to walk back to the house. It was too bad she'd decided against bringing those malted milk balls. Her stomach rumbled.

"Come on, Marmalade," she said aloud. She liked to imagine communing with the old calico cat's spirit, which she assumed still hung around the house after the cat had poisoned himself a few years ago by eating one blue-tailed skink too many.

The hawk was a large one and had landed in an oak tree not far away. From its field marks Nik had taught her, Margaret knew it to be a red-shouldered hawk: rust colored bars on the back and wings, white and brownish-black stripes across the tail, big as an owl. She half expected it to break into a loud *keehaaarrr*, but it had nothing to say. It sat perfectly still on the branch, as if stuffed. Margaret moved in closer, tromping through thigh-high hollies and bayberry bushes. She heard her mother's voice, drifting up from the pond, but she wasn't lost, so no big deal. She poked around under roots and in holes, tossed a limestone rock in the air, stopped to examine a worm-looking thing attached to the underside of a leaf. When she looked up, there was someone sitting on a tree stump a little ways away, looking back at her.

Actually, that wasn't right. The man's eyes were shut, but Margaret knew he could see her and Marmalade anyway. She also decided the man was a foreigner. The clothing was a clue – plain black suit, old-fashioned in a way that reminded her of the cover illustrations on those Charles Dickens books her grandmother gave her last Christmas. On his head was a black hat with a wide brim. Not a cowboy hat – it was wider and flatter, with no feather in the band. So he wasn't an Indian, as she'd first thought. But sure as sure, the man was watching her. With his eyes shut.

Margaret's heart was pounding, but she continued to stare. In her mind's eye she looked around for Marmalade's ghost, but he was gone. Twitching with the urge to run, she also felt unable to move, and as she stared, a branch fell from a tree overhead and clobbered the guy square on the head. Although the hat was squashed and knocked off, exposing his stiff black hair, the man sat motionless as if carved of rock. The branch should have knocked him to the ground, but it didn't. Her breath was coming in small gasps, and she felt the hidden eyes following her smallest movement. Margaret tore herself from the spot and galloped through the underbrush toward the pond, running flat out and heedless of brambles and snakes. She felt the hidden eyes boring into her back as she ran.

"Maaargaaaret!" Alice looked at her watch. "That's it. I'm going after—"

"Mom!" Margaret emerged from the trees on the far side of the pond, her chest heaving as though she'd run a marathon. She ran to them and threw her arms around Alice.

"Mom ..." she gasped, "you won't believe this ... there's a man sitting on a stump ... through the trees ... there." She pointed into the shadowed understory.

"What kind of man?" Nik asked, looking where she'd pointed.

"I don't know – an Indian ... or ..." she wheezed for breath and couldn't speak. "He didn't say anything. A tree limb hit him ... I think he's probably dead or something."

"You mean like a body?" Alice looked up at Nik in alarm. This was sounding more like they might need to get in touch with the sheriff.

Margaret was calming down now and pulled away from Alice. She looked at the trees expectantly, then back to Nik and Alice.

"He was just sitting on a stump. It wasn't anybody from around here."

Nik rummaged around in his backpack and pulled out his cell phone. He turned to Margaret and said, "Want to show me where? I'll call the authorities if we need to."

"Okay, but only if Mom goes too." Alice nodded and put her arm around Margaret's shoulders.

"We'll go look, but carefully, and not too close. If he's an escaped convict or something, he could be dangerous."

Nik touched a small bulge in the side pocket of his bag. "I'm not unarmed."

Alice stared at him. That was totally unexpected – he was the last person she expected to own a gun, much less carry one around with him. He gave her a tight smile.

"I never go in the woods without it. Just a precaution – you never know."

Alice felt her jaw must have dropped.

"Don't worry," he said, "it's registered and legal." He shrugged. "Let's go have a look."

He headed across the clearing as if he were just strolling through the park, Dawg at his heels. Alice was astonished and smitten with his utter cool-headedness in the presence of potential danger. This was a Nik she did not know. But now that he'd revealed himself, she willingly followed him into the trees. Margaret trailed behind them.

Margaret directed them as best she could remember, trying to recognize the huge old water oak where the hawk had landed.

"There," she said. "He was there." The spot she indicated was through a tangle of *Ilex* and small ironwood saplings and out into a space open to the sky. Another large oak lay upended, possibly from last summer's hurricane.

"Here?" said Nik, pointing to a weathered stump beside the felled oak.

"Yeah, but he's gone now." Margaret stood close to Alice and looked around at the encircling woods.

"What did he look like?" Alice asked. "What made you think he might be an Indian?"

Margaret hesitated. "I don't know ... his hair was straight black and his skin was dark brown."

Nik walked the perimeter of the clearing. Dawg sniffed eagerly all over the ground and trees, but did not appear to be aware of anything out of the ordinary. He loped around Nik and banged his tail cheerfully against his master's leg. Nik looked up at the sky. "Well, nothing here now to see."

"You're sure this was a real person, and not one of your ... mental encounters?"

"Mom! I *saw* him, just sitting there! I DID!" Margaret's face was flushing pinkish red.

"I just thought you might have imagined it."

"That is *so* not fair! I wouldn't make something like that up." She walked off ahead of them, kicking leaves out of her way.

Alice looked at Nik, feeling a sudden urgency to be out of the woods and back in her own yard. It was nothing she could put her finger on, just a feeling of eyes watching, or something waiting. The air felt charged for no reason she could point to, but she found herself stifling the urge to run.

"Let's go home," she said.

They headed back to the pond at a steady walk and hit the trail again that led back to Alice's property. When she and Whit had bought their home site out here, it had been against the realtor's advice. They'd been wavering between some much more attractive, and expensive, acreage in the rolling hills north of Citrus Park, and the cheaper wooded plots south of town. They'd opted for the latter, not just because it cost less or was close to the beach, but because of the trees. Alice felt drawn to the woods and land, and somehow couldn't see building a house anywhere else, even though her mother had fretted about it being out in the middle of nowhere. Soon, though, Raine and her husband, and a few other couples had bought the surrounding five- and ten-acre plots, so that they were now in the middle of somewhere, with neighbors.

They walked in silence, each chewing over their own thoughts. Alice was a little concerned about Margaret. It was possible she might have imagined seeing someone, especially with all their talk about camper's ghost stories. She knew that Margaret claimed to be able to "see" the spirits of her dead pets, but this was something different, and she didn't like the feel of it.

She was planning to finish her photo documentary of the sites needed for background material this afternoon by driving around to the two churches at the crossroads, the small county graveyard near Magnolia, maybe the courthouse, and library building as well. She cast a look over her shoulder at the trail behind her, but there was nothing unusual ... just trees and late afternoon sun. Still, the feeling of menace lingered, setting her teeth on edge.

In the bathroom, Alice stripped off her sweat suit and did a quick tick check. She'd gotten adept at distinguishing ticks from freckles – ticks eventually moved or bit in. She was pleased not to find any, but wished she didn't have to be reminded that her job was making her too sedentary. That little bulge of cellulite at the top of her thighs was the price.

She studied her face in the mirror over the sink. The eyes weren't bad. On her driver's license they were listed as hazel, but up close you could see that the iris was yellow, ringed in aqua blue. From a distance they looked brown. She wondered if they were her father's eyes. There were no photos of him, not even of her mother and him together. After his death, Suzanne Waterston never remarried. Alice wished she could have known him or even a little something about him, beyond the few facts her mother was willing to share.

She sighed and pulled on clean clothes. The afternoon was getting on, and she didn't want to lose any more time while the light was still good. She went to the study and packed up her backpack with camera, last roll of high-speed film, telephoto and wide-angle lenses, tripod, and notebook.

"I'm going out to take pictures of the old church," she announced. Margaret and Nik were seated at the table. As he sorted through the mushrooms he'd collected, Margaret was sketching them with colored pencils.

"Can I go?" Margaret put down her pencil.

Alice didn't answer; she looked at Nik.

"Not me," he said. He had four mushroom caps lined up on a sheet of newspaper making spore prints while he thumbed through his dog-eared guidebooks, verifying his field identifications.

"I might wanna go," Margaret repeated. "soon as I finish this."

"I'm not waiting around, the light's fading."

Margaret pursed her mouth. "Guess I'll stay, then."

"I'll be back in a bit," Alice said, relieved. "Shouldn't take long."

She went down the stairs to the car and put the backpack on the seat beside her. With a sense of purpose and more than a dash of jitters, she headed down the driveway.

Out on the parkway, she realized she was speeding again, gripping the steering wheel as the speedometer needle edged over 60, then 70. The church was only five or so miles away, so what was the hurry?

Turning onto the county road at the Coastal Small Engine Repair garage, a small shop run by local shade-tree mechanics, she passed through the unincorporated settlement of Snake Bite, a community containing the store, a couple of cement block duplexes, and half a dozen ageing wooden houses with old cars in their yards. She cruised around another curve, coming up on one of the county dumpsites. Right there by the side of the road, it was an assault to the senses: an open boxcar on giant wheels, more often than not overflowing with household garbage, road kills, mangled furniture, rotting kitchen refuse, an army of flies, and other unspeakables. She held her breath till she was well past it.

Almost to the end of the county road, she spotted the trees – a semicircular grove of pines, guardians of the first church. Sentinels, thought Alice, watching it year by year rotting back into the land. The shoulder of the road was newly mowed by county maintenance and smelled of cut grass, but beyond the strip of manicured Bahia, a profusion of weeds and brush filled the gaps between the pines. Alice pulled onto the roadside landing strip and parked about ten yards from the site, feeling a little self-conscious, even though the road was deserted.

She got out with her camera and locked the car. A battered pickup truck rattled by, the driver staring curiously at her as he passed. She waited nervously near the car, but the truck kept going so she turned her attention back to the church. Walking the few yards to the entrance, she was reminded of Cadjer Harrow pacing the area with his dowsing rod ... and this was the spot he had chosen.

"Dig here," she breathed, scanning the sagging steps and doorless entryway. Mid-afternoon westerly sunlight slanted in, highlighting interior angles and improving the depth of field – good enough for shooting. She brought the camera up to her eye and focused, framing the doorway and roof, but the bell tower was cut off, so she backed out nearly to the road. The angle was better; she clicked the shutter. First shot.

Then she moved in closer to get detailing on the entrance and weathered boards of the steps, the smell of dust and termite-riddled wood sharp in her nostrils. She aimed and shot again, the shutter release on her old manual Nikon sounding monstrously loud in the silence of the grove. Like a guillotine coming down – ka-chunk. No trucks passing, no birds, no woods noises. It was unnerving, and she wished now that she'd brought someone else along. This one photo documentary would have to do it – she wasn't coming back.

Peering in, she could see that the building was empty just the way she'd described it in her first story attempt. Every piece of furniture was long gone and so were both doors, but surprisingly most of the windowpanes remained unbroken in their frames. Probably coated so thick with cobwebs and spider shit they were as good as safety glass. She considered climbing the few steps up into the church, but just couldn't make herself do it. The silence was getting too damned loud.

Determined to finish the roll and get the hell out, she sat on the bottom step and propped her elbows on the threshold to steady her grip, then aimed into the gloom and clicked. It would have been better to set up the tripod since the light meter reading was so low, but she didn't want to take the time. She was feeling a low-level sense of urgency again ... just do it quick and get out ... so she braced her shoulder against the door frame and looked for something to set her focus by. The best bet was the bright rectangle of light cut sharply into the far wall by the back doorway.

Her finger hovered over the shutter release, but for some reason she was afraid to press it; there was the barest whiff of menace from the darkened interior. It eddied around her like fog filling a dip in the road. She hesitated, then twitched and the shutter mechanism chunked loudly, open and then closed, sending ripples of sound outward into the still air shrouded in shadow. And suddenly she was convinced she'd made a terrible mistake, invaded some space she had no business disturbing. Every movement, every miniscule eye blink and exhaled breath, sounded too loud; she heard as well as felt her beating heart. The interior of the church had become vibrant, and she couldn't hold still enough to focus. Stumbling backward, she unslung the camera strap from her neck and swallowed, panic rising in her like a tide.

"Idiot," she muttered. "Get a grip." Even her whisper sounded shockingly loud and obtrusive. Backing away from the entrance, she looked up at the tower. It speared the sky above her, rising from the roof peak near the front door. Unlike the church roof, which was tin, the bell tower was shingled in wood. It was caved in on one side, open to the sky and rain. Alice stared and stared until her eyes stung, watching it watching her. And suddenly her teeth were on edge again, the screech too high and faint to really hear this time – she felt rather than heard it.

"Dammit, I won't be spooked," she announced and slowly raised her camera. A crack like a shotgun blasted the air, punching her heart against the walls of her chest. A passing car had backfired. Alice turned and fled back to her car, fumbled in her pocket for the key, struggled with the lock, and wrenching the door open, dropped into the driver's seat. Heedless of its delicate mechanisms and expensive lens, she tossed her camera onto the passenger seat, a sin for which she would have threatened anyone else with death or dismemberment.

With both doors locked and the car cranked, she suddenly felt ridiculous and sat for a moment with the engine idling. She was safe, nothing was coming after her ... stupid to be frightened over empty air. Her breath was leveling out now, and the constriction in her chest was letting go. Alice turned around in the seat and looked at the church. Nothing. It was innocent, its trees stately in the late afternoon sun. Goddamn, she was worse than Margaret.

Feeling extremely foolish, she put the car in gear and pulled out onto the road. Her next stop was the small county graveyard on the outskirts of Magnolia, and she intended to handle it with complete journalistic detachment. Turning onto the parkway, driving slowly, she passed the entrance to her own mile of pot-holed dirt road, and kept going toward Magnolia, still jumpy from her case of the frights.

And then she realized with dread that she would have to go back – she hadn't taken any pictures of the fieldstone church down at the intersection of the county road and State Road 87. It was fairly unusual, from an architectural standpoint, and she wanted it for the pictorial record. But maybe she could do without it.

Magnolia was just six miles from Snake Bite, and Alice was soon approaching the graveyard off to her right. There was no sign marking it, and the location was less than choice; it seemed, in fact, to have been carved out of the surrounding pastureland and set off by post and wire fencing. Small unassuming graves marked with plain white stones or slabs filled most of the area beneath half a dozen century-old pecan trees, their massive branches moss-draped and bent with age. Plastic flower arrangements in marbelite vases were fading on many of the plots. All in all, the place was a small ragged island of suspended time.

Not far beyond it, Alice pulled into a one-pump gas station and got a diet cola from the outside vending machine. Feeling fine now, she sat in her car and sipped the drink, and checked to see how many shots were left on the roll. Five to go. Satisfied, she got out, locked the car, and walked down the shoulder of the road to the graveyard. She could see fenced pastureland stretching for several miles behind the graveyard, dotted by three magnificent oaks that spread their branches outward for yards and then drooped down, nearly touching the ground. They could easily be hundreds of years old, which added to the sense of timelessness as she stood among the stones. Although an occasionally vehicle whizzed by along the parkway, it was a restful spot.

Nearing 5:00, the sun was much lower now and the air was turning cold again. She considered going back to the car for her flannel jacket that she'd left on the floorboard to cover her backpack, but it was too much trouble. Ten more minutes and she'd be heading home where it was warm. Alice aimed and took two wide-angle shots from where she was standing, just to get the lay of the land. The distant trees were framed nicely against the sky. Then she began to wander among the headstones, on the lookout for the two described in the library material.

Though the two markers were supposed to have been erected in 1945, the brown sandstone requested for them was an odd choice, given that marbles and granites were much more popular in modern headstones. She wondered if it had been a cost-saving decision or some more personal decision. The surnames on the respectable white monuments were all familiar – county founding fathers whose descendants were still heavy into local politics and positions of influence. Then, near the back of the cemetery, she saw a plot set off by a low iron fence.

Stepping around slabs and over fallen wreaths, she reached a weedy, untended area. Here the property abutted the pasture fence where a line of pecans and white oaks arched along the fencerow, forming a canopy over the forgotten interments. The rusted plot fence was about knee high, with rows of fluted spear points along the top; inside were two stones, mottled brown and stained green along the base by lichens. Alice felt the old fieldwork thrill of discovery she hadn't experienced since her archaeology graduate student days. She stepped around the gate, fallen off its hinges and leaning at an angle, and then she was inside the tiny compound.

Alice knelt down in the dried grass and leaves and cleared away a tangle of woodbine and old blackberry canes to read the inscriptions on the headstones. The smaller stone was cut in what Alice recognized as the old-fashioned bed-board shape with urn-and-willow design across the top. Its epitaph read simply "In Memoriam Forgive Us." No name and no date. She wondered if this belonged to the unnamed recipient listed on one of the gravestone receipts. The other, larger stele should be Harrow's, if indeed this was the right plot. This stone followed the more elaborate "cradle" shape popular in the late 1800s and bore an equally elaborate inscription:

HERE LIE The Mortal Remains Of Reverend Cadjer Harrow Struck Down In His Prime By The Hand of God. He Whom THE LORD Laid Low Neither Man Nor Beast Shall Disturb Until the End.
AMEN

Alice could scarcely contain her excitement – here was her man, although she wasn't so sure she was glad to find him. She raised the camera to her eye, intending to shoot quickly and get out of there. She focused and pressed the release button. The shutter engaged, but the window stayed black and the shutter refused to open. Perplexed, she advanced the film to the next frame and heard the shutter click open. Damn! One picture wasted. Alice checked her meter settings, then aimed at the tombstones again and focused carefully. Locking her elbows to her sides, she pressed the release button smoothly and held still. Again, black filled the viewfinder and stayed that way.

"Shit!" Again she advanced the film and heard the shutter click open. Exasperated, her favorite expletive still on her lips, she slung the camera over her shoulder and stalked back along the two-rut lane that cars had worn as a short cut from the cemetery to the convenience store. Fuming, she got in her car and drove the four miles to Black Creek Ferry Road in a foul mood.

Alice pulled into the yard in front of her house and stopped. Sitting in the car, she carefully manipulated the lens on her camera. Nothing seemed to be wrong – no Florida crud growing behind the lens filter, no sand in the mount. She got out of the car and slammed the door a little harder than necessary, then felt like an idiot. Getting mad wouldn't fix whatever was wrong with the camera.

Dawg came sidling up to meet her with a welcoming canine smile, his feathered tail beating the air. On impulse, Alice aimed the camera at him, focused on his wet nose, and fired the last shot on the roll. The shutter worked perfectly, with the satisfying click of a well-lubricated, precision instrument. Baffled, she climbed the stairs to the deck, a monster headache settling firmly into place for the remainder of the day.

CHAPTER 12

ON SUNDAY afternoon, Alice and Margaret hiked down their driveway out to the dirt road. It wasn't the quickest way to get to Raine's house – they could have cut straight through the woods – but the old survey trail that ran between Alice's property and the neighbor's all the way through to the next road over was easier and less buggy.

"Are you sure Raine said I would get five dollars a day for taking care of their cats?"

"Absolutely."

"How long're they gonna be gone?"

"Ten days. They'll be back just before Christmas."

Margaret was quiet, doing the math. "So, that's fifty dollars."

"Yup. You okay with that bag?"

Margaret carried a seven-pound bag of cat food under her arm. "Uh huh."

They walked in silence down the dirt road for several minutes, comfortable in each other's company.

"When do you get your pictures back?" Margaret asked.

"Tomorrow. I'll pick them up on the way home from work."

Alice had told them only the bare essentials of her photo-taking expedition, that she'd found the gravesite of the preacher mentioned in the clipping and taken a few shots of the old wooden church. Her moment of complete panic over a car backfire she kept to herself. And then there was that bit with the shutter not working. There were patterns in the deep structure of events, she could feel them flowing together but the shape was too amorphous for her to see it. It was like being in a side spiral of a huge Mandelbrot set, an image she'd recently looked at on Nik's *Beauties of Math calendar*. The bigger pattern was out there somewhere.

"There's the tree," said Margaret.

Just off the road, the massive trunk of an ancient magnolia forked so that the main trunk continued on into the canopy of thick branches and polished dark leaves while the secondary trunk stretched out for about ten feet, head-high, and finally sloped toward the ground so that you could climb up onto it. It was a living tree house that kids all over the neighborhood climbed in and carved their initials on. It also marked the old survey trail cut when the woods were parceled up into tracts. They could follow the trail right to the Crandell's back gate.

They ducked under the trunk and headed down the trail, Margaret in the lead. The sun was still fairly high, but Alice intended to make sure they came back well before sundown. They pushed aside scrub and vines and stepped over fallen branches, always sticking to the middle of the trail. Margaret suddenly jerked back with a loud, "OWW!" and dropped the cat food bag.

Alice grabbed her in seconds. "What?"

"Twig got me in the eye," she moaned.

"Let me see." Alice held her chin and brushed her red frizz back from her face. The eye was weepy but otherwise okay. Alice gave her a squeeze and picked up the cat crunchies.

"C'mon, Munch, it's not too much farther." Margaret sniffed and trudged behind her.

Alice was listening to the heavy crunching of leaves and dry twigs behind her and thinking it didn't seem like one small girl could make that much noise.

"I wish you wouldn't call me that," said Margaret.

"What? Munchkin?"

"It just sounds child—"

"Shhh!" Alice stopped, listening. Now that they had halted, the woods were silent – not even frog croaks or bird chirps.

"What is it?"

"Nothing. Let's get moving." She stepped forward and immediately heard scratchings in the underbrush behind them. She whirled and Margaret collided with her.

"Mom—"

"Shhh," she whispered. She scanned the trees, but there was no movement.

Margaret looked around, too. The woods were not all that dense at this time of year, and there were small clear areas where trees had fallen, so that you could see for some distance.

"What are you looking for?" Margaret's voice was edgy.

"I don't know, I thought I heard something ... like an animal, maybe."

"What kind of animal?"

"How should I know? I don't *see* anything."

Alice was immediately sorry to be so short with her, but she was nervous. There had once been wild pigs in the woods before people moved in. One had even trundled across the clearing that was now her yard when Alice had been sunning on a towel right after the house was built. They had stared at each other in fright, and the pig had galloped past her into the trees. She could still remember its hairy muzzle and beady eyes. Maybe her tale of that encounter had influenced Margaret's dreams. She made a mental note to ask about it after they got back home.

Looking around now, she judged several nearby oaks adequate for climbing, if need be. Not that she really believed there were wild pigs in the woods anymore. Too many people had moved in and built houses; nothing bigger than raccoons or possums would want to hang around. Hurrying forward again with Margaret in front, she kept her thoughts to herself and listened intently for the following presence that stopped when they stopped and resumed when they did. At last they reached the wooden gate in Tim and Raine's electrified fence. Alice held it open and they passed through into a half-acre of mowed yard surrounding the Crandell's house, a pole and deck construction similar to Alice's, but considerably larger and more expensive.

She walked slowly across the yard, listening. Nothing seemed to be following, and Sesshomaru, Raine's massive white Persian cat, meowed loudly at them from the deck railing.

"Dinner's coming!" Margaret called out and ran up the steps with the cat food bag.

"Did you bring the house key?" Alice shouted after her.

"Got it."

Alice stopped beside an azalea hedge that clustered around the base of the stairs. The poor things were trying to bud out, fooled by the temporary warmish, humid weather that occurred around Thanksgiving. She stared back at the line of trees where she and Margaret had come through the fence – the treetops were still bright in the late afternoon sun, although it was getting dark underneath. Everything looked and felt perfectly normal, but a moment ago her heart had been thudding, and she'd had to fight the urge to break into a run. Alice bit her lip; got to be careful, she was starting to spook herself again. She wandered around the yard, inspecting Raine's planting of paper-whites, tiny members of the daffodil family that were just about bloomed out. A few lingering trumpets remained on the withering stalks.

Margaret came pounding back down the stairs. "All done. Sesshy was complaining a lot. Said we made him wait too long."

"Any sign of Tux?"

Margaret shook her head. Raine's other cat, a rangy black tom with a white front that resembled a tuxedo bib, spent most of his time out and about, and only came home to eat and occasionally sleep.

"Well, he can come in through the cat door when he's ready. I left all their bowls full and changed their water," Margaret said.

"Good, let's go home before it gets dark."

"Did you figure out what you heard in the woods?"

"No. I'm not sure I heard anything."

Margaret said nothing, looking at Alice with that look.

Alice headed briskly toward the gate. "Come on, we'll trot and it won't take five minutes to get back to the dirt road."

"If you say so."

The sun was lower and the woods shady. Her heart rate was up again as she held the gate open for Margaret and then stepped through. They stood still a moment, listening. Nothing.

"It's okay. Let's go."

Margaret started off at a quick walk. Alice was right behind her, pushing her thoughts ahead to the house where Nik would have a fire going by now and maybe even some sliced mushrooms sautéeing in butter. She could almost smell their aroma when she distinctly heard a snuffling sound.

"Are you all right, Munch?"

"Huh?"

"I ... thought you were coughing or something."

"No."

Alice broke into a sweat even though it was getting chilly under the trees. There it was again – sniffing, gruffing sounds on the trail behind them, and brush crackling under a heavy body. She whipped her head around and barely glimpsed a dark shape sidling off the trail into the brush. Or maybe she hadn't. She looked at the spot unblinking till her eyes watered, but nothing moved.

"Run," she said and pushed Margaret with her hand. Needing no encouragement, Margaret sped away, running and leaping heedless of brambles and underbrush. Alice was right on her heels, listening to the heavy panting noises getting louder behind her. Then suddenly the old leaning magnolia loomed ahead, with the bright ribbon of road showing through the smaller trees beyond it. They burst out onto the road and kept running. A hasty glance over her shoulder showed Alice that whatever it was had not followed them into the open. Margaret stopped not far ahead, holding her sides and gasping for air.

"Don't stop," Alice ordered and kept jogging. Margaret followed, running with a pained expression on her face.

At last their mailbox came into sight, its aluminum surface shining in a lingering pool of sunlight like a beacon. A quick sprint down the driveway and they finally stood sucking in great gulps of air at the base of the stairs. Dawg cavorted around the yard, excited by the sight of his humans running. Nik appeared at the top of the landing.

"I was starting to get a little concerned – it's nearly dark."

"I know, we stayed at Raine's longer than I expected. Probably should have just driven over there. Next time I will." She came up the stairs, somewhat recovered and glad of the glimpse of yellow fireplace warmth and flickering Christmas tree lights inside. "Nik, there was ... an animal in the woods. It chased us on the way back from Tim and Raine's house."

"Did you get a good look at it?" Nik scanned the yard for a moment, then came in and closed the door after them.

Once inside the house, Margaret no longer seemed afraid. "I didn't see anything, but Mom said to run, so I did." She scooped up Figaro and went back to the study; in a moment Alice heard the computer booting up.

Nik knelt to stoke the fire, and Alice sat down on the floor beside him. "I thought something moved off the trail when I turned around, but I don't know what ... just a glimpse."

"Large or small?"

Alice shook her head. "I just didn't get that good a look – but I'm pretty sure the bushes moved, so it was something."

"Make any noises?"

"Actually, that's what alerted me in the first place. I heard snuffling sounds and something walking on the trail behind us – I thought at first that Dawg had followed us, but then I remembered you took him with you into town. Coming back, the sounds were louder, harsh panting, huffing. I thought Margaret heard it too, but maybe not."

Alice watched Nik poking the coals around. "I'm really glad you're here."

He laid the fire tongs aside and turned to face her. "So am I. You don't seem overly safe out here."

"But it's never been like this. I've always felt completely safe – half the time we never even lock the door at night ... until now."

"It might be worth a call to the sheriff's office, or at least animal control. Find out if anyone else has reported trespassers or marauding ferals."

Alice smiled. "When you put it that way it sounds so matter-of-fact."

"And you think it's not?" Nik stretched out on the floor. Figaro padded over to them and settled down on his stomach, kneading his claws gently into the flannel shirt. Nik put up with it longer than Alice usually could. She had assumed he was basically a dog person, but the way he'd charmed Figaro was making her rethink that.

"I just think a large chunk of my life has been damn weird recently, that's all. And it started when the exhibit blew into town ... since then, everything connected with work has been weird. Then I started writing this story, and now my home space has turned bizarro, too. Maybe I'm cursed."

"You seem quite normal to me."

"Good, I was starting to have my doubts. But still ..." No matter how she spun it, she couldn't make that screeching noise in the gallery sound in any way normal.

"Still what?"

Alice was silent. If no one heard the screeching wind noises but her, how could she possibly talk about it without sounding delusional, and she had no intention of going there.

"I'm starved," she said instead. "Is there anything to eat around here?"

"I collected some mushrooms."

"Can we eat them?"

He nodded. "You can eat any mushroom ... once."

Alice blinked. There was not a ghost of a smile on his face, but he'd scored. "Gah!" She poked him in the ribs with her foot. Nik flinched, and Figaro dug in with all four feet.

"Ouch!"

Alice was satisfied. Now they were even.

CHAPTER 13

LATE IN the night, Nik shook Alice awake, scattering her dream of rain and thunder into fragments.

"Whaa?"

"Margaret's calling you."

"Oh, okay." She sat up, groggy. She'd really been out, like being drugged.

"Mommm." An urgent yet despairing tone that Alice knew only too well. She got out of bed and pulled on her bathrobe. Fumbling for the light switch in the hallway, she shivered violently. She should have left the heater on when they went to bed. The weather report had predicted an overnight drop into the 40s, but it felt much colder.

"Coming," she called.

She stumbled into Margaret's bedroom and tripped over mounds of girl stuff. Although the nightlight was plugged in, shadows lay too deep along the floor to show a clear path to the bed.

"Whatza matter?" Alice yawned hugely. She could see that Margaret sat huddled with the covers drawn up around her. "Bad dream?"

"I had the *worst* dream."

Alice sat down on the side of the bed, and Margaret grabbed her and held her close. The girl was drenched in sweat, although the night was chilly. Alice was starting to come awake.

"My head hurts."

"Do you need one of your pills?"

Margaret nodded. Alice got up and went to the bathroom, squinting painfully against the light as she got the phenobarb tablet and filled a cup with water. She elbowed the light off and went back into Margaret's darkened room.

"Here you go."

"Thanks." Margaret swallowed. "Can you rub the back of my head – it hurts so much."

"All right. Here, let me sit behind you." Alice propped up the pillows and settled into the warm spot Margaret had occupied. She put her hands on the girl's shoulders and squeezed gently, rubbing with her thumbs and then moving up to the base of the skull under the tangled frizz of curls. "Better?"

"Um." Margaret nodded.

"So. What was your dream about?"

Margaret was leaning against her, silent and drooping. They'd tried all manner of migraine remedies and treatments, from black cohosh tea to biofeedback, but the only thing that seemed to produce reliable, instant relief was the thing they least welcomed – controlled substance drugs. It was hard, watching her doubled up in pain and nausea.

Alice cupped her hands around Margaret's forehead and squeezed with even, steady pressure, in strokes that moved over the temples and up toward the top of the skull. It was all she could do, physically, to help, which left her feeling mostly useless whenever an episode took hold. Sometimes when Margaret could sense that pre-migraine light sensitivity coming on, she could derail the headache by taking the medication before the pain got too bad, but when it happened in the night like this, there wasn't much to do but slowly live through it. Alice rearranged the covers, pulling the comforter up around Margaret's neck.

"It helps dissolve a nightmare if you tell it."

"You and me and grandma were locked in this room, and Dad was there too, off in the corner and he wouldn't talk to us, and there was a giant outside trying to smash the room to bits ... his fist came through the ceiling."

Alice hugged her firmly. It sounded like a first-class horrorshow. The part about Whit bothered her more than the roof-bashing giant – separation anxiety symptoms? Whit had been gone for three years now and called Margaret on her birthday and appropriate holidays, but maybe she missed him more than she let on.

Alice rubbed her hands down over Margaret's slender shoulders. She had to be careful; the pressure needed to ease muscle knots she felt under her fingers might cause worse pain if applied too hard.

"Up here, that feels good." Margaret moved her mother's hands up to her forehead. Alice pressed over the eye ridges and down the temples on either side. Margaret was starting to relax, but Alice's back was complaining. She was too cold.

"Wait a minute, Munch, while I light the heater." She disentangled herself from the blankets and went into the hallway. Kneeling down, she fumbled for the long matches needed to light the pilot light on the gas heater. As soon as it caught, she turned the flame up to a reasonable height.

Alice stood for a moment with her back to the heater, soaking up reserves of warmth. Margaret's nightmares were cyclic, usually involving menacing creatures of the deep, giant sharks and whatever else swam up out of the black depths of the dreamscape ocean. Often they preceded or followed a migraine attack. Drugs combated the symptoms, but the root cause was another matter, one she didn't know how to tackle. She tried to think when, exactly, Margaret had started to dream like that, but she couldn't remember. Pre- or post-divorce? Maybe she'd always had them.

She went back to the bedroom.

"Anything else you want to tell me?"

"Yeah. That horrible pig-dog was chewing my ankle and laughing, and there was like a pack of dogs howling outside. Then the room turned into a cave and it was just me and some old guy I didn't know. His hands were stuck in the rock and the rest of him was turning to rock. He was screaming something at me but I couldn't understand him. Then I woke up. It felt so real, especially that last part."

Margaret pressed against Alice's chest.

"What do you think it means?" she asked, her face buried in Alice's bathrobe.

Alice had no idea what to say. "Well, I could give you an explanation for the first part – about how your dad was separated from the rest of us – but I don't have a clue about the other part. Why does that dog thing keep showing up in your dreams?"

"I don't know."

"Can you remember the first time you saw it?"

"Yeah. When I was five, right after we moved here. It came out of the closet."

"In your dream."

"Not exactly. I mean, I wasn't asleep. It was like a waking dream, or being half asleep and seeing something you know isn't there in real life. Like when I talk to Marmalade."

"So it's connected with living here?"

Margaret was heavy against Alice's shoulder, beginning to relax now that her fright was tapering off.

"I don't know. Maybe."

That was something to chew on. Alice hadn't wanted to admit that it might be frightening for Margaret to live out here in the woods, because she loved it so much herself.

Margaret sighed and lay back on the pillow, pulling the covers up around her face. Alice got up.

"You're okay now, right?"

"No. I wish you would sleep with me tonight."

"Look, I'll just sit here with you for awhile, until you get sleepy again." She pushed some of Margaret's stuffed animals out of the way and settled back against the headboard.

"You'll have to sit there all night then, 'cause I'm not going back to sleep."

"Just relax. You will." Alice's own eyelids were heavy, and although she was chilled to the bone in her thin bathrobe, she was already drowsing. Margaret settled into the hollow of her arm and pulled the covers over her head. One arm clutched the life out of her extra pillow.

"Goodnight," Alice said, and sat nodding in a fog that hung between sleep and waking, waiting for Margaret's breathing to turn slow and regular. Finally, she slipped her arm out from under her daughter's head and went shivering and numb back to the warmth of her own bedroom.

Climbing back into bed, she curled into a tight ball against Nik's back, waiting for her body's heat to invade the chill of the sheets. If Figaro would come get on the other side of her, then she'd be warm enough. Figaro usually slept with Margaret, although she complained that he split in a hurry when she was having one of those dreams. Alice had asked, joking, if Margaret could see him while asleep, and the answer had been a simple yes.

Alice lay in bed, now wide awake. It didn't seem fair – Margaret was a bright, sweet kid but there was a flaw somewhere. Why did she dream like that? Alice herself rarely dreamed, or if she did, nothing remained of it when she woke up.

Gray light was beginning to outline the bedroom window. The harder she tried to go back to sleep, the more awake she felt. She needed to be rested for work tomorrow, but that seemed unlikely at this point. Suddenly she felt a slight thump at the foot of the bed, then soft feet padding up toward her. Figaro settled into the small of her back and began to purr.

Alice relaxed against him and smiled to herself at the mental image of twelve pounds of tabby tomcat kneading the blankets like a kitten. She sent him a mental thank-you and drifted away.

"Is your name Tatji?"

The lizard-dog expanded his frill, then flattened it against his back and smiled a snarly grin that exposed sharp canines. "What's this? The stupid girl has been doing some research. Shall I be impressed?"

"Well, is it?"

Margaret sat in the rust-colored sand, so hot in her jeans and T-shirt she could barely move. She'd kicked off her shoes way back there – a moment's pang of regret, those were her favorite China flats and now they were gone. Above her towered the structure she had first thought was a sand castle but was now revealed to be a termite mound. The lizard-dog had popped out of a hole near the base.

"Why don't you go naked?" it said, reading her thoughts. "Everybody else around here does."

"Where is this place?" Margaret pulled up her shirtfront and wiped sweat out of her eyes.

"Well, it's not Oz, Dorothy." It made a cackling, barking noise. "Or maybe it is."

"You didn't answer my first question. Are you Tatji, the Red Lizard spirit?"

"I can take that form, if I want to. But maybe you'd prefer this one." The head disappeared back inside the mound. There was a scuffling, digging sound, and a huge tawny dingo emerged from behind the mound and sat down just inches away from her feet. "Better? Maybe you don't like reptiles."

"I don't mind reptiles – I just don't like you. I want you to go away."

The dingo shook its head in a very human gesture. "Not a chance. Not yet, anyway."

"Why do you hang out in my closet?"

"I don't. It's just a gateway – don't you know anything? Some psychic you are. You know what, you're so wide open, anything could come through. Doesn't that alarm you?" By the look on her face, the dingo could tell that it did. It settled down on its belly in the sand, panting. "Is this a proper position for a Sphinx? Or maybe I could pass for Anubis?"

"How would I know?" Margaret said. She watched the beast with sullen wariness.

The dingo licked its paws and scratched at its scruffy hide. "You're the one looking for mythical creatures on the Internet."

Margaret wiped her face, and then lifted her hair up off her neck. This time the desert was as still as a snapshot – not a whisper of air stirring. She felt faint. "What are you?" she asked again.

"I'm the link you're looking for."

"I'm not looking for any link. I don't understand what you mean."

"Well, see? I said you were stupid, didn't I? G'day."

It popped back into the hole in the mound, and the entire landscape vanished. Margaret was floating in cool blackness, and she was alone. It was heaven.

CHAPTER 14

"YOU'RE NOT going to blow off the Christmas party, are you? If nothing else, the food will be spectacular. I heard Shelton got Rigatoni's to cater this time."

"I don't know. I have a thousand things to do before we take off for the holidays."

"When are you leaving?"

"Probably day after tomorrow, depending on Nik's schedule. Margaret's already out of school for the whole week. Nik's never met my mother – should be a true test of his affection for me." Alice looked sidelong at Faye.

They were taking a break in the Florida Shipwrecks room, a side gallery that was a permanent installation. Sitting high up in the captain's quarters built into the cutaway model of the *Santisima Trinidad*'s mid-section, one of Spain's most formidable warships from the eighteenth century, you could see out over the entire room. Built at Havana in 1769 out of mahogany and pine, the *Trinidad* had been a 1,900-ton floating cannon platform with a hull two feet thick. It represented the culmination of 300 years of superb ship construction: the Spanish *navio* or warship, a durable ship of the line that occupied the forward position in most naval battles. Alice had tons of research under her belt on Spanish ships like this.

Sipping her coffee in the elegantly replicated officer's quarters, reproduced as closely as possible to the shipbuilder's specs obtained from the Archives in Seville, Alice was morose. Normally she would be enjoying herself because it was a wonderful place to escape for a few moments – like a Disneyworld set, only better. No oversized singing mice.

She looked down over the rail at a couple of museum tourists strolling beneath them. "Do you know," she said, "that this particular ship was never sunk in battle, even though it was in service for over forty years?"

"That so?" Faye said.

"True. It was the only warship in service with four gun decks. Potentially could have carried up to a hundred and forty-four cannons."

"You're a walking encyclopedia."

"Part of my job description."

Faye smiled. "And here you thought your promotion was just a stroke of good luck. Shelton knew what he was after."

"I just wish the main exhibit hadn't gotten off to such a bad start. I want people who walk through it to be blown away by the artwork of those Aboriginal people – I mean, what you see there is over thousands of years of vibrant, conceptual artwork that's stylish and spiritual at the same time. Instead all they can talk about is the haunted exhibit and its monsters." She rested her chin in her hand. "It's not at all what I wanted."

Faye wiped a plum lipstick smear from the rim of her cup. "The prints are selling. Everybody wants one of the Lightning Man or the Wandjinas."

"It figures, they're the most imposing. Not sure I'd want them staring down at me from a wall in my house, though." The mere idea of it made her uneasy. "Faye ... you haven't noticed anything weird yourself, have you? Around the exhibit, I mean."

Faye's eyes narrowed, and she shook her head. "Not unless you count the way everybody keeps wanting to reach over the ropes and touch the stuff. Security guards were talking about it; Shelton told them to keep a closer watch on the show during peak hours. How about yourself?"

Alice wondered how much she dared tell. "It's funny – I'm nervous around some of the panels, especially if I'm in there alone. I ... thought I heard some funny noises in there a few times." She immediately felt ridiculous.

"Funny how?"

"A kind of ringing in my ears or whistling wind, like you'd hear outside during a hurricane."

"Sounds like stress symptoms to me."

"Could be. Nothing a good Christmas break won't fix, I guess."

"So what else is new in your life?"

Alice sighed, and took a breath. "I'm writing a novel."

"Yeah? About what?" Faye seemed genuinely interested.

"Oh, some piece of local history that's basically a rural legend, an old church that seems to be haunted. Only it's not turning out like I expected either."

"How so?"

"I'm not sure how to explain it. I have these ideas in my head about how

I think it should go and what the storyline is, but when I start writing, it goes off plumb ... skewed in a way that makes the story darker or the characters more peculiar. Stuff I never even thought of starts showing up."

"Peculiar is good, especially if you're writing a horror story. Even if it's based on history, a bit of gothic couldn't hurt. I'd read something like that."

"You would?"

"Sure. Especially if it has a sexy villain or two in it. Does it have any sexy villains?"

"Not that I know of." Alice was mildly appalled. She was pretty sure that her preacher was the villain of the tale, but there was no way she could paint him as sexy.

"You know," said Faye, "for somebody as spooked as you are about spirits haunting the museum, I can't believe you're writing a story about more spirits haunting an old church."

"I'm not superstitious that way."

"I'm just sayin' ..."

"Don't worry. I haven't invited any demons over my threshold."

"Well, that's a relief." Faye's expression was neutral. "How's the time?" Faye frequently wore elaborate, unusual jewelry, but no watch.

"Two-thirty."

"Gotta go. I don't want to be losing my job, intellectually degrading as it may be."

Alice smiled at her. Faye liked to downplay her smarts, but Alice wasn't fooled. Faye got up from the captain's chair and had to stoop in the tiny low-ceilinged cabin to reach the narrow staircase spiraling down to the gallery floor. Alice followed behind her.

"I want a signed copy when it's published," Faye said.

"You'll get the first one." She couldn't tell if Faye really meant the flattery, but she decided to take it at face value. Smiling, she walked with Faye back to the museum shop. The entrance to the Dreamtime exhibit was just beyond Faye's glass cubicle.

Alice went down the ramp and stared suspiciously at the silent panels. As predicted, a lot of people were wandering around them, pointing and staring. Walking through the exhibit was like entering the 30,000-year-old caves of Koonalda, Ngama, Ruguri, Yourambulla. Alice loved those rolling, tongue-tripping names. They were like water splashing down mountain crevices, and their intonation sent shivers up her spine, but now she hesitated to even think them, much less say them aloud. She strongly wanted to see those locations for real, but didn't figure there was any way she'd ever be able to go there.

She noted it was indeed true that visitors couldn't seem to resist wanting to touch the panels and paintings, reaching their hands out over the velvet ropes toward the images although such actions were strictly prohibited by museum regulations. She wondered if the ritual masters in the original cave sites had similar problems from the uninitiated and the curious. Were designated elders the only ones allowed to touch the rock paintings and petroglyphs? What then happened to modern-day archeologists or tourists who invaded sacred sites on a daily basis – did the ancestral spirits still inhabit those places? For the sake of the Aboriginals, she hoped they did.

Passing out of the gallery, she walked across the lobby and took the elevator up to her office, mentally composing a book proposal letter she intended to send off to a couple of publishers whose write-ups looked like a good match for the type of book she now seemed to be writing. She wanted to get something in the mail to the first one on the list before leaving town for the Christmas vacation ritual.

Entering her office, Alice sat down at the computer, situated on a table separate from her desk so that she could see out the window. It put her back to the doorway, which Hannah told her was bad feng shui, but it was the only way she could work at the computer and still be able to rest her eyes occasionally by looking out at the sky and trees. She opened a file labeled "proposal," stared at the screen for a moment, and then began, "Dear Mr. Edmundson: As an experienced historian, I've been working on a novel based on facts recently discovered" and then paused. That was a terrible start. Dorky, Margaret would have said. She erased everything except the salutation and sat looking out the window, thinking. What if she actually got a bite on this manuscript? Then she'd be committed to finishing it and, assuming anyone bought it, having it read by strangers.

"Earth to Alice?"

Alice hit a couple of wrong keys and managed to minimize the screen.

"Gene, can't you announce yourself like a real human?"

"I did, but you were obviously too deep into whatever you've got going there."

"It's ... just something I'm working on in my spare time."

"*You* have spare time?" He sidled close to her, his hand resting on the back of her chair, only inches away from her shoulder.

She swiveled around to face him. "No coffee left – I only made a small amount, but I'm sure you can find some at the office party. You are going, aren't you?"

"Why not? MacBeth's providing the liquor."

"Gene, I didn't know you touched the hard stuff."

"I make an occasional exception." He made no move to leave. "It's probably already started. You want to go? I can wait around if you got something to finish."

Alice sighed. No more work was going to get done here; she deleted the file and powered off. "I don't suppose you've seen any attendance figures yet, have you? On the Dreamtime show? I'm just curious."

"Greater than expected," he said, hovering. "Shelton's a happy man."

"Well, good. I'm glad somebody is."

"You should be, too – you've got a success on the books. Congrats. Um, the food's in the conference room. Wanna go? We can watch Jessie try to get Faye under the mistletoe."

Alice gave him a look, and then gathered up her belongings and office keys. "I guess I can make a quick appearance." And I'll be watching out for you, she thought, as she snapped off the light and followed him into the hallway, closing her office for the next ten days.

CHAPTER 15

INSTEAD OF the early departure planned for Christmas Eve morning, Alice, Margaret, and Nik stumbled around and over each other in a frustrating series of delays that finally put them on the road well after lunchtime. Nik had offered to take them in his truck since it had more room than Alice's car, which had no real back seat, but it meant gassing it up, stowing camping gear in the laundry room, and convincing Dawg that he couldn't ride shotgun this time. Margaret had been crushed by his quizzical face and drooping tail as they drove away, leaving him standing in the yard. Nik assured her Dawg would be fine. Although Alice and Margaret were planning to stay for a week, Nik was coming back the next day.

As Alice had feared, the line of cars clogging the highway to Gull Harbor seemed unending. What should have been a three-hour drive from Citrus Park stretched into four, and it was late afternoon by the time they took the Periwinkle Beach cutoff and rolled into her mother's driveway fifteen minutes later. Suzanne Waterston was sitting on the steps, waiting.

"What on earth kept you? Hal and I were just about ready to call the highway patrol to go look for you." She opened the passenger door of the truck and gathered Margaret into her arms.

"Grandma!"

"You've gotten bigger! Now I wonder if some of those gifts under the tree will fit you! Carlisle, get down!" She hugged Margaret, nudged the old Afghan hound out of the way, and hustled her only grandchild up onto the porch and into the house.

"Good to see you too, Mom," Alice said as the door banged shut. "We could have just sent her Margaret and stayed home ourselves."

Nik was impassive. Alice recognized that he was in neutral, just going along with whatever happened. It wasn't his family, and he had no emotional connection to the scene in Gull Harbor. He extricated their luggage from under a tarp in the truck bed, leaving for Alice the cardboard box crammed with wrapped gifts.

She led the way up onto the porch and into the house, plunking the box down at the foot of the bed in the guest room. Actually, all the bedrooms were guest rooms to her. This wasn't the house she grew up in; that one was back in Miami. After Alice had left home for the university, her uncle Hal retired from his business and her mother became interested in Gulf Coast real estate, which led them here. The upscale split-level beach house they shared was called Dunescape. All the nice houses in Gull Harbor had names on plaques in front of their drives. It was a beautiful place to live, but it wasn't home.

It was a great place to visit, though. She went through the kitchen and out onto the patio at the back of the house, Nik following. The patio was unscreened and larger than Alice's entire living room and offered a panoramic view of the white sands and turquoise waters of the Gulf of Mexico. She breathed in the crisp sea air with joy.

"There you are," said her uncle from his reclining deck chair. He folded an issue of the *Wall Street Journal* and stood up.

Nearly as tall as Nik, but a good bit heavier around the middle now that he was in his seventies, Harold Blacksburg came to meet them. It was clear that Margaret resembled his side of the family. His hair had once been red, a metallic copper with darker highlights that faded to cinnamon under months in the summer sun, and now was streaked with yellowish white. His freckles were turning to the liver spots of old age, and squint lines around his eyes and across his forehead were deeply creased into the skin.

"Hi," she said, and lifted her face. He bent over and gave her a kiss on the cheek. He smelled of Old Spice, Lucky Strikes, and Wild Turkey, a wicked combination that assaulted her senses and brought sudden tears to her eyes – it was a vague aroma of home that lingered in her memory banks and guaranteed an emotional response whenever she smelled it. She'd grown up thinking Hal was her father because her mother lived in Hal's house. When it was finally explained to her that no, Hal was her uncle – brother, not husband, to her mother – but that he loved her as his own daughter, she loved him no less.

"Hal, this is Nikolas Thorens – um, Nik."

"So this is your young man, eh?" They shook hands, and Hal Blacksburg appraised Nik frankly. "Good handshake. If you like him, then so do I." The scene was a bit awkward, but not as bad as Alice had been dreading.

Nik was the first man she'd gotten seriously involved with since the divorce, which meant eventually having to introduce him to her equivalent of the parents.

Hal put his arm around Alice's shoulders. "Have you met any of Nik's family?"

"Um, no—"

Nik stepped in. "My parents and sisters live in Stockholm. But we've promised to visit when we can afford it."

"Swedes, eh? I traveled throughout Scandinavia when I was younger and in better shape," Hal responded. "Stayed at the Grande Hotel during the Nobel Prize festivities one year – met some fascinating people. Excellent theater there as well."

Nik was nodding and smiling. "To be accurate, our family is Swiss, but moved to Sweden around the time my grandfather and grandmother got married."

"Interesting. Any relation to the Thorens sound equipment dynasty?"

"Not that I'm aware of."

"Where's Mom?" Alice asked.

Hal shaded his eyes and looked out at the silver line of sand. "I think she and Margaret went off down the beach."

Alice set her mouth into a line. When her mother didn't want to deal with something, she simply removed herself from its proximity if she could. Well, she'd have to deal with it eventually because Nik was spending the night, and Alice had no intention of putting him on the couch.

Hal relaxed back into his recliner. "How've you been?"

Alice sat on a stone bench, and pulled Nik down beside her. "Fine. Just great. Margaret got a blue ribbon in the school science fair – beans growing in a jar or something. Nik helped her." She was instantly on edge for having said that, for implying that Nik was an acknowledged member of the household. Not that either Hal or her mother were prudish about who she lived with or didn't, but Suzanne had liked Whit a lot and was possibly more upset about the divorce than Alice. It was simply heartless, she'd said, that Alice had deprived her only granddaughter of growing up with a father.

"That's wonderful. You must be proud – all three of you."

He smiled broadly, reminding Alice once again why she missed being around him. Friends in Miami said it was too bad Hal never had any children of his own, but Alice begged to differ because it would have meant having to share him with kids that really belonged to him. Generous, solicitous, capable – he was all those things children wished their fathers to be, and Alice knew it would be traumatic for her when he died.

That event wasn't as imminent now as it once had been, since his pacemaker had been installed and he'd gone back to a moderately active lifestyle.

"How're you?" she asked, with all its implied meanings.

"Doing well, thank you. I manage to bat the ball around several times a week without getting winded." Alice knew he played "cyborg tennis" with a business associate who also wore a tiny battery in his left breast.

Hal reached into his shirt pocket and lit up a Lucky. It was the one vice he couldn't, or wouldn't, give up. So, the reaper still waited in the wings.

"Nik's going to Norway next year. Giving a paper at a foray sponsored by the University of Oslo's Botanical Museum and the International Mycology Association," she said, making conversation. "It's a big honor for a graduate student to be invited."

"Indeed," said Hal. "Will you be going, too?"

"No, can't afford it. And what would Margaret do for two and a half weeks?"

"Your mother and I—"

"I know, Mom would come get her and not give her back. She might even be willing to live in our house for three weeks just to have Margaret all to herself."

"She loves her granddaughter very much, as do I."

"She goes overboard. Funny, I don't remember her treating me that way."

A trace of a frown passed over her uncle's face. "That's not quite fair." He looked pained, but let it go. "I liked the promotional materials you sent me for the Australian art exhibit," he said, changing the subject. "It was very polished work."

Alice's spirits took wing; her uncle was in advertising and a business compliment from him was worth gold. She'd have to remember to pass this on to the museum's publicity design staff.

"Thanks. I didn't have much to do with it, I'm afraid. I just drafted the text. But you're right, the design department outdid itself." She was settling in now, readjusting to the rhythm of the surf and falling under her uncle's spell. He had a media voice, like that of a trusted newscaster, that coaxed her into believing someone was firmly, securely in control of the facts and understood anything anyone would ever want to know about them.

Nik touched her hand. "I think I'll take a short walk down the beach."

He stood up and headed down the private boardwalk that led from the patio out to the low dunes.

"Doesn't have much to say, does he," observed Hal. "Seems like a nice fellow, though."

"Absolutely. I really want you to like him ... Mother too, if that's possible. Of course, it doesn't matter whether she does or not because he's moved in and that's that."

"As long as you and Margaret are happy – then I'm satisfied."

They were silent for a few minutes, listening to the surf splash, rebound, and splash against the sand as the tide came in.

"Are you happy, Alice?"

"Yes, and no." She stared at her feet.

"I thought so ... what's bothering you? You're putting on a good face for us, but I see something underneath that makes me wonder."

Alice gave him a wan smile. "I never could hide anything you, could I?"

"I see lines around your eyes and a tightness in your mouth I don't remember. Whatever it is, it hasn't been kind to your pretty face."

"There's a lot of ... stress going on at work. I'm not sure how to deal with it."

"Can you talk to your boss?"

Alice shook her head. "It's not something I'd feel comfortable sharing with him. It's really important for him to know he can rely on me, that I can take care of whatever comes up as curator of this exhibit. The problem is, we've had two really nasty accidents in connection with it, but in both cases they weren't something anyone could see coming, so there was no way to prevent them. But in both cases, people got badly hurt and the only advance warning were these screeching noises in my head that nobody else heard. Want to analyze that for me?"

Hal sat quietly, looking at her and swirling the ice around in his glass.

"That doesn't sound like anything I have an answer for," he said finally.

"Right. So there we are. I'm trying to carry on like everything is normal, but just when I let my guard down, some other cosmic shoe drops and ...." She made a helpless gesture.

They sat in silence for a moment, and at last her uncle pushed himself out of the recliner. He sat down beside her and put an arm around her shoulders. She leaned against him, remembering all the times he'd comforted her like this when she'd been a girl.

"I want so much for you to be happy and fulfilled in your life," he said. "If I can do anything, you will ask, won't you?"

"You know I will. Don't tell Mother about any of this, okay? She would only make things worse for me."

Hal sighed heavily. "One of the things I most wish I could do would be to bring the two of you together, at least to a point where you could enjoy each other's company."

"Why does she hate me?"

"Alice," Hal's voice was reproachful, "I can assure you that she absolutely does not feel that way toward you. Suzanne has had some terrible things to live through and to cope with – perhaps you remind her of some of those things, but she also cares for you, and her beautiful granddaughter."

Alice pursed her lips. "That much I'll give you – she's crazy about Margaret. I wish she'd given me even a scrap of that kind of affection when I was that age. Was I really such a bad kid?"

Hal gave her a squeeze. "You know that's unfair. Suzanne did the best she could, given her circumstances. She's made a remarkable recovery, actually. For the first few months after her return, before you were born, she was quite suicidal. I think the fact that she was able to bring a lovely, smart, accomplished daughter into the world and eventually find a profession for herself is more than anyone expected she would be able to do. You judge her a little too harshly."

"You know, you always manage to turn me around whenever I get on one of my Suzanne rants. I should hang around you more often."

Hal kissed the top of her head. "You'll always be my beautiful Alice. Don't let yourself forget that." He got to his feet stiffly and stretched. "How long can you stay?"

"Less than a week. Mother said she would drive us back to Magnolia. Nik's just staying tonight. Somebody has to feed our dog and the neighbor's cats tomorrow."

"Stay as long as you want. We hardly ever get to see you anymore."

Alice followed him to the kitchen door. "Need any help with dinner?"

"None. You're here on vacation. Go find your fellow and bring him back for some eggnog. Made it with VSQ this time. It's quite lethal." He squeezed her shoulders and went inside.

Alice zipped up her jacket and went down the winding boardwalk to the sand. A stiff offshore breeze whipped her hair into a tangled mess, but who cared. She was on vacation.

The western sky was all red and purple, with a line of palms black against the palette. Nik was walking back toward her, so she went down to the damp margin of sand where the tide was rolling in and waited for him. The wind had a bite to it, and she shivered in her light jacket. Her feet were chilled but she didn't much care; the crunchy-wet sand felt good under her toes and she dug in, letting the tide fill the holes around her feet with each push of green water toward the shore.

Tonight they would stack all the gifts around the tree and drink eggnog made from Uncle Hal's recipe that was so rich it could make you sick if you drank too much, which was easy to do because it tasted so good. Then she would wait for Margaret to fall asleep so her bicycle, chemistry set, and dinosaur models could be set out. Of course, as a savvy twelve-year-old, Margaret knew the scoop on Santa Claus, but insisted on keeping the ritual anyway. That was all right – Alice could use the quiet time in the late night hours to work on her book.

She was into the third chapter now. The church building was completed, the first sermon had been preached in it, and although she had at first assumed the congregation to be all black, she'd been surprised to discover that this was not the case. There were indeed many members of the surrounding black community in attendance, but there were also white farmers and laborers, half-breed Seminoles, and drifters of undecipherable origin. It was a completely integrated social grouping, way before its time, the attraction being its charismatic preacher and founder. And Belinda Rider had emerged as a more significant character than expected. Although the narrative was basically omniscient, Alice found it easy to describe the other characters and speculate on their actions through the young girl's eyes, which apprehended events around her with both adolescent innocence and a fearful suspicion that was cagey beyond her years.

Also, a man Alice called Jeral Maunder had begun to court Yula Rider, Belinda's widowed mother, and Alice suspected they would marry soon, perhaps in the next chapter. Maunder's Grocery and Dry Goods would become a successful business operated by Jeral and his brother (this was fact, gathered from advertisements appearing in the *Massalina Countian* issues for 1887 and 1888, which Sandra Potts had photocopied for her) and marriage into the Maunder clan would alleviate Yula's struggle against her poverty-stricken circumstances. Belinda had never known a father nor had her younger brother Antoine, their mother's first husband having died during a typhoid epidemic and the second leaving shortly after his son's birth on a hot, steamy night in July, 1892, never to return.

The tide rushed in over Alice's feet and sucked the sand away again. She looked for Nik and was startled to see a huge black man stalking along the beach toward her. He stopped a dozen yards away and stood, hands on hips, looking her over. The setting sun at his back made it difficult to distinguish his features, but he seemed to have some kind of scar along his left cheek that snaked down his jaw line to the veins in his neck. Alice rubbed salt spray out of her eyes and saw with surprise that the figure coming toward her was only Nik.

"Found an interesting echinoderm in the seaweed," he began, coming up to her. "It's not usually this color ... what's wrong?"

"It must have been a trick of the light. For a minute I thought you were somebody else." She felt the urge to touch him and see his face up close to convince herself the other had been an illusion.

"*Ja*, it's only me." He was looking at her with eyes narrowed.

"I guess the way you were silhouetted made you look different. Weird. I really was convinced you were a tall black man."

Nik laughed in astonishment. "Not even close."

"Well, I'm glad it's you – the other guy was really unpleasant looking."

"Have you been hitting your uncle's whiskey?"

"I have not. Just forget I said anything at all. What's that smelly thing in your hand?"

"Sea urchin shell. I just wanted to show you the color – you don't usually find them in a shade of blue like this."

"Periwinkle."

He tossed it into the water and they headed up through the dunes toward the house where lights were being turned on. Alice could see blue and gold blinking on this year's Christmas tree, which was a damn sight better than last year's solid pink creation. She actually preferred no tree at all, and hoped Margaret would outgrow her need for one before she reached college age and moved away.

Later that evening, Alice stood at the kitchen sink washing out her cup; it was the only way to avoid a fifth serving of eggnog. Her head had a buzz on and her tongue felt fuzzy, but the stuff was so delicious sliding down you didn't realize it was going to knock you senseless until it was too late. Her mother sat on the couch, watching the tree lights blink on and off, with Margaret asleep in her lap under a crocheted coverlet. Hal had already gone to bed, and Nik had buried himself in a journal he'd brought. He was getting along with Suzanne surprisingly well, considering.

"Can we put her to bed now?" Alice said, coming over to Margaret and brushing the hair away from her face. She envied the smooth, unblemished skin children came blessed with. Margaret's was almost transparent with a tracery of tiny blue veins and faintest pink rouged into the cheeks – a doll's face.

Suzanne nodded. "Help me lift her, maybe we can do it without waking her."

Nik was on his feet. "Here, let me do that. She's not that heavy, but it'll be easier for me to do it." He smiled at Suzanne, who was visibly charmed.

"Careful now, that's my only granddaughter," she said, and allowed Nik to slide his arms under Margaret and ease her up from the couch.

Suzanne led the way to her own bedroom where a twin-sized rollaway was set up, another ritual they had yet to abandon. Someday they would have to give it up, but for now neither Margaret nor Suzanne was willing. The room was cool, and Suzanne tucked the child in with a thick satin comforter pulled up to her chin.

"Do you think she'll be warm enough? I've got more blankets if you think—"

Alice sighed and realized she was extremely tired, on top of being dizzy-drunk. "Mother, it's plenty. You don't want to suffocate her."

"Keep your voice down, you might wake her up."

Alice shrugged and walked back to the den, her mother tiptoeing behind her. Nik had strategically retreated to the guest bedroom. Three down and one to go, then she'd have the house to herself.

"Are you going to bed now?" Suzanne asked. "I can set out Margaret's Santa Claus things by myself if you are."

"No, I'm not. I brought some work to do, and it'll keep me awake for awhile yet."

"Well, suit yourself. Goodnight then." She pecked Alice on the cheek and padded back down the hall to her room.

Alone at last. Alice went to the kitchen, nuked a cup of instant coffee, and returned to the den. Opening her briefcase, she pulled out all the notes and clippings brought along for use with the next few chapters. If she could work uninterrupted like this for at least a couple of hours each day while she was here, a good portion of the story could be drafted.

Settling onto the couch, she spread papers out on either side, with her legal pad and a wide flat art book from the coffee table balanced on her knees as a writing desk. With the gas logs turned up in the fireplace, the room was cozy, highlighted by the tree blinking on and off in the corner.

It invited her mind to wander away from the task in front of her and hang fire in the hypnotic flickering of blue and gold.

Sipping the coffee, she watched the lights, waiting for her eggnog buzz to smooth out. She wondered how the Little Shiloh church folk had celebrated their first Christmas Eve in their new church. The library file had a flyer, hand lettered in black ink, announcing services for December 24, 1894, and as she looked at it now, pictures of the dim church interior lit by warm yellow candle flame crept into her mind. Her pen hovered over the paper as she wrangled with an opening sentence, trying it out several ways and finally scrapping it. She closed her eyes and put herself into the scene, imagining that the pine tree smell filling the den was coming from the new church planking. Gradually she began to see the scene. Opening her eyes, she wrote down the chapter title and the words began to flow, almost faster than she could write them.

Chapter Four – First Christmas

The church was filled with the mingled aromas of pine boughs, candle smoke, and new wood. The congregation, now seventy strong, sat on long benches. Real pews would come later, made from straight-grained oaks felled when the church grounds were cleared.

There were some newcomers as well, people brought in by the nativity service announcements that Pudloe Brown had penned and distributed around the Little Shiloh community as well as the township of Magnolia. He had even tacked one to the outside door of the new county courthouse.

Pudloe was young and eager to please, offering his help and energy to Reverend Harrow almost from the first day. He aspired to the call himself and wanted to learn all he could about this preaching business. Clever and quick-witted, nothing of importance slipped by him, and he soon had his hand in most of the church operations. Harrow praised his dedication and promised to enlighten him in ways he'd never dreamt of.

The congregation coughed and shuffled with restless anticipation. At last the choir filed in through the rear door, a blast of cold air at their backs. Candle flames winked and stretched horizontal but regained intensity after the door was shut. The room fell silent, and then a dozen women raised their voices a cappella in the popular carol, "Silent night, holy night ...." The worshippers stood in quiet admiration of the swelling harmonies that took their minds off hay baling, wood cutting, sick children, and other troubles of daily life.

Then Reverend Harrow marched down the single long aisle formed between the rows of benches, with Deacon Rodney Lathe, his second in command, at his side. Lathe had preached informally to various small groups within the black community around Little Shiloh for a number of years, but had never known how to coalesce them into a unified church. The appearance of Cadjer Harrow, a burning flame of such divine inspiration that people seemed unable to resist him, gave Rodney the opportunity he needed.

Instead of trying to compete with the man, Rodney wisely offered to join forces with him to save souls, and their partnership was proving to be all he had hoped. He was occasionally annoyed with the way that youngster Pudloe Brown insisted on horning in, but it was also a useful situation because the young man was easily manipulated. Rodney Lathe was used to telling other people what to do, and since that wasn't possible with Harrow, who held complete control of the church, Pudloe Brown was a satisfactory substitute.

"... round yon virgin, mother and child," sang the choir, now supported by the congregation.

The preacher and his deacon took their places on the raised platform where the real pulpit and choir stalls would one day be built. The hymn died away, and the church fell silent. Deacon Lathe raised both arms and said in a strong voice, "Praise to the baby Jesus on his birthday." Scattered voices punctuated his words with "Amen."

"Everything we got on this Christmas Eve comes from the powers of the Lord." Murmurs of assent rippled through the standing worshippers. "And things can be even better for all of us. Listen to the voice of the Lord as it speaks through His servant here on this earth." He waved toward Harrow and backed away.

Harrow stepped forward. He had acquired a new black suit and shiny boots, and wore a snakeskin belt in his trousers. His black eyes scanned the crowd as they watched him, scarcely breathing.

"We are a new church," he said. "We are young and we are strong, God's army against the perils of this world. Like the infant Jesus, this is a new beginning." Heads nodded. "There is nothing we cannot accomplish when we think and feel as one. A church divided cannot stand, but this church will be a pillar of strength."

He took a step closer to the edge of the platform, leaning toward his mesmerized followers. "Just as Jesus was born on this night long ago, I declare that the First Church of the Heavenly Powers, founded in the blood of the divine, is newly born tonight."

Cries of "Amen!" and "Praise the Lord!" filled the church.

"Sweet Jesus," sobbed Yula Rider, moved to tears at the intensity of Harrow's delivery. Jeral Maunder stood beside her impassively, his huge arms folded over his old brown coat.

"Join with me as one Body and we will vanquish all our enemies!" shouted Harrow. "Join!" the congregation shouted back.

The choir burst into a chorus of "I am a soldier of the cross," augmented at once by the voices of men, women, and children. The church rang with the sound of the exultation as Harrow stepped down from the platform and walked briskly to the front entrance. He opened the door and wind blew in, extinguishing all the candles in a single blast.

"We come into this world from darkness," he said loudly, standing behind the last row of benches. "Carry the flame burning inside you out into the darkness of this world and know that a power greater than any of us is ours for the asking. All you must do is surrender yourself and believe."

The worshippers stood with bowed heads in the cold dark. Children whimpered and were shushed by their parents, muted coughs hung in throats. Finally, the choir began to hum "Away in a manger." They filed quietly down the aisle toward the open door, and the congregation flowed out of the rows behind them and into the churchyard where Harrow waited to bid them good night.

Well. That was the strangest Christmas Eve service Alice had ever encountered. The fact that it came from her own imagination didn't help – who did she think these people were, anyway? She had never been to a black church and didn't know what a typical Christmas Eve service would have been like, but she suspected it would bear little resemblance to what she had just written. She scratched her head.

The church in her story didn't seem to be very Christian, in spite of the external trappings of Christmas carols and such. Perhaps Harrow had invented his own brand of worship and convinced others to follow him. At least the scene she'd painted was colorful and drawn from some modicum of fact. The flyer *did* say it was to be a candlelight service. But her characterization of Harrow was bordering on the demonic, and she wondered how this was going to play out when she finally got to the crux of the story, the lynching of Old Joe. After all, she wasn't writing a documentary; it was a fictional history of a local legend, so she could warp the facts anyway she chose, but she had a growing suspicion that the story was telling itself and that she had less control over it than she wanted.

And where was Old Joe, for that matter? She hadn't even put him into the story yet and didn't know how he fit into the group of characters developed so far. This was a significant problem if she intended to stick with the Camper's Legend outline, but her mind was just too foggy to figure it out. A scratchiness in the back of her throat made her wonder if she was coming down with something. Yawning, she checked her watch and saw it was nearly 2 a.m. Quickly, she put her writing materials away and pulled Margaret's toys out of the laundry room where they'd been stashed.

Getting the bicycle out with no noise was tricky, but at last all was accomplished.

Her head was full of ideas and questions about the direction her book seemed to be taking in spite of the more mundane outline she'd made weeks ago, but she was too sleepy to bother writing them down. Maybe if she gave herself the proper suggestion once she got to bed, she could do the drafting work in her dreams.

CHAPTER 16

ALICE WOKE up Christmas morning with a sore throat that threatened to linger for the rest of the holidays.

"Not fair," she whined into her pillow, swallowing with effort. She sat up and coughed, recognizing that familiar acid taste that spoke of bronchial infection.

"Are you sick?" Nik asked, eyes barely open. It was 7:30, just after daylight. "You sound wheezy."

Alice groped for her inhaler, kept by the bed in case of emergency. She hadn't had a serious asthma attack in years, but any kind of respiratory infection could make her uncomfortably short of breath. "Just a sore throat, maybe it'll go away soon," she said, but knew that was wishful thinking.

Nik reached out, and she crawled into his circle of warmth, reluctant to move for the rest of the day. She was dozing off again when the door creaked open, and Margaret poked her head into the room.

"Mom, can we open presents yet? Everybody's up but you guys."

Alice sighed, but couldn't get her brains in gear. Nik lifted his head, but didn't respond.

"Can we?" Margaret repeated. Carlisle sidled around Margaret and tiptoed into the room, his nails clicking on the polished floor. He jumped up onto the foot of the bed and lay down with a sigh.

Alice sat up, shivering. "Okay, I'm up now. Go ask your grandma if she'll put on some coffee. We'll be there in a minute." Margaret bounded away, leaving the door ajar. Alice looked back at Nik.

"Well, Merry Christmas."

"*God Jul.* I'm sorry you're sick." He rubbed her back in gentle, circular strokes.

Alice was greatly tempted to lie back down, but sighed and reached for her bathrobe. "Shit happens. Well, let's go before we're summoned again. Welcome to the Waterston/Blacksburg family Christmas."

Wrapped in her robe, with heavy socks and slippers on her feet, Alice shuffled into the kitchen. Spanning most of the back of the house, the kitchen and dining area at Dunescape offered an invigorating plate-glass view of the Gulf of Mexico. Early morning sunlight streamed into the room. The coffeemaker light was on and fresh brew steamed in the pot. Just starting to feel human, Alice poured herself a cup, sipped tentatively, and verified its decaffeinated nonflavor—another regrettable facet of visiting her mother. She could hear Suzanne's voice in the living room, and knew from the lightness of the tone that she was talking to Margaret, the light of her life. Alice supposed it was a good thing that grandmother and granddaughter were so tight with each other; otherwise, she'd probably never visit and that meant depriving herself of Hal's company, which she prized.

Her mind drifted back to the chapter she'd written last night when everyone else had gone to bed. Once again, the story was taking bizarre meanderings off the track of her original outline, and more so every time she sat down to work on it. Last night's description of the Christmas Eve service was just plain creepy. It was still very present in her mind, and she wondered why her book plot was beginning to feel more real and compelling than her own current events. It was definitely getting in the way.

Nik came in, sniffed the coffee, and turned to the fridge, searching for some juice. Alice studied him in the bright natural light of the kitchen, admiring the silkiness of his white-blonde hair and his tall, lean body clad now in flannel shirt and jeans. His prominent, sharp nose and square jaw spoke to her of Danes and Swedes crossing the ice fjords of Scandinavia in search of adventure. He was her Nordic hero, straight out of the sagas, except that he was passive and unobtrusive almost to a fault. Alice smiled— no cleaving of berserker shields from this fellow. Although there was that bit with the gun in his backpack, which she still found unsettling. As much as Whit had carried on about being their protector out in the woods when their house was new, he had never carried a gun. In fact, she was pretty sure he'd never owned one. She'd asked Nik about it later, and he'd said it was common practice to go armed when hiking the snowclad forests of Scandinavia. She remembered his exact words: "You never know when you might come upon a bear or wolf." No wolves in the Florida woods that she knew of, but she supposed an unexpected cottonmouth or rattler could be just as dangerous.

Nik found his orange juice and poured a glass.

"Shall we?" He motioned toward the living room, where tree lights twinkled. Alice filled her coffee cup to the rim and followed him. Margaret was sitting on the floor, surrounded by a heap of packaging material and wrapping paper.

"Hey, Mom, check it out! The models I wanted." She held up several boxes with various colorful sauropods and raptors on the front. "I already got a good start on the brachiosaurus."

Nik was immediately on the floor beside her. "Hey, let's have a look. That's pretty accurate, nice detail, where's the head?"

Alice plopped down next to her uncle, laughing.

"Well, the children seem to be happy. Where's Mom? I heard her voice a minute ago."

"Grandma went back to bed," said Margaret. "She got up to make your coffee and watch me open my presents, but said it was too early to stay up."

Alice nodded. Her mother would sleep til mid-morning, then get up ravenous, expecting them all to eat breakfast with her, no matter what they might have consumed beforehand. She would hustle around the kitchen in an energetic frenzy, tossing her salon-maintained red hair, styled short for tennis playing, and complain that they had run out of this or that but hoping maybe they could make do with whatever it was she decided to cook. These behaviors never changed – just the environments in which they were acted out. There was some of that compulsiveness in Alice, but she tried to diffuse it when it threatened to go off the deep end.

Her mother, on the other hand, accepted such activity as normal and considered most other people to be either lazy or suffering from some physical infirmity that would explain their obvious sluggish condition. Alice envied Nik a little, heading back to Magnolia after breakfast. She wondered how long she could tolerate life in her mother's breathing space before she demanded to be driven home. Margaret, of course, would object, but the hell with it. Alice would be firm but pleasant, because it was Christmas, and not put up with any arguments when she was ready to leave.

Her uncle put his arm around her and gave her a brief squeeze. "Why the long face?"

"Hm?"

"You just looked very lost and lonely there, staring off into space." His expression was a question mark.

"Just thinking about Nik going back to Magnolia without me is all," she said.

"Nik's very welcome to stay. I don't see why he has to leave so soon."

"Field guide work," answered Nik. "I shouldn't have taken this much time away, but I'm glad I came."

"As are we." Hal felt Alice's forehead. "But I'm wondering if you shouldn't go back to bed, dear. You look very run-down. I think you've been working too hard. Can't the exhibit get along without you for a week or two?"

Alice shook her head. She had not planned to take time off until the Wandjinas were packed and gone to galleries overseas in March. Right now that couldn't come a moment too soon.

Later that morning they packed up Nik's truck with most of the Christmas gifts, a large cardboard box filled with meticulously container-ized remains of the elaborate holiday dinner Suzanne and Hal had created the night before as a tag team (after so many years together, they navigated that performance with oiled precision), and Margaret's new bicycle, a gift from Hal. Alice watched with a sinking heart as Nik said his goodbyes to her mother and uncle, then solemnly kissed Margaret's hand, which made her giggle and snatch it away. Alice followed him out to the truck.

"Drive safely," she said.

"Maybe you should come, too. Go see a doctor—you might have bronchitis."

"Uh uh. I'm not sitting around in a crowded waiting room with a bunch of sick people. I'll take some aspirins and go back to bed. You go on."

She said this knowing the ride back to Magnolia at the end of the week with her mother, Margaret, new toys, and Carlisle was going to be an event that would test her patience. "I feel obligated to give Margaret and Mother some quality time. And I'll get to hang out with Hal, which I haven't done enough of lately."

"Your mother and uncle have an interesting relationship." Nik's simple statement encompassed all the questions he must have been thinking.

"Don't worry, it's platonic. She's a widow, and he's never been married, but they know each other better than anyone else ever could. It's a perfect setup. When I was little I thought Hal was my dad until I was old enough to understand 'uncle.' I've always interacted with him as a sort of stepfather. It never felt strange to me."

"What was your real dad like?"

"Who knows? He was dead by the time I showed up. Mom only ever said he was some painter who swept her off her feet, married her, took her to Australia, and then died, only she didn't put it quite that crassly."

"Your father was Australian?"

"Well, I 'm not sure about that. I don't think he was actually born there, but he may have had relatives in Queensland. Funny, huh? This exhibit makes me think about him. Funny."

He put his long arms around her for a moment. Alice leaned against him.

"So, what did you think of the Witch of Endor?"

"Your mother's not as bad as you led me to believe."

"Yeah, I noticed she went all girly when you offered to carry Margaret to bed. You *are* subtle, like I said, only I'm onto you now, so watch out."

He leaned down and kissed her with his mouth closed. "I have no secrets," he said. A corner of his mouth might have smiled, but by the time it registered in Alice's brain, it was gone.

"I don't understand why you treat your mother with such coldness. She seemed nice enough to me," he said.

"Nik, what was your family life like when you were little?"

He shrugged. "Pretty typical, I think – we siblings teased each other, parents disciplined us all, but loved us, too."

"Yeah, well, see ... I never got any of that from her, not even the discipline. And in particular not the love. When I was a preschooler, she acted like she didn't know me. I never went in her room, never sat on the swing with her like Margaret and I do, never got hugged when something made me cry. All that was Hal's job. He was really good at it, too."

Nik was silent. Perhaps this was more than he'd really wanted to know. Alice cleared her throat.

"You'd better get on the road. The critters'll be starved by the time you get back."

"Poor old Dawg, he couldn't believe we didn't take him with us."

"Please be careful going back." Alice held onto him. "Holiday traffic might be bad."

The door banged and Margaret came running down the steps. "Bye, Nik. Thanks for the paint set. I *love* it!"

She reached up and gave his neck a hug, then ran back up the steps and into the house, the screen door banging behind her. Alice could see it; Nik had won her daughter over completely.

"That was very cool of you, by the way," she said. "Giving her some art supplies. You're a good influence."

"I like Margaret. She has talent, you should encourage her."

"To be honest, I was worried about how she'd react to you moving in with us ... you know what I mean."

Nik's pale eyes were unreadable, like fjords reflecting the winter sky overhead. "Obviously she knows we have sex. I assume she's known for the past year. You should have said something if you have reservations."

"No reservations. Drive safely. Give Figaro a hug for me." She squeezed him once more and stepped away.

Watching the truck disappear down the gravel drive, she immediately felt worse. Maybe she did love him. She had successfully resisted loving anyone for so long, she wasn't sure. It was hard to tell where this relationship was going, but it was clear that it wasn't short-term.

She went back inside and saw Margaret rolling up her pants legs.

"Going somewhere?"

"Down the beach with Grandma. She said we could go around to the cove, okay?"

"Take a jacket. I don't want you to catch cold, too. One sickie in the house is enough."

She wandered back to the kitchen, intending to drink the rest of the orange juice. Through the wide windows she could see Margaret and her mother walking briskly down the boardwalk toward the margin of sand, made wider by the receding tide. The sun beat down on the water from a cloudless sky; by noon it would be too warm for a jacket. On the back patio she could just see her uncle's feet hanging several inches over the end of his lounger. The house was quiet except for Carlisle's snoring and doggie-dream paddling where he'd nested in a mound of Christmas wrapping pushed under the tree.

Alice dressed in her usual sweat suit, then took her briefcase with all her writing materials into the kitchen, intending to spread everything across the table, but then changed her mind and went out the back door. The air was warming gradually, producing a shimmer out over the water as the sun rose toward noon. She had been shivering slightly from a low-grade fever, but the sun on her face felt so good she headed down the boardwalk. Not far away was a screened cabana and boathouse where her uncle's outboard was tied up. A long picnic table filled one end of the cabana where she could work undisturbed. She wanted to study her outline again and give some serious thought to where it was all going. She also needed to work the basic Camper's Legend into it, but hadn't quite figured out how.

The cabana was clean but a bit unused looking. She dusted off the tabletop, spread out her materials, and went though the library folder piece by piece, consolidating every scrap of material dealing with the lynching of the man called Old Joe or, in one case, his Indian name of O'Shawnie, which quick research in the museum's Florida History archives had revealed was probably O-Sha-Nee, a Miccosuki word for "otter." There weren't many clues as to who he was and what his connection with the church people might have been. She reread the news announcement about the selection of the church site and realized there was a small item she could build on. It stated that "a curious crowd of Snake Bite citizens and a few Red Indians" had been witness to Harrow's dowsing event.

What type of Indians could they have been? She knew that Creek, Miccosukee, and Seminole descendants would have been in the area, even after the Trail of Tears relocation to Oklahoma in the 1830s. There was nothing to prove one of these Indians had been the hanged man, but for the flow of her storyline, it could be useful. Perhaps Otter had been impressed by the shamanistic ritual of the dowsing rod and wanted to join the church? Although Snake Bite had been (and still was) a mostly black community, there was no indication that other ethnic groups were excluded from the church. Hadn't Harrow's obituary suggested that he was himself of mixed blood? Maybe that was a better reason for the Old Joe character to attach himself to the new minister and his flock.

She wondered what Joe or Otter should look like. A grainy photo accompanied the lynching article, showing his body laid out on the ground, surrounded by the posse members who'd hunted him down, but she could distinguish no details of face or figure. Then she remembered Margaret's supposed sighting of an "Indian" in the woods near the pond. What had she said . . . that the fellow had brownish skin with stiff dark hair, wore a black suit and a wide-brimmed hat, and looked sort of like an Indian. Then it struck her: Margaret hadn't been talking about Old Joe or O-Sha-Nee at all—the person Margaret described was Harrow. Alice dropped her pen.

How could Margaret know those details? Alice had sat at the computer and visualized Harrow before they all went for the walk to the pond, but she hadn't shared it with them. They had only read her draft of the Camper's Legend story, not any of her book chapters. She felt tingly, like an electrical charge was building up. She half expected her hair to float upwards.

Alice rubbed her eyes and tried to think. Margaret had said the creature didn't move or speak to her or anything like that; there was just the visual image of it sitting on a stump, and of course it was gone when they all went back looking for it. How could that be possible? Alice massaged her temples. Telling ghost stories and writing about them was one thing, even fun in a daring sort of way, but it didn't make them real. There was supposed to be a line where imagination stopped and cold reality existed— if you couldn't tell where the thin line between them was, you were judged insane or deluded or, in the old days, possessed.

Chin in hand, she looked out at the shining water rippling gently with the tide. On this still, cloudless day, the Gulf looked two-dimensional, flat greenish blue with no depth. A line of brown pelicans dipped and coasted, dipped and flapped their way toward the sandbar out near the channel. Alice shut her eyes. The scene behind her lids went black, with pinpoints of phosphenes floating. Then a lean-to constructed from pieces of tattered canvas appeared sharply as if shown through a projector onto the back of her lids. A man sat under the canvas, smoking a pipe.

He was filthy in a way that only years of neglect or indifference could achieve, smoking placidly with seeming insensitivity to the insects that crawled on and bit his body. Untended wounds festered on his legs where brambles had lacerated the flesh above his ankles. With soft brown eyes hidden under the jutting brow of his round moon face, he studied the ground in front of his feet. A circular design was drawn in the dirt where, sitting cross-legged, he tossed small pieces of bone onto the roughly drawn arcs and arrows. Alice's eyes popped open. She grabbed her pen and began to scribble words as fast as she could before the image faded.

Chapter Five – Spirit Guide

Otter sat under his makeshift tent and watched the rain fall. His fire was gone and it would take him a long time, maybe hours, to start another once the drizzle stopped. The tent wasn't good, but he didn't know how to make a proper house like the one his mother had lived in. That house had been up on stilts and thatched with palm fronds, open-sided so that no walls stopped the flow of cooling breezes. They hadn't lived on a river with woods all around like this, but on a sandy hillside with unbroken water that stretched out from sand to the end of the world. But his mother was dead and now he lived on his own.

Otter was an ingenious hunter. He could fashion arrows from the tough rushes growing at the river's edge and make tools from bones of the animals he killed and ate. His mother had taught him how to make impoundments for fish, to keep them alive until he was ready to eat them, and he still remembered how to do it even though she had been dead for more seasons than he had fingers. He lived with the rhythm of the river and its ebbing and flowing, in the rain and the dry times, with his mother's spirit to guide him.

Once in a while he crossed the river to visit a witch who lived on the other side. She was kind and shared food with him if she had any. She gave him spells and charms to help him bring the fish to the surface of the water where he could wade in and catch them with his hands, and once she told him how to work a misfortune on two white men, hunters from a nearby town, who had threatened to run him off his tiny spot of land because they didn't like his smell. He had weighted their dead bodies down in the water with large smooth river rocks, food for his brother fishes.

The witch had a daughter, old enough to marry and young enough to be pretty. He longed for her in a man's way but said and did nothing for fear the witch would strike him dead if she knew what was in his secret heart. The young girl's skin was smooth and black as night, her teeth white like shark's teeth. He figured her to be as old as two hands plus two fingers perhaps. She was kind to him too, and they cleaned fish together on the riverbank. He liked the feelings that ebbed and flowed like river current through his body when they sat together, and he would have protected her with his life. He knew her name but couldn't make his tongue say the sounds, so he called her Little Stick of Burned Wood in his own tongue, a name she didn't seem to mind.

Lately, though, she had been less friendly and the witch less willing to work her spells. They seemed afraid or on guard in some way, although surely they must have known no harm would come to them from him. He missed the girl terribly and took to following her at a suitable distance, far enough for her not to see him yet close enough to know where she went. She went often to the new spirit dwelling rising tall out of the cleared patch some distance from the place where the river went underground. There she and many others of her kind invoked the spirit world for help in the growth of their crops and the health of their children.

Otter wasn't interested in the religion of the riverbottom people, but his need to be near the witch's daughter drove him to the vicinity of the building and its strange shaman with the black holes for eyes. He was an evil man, Otter was sure, and his hand rested more than once on the shoulder of Little Stick in a way that made Otter crazy with anger. He considered approaching the witch for a powerful spell to thwart the shaman's possible designs, but then he would have to reveal his own desires and this he was afraid to do. So he waited and watched.

The rain pounded his tent. He felt sorry for himself and wished the water would stop pouring so he could cast the bones and ask his mother's spirit what to do about Little Stick and her mother. He heartily disapproved of the shaman and his circle of warriors, convinced that the Great Spirit they gathered to invoke was not the same as that of his own people. He had tried to think of a way to protect the girl without letting anyone know what he was doing, but it was too hard; he couldn't untangle a plan from his wandering thoughts. That was why he needed to ask his mother what to do.

He dozed, knees drawn up to his chin, and finally the rain stopped and sunlight came down in its place. He unfolded his legs and stepped out into the bare scraped area in front of his lean-to. The ground was damp, but as soon as most of the water had soaked through the sand he could make the spirit-trap the witch had taught him to draw. Under the palmetto mat in his shelter was the stylus she gave him to use—a sharpened sassafras twig blackened on one end where it had been hardened in the fire. He pulled it out and squatted down.

First he made the circle. Then he drew the four points like arrows aiming north, east, south, and west. Finally, he pulled from underneath his shirt a small bag made of animal skin and tipped a tiny bit of its contents into the palm of his hand. The witch's magic powder it was, something she made from certain plants and snippings of his own hair. He wet his thumb and pressed it into the powder, then to his forehead. He blew the remaining powder from his palm into the circle and took out the bones.

The bones. He held the three small, smooth finger bones taken from his mother's hand when she died. It was all he could think to do before he set the body up on a ridge of white limestone for his brother vultures. He had asked her later when he was miles away and had slept and eaten many times if it was an evil thing he had done. She told him no.

Otter cast the bones into the circle and called her name. "Wah-ko-la." Leaves rustled and water dripped from their tips, but not because of his mother's presence. He could wait; she would come. He had called her once when the witch's daughter was with him, and his mother had stayed hidden until Little Stick got weary of waiting and swam back across the river. Then she had come.

"O-Sha-Nee . . ." Her voice whispered in his ear. Otter spread his palms over the circle and put his forehead down on the bones.

"The young one is not your burden. Let it go."

He frowned and shook his head. He tried to hold the thought of what he wanted steady in his mind.

"She loves you, but not as you think . . . it is a child's love."

Tears ran down his face, thinking about Little Stick in her white dress. She was an egret in his mind.

"Are you unmoved, son of otters?" His mother spoke the name of his spirit animal, so chosen because shortly after his birth a mother otter had crawled into the blankets with two duck eggs in her jaws and eaten them both, leaving the cracked shells and slippery pieces of yolk across his infant face. The elders said later it was the reason for his slowness in comprehending things every child knew.

"Then you must go to the shaman and offer him your service. The risk is unlucky but may accomplish what you wish, son of otters."

Otter sat up and nodded—he understood. He gathered the bones and climbed to his feet, scuffing out the design on the ground with his feet lest someone should come and see it. The witch had impressed on him that it must be kept secret or the spell would cease to work.

"We'll keep it a secret." Margaret's voice came up from the beach and wedged its way into Alice's consciousness. "Just you and me know where our special spot is, Grandma. Hey, Mom's there."

Suzanne pushed open the screen door of the cabana. "What a surprise. I thought you were too ill to be out and about."

The lean-to in the woods vanished from Alice's mind, but her emotions were still meshed to Otter's vision and for a moment she couldn't recognize the two people surrounding her with meaningless talk. On his mother's advice, Otter had made some decision concerning his dilemma but what was it? The answer was gone from her head, and so was the mental link.

"Margaret, why are your jeans wet?" she asked, irritated. She looked at Suzanne. "Did you let her go swimming in her clothes?"

"We buried some treasure—" Margaret began.

"She slipped and sat down in a pool on the flats," said Suzanne. "She's going to change as soon as we get back—"

"—and it's in a secret place that only we know about—"

"—so don't be angry. It was a simple accident, and it's so warm today nobody's going to get pneumonia from wet clothes anyway—"

"—just like pirates wrecked on a desert island—"

"All right!" Alice put down her pen and pulled her notebook closed. "I'm not mad," she lied, putting her writing materials back into the briefcase and repacking the library folder.

"Don't get up just on account of us," said her mother. "We're leaving, you can go back to your papers. What *are* you working on so secretively, anyway?"

"Just stuff from the museum. Research for a shipwreck that got found off the Keys."

"Pirate treasure!" said Margaret.

"They weren't pirates, just travelers who met a bad end."

"That's very interesting," her mother said. "*Was* there any treasure?"

"Some. Silver bars and things like that, whatever was loaded on board in Vera Cruz to go back to Spain."

"Will any of it go on display? I'd like to drive over and see it." Her interest probably was genuine, although secondary to another visit with her granddaughter.

"Eventually, I guess. But it'll take months—maybe years—to get everything cleaned and catalogued. Jessie and I are going to be busy for most of this year on it. Once the Wandjinas are packed and gone."

"Who's Jessie?" Her mother's prying curiosity hadn't changed. It seemed that once Alice moved away, first to college and then to Boston as a young bride, Suzanne always wanted to know who Alice's friends were and what they were doing. She rarely forgot any of them once she acquired some detail that would fix the person in her memory. The fact that most of them were faceless names she would never meet was beside the point. She was having a vicarious relationship with her daughter through knowledge of Alice's acquaintances.

"He's the laboratory conservator."

"How's a conservator different from a curator?"

"I know," said Margaret. "The lab dude gets to play with the artifacts and the other one has to organize them."

"I see." Suzanne beamed at her.

"Jessie Birch is Canadian with a degree from Queens College in England. He's very bright and well-thought-of in his field," Alice added, then wished she'd bitten her tongue off. Why was she telling her mother about Jessie? It was just asking for trouble.

"Really?" Her mother was looking at her with interest. Alice returned the look, unblinking, arms crossed over her chest. Her head was hurting, muscles twitching with that subtle ache that meant high fever, delirium, coma. She felt in no mood to play the personal guessing games her mother thrived on.

"Have I met this Jessie person?" Suzanne nibbled a manicured fingernail.

"I doubt it. He never comes up into the part of the museum where the real people in offices live."

Suzanne was undeterred. "I remember meeting a very distinguished, handsome man when we came to see your Florida history show last summer."

Alice stood up, briefcase under her arm. "That was Shelton MacBeth, the museum director."

"Hey, can we go now? My butt's wet."

Bless Margaret. "You bet, Munch." Alice went out to the sandy dock and started trudging down the boardwalk toward the house. She had an image of Suzanne following, looking thoughtful and probably plotting some unpleasant way to bring up the subject again at dinner. She could tell; it was going to be a four-aspirin evening.

CHAPTER 17

NIK DID a lot of thinking on the drive back to Magnolia, and by the time he turned off Magnolia Parkway onto Black Creek Ferry Road, he had come to some conclusions. Alice's family was odd, but maybe not as dysfunctional as he had been led to believe. Hal Blacksburg was a straight shooter and could be counted on to treat people decently, or at least he gave the impression of genuine interest in those around him. The mother was much more complicated, secretive actually, with strong self-preservation instincts. Nik suspected those instincts took precedence over the needs of others, even her own offspring. Her interaction with Alice was complicated as well, with obvious tension on the surface but something else at play that was only hinted at. He wasn't sure either of them was aware of it, like a subconscious taboo that neither of them had been willing to acknowledge. It probably had to do with the dead husband/father, but that wasn't his business and he didn't intend to pry into it.

Having now met the mother, he could see some of her in Alice, especially the tendency toward secretiveness. Not that he minded that much, it was one of the traits that made Alice interesting to him. Her personality had layers. He liked having sex with her and found her libido surprisingly responsive once they'd allowed their relationship to go that far, although in the early days he had been somewhat put off by her situation of being newly divorced with a child. But he'd since come to the conclusion that Margaret was an asset to their relationship rather than a hindrance. Margaret was intelligent, curious, and had her own secrets as well, although she and Alice were more forthright with each other than your typical parent-child involvement. What one thought was often mirrored in the opinions of the other, with interesting degrees of difference. He enjoyed fostering Margaret's scientific and artistic endeavors.

Having met the "parents," he could also see the source for what he considered Alice's odd blend of open mindedness and willingness to entertain new ideas tempered by a suspicious cynicism that had been an early stumbling block in their commitment to each other. Alice could be sarcastic like no one else he knew. He was not a complete cynic himself, and preferred to try to look at things from more than one point of view. Nik considered himself a realist, if anything, and he and Alice were happily compatible on a number of points. Both were mostly apolitical and nonreligious, with occasional bouts of passionate bias on particular issues, typically involving protection of the environment.

They had similar taste in music (mostly jazz and world beat artists, with some classical) and literature (standards such as Shakespeare and novelists like Hermann Hesse), although the range of his reading was not as wide as hers and tended more toward the scientific and nonfiction. He remembered the happy discovery that they'd both read and admired *Foucault's Pendulum*. Both avoided chick flicks and jock movies, preferring an occasional foreign film or movie classic on the Arts & Entertainment channel.

Margaret had initiated him into the mysteries of Japanese anime, which he found both confusing and stimulating, so he was willing to try to find out what it was all about. The character design and background artwork in some of the series they'd exposed him to was excellent and well worth watching. Margaret and Alice claimed that the storylines were deep as well, but some of them just put him to sleep. But he could tell that a few were works of art and deserving of the praise heaped on them. He preferred to watch them in subtitle mode so he could hear the performances of the original Japanese voice actors.

Dawg met him at the head of the driveway and galloped around the truck, exuding such dog joy at his master's return that Nik was contrite for having left him behind. He stopped the truck and got out.

"Hey, old fella, did you miss me, then?" Dawg slobbered him properly as Nik bent down to rub him under the chin.

"Let's go check the mail, okay?"

He walked across the dirt road to the box, Dawg at his heels. The postal service was closed for Christmas Day, but yesterday's mail was crammed into the box, and he pulled out at least a dozen holiday catalogs selling crap he wouldn't even consider buying in a million years. Hiding amongst them were credit card bills for Alice, a utilities bill, a handful of Christmas cards to Alice and Margaret, and one from his parents. He separated that one from the rest of the stack.

He got back in the truck, and Dawg promptly jumped up into his place on the passenger side. Nik felt around in the glove box and found a bag of dog biscuits, from which he extracted two and let Dawg slurp them up from his open palm.

"No, I won't leave you next time, no matter how much the girls complain," he said, wiping his hand on his jeans.

He pulled up under the house in the parking bay nearest the steps and got out. Nik was still amused at the mental image of them all crammed into the truck as he climbed the stairs to the front door. Who would collect the most dog drool? He let himself in with the extra key, making sure not to allow Dawg in behind him. He wasn't willing to push Alice's tolerance that far.

"Sorry fella. Just wait – I'll be back in a minute."

He had to piss severely and had been holding it for the past thirty minutes. He hit the bathroom in seconds.

Relieved, Nik wandered back out to the living room and stood looking around. It gave him an odd feeling, being here alone in a house that belonged to someone else. Like staying in a hotel room or something. Although he enjoyed being by himself and had no trouble finding ways to keep from being bored, he hoped Alice wouldn't stay too long, and not just because he felt ill at ease sleeping alone in her ex-husband's bed. He actually missed her company. It was a unique experience for him, and he savored the way it felt. Was it love? He'd been willing to move in with her in order to find out.

He put the mail on the kitchen counter and opened the envelope from his parents. It was a card, as expected, with a note in his mother's handwriting admonishing him for not coming home for Christmas. Enclosed was a crisp hundred-dollar bill. Well, that would require a phone call. Nik put the bill in his wallet, calculating how much dog food he could buy with a hundred USD.

After making himself a sandwich and finishing off a bowl of soup he found in the fridge, he was ready to spend the afternoon doing exactly what he liked best – foraging for mushrooms in the woods and photographing them in their natural setting. He wound film onto the take-up spool of his camera and snapped the back shut, then checked the batteries in his mini-recorder, so that in addition to the photographic record, he could tape descriptions and any other pertinent field notes for each shot.

Dawg was waiting for him at the bottom of the stairs. The sun was still above the trees and the light was perfect for the type of pictures he liked to shoot, indirect and not too yellow. The subtle violet and roseate shadings found on certain mushroom caps reproduced best with automatic timer shots. Sometimes he exposed them as long as twenty to thirty seconds in afternoon conditions like this. Brighter sunlight tended to whiten and wash them out.

He took a few minutes to lift Margaret's new bicycle out of the truck and stow it safely under the house. He was pleased to see that whoever had bought the bike knew enough to get wide nobby tires on it, which was much more practical for cycling around the neighborhood's dirt roads than her old one with its thin sidewalk-friendly tires.

Nik pondered whether to go down to the bog where he knew he could find bluets and parasols or to try his alternate site, a group of rotted oaks toppled hear the northern edge of the property. It often supported large colonies of oyster fungi, a decent edible. But it was a longer walk that way. He knew that Alice and Whit, like most homeowners in the Black Creek area, had bought a ten-acre tract and put their house in the exact middle, protecting their privacy from the road and passers-by. It was nearly twice as far from the house to the rotted oaks as it was to the pond. He also had a secondary mission: to reconnoiter the property just to make sure nothing was amiss. He did not expect to meet anything supernatural or unexplainable, but feral pigs or dogs he was prepared to deal with. After dusting his ankles and waistband with a sock filled with sulfur powder to discourage crawling bloodsuckers, he turned upland toward the oaks.

"Off we go," he said, and as soon as he started walking toward the trail, Dawg bounded ahead of him.

One of these days he was going to suggest that Alice fence the whole thing in. It would be worth taking out a loan for a good wire and post fence, in his opinion, if she didn't have the money readily available. Although his graduate assistantship was just a fraction of her museum salary, he was willing to chip in what he could to get it done. In his mind, it was a safety issue, not so crucial now that he was living there, but just the two of them out here didn't seem like the best idea, even with a few fairly close neighbors. It just made good sense to take precautions.

Dawg ran ahead, then trotted back to walk beside Nik, his tail beating time to his strides. They were best pals, and Nik continually thanked the luck that had brought them together when he'd gone dog hunting at the animal shelter. Dawg was a mix of breeds, part golden retriever, German shepherd, bird dog, Labrador, and who knew what else, which resulted in a short-haired, medium-sized black and tan mutt who was tough as nails, fearless, loyal, people-oriented, and easy-going. Nik took him everywhere and was willing to overlook his smell.

Nik walked slowly, looking to either side of the trail. He thought about his trip to Norway, which wasn't all that far away now, and what he intended to say for his presentation. The slides for the field guide demo would sell themselves, but his discussion of Gulf Coast fungi had to be as tight as he could make it. There would be plenty of name mycologists there ready to ask questions and pose their own opinions. Professionally, it was an important event for him; he might even make a name for himself. Alice had offered to edit his presentation because she thought his writing was a little too stilted, but he didn't imagine any of his target audience would notice; they might even find it exciting reading, a notion which amused him. For the layperson, the topic of mushrooms was probably deadly dull, and maybe that included Alice. If it was true, she didn't say so. Margaret, however, did so often, in a teasing sort of way.

Dawg barked sharply and stopped short in front of him.

"Yeah, I see it," he said and caught a glimpse of a diamond-patterned shape whipping away under the leaves. Unlike birders, mushroomers were not likely to get bitten by snakes. He wasn't afraid of snakes and in fact found them quite beautiful, but he did have a healthy respect for the venomous ones. He was pleased that Margaret seemed to share his interest in reptiles.

He thought about her with genuine affection. Generally he was standoffish where children were concerned, but she didn't seem all that childish. He was intrigued by the way she knew there was no Santa Claus, and known for years, but willingly suspended her disbelief to make her Christmas more exciting. He also wondered about her tendency toward nightmares. In the few weeks he'd been living in their house, Alice had been called out of bed more than once to calm her fright. When questioned about it, Alice had insisted it was a common way for children to deal with their fears without having to face them in the real world. Nik wasn't convinced – if that assumption were true, it was an inelegant flaw in the cosmos. There should have been a better design.

"Hello, there." He stopped in his tracks just in front of a perfectly formed slender parasol standing by itself in a mound of leaves. Nik sat down on the ground next to it. Dawg came and stood beside him, whining.

"What's the matter? It's only a mushroom. *Lepiota procera*," Nik said into his recorder. "Perfect specimen, no animal chews, upright in partial shade, beech and oak leaves in situ, appears to be about six inches tall."

The fawn-colored cap was fully opened with broad flat scales across the top, and he noted with satisfaction the characteristic double-edged annulus and swollen base of the stalk, a real beauty. He began pushing away some of the obscuring leaves in preparation for a prize-winning photo. Dawg looked off into the tangle of vines and underbrush and continued to whimper.

"Not going to give it up, are you ... so what is it? Snake?"

Nik craned his neck and tried to see where Dawg was looking. Then he spotted a small grouping of mushrooms among the leaves piled between the exposed roots of a leaning oak.

"*Hej–*"

About two inches tall with flat, cinnamon-brown slimy caps on thick cottony stalks, their curling edges caught the light. Nik could barely believe his eyes because this particular mushroom was fairly rare, requiring highly specialized conditions for growth.

"*Hebeloma syriense*, if I'm not mistaken," he breathed. The Corpse Finder mushroom, so named because of its tendency to grow from the remains of carcasses.

Then the smell hit him – death.

Nik put the camera down. He stood up and took a few steps toward the source of the stench, which he could now see was a mottled lump of fur and bones. A raccoon? No, the fur was solid black, with a little white patch. It was the remains of a cat's body, with the head torn off. Nik stood staring, breathing through his mouth. He reached out and rubbed Dawg between the ears.

"Good boy, *tack* for not rolling in it."

What was large enough to kill a cat this way? He didn't for a moment suspect Dawg, who was trained to live with cats and not chase them. Marauding dog pack? If that was the case, he needed to call the sheriff's office. There was no separate animal control agency out here for the rural part of the county, so he knew that most people relied on a sheriff's deputy or more likely their own skill with a .22 to take care of such problems.

Nik stood up, holding his nose. Flies had already blown the body, and what was left was puffy with maggots. Even so, he could see the head had been twisted off rather than chewed away, so whatever killed the cat hadn't been interested in eating it. The evidence lay about two feet beyond the body, looking up at him with sightless sockets. Nik was dispassionately curious to unravel the truth of what had occurred here although he knew Raine would be distraught over the discovery. He took a photo of the remains and recorded a brief observation of the details into his tape cassette. He was about to stow the camera back in his bag when he realized he'd nearly forgotten the parasol that had first attracted his attention.

He got down on the ground again and made the shot, but his concentration wasn't there. Disquieted, Nik decided to pack it in for the day and headed back up the trail toward the house. He wanted to look up the county authorities in the phone book and also thought about calling Alice, but immediately discarded the idea. She seemed to have enough on her mind without this. Time enough to share the news of Tuxedo's grisly death when she returned.

CHAPTER 18

SUZANNE WATERSTON adjusted her sunglasses and wheeled her Lincoln Towncar out of the driveway and onto the back beach road in one smooth motion. Margaret sat in front beside her, her lap full of dinosaur models, books, and her new paint set. That was fine with Alice — she needed the back seat to spread out her writing materials, except that Carlisle wasn't cooperating.

"Get down, you!" She tried to push him off the seat, but his front legs went poker-stiff, and he made himself twice as heavy.

"Just speak to him in a reasonable voice," said Suzanne over her shoulder. "He doesn't like to be scolded."

"He's stone deaf, he'll never even hear a reasonable voice. But I'm not going to ride a hundred and fifty miles with him lying on my notes." She tried pushing him from behind, which made his nose go down and his tail hike up, but he didn't budge off the seat. "I'm gonna throttle you!" she said to the dog. He looked at her lovingly and bent around to chew at the root of his silky tail.

"Mother, tell your dog to move," she complained.

Margaret reached her hand down between the front bucket seats and held her palm open near the floorboard.

"Here, Carlisle," she said. Immediately the dog slid off the seat and settled himself across Alice's feet, his feathered tail thumping.

"How'd you do that?" Alice couldn't see the dog's face, but he seemed to be chewing.

"I gave him a pickle."

"The dog's eating a pickle on my foot?"

"Yeah, a kosher dill."

"He likes those best," Suzanne added.

Alice tried to pull her feet out from under him but there wasn't enough room to maneuver.

"Explains why he's a sour puss," said Margaret.

Alice whapped her across the top of her head with the rolled front page of the *Harbor Herald*. "I can't take adolescent humor this early in the morning, thank you."

Margaret slunk down in the seat with her Rubik's cube, a gift from Hal, while Alice tried to adjust her feet under the warm dog belly.

"Don't slobber," she ordered him.

If this was an indication of how the trip was going to go, she didn't have much hope of getting any real work done during the drive. She had hoped for three hours of writing time, but at this rate it would be a struggle. She was still fighting off a cold, and this wasn't making her feel any better.

Nauseating noises emerged from Carlisle's front end as he smacked his lips and licked her ankles, then heaved a monumental sigh and stretched out across the floorboard. She eased her feet out from under his chest and pulled them up beneath her on the seat, Indian-fashion. She thought about Otter sitting in his lean-to. She decided he probably sat with his knees drawn up under his chin so he could stare at the ground for long periods of time. She wasn't sure why he did that, maybe he was thinking ... or dreaming. She opened her legal pad, her pen hovering. What would he dream about?

Chapter Six – Picture Magic

Otter stood at the edge of the clearing and watched the church with wary eyes. Little Stick and her mother had been inside long enough for the shadows cast by the sun to double in length. He wished they would come out. The waiting itself wasn't hard, he was patient and knew how to make time go still, but he couldn't quiet the inner voice that worried.

Suddenly the witch emerged, her daughter behind her. He thought the woman's face looked sad, that perhaps she had shed tears. If the black shaman had made her weep for some reason, then the need to follow his plan through, no matter how distasteful, was stronger than ever. He stepped out of the trees and into the witch's path.

"Joe!" she said, looking up. "You gave me a fright."

Otter spread his palms out in a gesture of well-meaning innocence and Little Stick smiled at him.

"It's all right," said her mother, touching her fingers to her eyes. "I know you didn't mean any harm." He continued to stand before her, looking from her face to the church and back again.

"Did you want something?" she asked.

"No," he said and shook his head. "Not here. There," he said, pointing to the church.

"What would you want in there?" asked Yula. "You don't have no business with Pastor Harrow. Just go on home now."

"Work," said Otter.

"Don't be foolish," said Yula. "There ain't any work you can do for them."

Otter looked closely at her face and touched the corners of his eyes. "Why?"

"Mama started crying because they told her she couldn't work her roots no more," said Little Stick. "They said it was evil."

"Hush, don't talk about things you don't understand." The witch put her hand over her daughter's mouth.

"I ... work there," said Otter, pointing again. "Watch. Listen."

Yula looked at him, trying to understand. "Listen? I don't hear a thing."

"No, Mama, he means he'll spy for us ... don't you, Joe?" Otter smiled.

"Well, girl, you understand him better than me," her mother replied. "I just hope he won't get himself in trouble. The Deacon and that Pudloe Brown are bad business."

"No trouble," said Otter and stepped around them, heading for the church.

"Be careful," said Little Stick as he walked away from them.

Otter waved to her, proud of her concern and his bravery. He wasn't afraid of the shaman's clan; his mother protected him. His spirit brothers protected him. He would be all right.

He went around to the front entrance of the building and climbed the wooden steps to the door. The spirit house smelled good, of pine and smoke like a proper lodge – he could work in here. He stood in the open doorway and waited for the shaman or one of his warriors to come. If they were truly men of the spirit world, they would know he was there, they had only to feel his presence because he had said a prayer to the Great Spirit upon entering the doorway. He waited.

Yes, here came the dark one, the black-eyed shaman. Otter had not seen how the man entered the main room of the church, but suddenly he was there striding down between the rows of benches.

"What do you want?" asked the man, coming into the light from the open door.

"Work."

"This church does not pay anyone to labor for it, we do so of our free will, not for money."

"For food. For ... keep warm," answered Otter. The shaman looked thoughtful.

"What can you do? Work how?"

Otter made a chopping motion with his hands and said, "Cut wood." He swept with an imaginary broom. "Make dirt go away."

The shaman was nodding. "What else?"

Otter looked around, casting for some other bit of meat to dangle before this wolf's nose. He had to be careful.

"Paint," he said, using a word the witch had taught him.

"Is that so, now? A painter? Of what sort, I wonder. What would the likes of you be painting?" The shaman seemed to be talking more to himself than Otter. "What is your name?"

Otter stood blinking for a moment. He did not think he should give this powerful spirit worker his true name, so he said the strange syllable by which Little Stick and her mother called him. "Jo."

The black shaman nodded again. "What do you paint, Joseph?"

"Earth," His fingers balled into a fist. "Sky," he said, sweeping his other hand in an arc over the fist.

Understanding dawned in the dark eyes of the shaman. "You mean pictures."

Otter was trembling slightly and wished to take a step backward, away from the light he saw flickering in the black orbs. But he stood his ground. The shaman looked at Otter some more and ran his tongue over what looked like shark's teeth. They were whiter than those of Little Stick.

"All right, Joseph. You may work for the First Church of the Heavenly Powers, and in return you shall be fed and given a place to sleep. But you must touch nothing unless I bid you do it, and you must do exactly what I ask without questions. Do you understand?"

Otter did not follow much of the man's speech, but he heard the word *understand*, and nodded.

"Good. I shall inform my assistants, Deacon Lathe and Warden Brown, whom you must also obey in my stead. Do you understand?"

Otter nodded again. He trusted the ambitious young brave and the gray-haired elder even less than this one; he would need to be patient and turn his thoughts inward while his eyes and ears turned outward. It would be no small trick.

"I have a task you can do for me now," said the black shaman, turning away and walking down one side of the room to a small area set off by a tall wooden screen. Behind the screen was what seemed to be a long piece of white deerskin, except that it was too stiff and rough. All across it were shapes and designs painted in black and red. Some of the four-leggeds he recognized, but others were completely unknown to him. Otter suspected they were magical emblems, totems of power belonging to the black shaman's tribe.

"Do you know how to mix colors? Red, black, white, yellow? These I need." The man pointed to the paint pots and mimed the movements of mortar and pestle.

Otter nodded. They were all tints supplied by Earth Mother, red from clay, black from burned sticks, white from the soft rocks along the river's edge, yellow from plants boiled until the water was almost gone.

"Then here is your first task. Mix me pots of those four colors and bring them here. But take care not to spill any on the canvas. Understand me?"

Otter was puzzled – what was canvas? The shaman pointed to the deerskin and he understood. It *was* magic, or at least it was a design for spell casting – that much he kenned. He appreciated the shaman's concern for care; there must be no room for mistakes or clumsiness where invocations were concerned.

"No trouble," he said and nodded.

"That is well. Have the paints mixed by tomorrow, and I will show you what to do with them. Come to the supply house this evening, the square building behind this one." The shaman pointed toward the back of the building. "You will find food there."

Otter turned to go. He felt the shaman's black eyes on him, trying to read his heart and his thoughts. But those were cloaked like night and not readable by anyone except his mother.

Springing down the steps, Otter squinted into the afternoon sunlight. There was still plenty of time to gather the materials he need for mixing pigments. He walked away from the church toward the woods feeling highly satisfied with himself. He had been clever like his spirit totem, his brother otter … he wondered what his mother would have to say.

"So don't answer me. I'm only your mother." Suzanne's voice finally made contact.

"What? I'm sorry, I didn't hear you."

"Well, I don't now why not. I called you twice."

"Carlisle's snoring is too loud," she answered and poked him with her toe. There was no response.

"Carlisle!" shouted Margaret. The dog heaved to his feet, cascading neatly stacked papers and clippings off the seat onto his head.

"That does it," said Alice, reaching underneath him for the pages. "As soon as we stop somewhere, he's going up front."

"That's what I was trying to tell you," said Suzanne, craning to look over her shoulder. "Food's just up ahead. Where do you want to stop – McDonald's, Burger King, or Hardee's?"

"Ugh." She couldn't get a decent fruit salad in any of those places. "It doesn't matter."

"Hardee's," said Margaret. "We can get whole pickles there."

Alice frowned. "He eats them in your lap this time."

"Great. I want him anyway."

Pulling into the Hardee's parking lot, they locked the dog in the car and went inside. Finishing their food in a few hasty gulps, they were back on the road within twenty minutes. Margaret pushed her seat back as far as it would go and stuffed the Afghan hound on the floorboard between her legs where she could hand feed him bits of fries with pickle. Alice slouched down in the back seat so she wouldn't have to watch. She'd offered to drive out of courtesy, but knew her mother wouldn't take her up on it. Suzanne loved to drive, and once she was settled into the cockpit of her car, she would willingly cruise for hours. Besides which, she never let anyone else drive her car.

Alice read over what she'd written and liked it okay. There was a surprising dignity to the Old Joe character she hadn't planned on, and it worked well in contrast to the other characters. It had taken two chapters to successfully introduce him into the story, but now she felt that his presence was both organic and necessary to the plot from here on. In fact, satisfactory character sketches now existed for all the people living in her nineteenth-century church community.

Now that Alice had sifted through all the letters of parishioners and news stories about the church, as well as the odd little notebook which she found especially disturbing, a picture had emerged of Cadjer Harrow as a fierce fire and brimstone preacher that no one dared contradict. Several passing comments alluded to the fact that he was constantly accompanied by a vicious black dog big enough to look school-age children in the eyes. The dog had become his inseparable companion shortly after the founding of the church, and Alice realized with a shiver that she had almost seen it straining at the leash in her first visualization of him. Settling back into book mode, she consulted her outline to see what came next and if there was anything else that needed taking care of before she moved on in the story.

Actually, there was, and now that she thought about it, she'd been avoiding dealing with it. Harrow's notebook, a small bound book with thick unlined pages between flexible leather covers, lay unopened on the seat beside her. In curator's terms, it was an octavo, about six by nine inches, with flexible calfskin covers. She knew that in the early nineteenth century, limp leather covers were commonly used for books intended to be carried on one's person in a pocket or satchel.

The pages had not been trimmed flush, producing deckle edges, a rough, uneven effect. Many of the pages showed a condition known as "foxing," where reddish-brown spots freckled the surface, especially near the edges, indicating storage that encouraged the growth of microorganisms. Maybe he'd used it in the rain and then stowed it in the pocket of his coat. About thirty pages in the front contained typical church information and notes, and many of the pages in the middle were blank, but it was the dozen or so near the back where she'd discovered something entirely different. She'd thought about it a lot, but hadn't come to grips with what it implied about Harrow and his church. Maybe now was the time.

Chapter Seven – Initiation

Monday morning, January 1, 1900: Rain poured in torrents, turning the bare area in front of the Heavenly Powers church to mud. Members of the congregation splashed their way to the entrance and stacked their umbrellas just inside the door. It was Initiation Sunday and the church was packed full; nearly every bench seat was occupied.

Initiation Day took place at the beginning of each new year, and this, the fourth and best attended, would see fifteen men and women taken into the Body. This was the name Harrow had given to his inner circle in the year of the church's founding. He made no distinction of sex or age among the people he chose, and his criteria for selection were not revealed. It was said he could look into their souls and see what he was looking for.

Membership in the Body was coveted by all because its initiates were powerful, not only within the church but in their daily business as well. Jeral Maunder, recently named sexton, which placed him next to the Deacon and the Warden among the Hands (as Harrow's closest assistants were called), had parlayed his feed store into a commercial enterprise of significant volume, dealing in farm equipment, foodstuffs, building materials, and the finest saddles and riding tack available in the county.

Maunder stood now by the church entrance, watching the congregation dash in from the rain and take their seats. He searched the crowd of faces and scowled because Yula Rider and her daughter Belinda were not present. Two days before, she had turned down his offer of marriage but he would try again, partly because he was as interested in the daughter as he was the mother.

The choir marched up the platform steps and into their new stalls made of oak that had been oiled and rubbed to a dull gleam. There was a new German-made pump organ as well, which had been brought by rail all the way from the port in Savannah. It was well known that Preacher Harrow was a wealthy man and could afford the best when he wanted it. Where the wealth came from was a subject of constant debate and gossip, but it was clear he'd brought it with him into the county. One rancher even claimed to have been paid with a gold nugget, which was likely worth far more than the ill-tempered stallion he'd sold for it. Taking one last dissatisfied look around, Jeral Maunder hurried to join the Body members assembled along the back two benches. As bell ringer, he would stay by the door until the real ceremony began. The candidates for initiation sat silently in a row along the back wall, their faces hidden in hooded robes of rough dark cloth.

Harrow ascended the pulpit, which was also newly made of gleaming oak. He wore the black and red robe of the Hand, as did Deacon Lathe and Pudloe Brown, who stood beside him like sentries. A single voice from the choir began the familiar hymn, "Promised land, heavenly home," in a clear strong soprano, with the organist and the rest of the choir joining in after the first verse. When they reached the chorus, the congregation was directed to sing, and a hundred and thirty voices sang out the words, "show me the way, make plain the path, take me home on the lonely day of wrath."

The song died away and everyone sat down. Reverend Harrow motioned for the candidate initiates to come forward. At once the fifteen chosen ones left their benches, coming down the long central aisle to stand in front of the platform.

"God has blessed us," he said to the congregation in his hard, rasping voice to which all had become accustomed. "Each year finds us stronger as our numbers grow. This year is momentous, as we move from an old century into a new one. This year fifteen of the chosen best stand before you, the most ever selected for initiation into the Body of the church. They have been tested and found to be worthy additions to God's host upon earth."

Scattered cries of "Amen" punctuated his sentences.

He gripped the lectern and continued. "It is my fervent hope that one day all of you here will become part of the Body. Then we shall indeed be a power to reckon with – none shall oppose us."

Harrow paused and let his words sink in. What he did not say was that eventually those who did not make it into the Body would be driven out or otherwise eliminated. It took one hundred percent cooperation and belief to make the power flow, and he intended that it should do so at his command. It resisted control, but he was strong and completely unafraid, and he had allies.

"Let the Sisters of the Blood sing the invocation," Deacon Lathe commanded.

The choir stood and began to chant the single word "Come" on one long sustained breath that hovered on the chosen note for several minutes. At random, singers slipped out of the chant to snatch a breath and eased back in. The chant had taken them many hours of practice, and Harrow would not be satisfied until he heard the note held with unwavering intensity. Forming a ring in front of the pulpit, the candidates joined hands and lifted them toward the high ceiling. The note hung suspended in the rafters as the singers continued the invocation, the congregation sitting as if carved from granite. The timbers of the church resonated with the frequency of the one note, their very molecules and atoms attending to its siren call. All eyes were straining to see into the circle of uplifted arms.

Dimly at first and gradually becoming more discernible, a yellow haze began to pulse within the circle. Then it became pale lemon and finally dazzling white so that worshippers were forced to turn their gaze aside. The hairs along their arms tingled and those seated closest to the circle felt their ears ringing with a sound beyond or above that created by the choir.

Harrow stepped into the center of the circle, engulfed in the white-hot star held in suspension by the chant. Only his outline could be seen, if any dared to look. The fifteen chosen ones stared into the ball of fire with temporarily sightless eyes. When the blindness faded later, as all knew, the initiation would be complete. For some it lasted just a few hours while others took longer. Jeral Maunder, it was rumored, had been blind for a week, such was the concentration of his exposure. It was also believed to be the reason for his growing personal power. Some thought he might become an eventual challenge to Lathe or Brown, or even the Reverend himself, although most would have denied even thinking such thoughts.

His relentless courtship of the local voodoo mistress was another thing no one dared speak about. Her position was both enviable and perilous, and her friends feared to speculate which it would turn out to be.

Some of the initiates cried out as pain beyond imagining stabbed through their sightless sockets into their brains. Harrow struggled to hold the inferno, to bend it to his will. Lines of electricity snaked outward from it, touching the circle of fifteen. This was the moment of peril, for those not completely worthy would be burned to a cinder on the spot. After heart-stopping moments, the star began to dim. Finally the light was gone and Harrow staggered back to the pulpit. Hands still joined, the now-blind initiates were guided by Lathe and Brown up onto the platform where they knelt in a single line, new members of the Body, with their backs to the congregation.

"Let there be light!" shouted Harrow.

"Amen!" responded the hundred and thirty voices.

"Thy will be done," he said and motioned to Maunder, who hauled on a long rope that rang the new bell up in the tower. The singers closed their songbooks, filed out of their pews, and left the church by the back door. Thunder crashed overhead as rain pounded the tin roof, and the choir members ran for cover to the newly expanded out-building to hang up their robes and dry their faces.

The congregation stood to receive Harrow's parting benediction.

"Once again you have witnessed another miracle of the Lord's presence among you. This year, all the chosen ones have been accepted. Know that you are privileged to belong to the First Church of the Heavenly Powers and that no one -not the rich farmers whose fields you plow, or puny scheming politicians who wield merely an illusion of power, not the workers of false magic, and especially not the members of the fancy churches with colored glass in their windows who would try to seduce you away from this path of power – not one of them will do for you as I can." Harrow wiped his brow and added, "Through the power of the Lord. Amen."

Murmured voices responded in kind and the service was over. Umbrellas were reclaimed and once again church members ran through the rain to their wagons and horses for the wet ride homeward. Only the initiates remained where they were, as they had been instructed, knowing the true conclusion to the ceremony would not come until everyone else was gone. They knelt unmoving, cowls hiding their faces.

"We'll begin now," said Harrow to Deacon Lathe, who nodded and lit two tall red tapers, handing one to Brown and keeping the other. He took up his position at the front of the row, as Brown went to the other end. Lathe nodded, his signal that all was in readiness. The light from the candle threw his ebony face into strong relief, the jagged scar down his cheek prominent.

Out of the shadows, a darker shadow coalesced into a form that settled into the shape of a monstrous canine, red-eyed and prick-eared with a scrofulous hide that seemed more reptilian than mammalian. It took up a position just behind Harrow, and had any of the initiates been able to watch, they would have observed that Lathe was careful to keep his distance from the beast.

Harrow walked to the head of the row and stopped in front of the first of the kneeling figures. He threw back the cowl and lifted the face of a young woman of uncommon beauty, with small features and skin the color of pale cream. He felt his manhood stirring, and put his cold hand on her shoulder. Harrow knelt in front of her, parted her robe, and reached to lift her skirts. Her sightless eyes went wide with fear, but she made no sound.

"What is your name?" he croaked, a black carrion crow leaning over a dove. He drank in her beauty with his black eyes.

"Elise," she whispered.

"We shall make a child, Elise," he said in his rasping voice. "I would have my blood carried on, now that my work here is well in hand. If you are a virgin, so much the better." He could tell from the look on her face that it was so.

"If you bear me a son, Elise, your family will prosper and you will lack for nothing. If you fail, I shall have to try another, but I do not think you will fail me."

Brown and Lathe watched, rapt, as he took her with brutal efficiency. They knew they were not allowed to touch the chosen ones – that was Harrow's prerogative, but they also knew there was no taboo on anyone else.

Sated, Harrow stood up and rearranged his clothing. Elise got to her knees and pulled her robe about her slim body with trembling hands, but uttered no sound. Then he took the young woman's face in his hands and turned her left cheek up to the light of Deacon Lathe's candle. Her eyes were tightly shut, and her mouth clamped into a grimace that marred her delicate face. His monstrous slavering dog at his heels, Harrow stood over the woman and drew out a slim sharp blade.

Alice screamed as the knife traced a serpentine line of fire down the woman's face, incising the coils of a serpent into the flesh. Experiencing the woman's white-hot pain as if it were her own, she frantically struggled to pull herself out of the vision.

Suzanne jerked the wheel and aimed the car onto the shoulder of the highway.

"Mom, what's wrong?" Margaret's frightened face popped up over the seat, the dog floundering around under her feet.

"Alice ... what on earth?"

She heard their voices and knew the car had stopped, but she couldn't get free. Someone had her by the shoulder, shaking her loose from the nightmare, and then mercifully it was gone. She sat up and put her hand to her face, expecting to touch blood, but there was nothing. Carlisle whined and licked at the knees of her jeans, his long pointy snout poked between the front seats.

"My God, Alice, you scared hell out of me. What happened back there?" Her mother's face wore an expression that could best be described as genuine fright tempered with utter annoyance. For Suzanne, one simply didn't create scenes. It was unseemly, even in the privacy of one's car where there were no outsiders to observe the embarrassing behavior.

"I guess I fell asleep ... I think I was dreaming." Her hands were shaking as she tried to gather up her scattered notes and papers. "I'm all right now."

"Mom, can I ride back there with you?" Margaret asked, chewing her lip in a way that looked very familiar to Alice.

"Yes, Munch, you certainly may." She packed all her materials into her briefcase. Margaret scrabbled between the bucket seats and settled onto the back seat beside her. Comforted by the warmth of her daughter's body, Alice took a deep breath. It had been no dream – that pain was too real. Even now her cheek throbbed with an ache that went all the way down her neck, and her vision was blurred with tears.

"Just a minute," she said, reaching for her purse. She pulled out a small mirror and examined the left side of her face. There was absolutely nothing out of the ordinary, yet the sensations lingered.

"What're you looking for, Mom?"

"Nothing." She put the mirror away. Alice leaned back against the seat, her mind in denial.

177

Suzanne cranked the car. "Is everything under control back there? Carlisle, down!" Obediently, he curled up on the floorboard with a moist yawn, his head in the seat where Margaret's butt had been. She guided the car back onto the highway.

"How far are we from home?" Alice asked.

"About thirty-five minutes."

"Okay." Alice leaned against Margaret; she'd had enough of this car trip. Two more chapters had been drafted, but her empathy with the characters was clearly out of hand. She was fully committed to the story now, and looked forward to its unfolding with a voyeuristic anticipation, but it also now haunted her thoughts. She wondered what would happen when she tried to type the scene she'd just written into the computer ... would she experience the sensation again? Maybe she could get someone else to type it for her – someone who wasn't emotionally attached to the material the way she had become. Which made her think of Nik. Suddenly she ached to be home. She'd stayed away too long.

CHAPTER 19

FIREWORKS ROSE and exploded in showers of sparkling pink and green over the lake, their reflected evanescence bright on the glassy surface. More shot up in a volley – shells exploding in flowery star bursts, Girandole clusters spinning into the air like flying saucers, and ear-shocking bangs giving the impression of a battle in the clouds. Another year had been banished and the new one duly welcomed. Eve and Dan Lee's annual New Year's Eve festivities got off to a roaring start each year with the Neighborhood Association's fireworks display. With the night clear and cold, this one was particularly spectacular.

"Happy New Year!" shouted Dan Lee over the television Times Square broadcast and distant pops and bangs outside from rockets and Roman candles. He popped the cork on a bottle of expensive champagne and began filling glasses.

Alice and Nik arrived just after the countdown and were now squeezing their way into the foyer. Alice loathed New Year's Eve parties and found them depressing, but for tradition's sake and because the Lee family had made the trek out to her little Thanksgiving Day fest, she felt obligated to attend. She hung her coat on a peg in the entryway and scanned the crowd. Some of the faces she knew, most she didn't: lobbyists, politicians, local celebrities, university bigwigs, and a few nobodies like herself.

"Are you going to be okay?" Nik felt her forehead, and she gave him a grim smile. She was feeling a little weird, slightly fevered and achy, plus a general fuzziness from the flu medication she'd taken just before they left home. "Maybe you should have stayed in bed."

"No, I'm glad I came now that we're here. We won't stay long."

"Suits me," he said. This was definitely not his territory, and he was there only because of his concern for Alice. It was another test of his loyalty, which so far he'd passed with uncomplaining good humor. In her fevered paranoid state, she wondered what it would take to drive him away, and then immediately hoped if there was such a thing that she wouldn't find it.

She led the way through the press of bodies in search of Eve and found her in the kitchen, which was filled to capacity with more bodies, most of them female in figure-slimming varieties of the basic black dress. Alice felt hopelessly frumpish in her blue velvet. It was supposed to be a good color for her, but here it looked overstated. At least it was warm.

"Alice!" Eve waved around the refrigerator door where she was trying to refill an ice bucket and hold her wine glass at the same time. She was dangerously close to spilling them over the floor and her designer frock but miraculously managed to do neither. "How's your cold?"

"Hanging in there," said Alice. "Don't let me breathe on you."

Several guests closest to her gave her a second look and sidled away. Fatigue settling in, she started looking around for a place to sit. Not a chance. All the chairs were taken, and some guests even sat on the carpeted stairs leading to the second floor.

"Talk to you later," she said and maneuvered her way out to the living room, Nik following.

More people. Their faces bobbed in front of her, mouths moving, eyes blinking, undifferentiated babble surrounding them; she was in a rehearsal for a Fellini movie. She pressed the back of her hand to her cheek and felt heat. Might have to leave sooner than planned. Out in the so-called "great room," purple and red balloons were everywhere, having been released at the stroke of midnight from a canopy of netting strung across the ceiling. Across the room she spotted Shelton MacBeth, half a head taller than his circle of admirers. She thought about joining him – at least he was someone Nik knew – but she just didn't have the energy.

"Hey, Alice! Where's your hat?" Dan touched her shoulder.

"I don't—"

"Not to worry, I'll get you one." Alice swore silently. There was no way she was going to wear any stupid paper party hat.

She looked for a way to disappear before Dan could find her again. Wandering back out to the dining room, she found an astonishing variety of finger foods crowded onto a banquet table. Too sick to eat anything, she turned her back on the table and stared through tall windows out at the brightly lit terrace and the lake beyond.

"Do you want anything, like a soda or something?" The fact that Nik was willing to brave the kitchen by himself for her sake made Alice think she might survive the night after all.

"A ginger ale would be good, I'm really thirsty." She leaned against the window frame and saw there were some unoccupied chairs on the terrace.

Nik gave her hand a squeeze. "I'll be right back."

Alice waited, listening to the cacophony swirling around her head. Someone thrust a champagne glass into her hand and wished her something or other. She gulped it like water and felt it bubble through her sinuses. That was interesting. She gulped some more and headed for the back door.

Out on the terrace the crowd was thinner. A contingent of smokers had convened near one end, so she found a seat away from them and was about to plop, groggy, down on a cushioned pool chair when a figure emerging from the shadows shocked her wide awake.

It couldn't be. She stood rock-still beside the pool and watched him walk across the yard, around the pool, and up the patio steps. He placed an empty champagne glass on the terrace refreshment table, and clamped a cigar between his teeth, feeling around in the pockets of his black coat for a light. He extracted a long match, struck it precisely on the sole of his black riding boot and turned his back to the house with its people and lights. For heart-stopping moments they regarded each other, and her head began to vibrate with that high hum she hadn't heard in days. Even from that distance she could feel his eyes on her, see the stiff shock of dark hair, the cruel mouth. She told herself it couldn't be; characters from novels didn't materialize in the real world and follow you around. But who in the world could look like that? Surely not anyone Eve or Dan knew. She began to shiver, not just from the cold.

She opened her mouth to speak to him and deny the evidence of her eyes, but no words came out. At that moment, two women accosted him and drew him away. They laughed heartily at something he said, and all three went inside. Her first impulse was to run to the car, lock herself in, and get out of there. The urge lasted just seconds, to be replaced by a determined fury. It was time to confront the man, if man he were – she'd had enough. She downed the rest of her champagne.

"'Scuse me," she said, elbowing her way through the crowd. He wasn't in the dining room or the great room, where most of the party had congregated. She saw Nik and motioned to him frantically as she spotted the two women disappearing into the game room. Harrow wasn't with them, but then she saw him bent over the pool table, lining up his next shot. Although her courage was draining away, she approached the black-suited figure. At that moment, shouts and several muted screams punctuated the background party noise so that Alice turned toward the doorway. Voices were issuing orders, but in such confusion she couldn't tell what was happening. A look back at the pool table revealed the startled face of the player in black, who wasn't Harrow, not even close. The man looked at her curiously, then toward the door where the sounds of confusion grew louder.

"Sorry, I thought ... you were someone else," she stammered. Alice fled the pool room, her cheeks flaming. Her head was pounding, eyeballs aching with every pulse, and she knew she wasn't going to make it back out to the dining room to find Nik. Leaning against the wall in the hallway, she closed her eyes and thought it would be easier just to faint on the spot.

She felt herself slipping, drowsily ignoring the sounds of disturbance coming from the direction of the balloon room. Nik's face swam in front of her and hands caught her just as she decided to let gravity do its thing. His grip on her waist brought her awake. "I knew you should have stayed home," he said, scolding.

"Do I smell smoke?"

He nodded. "Somehow some candles got turned over and set a stack of paper hats on fire. Your friend Dan doused it with champagne, then smothered it with couch cushions. Nobody was hurt."

She leaned into him and shut her eyes. "Let's go. I'm losing it."

With his arm around her, Nik guided them back to the foyer and retrieved their coats. The proper thing to do would be to find Eve and give her regrets for leaving so early, but she couldn't do it. Her head hurt so bad, so bad. Maybe she imagined seeing the preacher's doppelganger. There was no telling what a combination of fever, drugs, and alcohol could make you see. But that wasn't much comfort – it still meant her imagination was out of control.

Alice folded her arms over her chest to control her shaking. Too bad about the fire. She was glad no one had been injured, but there was no denying the fact that the new year had gotten off to a grim start.

JANUARY

CHAPTER 20

ON THE second day of January it snowed. After two months of moderate winter, a blast of icy air forecasters dubbed the Alberta Clipper sailed down from Canada across the Midwest, heading south. The first serious freeze of the season, it wasn't as bad as a Siberian cold front, meteorologists said, but almost.

Alice, Nik, and Margaret were having a late breakfast in the cozy dining room of the Pelican's Roost café. A favorite eating spot for locals on or near the coast, the Roost was a fifteen-minute drive from Alice's house and was a Sunday morning habit she'd acquired when the family had first moved to the area.

An ordinary cinder-block building with a wide wooden deck appended to the beach side, the Roost hosted country-conch bands like the Dipsticks every weekend, but its best-kept secret was a plate-sized concoction called the Panhandle Omelet, which came with everything in it and a bottle of Tabasco sauce on the side. In summer, the narrow beach and the café were crowded with pink-fleshed tourists and romping dogs, but in the off-season, like now, it was blessedly quiet and the service was better. With its oversized plain wooden booths and non-matching cutlery, Nik immediately embraced it as his kind of place.

Alice sipped coffee laced with some of Margaret's hot chocolate and stared out the wide plate-glass window at the empty shoreline. She had slept most of New Year's Day, and this morning felt worlds better. She owed Eve and Dan a call explaining her hasty exit from their party, but that could wait.

"There's a cold front moving in by tomorrow, according to this," Nik said, flattening the weather page of the newspaper so they could see.

"I think it's coming in early," said Alice, watching the palms along the beach whipping in the wind. She put her hand to the window; the glass felt

cold. Earlier that morning it had rained, and now leaden stratus forma-
tions blanketed the horizon and changed the gulf to the color of dark
dishwater. Waves were froth-tipped and rolling in with increasing intensity, clawing at the deserted beach. Nik continued to read from the paper.

"It says here that the wind chill factor in North Dakota last night was
minus eighty-six degrees. Here in the South we can expect a rapid drop into
the twenties, maybe into the low teens, by late tonight."

"Will it snow?" Margaret asked.

Nik looked out the window at the massing cloudbank. "If the temperature keeps dropping and it starts to rain, it might."

"Wow! Snow!"

"I think the last time we had snow here was before you were born," said
Alice. "It probably won't stick very long, but it would be fun to see, at least
for you and me."

Nik laughed. "At least I won't have to shovel it."

"I bet you shoveled a lot of snow in Sweden, huh?" Margaret asked.

"Yes, if I wanted to get out the door."

"Wow, I wanna see snow like that," said Margaret. "Let's go to Sweden
next Christmas."

Alice glanced at Nik. Margaret was already assuming they would still
be a trio a year from now. That was good, because she was beginning to
think along those lines herself.

"Save your pennies," Nik said. His tone was noncommittal.

Alice looked at the clouds again. "Well, this is going to be a good day
to hole up with a fire going and a book to write."

"Maybe we should head home then. It's getting darker." Nik stood up
and brushed crumbs off his lap.

Alice made a mental note of the fact that he'd said "home" rather than
"to the house." They were starting to act as a family unit, and she was both
freaked and pleased by the idea.

"Wish I could stay home tomorrow," she said aloud.

"Me too," said Margaret.

"So do I," said Nik. They shared a good laugh and got out of the booth.

"Shelton e-mailed me that the *Marquesa* stuff is due up from south
Florida this coming week, so we'll be busy," Alice said, grabbing the bill and
heading for the cashier.

The others followed, and Margaret leaned on the counter. "Can I have
some gum?"

"I guess." Alice paid the bill, and bought two chocolate bars in addition to the gum. She followed Margaret out the door and joined Nik, who had gone out to look at the sky. A fine misty rain moistened their faces. The gulf was becoming more turbulent as waves thrashed in all directions, throwing spray high in the air. Wind whipping her hair into a bird's nest of tangles, Alice ran for the car, the others close behind her, an icy gust at their backs.

On the drive home, winds out of the northeast pushed the car relentlessly toward the wrong lane. Alice gripped the wheel, forcing a straight path through torrents of rain that momentarily blinded her view of the road. Silently, she commanded the car to dig its tires in and get them home safely.

"We're going to need to cover the pipes that are exposed," Nik said, "if we don't want to be without water when the freeze line hits."

"I think there's a roll of ceiling insulation in the storeroom. If it's too grungy, I guess we could use blankets or something."

"Is that snow?" Margaret's face was pressed to the window.

"Sleet," said Nik, "but if this keeps up it won't be far behind."

Turning into their driveway, Alice careened around the curves, leaves and twigs falling across the windshield with each gust, and wheeled into the open turnaround a bit too fast perhaps. Dawg scrambled out of the way, wagging and jumping at the return of his adopted family. Alice had to admit that he was now as much a part of the household as Nik.

"I love the way Dawg always seems so happy to see us," she said.

"Me, too," said Margaret. "He even likes Figaro!"

"And he'll defend you with his life," said Nik.

Alice gave him a look. "Jeez, I hope it never comes to that."

It was turning colder by the minute with icy blasts out of the north that cut through her flannel windbreaker and sent shivers up her back as she scampered up the stairs. She could hear Nik coaxing Dawg into the downstairs laundry room for shelter. Hunched over the doorknob, Alice worked to insert the key with shaking fingers.

"Hurry, Mom, I'm freezing!" Margaret huddled against her and sneezed wetly.

"Got it." They darted through, and she slammed the door shut against the push of the wind.

Inside, she turned up the gas heat and checked the wood supply. Just a few small pieces remained stacked in the hopper. Lacking central heat, they were going to need the fireplace to get the living room warmed up. She opened the door to call down to Nik, but saw him walking out to the margin of trees carrying Whit's old chainsaw. Another blast of cold blew the door wide open. Alice pushed it shut, thinking she knew exactly what chilled to the bone meant. The saw thragged to life for a couple of earsplitting seconds and then died. In a moment, she heard footsteps coming back up the stairs.

"*Skit också!*" Nik muttered under his breath as he came in.

"Pardon?"

"The saw has no gas," he said. " I'll have to go buy some, and two-cycle oil as well."

"I'll give you some cash."

He shook his head. "I've got enough."

"Do you have a gas can?"

"*Ja,* in the truck."

He disappeared back out the door before she could protest. Nik tended to lapse into Swedish when he was frustrated or angry, and she couldn't blame him for being put out about having to drive into town just to get the saw working. Her offer to pay probably hadn't helped; she'd already paid for breakfast.

They tiptoed around the issue of money, not wanting it to become a wedge between them. As a doctoral student, Nik lived on a graduate teaching assistantship, which he supplemented with freelance illustration work, but it was far below what she brought in. It didn't bother her to pay for everything, but maybe he didn't like being a kept man. Alice smiled – she liked the racy sensation of that notion.

She hovered over the hallway heater, nudging Figaro out of the way with her toe. "Heater hog," she said, pushing his tail plume away from the grate.

Margaret pushed herself in next to Alice. "I don't feel too good," she said. Alice felt her forehead.

"You're a little warm ... when did that start up?"

"This morning, but it wasn't bad until just now."

"I guess I gave you my plague. Sorry. Why don't you go back to bed?"

"I'll just lie down on the couch," she said, scooping up Figaro. He squeaked in protest, but Margaret held him in both arms. "I need a cat."

She went to the couch and curled up on her side, hugging Figaro to her chest.

Alice retrieved a blanket from her bed and tucked it in around her. "Okay now?"

Margaret nodded, bleary eyed, and sneezed again. Alice put the Kleenex box beside her and frowned. She was just getting well from whatever she'd picked at her mother's house, and now Margaret was sick. She supposed Nik was next.

Shivering, Alice sat down on the floor and rolled up some newspaper logs to make a small blaze in the fireplace that she could probably keep going until Nik got back and cut up some proper logs. She got up and went into the kitchen to put on a pot of water for tea. Nik had told her that hyssop helped relieve the symptoms, especially if you inhaled the steam from the mug. She had tried it, and was surprised to find he was right. If Margaret would drink some, it might work enough to let her fall asleep.

Sitting down in the breakfast nook, she waited for the kettle to whistle and started thinking about her book. In spite of her plan to stay away from it for a while, it was a lure she couldn't keep out of her mind. The urge to work on it was so strong that even when it was put away out of sight, pieces of chapters were writing themselves in her mind. The dark face of Harrow figured prominently in most of them.

That chapter she wrote in the car was awful – not in the words she'd chosen, but in the content. She hadn't intended to write anything like that, but it's what she saw played out in her eyelid movie and it's what got written down. There was no denying that the Rev. Cadjer Harrow was a villain ... more than that ... he was becoming a truly evil creation. If this was really a horror story she was writing, maybe he wasn't completely human, and if that were the case, what was he? She thought back to the chapter where Otter had been employed to mix paints for some project of Harrow's. She could almost see what was on the long canvas Otter had called a deerskin, but not quite. What sort of magic symbols might he use if he were a black shaman, as Otter had called him? There were some designs drawn in the back of that little notebook – geometric shapes, spirals with crosshatchings and parallel lines in waves, and an oblong leaf-shaped design that contained seven dots inside a circle beside a line of three sun devices – but she hadn't known what to make of them. Maybe it was time to take a closer look.

The kettle's whistling pulled her back to the here and now, bringing the kitchen into sharp focus and pushing Harrow's world into the shadowy background where it lurked most of her waking hours. The tea steeping, she checked on Margaret, who appeared to be dozing off. Just the tips of Figaro's ears stuck out from the cover around her face. The house was quiet except for the crackling from the fireplace.

Margaret shivered in the dark. The cave, or whatever this place was, seeped cold into her skin and chilled her blood. It was black as night, like being underground, but feeling around and touching rough rock ledges helped her see with her hands. Ahead somewhere she could hear a wet noise, like slurping.

The ground under her bare feet was firm and felt like damp hard-packed sand. Feeling her way around a bend, she stepped in an icy pool of water, danced out of it, and then stuck her toe back in, determining that it was only a shallow puddle and could be stepped over quickly. Reaching out, Margaret touched damp boulders piled one on another to her left. To her right, there was nothing. The sound of trickling water mingled with the slurping, and she stopped for a moment, just listening. She decided the trickling came from above; maybe there was a waterfall high overhead and out of sight. But the smacking sounds were not far away at all. As her eyes grew more accustomed to the gloom, she thought there might be a faint patch of something luminous on a ledge just a few yards away.

"I'd share with you, but I'm a bit starved, y'know, and this was all I could catch."

Margaret shuddered. She knew that voice.

"Good of you to join me at home, this time." The Quinkan started to cackle, its eyes flickering wickedly in the semi-darkness. Its shape was hidden, a smear on the rocks.

"G'day. All thet desert sand, thet's just not moy turf. Sorry, oy don't have a barbee on the patio, but well, oy make do the best oy can, yes."

It barked another laugh and spat out a finger bone, which landed near Margaret's foot. She yelped and jumped back.

The Quinkan made a nauseating sucking noise and then leapt down from its perch. Margaret stumbled backward over a pile of bones, and squeaked again.

"Ahh, y'see, there's no rubbish bin, so one just has to make do, one does." It had assumed a shape she could see, a dingo about the size of a full-grown buffalo. It came toward her and sat down, blocking the passage.

"What's up, cat got your tongue?" it snarled.

"You're horrible! You're a horrible stinking ... thing, and I know you eat children who don't know what you are. But I know."

"You don't know shit. But I'll grant you this, you're persistent. You might eventually figure things out."

The Quinkan stood up, and cocked its head, looking down at her. "Hey, you want to see something interesting?" it said in a young man's voice

189

that she didn't recognize. "C'mon, I'll show you, and I promise not to eat you on the way."

It turned tail and trotted along the path into the gloom. Margaret followed, repulsed and angry, and unable to resist. A part of her fevered sleeping brain knew this to be a dream state, but it could only watch helplessly as the Quinkan drew her onward into the tunnel.

As they wound their way among piles of rocks and slits through high sandstone walls, the light grew brighter, and suddenly they stepped out onto a narrow margin of rocky shoreline no more than a yard wide. A deep clear pool still as glass filled the narrow canyon open to the sky. It was hot as blazes under the noonday sun, and Margaret shaded her eyes, squinting against the light. Somewhere she could hear the whisper and rush of falling water, but it wasn't on this side of the rock wall because not a ripple disturbed the surface of the pool. The Quinkan darted along the edge of the pool at a run and slipped back into a crevice where the canyon wall was split. Margaret ran after it.

Back in the cool darkness, she was hit by a wave of nausea and horror that dropped her to her knees. She promptly lost her breakfast on the trail.

"Well, that's a nice mess. You wouldn't want to clean that up, would you?" The dingo stood over her, its tail lashing its hindquarters.

"What's here? Why's it got that smell?" Margaret was promptly sick again.

"Secret place nobody knows about. What a baby," the creature sneered in its own whining voice. "I was going to show you something truly important, something your dumb mother-human would love to know, but guess what? I've changed my mind. Out!" It snapped at her with blood-stained fangs.

Margaret scrambled to her feet and fled out of the cut, back to the pool. Heavy paws hit her in the back, and then she was tumbling into the icy waters and down down sooo cold down down freezing sooooo cooooooolddddd....

Suddenly the phone rang. Alice nearly jumped out of her skin and grabbed it on the second ring. Margaret murmured and turned over, her face toward the couch cushions. Figaro disappeared completely under the blanket.

"Alice?" It was Eve Lee.

"Oh. I've been meaning to call you." Guilt settled in. "Sorry we left without saying goodbye—"

"Well, who could blame you? I wanted to apologize for the party – what a mess! That smoke stink was everywhere. No more open candle flames next time!"

"It wasn't that. I would have stayed, it was just this flu that I thought was gone, but wasn't."

"Ah," said Eve, "I was right, then. I told Dan I didn't think you looked well, kind of pale and flushed at the same time, if you can have such a thing."

"You can. I'm much better today, but now Margaret has it."

"Well, listen, if you need anything at all, please let me know. You're still family to me, and I would do anything to help, if you want me to."

Alice was thinking how much she wished there was someone she could talk to plainly about her exhibit problems or her book creepiness, but she didn't think Eve was that person. She would love for Nik to be that person, but he clearly wasn't. That left Margaret, and she was too sick. Still, she could ask obliquely.

"There is one thing ...."

"Yes?"

"There was this guy I saw at the party, black suit, riding boots, wide black hat. Who was he?"

"I have no idea, I'm sure I didn't see anyone who looked like that. Not anybody I know. But I guess he could've come with someone else ... a lot of people bring dates we don't know personally. Why?"

Alice hesitated. "He just reminded me of someone. Turns out it wasn't who I thought after all."

"Sorry I'm not more help. I could ask Dan about him."

"No, don't bother to do that," Alice said. "I have your number. We'll be in touch."

"Great. You and Margaret take care of yourselves."

As she hung up the phone, Alice realized she was more engaged with the church story than what was happening around her; the urge to get back to her fictional world lest she miss some crucial piece of action that was going on while she paid attention to her waking life was overwhelming. She went to the study and turned on the computer. The Initiation chapter was still untyped, but she didn't have the nerve to tackle it yet. When she wrote from Harrow's point of view, it was frightening and created a sense of anxiety in the pit of her stomach. Shifting point of view among the characters was not what she had planned to do originally, but so much of the story seemed to be unfolding that way, it would now be hard to go back to the narrator as mere outside observer.

191

The characters were all so unusual, warped even, that she couldn't stay out of their thoughts, although she'd gone a bit too far in that last episode. That experience in the car was a nagging morsel of dread that she still hadn't come to terms with; it was hard not to keep checking in the mirror to see if there was a mark on her cheek. Although the plot veered off in strange directions, its progression toward the lynching now seemed inevitable. Her sympathy lay with poor Joe, and she was pretty sure now that he had been innocent of any crime, both in her novel and in real life. There were still some questions about him, though, and she wanted to talk to the pastor of the present-day St. Christopher's church if she could ever get him on the phone. So far, he had not been in his office when she called.

At the climax of the story, which was still somewhat under dispute in her mind, she figured Old Joe would be found not guilty after his execution. She speculated that out of remorse for the poor soul, Reverend Harrow might regret his part in the lynching and end his own life. His obituary and tombstone epitaph weren't specific about his cause of death, so she could invent anything that would further the plot and give it a fitting end.

She sat down on the floor beside the computer desk and spread out all the material from the library folder, arranging it in appropriate piles such as letters, newspaper clippings, church documents, real estate papers, and the small book of notes in Harrow's own hand. This latter was the most revealing of all, and she wondered how it had come to be preserved all these years. Entries toward the front of the book were accounting statistics having to do with the church, and some were personal notes about things to do and take care of. Some things further toward the back of the book, especially the sign and symbols, reeked of black magic, and some of it just sounded like the ravings of a nut case with delusions of grandeur. But of one thing she had no doubt: the Rev. Harrow was not a happy soul.

From a curator's standpoint, some of the folder items had actual historical value just because of their age. She'd been meaning to contact Sandra at the library and find out who put the file together, and why very old and modern things were jumbled in together. Maybe this week she could follow up both with Sandra and the current church pastor and ask some of those thousand questions she'd been storing up since delving into this whole mystery. Her mental list of people to get in touch with was growing, not to mention the salvage people connected with the *Marquesa*, which she'd almost entirely forgotten about. And there were the daily requests for tours through the *Land of Legends* exhibit, and the fact that all the Wandjina prints were sold out. But none of that was important right now – Old Joe was.

Now that she thought about it, he was the crux of what bothered her about the entire business. Why had the congregation of the church been moved to vigilante violence against a halfwit Seminole or Miccosukee, who probably hadn't even understood what crime he'd been accused of, much less actually been able to perform it. There were several slightly differing accounts of the lynching, but all seemed agreed on the point of Joe's incompetency. One story suggested the local law establishment had been less than helpful in finding the young girl's rapist and killer, and justice had been sought in the manner described. It made some sense. But there was something else.

She found the clipping and read Harrow's quoted words again, "There is indisputable evidence that this godless savage is the one you seek." It had been Harrow who publicly accused Old Joe of the crime. It was now beginning to dawn on Alice that Joe was probably the scapegoat for someone else's crime, and she was pretty sure who that someone was. Harrow had been the poor man's most adamant persecutor.

Alice could see the preacher easily in her mind now, and he gave her the willies. It was strange how all the actual figures from the library material appeared so easily in her mind as real people. She felt she knew them, whether she wanted to or not – Harrow, Deacon Lathe, and Pudloe Brown, the obsequious churchwarden – they all lived vividly in her imagination. And she'd added an invention of her own, Maunder, who'd provided the rope for the hanging, which was, of course, the belfry pull-rope.

"Mom? Can I have some aspirin?"

Margaret's voice snapped her back to the present, and it took her a minute to feel firmly seated back in her body.

"Coming," she called. She got up and stretched carefully; her leg had gone to sleep, she'd been sitting so still. She went to Margaret and felt her face. "How're you doing?" Burning up. Alice went to the bathroom for the aspirin.

When she came back, Margaret asked, "Will you sit with me?"

"Okay, let me get comfortable." She put Margaret's pillow in her lap, got the blanket readjusted around them, and turned on the television with the remote, searching for a weather report. The forecaster was in mid-stride when she found one.

"... high pressure ridge here moving east, just enough to let that Canadian cold air mass swoop down. Texas is under the heaviest snowfall in a hundred years." Alice remembered back when their house was being built that she had gotten up on a ladder on Christmas Day trying to thaw out the frozen water pipes under the house with her hair dryer. It had worked, too. She might have to use that technique again this year from the sound of things. Most of the pipes were enclosed by the new downstairs laundry room, but there was a bit of outside plumbing still at risk.

The meteorologist was consulting his computer-enhanced grid of the Florida Gulf Coast: "... possible snow flurries, but twenty-to-thirty mile an hour winds will prevent any accumulation. The chance for rain should diminish by early afternoon." Alice felt colder, listening to him drone on. She wanted to turn the heater up again, but Margaret seemed to be cruising off to sleep, so she sat still, her feet numb.

"... citrus growers will have oil-burning smudge pots out in the groves tonight. Expect Monday to be fair and cold, highs in the twenties with a hard freeze through Thursday—" Alice clicked him off. Enough was enough.

Quietly she slipped out from under the pillow and settled it back into place. In the hallway, she upped the gas until blue flames turned orange and licked the top of the firebrick shield. She stood as close to it as she dared. Images appeared in her mind, figures talking and interacting with each other – she imagined herself standing in the wings with a half-written script that the actors didn't need anyway. They were playing out this story for her benefit; all she had to do was document what she saw.

She went back to the computer and sat down, noting that some warmth had begun to infiltrate the study. It took a minute to gather her thoughts again, to remember where she had been before Margaret called her. Far, far away, that's where. It had seemed like coming in for a landing from some foreign country. She sat quietly and tried to get it back, then put her hands to the keyboard.

... The church was dark inside except for one candle burning in its holder next to the pulpit. Harrow stood beside it and waited for the girl to approach. Several other figures sat nearby, hidden in the shadows.

"Belinda Rider, what business have you with me that cannot be dealt with by the church warden?" Harrow's voice was hard and unyielding. The girl came down the aisle toward him and stopped beside the first row of pews. She was only thirteen and afraid. She twisted the skirt of her gingham dress with nervous hands.

"I come to ast you to release my momma. Please, please—" Tears ran down her cheeks.

"Release! What do you mean, Belinda? Speak what you accuse me of plainly and have done with it." His words were like iron, his face a mask.

"I ... I know you got a spell on her for sayin' aginst you an' the brotherhood."

"Have a care ... have I not told you, all of you, that the Body is sacred? That the source of its power is greater than any of you?"

"Momma's dyin', she sweats blood and her eyes they roll up like a cow that's eat jimson weed. None of her conjure can make it go away ... she say you done it to punish her."

"Conjure is blasphemous – only the initiates of the Body are permitted to invoke the Powers. I am only the mouthpiece; her fate is her own."

"Please," Belinda cried softly.

Shadowy figures appeared at the base of the pulpit, and Harrow descended to join them. He reached out and took the girl roughly by the arm.

"Warden Brown," he said, "we have here a blasphemer by her very own admission. What say you?"

The girl's eyes shone with terror, and she wriggled to free herself, but the pastor held her with the strength of a bear. In fact, he somewhat resembled one as he loomed over her. Deacon Lathe was suddenly behind her. He slipped his belt around her neck and pulled it tight, but not enough to kill.

"I think," he said, his breath on her neck, "that she is a lost soul that will not bend to the will of the Powers."

Harrow nodded. "Perhaps she will bend to you, then. I leave you to it."

He turned his back on them and lit a match from the candle, then pulled a cigar from his coat pocket. The girl's screams strangled in her throat where the deacon's belt held her fast. Her feet kicked and thrashed, and Brown grunted.

"More bone than meat," said the warden. "A lost soul to be sure."

At that moment, a figure leapt out of the shadows, knocking Pudloe Brown to the floor. A long knife flashed out.

"Help me!" shouted Brown as he grappled with Otter. Harrow and Lathe were on the man in seconds, and a blow to his temple from Lathe's pistol butt ended the struggle.

"Bind him well," said Harrow. "He will be much more useful to me than mixing pigments." He adjusted his clothing and stalked from the church.

The heels of his boots pounded through the nave, covering the fading moans of Belinda Rider. Her bloodstained body lay in the shadow of the pulpit, and twitched only a little as Pudloe Brown reached out for her again.

Alice stared at the screen and couldn't believe what she had written. She had been so caught up in the girl's terror, writing for the first time in vernacular as if hearing it firsthand, feeling what she felt, that her fingers were shaking and she was short of breath. The images of violence and death were still neon-bright in her mind, and the living room with her sleeping child was a pale reflection of what was real. Alice got up and took a deep breath. She heard a thump downstairs like a car door closing, and then heavy footsteps on the stairs. Nik. It was about time.

She went to the front door to greet him, but opened it to nothing but wind and rain. There was no one coming up the steps. Perplexed, she took a few steps down the stairs and looked around. She could not see his truck in the extra parking bay – clearly Nik hadn't come home yet. Snowflakes were swirling in the air, disappearing as soon as they hit the deck railing. Too bad Margaret was missing this, but she wasn't about to go wake her up. Alice turned her face up and felt the crystals melting on her flushed forehead. That was monstrous, what she'd just written, and what was worse, she knew in her gut that it was closer to the truth than anything in the library folder news clippings.

The clouds were so thick it seemed like dusk although she knew the time was only mid-afternoon. Huddled in the rain, she didn't like the way the tops of the trees were whipping around in the storm. It had the sound and feel of gale-force winds, with a whine that rose and dropped as new gusts rolled up against old ones like breakers on the shore. The trees were taking a beating. A loud wooden crack came from beyond the clearing, and she could vaguely make out a huge oak limb splitting off from the main trunk. At that moment she heard the familiar rumble of Nik's truck coming down the driveway and an instant later spotted his headlights through the rain.

He pulled up under the house and this time came thumping up the steps for real.

"Sorry it took me so long – it was hard to drive in this," he said. "There's a tree down in the driveway out near the road. I had to work my way round it. I'll cut it up when the storm dies down."

"In the dark?"

"Sure, you can hold the flashlight. Unless you'd rather be stuck at home in the morning," he said.

"Don't tempt me."

Alice put her arm around him and drew him inside, into the warmth and safety of their shared space. Nik felt solid and real, and she intended to keep him.

CHAPTER 21

IT WAS so cold in the morning that Alice's car sputtered and refused to start. Perversely, Nik's old truck, which was ugly as sin and sounded like a bucket of bolts, had cranked without complaint half an hour ago just as the sun was coming up. He'd probably made it to his first class with time to spare.

She tried again and it nearly caught, but then died. "Don't do this to me," she said between her teeth. Alice weighed alternatives, and on her last try, just when she'd talked herself into calling the office and taking the day off because her child was sick with the flu, the engine fired up.

Reluctantly, she backed out from under the house, tires crunching on the thin blanket of snow and ice covering the yard. The end of the driveway was littered with small twigs where Nik had drawn and quartered the fallen basswood. A dozen or so two-foot sections from the larger branches lay in a pile on one side of the drive. Bless Nik. She would make sure to come down the drive with the wheelbarrow and carry them in when she got home from work. He had warned her that he might be late because of a graduate student departmental meeting at 5:00, so she intended to get the fire going herself.

Crossing the bridge over the Massalina River just short of the DeFlores County line, she was startled by great billowing clouds of steam rising on both sides of the bridge. It was an effect caused by early morning sun warming the river's icy surface, but to Alice's state of mind it seemed more like driving over a crack into Hades. With the way things were going lately, she could almost believe it. It was worrisome, the way her book (which had started out as an innocent young-adult short story, she reminded herself) had taken such a hold on her imagination that it colored even the most ordinary events with dread.

Reaching town, Alice had to park a block away from the museum and feared her feet would turn to blocks of ice before she could get inside. Snow was clumped several inches thick against the curb, pitiful by Stockholm standards, but remarkable for Florida. The storm was gone, leaving a blue sky washed clear of clouds; sunlight sparkled along frosted bushes and sidewalks. The bank sign on the corner read 23 degrees at nine o'clock – too cold for a thin-skinned Southerner to be out on the streets. She was also late, but didn't care.

She slipped inside the back door and blessed building maintenance for the greenhouse warmth that surrounded her. Later in the day it would probably feel too warm, but right now it was wonderful. She walked down the fallout-shelter hallway to the elevator, brewing a steaming pot of coffee in her mind.

In front of the elevator, Hannah and Jessie stood with their heads together, talking. Alice remembered hearing a rumor that they'd been an item back when she first came to work at the museum, although she'd never seen any tangible evidence. They seemed to be good friends, but that was all. If indeed there had been anything else going on behind the scenes, they'd kept it well hidden. Alice had almost asked her in an unguarded moment when she'd needed to unload about Whit and her recent divorce to someone, but the timing hadn't been right. She'd also wanted advice about letting her simmering attraction to Jessie come to a boil, but then she'd met Nik and gotten distracted.

They saw her coming, and Jessie motioned to her.

"I've been waiting for you to get here."

"Damn, I thought I might sneak in unnoticed. So fire me," she said.

Hannah looked her over. "I can't say you look rested – holidays that rough on you?"

Alice opened her mouth and then shut it. There was no way she could begin to describe what her holiday has been like. Instead she shrugged and gave a half smile she hoped wasn't too phony. "I assume the Wandjinas behaved themselves in my absence?"

Hannah nodded. "No accidents, no surprises. But then, the museum was closed, so no visitors either."

Jessie was grinning. "We might as well tell her."

"Tell me what?"

"Get some coffee in your veins," Jessie said. "How'd you like to be locked in the vault with me for a couple of hours?"

Alice's brain ground to a full stop. It was that teasing tone of voice he sometimes used, playful, maybe flirting, that could charm you into anything if you were female. Maybe male, too, for that matter.

"Do what?" she got out.

"The pirates have arrived," said Hannah, smiling. "The vault's full of stuff that'll make your eyes pop."

"Oh," Alice said, feeling stupid. "You need to reconcile the manifest."

"Righto," he said. "Most of the treasure's already in the vault – came in last night with a highway patrol escort from Miami. We took a sampling to the lab, to make some rubbings. They'll be back in a few minutes – security, that is – to move the rest of the bars. Want to see?"

"C'mon," said Hannah, "it'll wake you up."

She followed them away from the elevator and down the hallway to the conservation lab. Jessie pushed the doors open and Alice gasped. Two lab tables were stacked with silver bars, each about the size of a thick fantasy novel. They were being watched over by Victor and Cheryl.

"Whadda ya think?" said Cheryl, attempting to sound unimpressed at having a pirate's fortune not five feet from her desk. "I wanted to take a snapshot but the boss wouldn't let me. At least he let me help Randy put tags on 'em."

"There will be plenty of photos made once we start documenting everything, but not yet," said Victor.

"First somebody's got to sit in the vault with me and catalog every piece against the ship's manifest." Jessie looked at Alice. "You get the first shift, madam curator, if you're willing."

"Yeah, I am ...." she said, still staring. "Are they heavy?"

Jessie laughed. "Pick one up and see."

The bars were corroded and pitted where they had been exposed to sand and wave action. She hefted one in her hand.

"About ten pounds?"

"Good guess," he said.

"Same weight as my cat," she said, and smiled at the thought.

"But worth a whole lot more," Victor observed.

"Depends on whether you're a cat lover," said Hannah.

"No cat's worth that much," he snapped.

Pissy bastard, Alice thought, and wondered if Victor was still mad at her for rejecting his photos for the Karl Bodmer exhibit promo stuff. The advance slides sent to her from Tucson were much better than his, and she intended to use them instead.

Before she could probe him, two uniformed highway patrol officers and several museum security guards returned for the remainder of the treasure. A sergeant pushed a wide four-wheeled hand cart in through the lab doors.

Jessie helped them load up the cart. "I admit I was a little nervous to have it just sitting out in the open like this. I wonder what kind of insurance Shelton carries in case of theft?"

"No worries. We'll make sure it stays in the vault where it belongs until the State people come to divide it with the salvors," one of the guards responded. Alice noticed that all the security personnel were wearing sidearms. She believed him.

She followed Jessie and the security guys down to the vault, which was a large rectangular room at the end of the basement hallway. The reinforced door stood open with yet more guards outside. Inside, piled along the baseboards from one end of the long room to the other was a pirate's heaven. She scanned the room, making a quick mental assessment. Round copper ingots as large as garbage can lids were stacked five deep in a corner, intended for use in the minting of coins had they made it to Spain. There were plenty of pistols, muskets, swords, axe heads, other nameless tools, and ship's iron hardware.

Gleaming dully under the fluorescent lights were rows of silver "pies," round disks cut into six wedges, the pie shape being suitable for stowing in barrels. Next to them, stacked like bricks on a construction site, was the main cache of silver bars, how many hundreds she couldn't guess. Long folding tables held mounds of silver coins, some corroded into single large clumps as large as footballs, silver dinner plates and forks, dented pewter cups, jeweled snuff boxes, an ornate silver bottle stopper, numerous navigational devices (more valuable perhaps to the true archaeologist than all the gold and silver), stacks of K'ang Hsi blue and white porcelain as perfect as the day it was packed (Alice's fingers itched to touch the delicately fluted bowls), and finally, of course, the gold.

It was arranged on a separate table at the end of the room nearest the barred observation window in the steel time-lock door. Ropelike gold chains that looked to be yards long were coiled around gold disks and ornately worked pendants. Boxes held smaller jewelry pieces set with grassgreen emeralds, cabochons of carnelian and onyx, or empty studs that had likely held pearls; and most wondrous, a 21-karat solid gold bar weighing over five pounds according to its tag. Alice was overwhelmed by it all.

"So, ready when you are," Jessie said to her.

"Um, let me unlock my office and check the mail. I'll be right back down." Alice flashed him a quick smile, hoping she radiated complete calm although her pulse was racing.

"Okay, I'm not going anywhere. Hurry back." He grinned with unrestrained excitement.

"I will." She was tempted to call him Indiana, but resisted.

Alice rode the elevator to the third floor, grabbed the papers, letters, and trade magazines stuffed in her mailbox, and made it to her office in record time. She was about to slap a quick note on her door that she'd be unreachable for the next several hours when she realized she hadn't thought about the Dreamtime exhibit at all since encountering Jessie and Hannah in the hall. The sight of the dragon's horde in the vault had completely pushed it from her mind.

Getting back on the elevator, instead of going down to the basement she stopped at the main gallery. One quick look around and then she'd join Jessie in the vault. There was no sign of Faye in the shop, so she tiptoed into the stillness of the exhibit. The gallery wouldn't be open to the public for another hour, so she had it to herself. Although there was no weird ringing in her ears, Alice felt an atmosphere of tension, like something held in check, but only just. Her arms tingled, and the ends of her hair seemed charged and flyaway – it floated around her face as if a static charge were building up.

"What are you up to?" she breathed, keeping her eye on the looming Wandjina figures, kept company by Namarrkun, the Lightning Man, as she walked the length of the exhibit. The sense of expectancy was palpable, but she encountered nothing visibly out of place. Then she reached the series of red ochre hand stencils along the Split Rock mural. The handprints should have appeared white with red pigment outlining the shape of the hand, but they did not: all of the hands were black. Alice stared at the panel in disbelief. It simply was not possible. Had someone defaced the exhibit? But how? Security was all over the building, especially with the *Marquesa* treasure down below.

"Not possible," she repeated.

Resolutely, she filed this image away until she could pull out the exhibit slides and see for certain what color those hands were supposed to be. There was a point at which the abyss beckoned when you admitted there were things in your universe that did not play fair with the established laws of physics, and she did not intend to take that plunge. She turned her back on the panels and went out to the elevators and down to the Spanish shipwreck gold.

She got off the elevator and walked down the hall to the vault, where Jessie waited with the security guys.

"All set?" he asked.

She nodded, and went into the treasure room. The officers departed, locking them in.

"They won't be back until lunchtime," he said, " but there's a phone in here, in case of emergencies."

"Well, that's good to know," she said.

"Pull up a chair, and let's have a look." He sat down at a desk where the manifest pages were spread out. "Suppose you call out items and numbers, and I'll look for them. When you get tired, I'll call and you look."

"Fine. What do you want me to start with?" Alice was a little nervous around him, having his undivided attention.

He was dressed for manual labor today in rumpled khaki pants and a sweatshirt over a turtleneck T-shirt. She assumed some of the layers would come off as the room warmed up, which could be interesting in itself.

"Let's do the bars first – that should be easy enough. You'll have to check two lists, the manifest numbers to verify them and then our list with the museum tag numbers. It's possible some things might not be tagged, although we sent enough tags to Deep Six to cover the entire inventory."

"Do we add tags if they're missing?"

He nodded and gestured to the desk. "There's a ring of numbered tags in the drawer."

Alice looked and saw a wire loop with hundreds of yellow metal tags strung on it, numbered in sequence.

"Ready," she said and picked up the first page. The entries were penned in a style known to historians as Spanish accountant's script, a looping cursive style used by seventeenth and eighteenth century cargo laders. The words were all linked together into one continuous line with many flourishes and elaborate serifs. She'd learned to decipher it as part of her graduate thesis, but it had never been easy.

"Can you read that?" Jessie asked.

"Eh, we'll see. I'm a little out of practice, but maybe it'll come back." He turned his smile full on her. "See, that's why I need you here." He laughed and her heart melted. She focused on the page in front of her.

"A-1002, silver bar" she read. He stooped over the stack of bars, flipping tags, and eventually found it.

"Got it. Log in a check mark with your initials next to the entry."

For the next hour she read numbers, and he searched for them. Some of the silver bars were so corroded by salt water that the mint identification marks were gone, but they were able to locate and check off the majority of them. While he searched among the stacks of bars, Alice's mind wandered back to her book. She kept hearing dialogue and unusual phrases of description; often she had to stifle the urge to drop everything and write them down on the back of the manifest pages.

One particularly vivid mental image involved Old Joe struggling through deep woods and underbrush in the area that was now Camp Apalachee, a posse of the Body close on his heels. She could hear the horses snorting and stamping along the steep bank of the springs and hoped the imagery would stay in her mind long enough to be able to transcribe it when she got home.

They worked their way through the silver and then the porcelain, saving the gold for last. A good deal of the search work involved moving heavy pies of copper and silver around, not to mention the artifacts of iron and wood. By the time they reached page thirty of the manifest, Jessie flopped down onto the bare floor, stretching out full length.

"My back's killing me," he groaned.

"Stay there, I can work on the small stuff by myself," she said.

"Thanks." He pulled off his sweatshirt and rolled it up under his head, then settled back and closed his eyes.

Alice held up a heavy chain fashioned of hundreds of gold links shaped like tiny violets. She was confounded by the incredibly painstaking work some long-dead artisan had lavished on it. It was a rope of gold.

"Get the rope."

Alice jumped. The voice was guttural and sour, not Jessie's at all.

"What did you say?"

"Um?" He opened an eye.

"I ... thought you said something."

"Nope, not me."

She sat trembling, a wave of absolute fear and panic taking hold to the point that sweat broke out across her forehead and her breath came in shallow gasps. The gold chain fell to the floor. Jessie opened both eyes and sat up.

"Is something wrong?"

She shook her head. The sensation of paralyzing fright was receding. Reaching down to retrieve the chain, she was mortified at having dropped such a priceless object as if it were no more than a dog's choke-chain.

"I'm turning into a klutz ... all this gold, I guess."

"Sure, makes me nervous, too," he admitted.

Alice massaged her temples, squishing the tightness in her skull around but not getting rid of it.

"Let me ask you something. In the Dreamtime exhibit, do you recall what color the hand stencils are on the last photomural?"

He blinked for moment, shifting gears. She could tell he wasn't connecting to her train of thought.

"I mean that last big panel across the back, with all the animals – do you remember what the spatter-painted hand prints look like?"

"To be honest, I don't," he said. "You're much more familiar with the material than I am. I even heard you have relatives from the outback."

"No Australian relatives, just my dad, but I never met him. I don't even know for sure what his ties to Australia really were. Yeah, I know," she said, reading the look on his face, "hard to believe I know next to nothing about him. Ask me about the Blacksburgs, my mother's family, and I can give you the genealogy all the way back to Sir Walter Scott."

She shed her sweater and pushed up her shirt sleeves; it was getting damned hot in the vault.

"My mother was widowed before I was born, and according to my uncle it was traumatic enough to make her give up her singing career. She was treated for post-traumatic stress syndrome and diagnosed as clinically depressed for a number of years."

She was babbling about stuff she was sure Jessie had no interest in hearing – way too much information, she was certain – but she couldn't seem to shut up. "My mother had to move in with her brother ... my uncle Hal, and he sort of took care of us both. I thought he was my dad when I was a toddler, isn't that funny? Even when they tried to tell me otherwise, he still felt like my father. I didn't really make the emotional shift until I was a teenager." She cut her eyes up at him; he seemed to be genuinely interested.

"Miz Waterston, you are not half as ordinary as you'd have all of us believe. In point of fact, you're downright mysterious." He was half-smiling, with his head tilted to one side. She felt exposed.

"Sorry. That's personal drek I shouldn't be boring you with. Shit, I hope this isn't damaged."

She held the yards of golden links, warm and heavy in her hands, and heard that strange voice again, an echo with no substance – it was maddening. Get what rope? And there had been a fleeting smell in the room too, like someone had waved a bottle of bleach under her nose and quickly recapped it. She regarded Jessie, sitting there appraising her with such frank interest. Apparently he hadn't noticed any disembodied voices and phantom scents.

"So, I seem like a normal person to you, in the grand scheme of things?"

"Sure. You're one of the most practical, organized people I know. Efficient, no-nonsense, brain like a filing cabinet, completely dependable." He was looking at her too directly for comfort.

Dependable. Not exactly a compliment, coming from a guy regarded as the worst flirt and best catch on the museum staff, but in her current circumstances it was a welcome assessment. He was watching her with eyes slightly narrowed, probably wondering where this was leading. There was no way in hell she was going to tell she was hearing things that weren't there, although by thinking it she had finally acknowledged there was something wrong with her. It made her feel slightly nauseous and her palms were sweating again, but not from the warmth of the room. It was a gut-level fear of the unknown.

At noon the DeFlores County sheriff's patrol, replacing the state troopers, came to let them out.

"Eating lunch today?" Jessie said as they walked back to the lab.

"No ... I mean, not here. Margaret's home sick again so I'm only working a half-day today. She doesn't mind staying by herself, but it makes me a little uneasy."

"Ah, so you won't be here this afternoon. I guess Hannah will have to pinch hit for you then. Could I get you to fill her in on where you left off before you leave?"

She followed him to the lab, where bored Cheryl occupied space at her desk.

"Any calls while we were in lockup?"

She shook her head, dragging her attention away from a copy of *Soap Opera Digest*. Today her hair was too black and had been forced by a misapplied curling iron into sweeping ringlets that engulfed her round face.

Alice stared at the curls. "Can I use your phone for a sec?"

"Sure." Cheryl shoved it toward her.

Alice punched in Hannah's extension, but there was no answer. "I guess she's already gone to lunch. I'll leave a note on her desk to come down here when she gets back."

Jessie turned to Cheryl. "I'm going back to the vault around one-thirty, or whenever the cops show up. If Hannah comes back by then, don't let her get away. I need her to take Alice's place at the controls." Cheryl wrote a note to self and stuck it on the cover of the *Digest*.

205

He turned back to Alice. "Got a few minutes?"

"I guess," she said, checking her watch.

"I want you to see the salvor's report that came with the artifacts."

His office was a crowded fire-hazard of a room inside the conservation lab. Jessie pushed open the office door and nearly dislodged an Inuit shaman's mask hanging on a hook on the other side. Following him in, Alice looked around for a free surface to sit on and didn't see any. There was a narrow path to his desk through stacks of archaeological journals and conference proceedings, a crate of Florida Clovis-era native artifacts, a telescope on a tripod leaning against a stack of boxes marked BALLAST STONES/IRON FASTENERS, and his Swiss racing bike that didn't look strong enough to carry a child, let alone a full-grown man. A clunky analog chronograph watch was buckled around one handlebar. Everything about him seemed complicated, with layers of detail: his approach to his job, his equipment, even his toys.

She nudged a hugely expensive underwater camera, perilously sitting on a stack of computer manuals, to one side of his desk and perched on the edge. Also squeezed among the debris on the desk was a wide-screen flat panel monitor, the only one in the museum, needed for displaying special survey and cartography data that produced topographic drawings via the large-format plotter out in the lab. It was not an office for claustrophobics.

"Got room there?" he asked.

"No problem."

She evaluated his desk, a disaster zone of heaped papers with the potential to avalanche in any direction. Sticking out at odd angles from the piles were contact sheets of artifact photos, rough drafts of dozens of articles, a wall-sized chart of the Periodic Table of Elements, and a photocopy of the Florida Archives and History Act. It was a real-life example of sedimentary stratification in process. And everywhere there were books upon books – the eclectic shelvings of a voracious reader or compulsive collector.

"Have you actually read all this?" she asked, looking around.

"Nope. Well, that's a lie. Some of it all the way through, most of it not. I collect titles. If I need to know something, I'd rather look through my own collection first for anything useful. If I'm missing a resource, I acquire it. I'm sure you never do research that way. You seem like the type who'd rather takes notes than own the source."

"Not exactly. I have a lot of books in my office, too, but it's just as easy to access online databases or query libraries."

He leaned back in his computer chair, happily at home among all the clutter. "Ah, but these books are the arcane, the esoteric, the tomes that nobody else would think of wanting to own. Leads me down paths the ordinary mind would never imagine. Some say it makes me a little mad."

"You are that," she said and laughed. The room was a true rat's den of scientific detritus. She thought of Merlin with owls beshitting his books and lizards in his alchemy retorts.

"This office is ridiculous," she said, smiling, feeling the slightest bit flirty herself.

"No, it's convenient," he said. "Everything I need is right where I can reach it."

"Some of these journals are from the eighties, you'll never look at them again."

"I might."

"Never. I'm surprised the fire marshal hasn't condemned this room."

"He's never seen it."

She laughed again, unrestrained this time. It felt good and dispelled the pall of gloom traveling around with her.

"Well, I need to go," she said, wishing she didn't have something else that needed doing more than keeping him company. "What did you want to show me?"

He handed her a binder with over a hundred pages of typed material.

"Just scan through it and see if you find anything that sets off alarm bells. I can't decide if these guys are just incompetent or profoundly good at deception. Either way, we know they will try to keep as much of the good stuff as they can out of the state's coffers and in their own. Now that you've seen the hoard, let me know what you think of their report."

"Gotcha."

Still smiling, she shut the office door and went out to the hallway exit. Back in her office, she called Margaret.

"I'm going to be just a tad late getting home," she said.

"How come?" Margaret didn't sound concerned, just curious.

"If I can contact the minister of St. Christopher's, I'll try to get an interview with him on the way home. Shouldn't take too long."

"Okay. Can you bring pizza?"

"No, I don't want to stop by the Pizza Bin. I'll cook real food when I get there."

There was silence on the other end.

"Margaret? Are you still there?"

"Uh huh. Mom, when you come home, I wanna show you something. Okay?"

"What is it?"

"Just something. On the Internet."

That was typical of Margaret, simultaneously blunt and cryptic. It was hard to pry things out of her until she was ready to divulge; then, she would rattle on as if giving a dissertation defense. Alice endured a cringe-worthy moment, as she recognized that trait in herself.

"All right. Nik's going to be late, too, so you and Dawg and Figaro just sit tight. How's your cold?"

"Better. Bye."

Alice checked her watch. Getting the pastor of St. Christopher's United Christian Church checked off her to-do list, either with a phone interview or in person, shouldn't take that long. She just wanted to ask him if he knew any of the church history, especially the early part. Then she could get home. If he could tell her something about Harrow or Old Joe, that would be a bonus.

She hoped it would go quickly and that he would be cooperative. If not, well, she had a plan B.

CHAPTER 22

ALICE'S STOMACH was growling, but she ignored it and sat down at her desk with the phone book. She quickly found St. Christopher's listed in the Massalina County section and dialed the number. She counted the rings, almost holding her breath. On the ninth ring, a young female voice came on the line.

"Saint Christopher United."

Alice's brain hiccupped for a moment. "Ah, hello. Yes, ... I'd like to speak to the pastor, please." She hadn't really rehearsed what she would say, hoping the inspiration would carry her once she heard his voice.

"Reverend Rider isn't here right now. Is this an emergency? He won't be back till after lunch."

Rider. She was shocked. It hadn't occurred to her that a relative of someone from the folder documents might be leading the flock at the crossroads. Was this a descendant of the family whose daughter was supposedly murdered by Old Joe? The prospect made her giddy with discovery.

"Um, well, I just wanted to make an appointment with him, to talk about some church matters."

"Are you a church member?" the young woman asked.

"Well, um, no, I'm from the Hardison Museum," she said, hoping like hell this wouldn't get back to Shelton somehow, "and I wanted to just ask him about some pictures that we have in the Florida History Photo Archives, to ... help us with dating them and identifying people in them." The ruse was pretty thin, but she hoped that luck would win out over logic.

There was silence on the other end that seemed to run on for minutes, but was likely just a few seconds. She could imagine the receptionist trying to decide if she should get rid of this stranger or give her a break.

"I'll leave him a message that you called," she said at last. "You can stop by after one o'clock, he might be back by then. He's gone to have lunch with his daughter and her family. What was your name?"

"Alice Waterston."

"And you're from where?"

"The Hardison Museum, in Citrus Park. Thank you so much." She hoped she didn't sound too fawning, or too suspicious.

"All right, and have a beautiful day."

"Thank you, that would be nice." She hung up. There was just enough time to grab a quick bite somewhere and drive to the church.

On impulse, she dialed home again. She listened to the phone ring, then got her own answer message. That was not good – where was Margaret? She tried again, and when she heard her own voice again, she said after the tone, "Margaret? Hey, kiddo, are you there? Figaro? Will somebody pick up?"

Hanging up, she considered blowing off the visit to Reverend Rider and heading straight home, but she'd made an official appointment and really didn't want to call back and cancel. Finally she decided to keep the appointment and call Margaret again once she got to the church.

After inhaling a drive-through salad, she hit the road and twenty-five minutes later was pulling into the church parking lot. The building was affluent for its rural location. Of old brick and fieldstone construction, with a wide arc of steps leading up to a portico supported by columns, it had a solid, permanent presence. High windows set in solid blocks of green and blue glass looked out onto the highway. A covered walkway led from the main building to a smaller rectangular annex that she assumed contained offices and classrooms. The sand parking lot held just one other car, and she parked beside it.

Punching in the numbers on her cell phone, she bit her lip and waited. Margaret answered on the first ring.

"Where were you? I called twice—"

"Mom? Raine says Sesshomaru is missing. She stopped by here, to see if we've seen him."

"Oh no, that's terrible. They were so upset about Tux. You know, I don't think it's safe outside. There seems to be a cat-killing dog or something in the woods. I'd feel better if I knew you and Figaro would stay put inside, will you?"

"Yeah."

"I have this little errand at the church to take care of and then I'll be right there."

"Okay."

"Well, 'bye then."

"Bye."

Alice recognized this behavior; when Margaret was concerned or fixated on something, she responded in monosyllables. Well, it would come out when she was ready.

She got out of her car and walked around to the row of doors in the annex. The first was marked OFFICE, and she went in. No one was sitting at the metal desk in the center of the room. Flanked by two filing cabinets of the same gunmetal gray as the desk, a door led to yet another office, the pastor's, perhaps. The room was chilly, and an old electric space heater grinding away in a corner, its coils glowing orange, was little comfort. Alice didn't envy whoever held the secretary's job. This part of the church complex was Spartan in comparison to the main church. Had they run out of money once the main grand edifice was completed?

"Hello?" she called.

At once, a small black man came through the door of the adjoining office. He was quite elderly, with grizzled hair and lined face, but seemed agile enough. He could have been anywhere from sixty to eighty or more.

"Are you the lady from the museum?" His voice was surprisingly strong and well-pitched, inviting confidence and confession. A voice of honey and deep rivers.

"Yes, I'm Alice Waterston." She offered her hand, which he shook and then held for a moment.

"Cecil Rider," he said cordially. "It's nice to meet you. My study's a little warmer, won't you come on in and have a seat?"

"Thanks," she said and stepped past him into the inner room. Several worn leather armchairs were arranged in a rough semicircle facing a stone fireplace, and she sat down in the nearest one. Logs were burning in the grate in a high crackling flame, and the room was indeed appreciably warmer than the receptionist's. Bookshelves lined the walls, but there was no desk, and Rev. Rider took a seat in one of the chairs next to Alice.

He sat quietly, looking at her with interest, and finally said, "Well, what can I do for you?" He smiled at her with friendly good humor, an easily likeable person.

"I'm a historian," she began, "and I'm working on the history of this area – Massalina County, Magnolia, the early surrounding settlements, things like that." She hoped that wasn't sounding too vague. "I was wondering what you could tell me about your church, how it was founded and so on?" She waited, hopeful.

He continued to smile, but seemed to be deliberating over how to answer. He folded his brown hands over one knee and looked at her with bright eyes that she couldn't read.

"I became pastor of this congregation in 1945, just after this building was put up. That was certainly a glad time – war ending and the new church going up. Everyone pitched in. It was an honor for me to be given charge of such a fine church." Silence.

"I'm sure it was," she prompted. Was she going to have to pull information out of him? She'd hoped it would be easier.

"If you don't mind my asking, who were the previous ministers, before your term?" She realized with embarrassment that it sounded like she was interviewing someone in political office, but she didn't quite know how to phrase what she was really thinking, which was, how in blazes are you related to the Rider family?

"No, I don't mind. My father was leader of the flock before me. He brought me up in the church, and I never thought about doing anything else with my life. When he died, about a month after the church was finished, I just naturally took his place in the pulpit, a post these good people have seen fit to keep me in for the last fifty-nine years. I'm retiring this year, though."

Well, that was a little better, she thought, but still not enough. "And before him?"

He looked at her steadily. "There wasn't anyone else."

Alice was tongue-tied. She hadn't expected an answer like that. It was a blanket denial of everything she'd found in the library.

"Are you certain? I mean, wasn't that old plank church down the road where the original congregation met?"

"I think you must be mistaken," he said evenly.

"Then who wrote this?" she asked and reached in her purse for Cadjer Harrow's notebook. She handed it out to him; this was ambush tactics, she knew, but he'd forced her to resort to plan B.

Smiling, he took the book, looked at the cover, and then dropped it as if a snake had bitten him.

"What are you doing with this?" His smile was gone.

"I ... checked it out of the library."

The Reverend Cecil Rider frowned and stared at the book on the floor, as if the spot were an opening to the Pit. Sensing his intention, she scooped up the book before he could toss it into the fireplace. Shaking his head, he began to speak softly. Alice leaned in to hear him better.

"I haven't thought about that thing for years. I assume you must have the folder it was filed in. I had asked that it be withdrawn from circulation and destroyed. I see that is was not."

"Then, the folder belongs to you." This was a revelation she'd never anticipated.

"Yes," he said, with bowed head. "Most of it was collected by my father. Maybe that's why I never put it to the torch like I should have done, I should at least have made sure that book you hold was reduced to cinders." His voice was a whisper; he sounded as if he were confessing to some horrible crime. Alice felt embarrassed.

"Reverend, could you ..."

"Miss Waterston, I must ask you to take that folder back to the library and tell Miss Potts to incinerate it. In fact, I'll call her myself. It's the least I can do."

"I can't do that, I've only just started to understand "

"Young miss, let the past stay buried. It can only hurt those who don't deserve to be hurt. That's really all I can tell you." Or all you *will* tell me, she was thinking.

"I'm sorry. I didn't mean to cause trouble, for you or anybody else. I only wanted to hear from someone who might know what Cadjer Harrow's history was all about."

The room fell silent. She was alarmed to see that even the fire had shrunk, its flames dimmed to glowing coals.

"I beg you not to speak of that person," said the old man.

"I ... I'm sorry, I just thought you could tell me something useful."

"The most useful thing I can tell you is to stop whatever you have been doing with those documents and to put that thing you hold into the fireplace."

"But why?"

"Have you read that book? Do you have any idea what the person who wrote in those pages was trying to do?"

"No, that's why I'm here."

The Reverend Cecil Rider sat with his hands tightly clasped in his lap and his eyes closed so long Alice was afraid he might have gone to sleep. At length he opened his eyes. She saw that his hands were trembling. His face glistened with sweat, and he got up unsteadily.

"Miss Waterston, I'm not well and need to take some medication. I was not prepared for this, and I don't know how to deal with what you want from me. I'm going to have to ask you to leave me, if you don't mind. We'll speak again, but not now, please."

Flustered, Alice stumbled over the chairs and went out to the front office. He followed her to the doorway, his face suffused with pain.

"I'm pleased to have met you, Miss Waterston. I wish it could have been for a different reason. Perhaps it still can." Was this last a plea or a command? Impossible to tell from his voice or expression.

"Thank you for your time. I'm very sorry I troubled you," she said, backing out the door. "I'll call you again later, if it's all right."

He nodded, but said nothing.

She got in her car and pulled out onto the county road, her stomach in knots. In the rearview mirror she could see that he had walked out into the churchyard and stood hunched in the cold, watching her drive away with the gods knew what in her purse. He obviously knew who, or what, Harrow was. It was too bad he wasn't willing to tell her.

CHAPTER 23

"I KNOW what the pig-dog is," Margaret said.

"Um, a figment of your imagination?"

"No. Look here. It's a Quinkan."

They were sitting in the study, Margaret at the computer where Alice found her when she got home from her aborted interview with the reverend. Margaret pulled up a Web page on the Internet, and Alice leaned over to see. Aboriginal designs and images of familiar looking cave art filled the screen.

"It's a trickster spirit that's evil or just playful, depending on which type it is. The evil type tries to eat your body and suck out your soul to make new Quinkans – it goes after children 'cause they're easy to fool. The other kind plays jokes and tricks, but it tries to protect people from the evil kind."

Alice was looking at Margaret, not the screen. "And you believe this? That some creature from your dreams is trying to steal your soul?"

"Mom, this is serious." Margaret was starting to frown.

"I *am* being serious."

"No, you're not. You think I'm 'projecting my fears' or whatever onto some made-up monster, but I know it's a real thing. What do you think chased us in the woods?"

Alice's mind was stumbling into uncharted territory. "A feral dog or something," she said with little conviction.

Margaret shook her head. "It says here, 'a Quinkan is a mimic.' You know what that means?"

"Yes, I do know the definition of the word."

"It means it can talk like a human and look like whatever shape it wants when it's trying to trap you. Even a lizard or a dingo. I know, gut level, that's what it is. Listen to this."

She began to read from the screen. "'Gaiya the giant devil dog was a menacing ancestral spirit before its transformation into a benevolent spirit dingo kind to humans. The devil dog hunted for its mistress, Grasshopper Woman, and once it locked onto its prey, usually men, it hunted them with single-minded fury. Its howling could be heard for miles as it tracked its prey. Larger than any ordinary dog, it was the size of a horse and its footsteps shook the earth.'"

She paused, looking at Alice. "And I found some stories with the red frilled lizard in them; he's almost always a villain of some kind. The thing in my dreams is a Quinkan 'cause he's dangerous and shape-shifts into these other things. They're all in the Dreamtime myths."

"I'm still not following how you decided to go looking for Quinkans in the first place."

"I didn't. I just wanted to try and find something that looked like that creech from my dreams. Mostly it's a little pig shape of a thing with a round stomach and a head like a dog with sharp teeth, and once it was a huge dingo with a long tail. But sometimes it's a big red lizard the size of Figaro with a frill around its neck. So I just searched on those keywords: pig dog red lizard sharp teeth. All the top hits I got were websites about Dreamtime stories, like Tatji the Red Lizard, and man-eating dingoes and the two kinds of Quinkans."

They was silent for a moment. "Are there any Quinkans in your exhibit?"

This caught Alice by surprise. She hadn't made the connection, or hadn't allowed herself to make it, but as soon as Margaret said it, she could see the panel clearly. Actually, there were two, from the Cape York region in northern Queensland. One was the Split Rock site that included a jumble of ancient stick figures, later ancestor spirit beings, many hand stencils, and various animals such as birds, snakes, and fish. The other was from another cave system in the area, and among the many figures crowded and superimposed on each other was a manlike Ancestor with rays emanating from his head, accompanied by a dingo that was not unlike a pig. She remembered now that the area was called the Quinkan Reserves, in reference to the ancestor spirits depicted in the rock outcroppings.

"Yes," she said. "there are. It's an important public site. I'm not admitting there might be a connection, I just want to know what you're thinking. I mean, a dog is a dog ... you could be dreaming about anything, don't you think?"

"No. I know it's from Australia. Because of what the places look like when I dream about it. Like this," she said, and clicked on another bookmarked site. A large image of Australian red-sand desert country complete with termite mounds appeared.

"Sometimes I'm lost in the desert when I meet it, and other times it's dark all around us, like in a cave underground. Our voices echo and it's freezing cold. Sometimes it doesn't have a shape; I just feel it there in the dark. It has the most awful whiny voice – I hate it. It complains about having to come mess with me when it should be doing something more important. If I'm such a waste of time, why doesn't it just go away? That's what I want to know."

"I've read somewhere," said Alice, "that if you recognize a dream when you're in it, you can control it by saying something like, 'This is just a dream and I'm going to wake up now.'"

"Yeah, tried that. Doesn't work." Margaret looked at her directly. "I used to stay awake all night 'cause I was so scared that it would show up. Sometimes I could see it even when I wasn't asleep. It comes out of the closet, just like in *Monsters, Inc.*, only it's not friendly."

"Munchkin ...." Alice got up to put her arms around Margaret, who sat stiff and unresponsive, staring at the image on the computer monitor.

"It just pisses me off. Why is it doing this? I'm so tired of being scared I think sometimes I can't stand it. I'm gonna stop it, somehow. But I have to find out what to do," she said," and you have to help." She looked up at Alice with ginger eyes that were turning black.

"I will," Alice said, holding her. "Whatever it takes, we'll figure this out together."

"You know how we talked about manifesting things by thinking about them or doing some ritual to make something happen?"

Alice nodded, biting her lip. This was horror-movie real estate and every fiber of her reason was resisting it.

"What if one of us, or both of us, can really do that?" said Margaret.

Alice sat on the floor. "How? I don't believe in black magic, and I hope you don't either."

Margaret frowned again. "No, this is different. Black magic is something you make up in your own head, but I didn't make this thing up."

"I wonder why it only shows itself to you. I've never seen it or dreamed about it."

"Because that's what Quinkans do. Everything I read about them says they go after kids 'cause they're easiest to lure away. Kids hear what they think is their parent's voice and when they follow the sound, the Quinkan grabs them."

"Has it ever talked to you in my voice?"

"Yeah ... Dad's too."

Alice felt an ache in the back of her throat, unbidden tears of guilt and remorse. "I'm sorry you've had to stay here alone so much. I shouldn't do that to you."

"I'm twelve, I don't need a babysitter. What I need is somebody who knows an anti-Quinkan sorcery spell."

Alice stifled the urge to smile, and then realized a part of her brain was also thinking along those lines.

"One story I read said they eat adults, too, if they get in their way," Margaret continued.

"By story, what do you mean? Like, an eye-witness account?" Alice couldn't even believe she'd asked such a question – it meant she was that much closer to acceptance.

"I mean the legends that go with the cave paintings. They're on a lot of websites. I got confused at first 'cause there's so many different legends," Margaret said. "There's a bunch of different myths...they don't all believe the same thing. I thought the Dreamtime was just one thing for everybody, but it's not."

"It's all tied to geography," said Alice. " The landscape is a physical record of the Deamtime events, but each tree or hill or rock formation has its own story, depending on who lives near them. Take the Wandjinas or Lightning Man, for example – they're well-known to clans of some regions, but not others. You're a good researcher, you know that?"

Margaret smiled for the first time that evening. "Thanks."

Alice stood up too fast and felt lightheaded for a few seconds. An escalating throb at the back of her skull sent her to the bathroom for a painkiller. Glancing at her watch, she realized it was well past their normal suppertime. No wonder her stomach was growling. And Nik was much later than she had expected him to be. She wondered how a student-teacher meeting could last that long.

She swallowed three aspirins and went back to the study where Margaret was clicking intently through a site, scanning the rolling pages, looking for something.

"I'm just curious," said Alice as she settled onto the daybed. "What did you think when you saw the Dreamtime exhibit at the opening reception ... you know, did you feel or hear anything strange, not counting the shattered glass? Did you recognize your creature on the Quinkan panels?"

Margaret pursed her lips. "Well, I didn't really look at all the panels.

Nik and I mostly hung out by the food table because we were starving. I did look at the things in the middle where all the modern art was, but I don't remember what the panels looked like, except for the Lightning Man and the one next to him."

"Yeah, that one would be hard to miss."

"If I knew the pig-dog was a Quinkan, for sure I would've looked for it." She shrugged. "But here it is – look." She found the image she'd been searching for and pointed at the screen. "There's the pig-dog, only the caption calls it a dingo. The red lizard is here, too."

Alice looked at the figures jumbled one over another in ochres of red, yellow, white, brown, and black. She recognized it as a frieze from one of the cave "galleries" at the Quinkan Reserves site; in fact, its panoramic image was hanging against the east wall of the exhibit space. She also remembered with dread that all the hand stencils from the Quinkan panels, shown here as white and red, had inexplicably turned black.

"You don't happen to remember what the hand stencils looked like on the panel when you saw it, do you?" she asked. Margaret shook her head.

Alice folded her legs underneath her and hugged her ribcage, body language she recognized as protective. She had no coping mechanisms for the supernatural or even the metaphysical, but something had to be done.

"Look," she said, "I think we should try to approach this with some common sense, to keep from getting too spooked, so let's just get our thoughts organized first. Let's make a list of assumptions about the situation – what we know or suspect – and then look at them as a whole. That way it might be easier to see some kind of solution."

"Yeah, that sounds like a plan," said Margaret. "I was kind of doing that in my head already."

"Start a new file and type ASSUMPTIONS at the top of the page. Then we can start listing things."

Margaret did so, and typed in the first entry.

1. The thing in my dreams is a Quinkan.

"Let's rephrase that a little," Alice said, reading over her shoulder. "We don't know for certain that's what it is. Say that the dream creature seems to resemble the Australian Quinkan spirit being."

Margaret began typing. "What else?"

Alice thought for a moment. "List the most important characteristics of Quinkans that you read about – it's a trickster spirit, a shape-shifter, it's malicious, it goes after children ... and it has a counterpart spirit that's not evil, that might work against it. And then list the specific forms you've seen it take in your dreams." Margaret typed quickly, spelling be damned. Soon she had a list of nearly a dozen items.

"Go back a minute," Alice said, thinking. "The first thing we need to document is when this creature started showing up in your dreams. How old were you?"

"I've always had horrible dreams."

Alice sighed. "Yes, I know. But was this thing always there, or is it recent?"

Margaret chewed this over. "Five years back maybe. Before Dad left, if that's what you're thinking."

"I'm just trying to tie it to anything that might be significant, like what was going on in your life, or ours, at the time."

They sat in silence. It was raining again, and the sound of water sliding off the eaves and puddling on the concrete patio below was a constant white noise in the background. The temperature was slightly warmer than the night before, so there would be no snow this time.

"I think," Margaret said, "it started coming the summer I stayed with Grandma and you and Dad went to Boston. I tried to tell her about it and she shut me up quick. Didn't wanna hear it."

"Write that down." Margaret typed while Alice considered this new bit of information. Her mother never mentioned such an episode, but Alice was already planning to confront her with it the next time she saw her.

"Should I list the Indian-like guy I saw down at the pond?"

"What? Oh, well, that wasn't a dream event, was it? Are you sure what you saw was physically there?"

"Looked that way to me." Her tone was challenging.

"Okay, let's do this. Make a new list called UNEXPLAINED EVENTS and put it there. And you can add those two museum accidents there, too."

Margaret typed furiously, her jaw slack as she concentrated. Their tag-team effort felt good, Alice realized, no matter how off-the-wall the subject matter. Nik would be having a cow if he could hear them, which reminded her: where was he?

Margaret looked at her. "Anything else under EVENTS?"

Alice was silent.

"Mom?"

Alice clutched her hands together – it was now or not at all, so she stepped over the edge.

"There are a few more things ...."

"Like what?"

"A couple of things I just never mentioned, because ... I wasn't sure, um, if they really happened."

"Like my Indian." Margaret's I-told-you-so expression required no response.

Alice felt hot even though the room was cool. She tried to keep her voice even and matter-of-fact, but it was the first time she'd admitted aloud to anyone what she'd been dealing with internally since the *Land of Legends* exhibit arrived; her pulse was thudding against her skin.

"First thing," she said, "was when the unloading accident happened in the museum. I heard a shriek or wind whining, and I felt icy cold and couldn't breathe. Apparently nobody heard or felt anything like that but me." She looked quickly toward Margaret, but the girl's focus remained fixed on the screen as she typed. "I heard it again at the reception just before the glasses broke, and a few more times in the gallery, especially around the Namarrkun panel. Then about a month ago—"

"Wait," Margaret interjected. "I can't keep up."

Alice took a long breath, and waited while Margaret typed fast, her mouth set. "Okay," she said finally.

"Remember when I stopped by the library and found that folder with all the church records? On the way home in the dark, something flashed in front of my car just beyond the church – I swerved and nearly ran off the road. Scared the shit out of me. It was just a quick streak across the road in front of the car; in the fog, could have been anything, but ...."

She realized that Margaret had stopped typing and was staring at her. "Did you hit it?"

Alice shook her head. "There was nothing there. I backed up and looked. I could have imagined it, I guess."

"I think it belongs on the list."

Alice swallowed. "You're right. It does."

Now that they were into it, she was going to document everything, no holding back because somebody might think you were losing your good sense, even when that somebody was yourself.

Margaret began typing again. "I'm adding us getting chased through the woods from Raine's house by the Quinkan or whatever it was."

"And Tux getting killed," Alice added softly.

"And Sesshomaru missing."

"And that illusion on the beach in Gull Harbor."

"What illusion?"

"Um, Nik looked like a character in my book when he was backlit by the sun, walking toward me. It was almost like there was someone superimposed in front of him," she said, remembering the fright it had given her.

"I was meaning to ask you about that book," said Margaret. "Can I read some of it?"

Alice hesitated. "I don't know if that's a good idea."

"Why not? Is it that bad?"

"Not bad, just intense. The subject matter. It's rather adult." She knew Margaret would find that lame, but couldn't think of any other way to say what she was thinking.

"Have a clue, Mom ... I've read *Interview with the Vampire* and all Judy's Dark Hunter vampire books and a bunch of yaoi manga. It can't be any stronger than that."

"I had no idea you were reading such stuff."

"Well, duh. We just pass 'em around at school when class gets boring. Judy's older sister buys 'em. She got a bunch of Laurel Hamiltons from Lissa and I get 'em next—"

Alice stared at her daughter. She didn't even know what a "Laurel Hamilton" was; obviously not an author on her own reading list. From the tone of Margaret's voice, she assumed it wasn't something from the Young Adult section of the bookstore.

Margaret stared back. "What happened when we drove home with Grandma after Christmas? You were back there writing and then yelled bloody murder."

Alice hesitated, and then plunged ahead. "In the car, I was writing a passage where a vicious character cuts the cheek of another person with a knife, and I swear I felt it myself the moment I put the words on paper. I couldn't believe it was just imagination. I kept looking in the mirror for days afterward to be sure there wasn't any mark."

Margaret typed slowly, inputting the words that Alice felt branded her a lunatic. Finally Margaret turned to her. "I know what that's like. When the dingo-lizard chewed my ankle in my dream, I thought the pain was real. It shocked me awake and my leg was still hurting while I sat there in the dark. Did it scare you, when you felt the cut? It would me."

"Yes, I was really frightened. To be honest, I still am. Because I thought I saw the guy who did the cutting ... the preacher who founded the old church. Would you believe ... he walked across the lawn and into the house at Eve and Dan's New Year's Eve party. I followed him in and looked all through the crowd, but couldn't find him anywhere. Eve said she didn't know anybody like that when I described him to her."

"What does he look like?"

Alice ignored her question, continuing, "This morning, while Jessie and I were locked in the vault with the shipwreck goods, I distinctly heard his voice in my ear – the book guy, not Jessie. I experienced a sort of eyelid movie with vivid sound effects, of the chase leading up to Old Joe's lynching. And yesterday, while you were asleep on the couch and I was writing a really vile part of the book, I thought I heard Nik coming up the steps outside, but when I looked, there was no one. I think this book is starting to get to me."

"Can I read it?"

"Yes, but not tonight. It's not something I'd recommend before bedtime. I guess it's time I let you read it. Just remember, the subject is fascinating but it's not pretty."

They sat still for a few minutes, looking at the screen.

"There's something else," said Alice finally. "Just before Christmas, I sent off some query letters to publishers, but now I wish I hadn't. I'm not sure this story ought to be published."

"Let me add this to the list," Margaret said, turning back to the keyboard.

Alice sat quietly, with her inner ear on the rain outside. Now that she'd mentioned the sound of phantom footsteps on the stairs, she couldn't stop listening.

"Okay," said Margaret. "That's over two pages of stuff. There's a Quinkan at work, I know it."

"There's one last thing."

Margaret turned back to the keyboard.

"On my way home this afternoon, I stopped by St. Christopher's, to meet the pastor. You're not going to believe this – I didn't – the man is about ninety and is a direct descendant of somebody mentioned in the library folder, at least I think he is. I took the folder along with me to ask him about it and found out *he* put it there, in the library! So, I asked him about a notebook that was in the folder, and he wanted me to burn it on the spot. After that, he wouldn't talk to me about anything and in the space of a minute I found myself out the door and driving home."

"Did you show him those photos you took?"

"No, why?"

"I just wondered if he would've said it was haunted or something. Maybe he would've felt something when he looked at 'em."

"Did you?"

"Yeah, I did, like somebody was looking back at me, especially that one of the steeple. I didn't say anything because I didn't think you wanted to hear anything like that."

"I do want to hear it. I felt a presence too, when I was taking the photos. It was so strong I had to leave."

Margaret scrolled through the list. "You know what? You have way more things on this list than me. I thought I was the only one open to ... whatever, but I'm not. You are, too."

In the yard the sound of truck tires was distinct from the rain, and seconds later they heard Nik's truck door slam.

"I wonder if we should share this with Nik," said Alice.

"Dunno. You know him better than me."

"I'm not so sure about that. I think you see sides of him that I don't," Alice said, listening to the sound of his boots coming up onto the deck. "Whatever we tell him, I don't think he's going to be a believer. Hell, I'm not a believer, but we have over two pages of evidence for something that's not normal."

"Paranormal," said Margaret.

"Thank you, I was trying not to use that word." Alice smiled at her daughter; Margaret smiled back, their complicity confirmed.

The front door opened and Nik came in, shaking rain from his hair. It hung wet across his forehead, and his face appeared slightly flushed, Alice noted, as she came out of the study to meet him.

"Sorry I'm late," he began, "a group of us went to the University Center pub after the meeting."

"That's all right," she said. "Have you eaten?"

Nik sat down on the couch and pulled off his sodden boots, dislodging Figaro who'd dive-bombed his lap as soon as he hit the couch.

"Don't fix me anything; we had food."

"How's Stuart? Anybody else there I know?"

She was dancing around the issue at hand with small talk, waiting for an opening. Margaret hung in the background, watching.

"He sends his regards to you." Nik got up and put the boots outside on the deck. Padding back to her in his sock feet, he leaned down for a kiss. She responded, but with minimal enthusiasm.

"Nik, there's something we'd like to talk over with you," she said.

He stepped back, suspicious. "Uh oh, you're about to kick me out, right?"

"No! Of course not. We want you here, especially since ..." she cut her eyes at Margaret, "since there have been so many strange things going on."

Nik seemed relieved. "I'm perfectly willing to defend the homestead against marauding beasts," he said, his tongue stumbling over his teeth. Alice had never seen him loosened up like this, and she wasn't sure she liked it.

He flopped back down on the couch, smiling back at her. "You two look like you've been hatching a plot. I can tell - call it gent's radar ... opposite of women's intuition. What's up?"

Margaret faded back into the study, and Alice confronted him alone.

"I - we - think we might have a potentially dangerous situation developing." She was groping around for the right words, knowing that vague airy-fairy jargon wouldn't cut it with him.

"Don't forget that I told you we should have called the sheriff's office or animal control to come out and have a look around." Nik's tone became what Alice might have mistaken for condescending if she hadn't known he'd been out boozing with cohorts. "I wouldn't hesitate to shoot a wild dog or a coyote, but I don't feel too good about offing a human by mistake. That's law enforcement's job." He chuckled at his own wretched joke.

"No, that's not what I mean."

"Then what?" He smiled again, almost silly.

"What would you say if I told you I - we - think we have a haunting?"

Nik burst into a laugh. "I'd say you are not the Alice Waterston I know and that some alternate personality has possessed your body. Haunted by what, exactly?"

"We're not sure. But we did make a list of everything we couldn't explain."

"So that's what you've been up to. Conspiracy - I could smell it." He laughed again, and leaned his head back against the cushions, closing his eyes. "I'll tell you right up front that I don't believe in anything that can't be explained by physics or psychology. Which eliminates just about anything on that list, I imagine."

"Yeah, it does." This wasn't going very well, but she tried again. "Don't you at least want to know what we've been talking about?"

Nik sat up straight and ran his hand through his hair. "Okay, tell me. I'm listening."

Alice stood up. "You know, I think it would be easier if I just printed the list out and let you read it."

"Fine by me," he said, searching around under the couch cushions and extracting the television remote.

She heard him click on the Science Channel as she went into the study. She exchanged silent glances with Margaret and printed the file.

"Here you go," she said and handed him the pages. She sat down on the couch beside him and watched intently as he put on his glasses and read what they'd written. He finished, and sat staring at the last page before commenting.

"*För fan*, Alice," he said finally, "I can't respond to this. I'm not sure what you want from me, but this is nothing I can relate to." He took off his glasses. "Psychology might have something relevant to offer, but that's not my field."

"So, you think I'm delusional."

"If someone hears and sees phenomena that no one else does, would you not admit that's a possibility?" He was frowning slightly, his chin tilted, as if trying to see her from a different perspective.

"Nik, can't you admit there might be things beyond what our empirical scientific knowledge can demonstrate?

"No, quite frankly, I can't. Are there unexplained phenomena in science? Of course. But there must be an empirical basis for explaining everyday reality."

"Where does belief come into the equation, then?"

"Seeing is believing," he said, his jaw set.

He looked back down at the list. "It seems to me that you've bought into the cursed exhibit theory spread by the news stories. I thought that was exactly what you wanted to avoid."

"What if Namarrkun or a character out of my damned book walked through the door this minute and reached out and grabbed you by the shirt? Would you believe?"

"No, I would check myself into the first hospital I could get on the phone."

He was leaning toward her in a semi-aggressive posture, eyes unblinking. She wondered if he'd argued his graduate thesis this way. She heard Margaret's bedroom door close.

"If even half the things on this list seem real to you, I'd say you've been living on the edge of a dangerously irrational mental state. Get some help."

"Then I guess I can't rely on *you* for that help," she said hotly. "That's too bad, because right now I really need some support." She reached out and took the pages out of his hand.

"I can't support your belief in the supernatural, if that's what you want," he said, getting up. He went out to the deck and retrieved his boots.

"Where are you going?"

"Back to town. I can't deal with this. I have a lot on my agenda, and it doesn't include ghostbussn, eh, –busting. I have a dissertation to complete."

He went to the door and shrugged into his jacket. Alice could feel tears springing at the corners of her eyes, but she blinked and held them in check. "Nik ..." It was a plea, but not a grovel.

"I'll see you later. Call if you need anything that has to do with the real world," he said and shut the door.

She listened to his steps going down, and heard his voice calling for Dawg. Moments later the truck thragged to life. Only then did she allow the shock of his sudden removal to sink in. Figaro jumped into her lap, meowing, and she cried into his fur with fury and remorse.

CHAPTER 24

AS SHE'D feared, Nik stayed away all week. Alice poked forlornly among his things still scattered around the bedroom: socks and shoes in a jumble, a pile of coins from his pants pocket on the dresser, a stack of folded T-shirts and jeans, a heavy wool fisherman's sweater in the closet. Apparently he didn't need them enough to drive back out to retrieve them. At least there was no underwear to deal with since he didn't wear any, the remembrance of which fact gave her a sad lustful twinge. She really did miss him.

The only excitement all week was a determined possum that kept coming in through the cat door during the early morning hours to raid Figaro's food dish. Dawg would have prevented that from happening, but he'd gone with his master back to town. She blocked the cat door with a concrete block, which meant having to let the cat out manually, but they couldn't have a possum loose in the house while they were asleep, turning over garbage bags and nosing around.

Things were quiet at the museum as well, and she wrote no book pages, although Margaret was allowed to read what she had written so far. Then, on Friday, two letters came from separate publishing houses, one a form rejection and the other a handwritten note on *Libris* letterhead asking to see the first three chapters of the work she had proposed.

"Now what," she wondered aloud, handing the letter to Margaret.

"But that's cool, isn't it? A publisher might want your book."

"I'm not convinced anymore that they should."

"Well, I think it's cool, anyway." Margaret folded the letter and gave it back.

Alice thought about it for a moment and smiled. "You're right, it *is* cool. Let's go out for supper, just to celebrate the fact that someone somewhere thought my book proposal was cool."

"Can we go to the Roost? I can get hot chocolate!"

228

The Pelican's Roost carried no liquor license but cheerfully provided setups for customers bringing their own firewater, and the weekend crowd was predictably and regularly boisterous. Laughter and loud conversation rippled over the tables and around the crowd waiting to be seated during the Roost's peak supper hour. Every table was occupied, and a line of waiting diners slouched out the door and spilled onto the sandy path leading toward the parking lot.

By the time Alice and Margaret finished their crab cakes and downed their last hushpuppies, the volume of well-fed voices had reached a decibel level where shouting to one's neighbor was not only permissible but necessary. Margaret was still sucking her hot chocolate and whipped cream when Alice suddenly got up.

"I've got to go stand outside for a minute," she said close to Margaret's ear. "I just need a breath of fresh air – be back in a minute. Just stay put, okay?"

Margaret looked concerned, but nodded, her mouth full of chocolate. Alice turned and moved unsteadily toward the door. The house wine and the bacon-broiled soft-shell crab and potatoes with sour cream were making a vicious wizard's brew in her stomach. Oooh, she thought, as her dinner ingredients collided unhappily. She squeezed through the waiting crowd and made it out to the front steps. The sunset air was frosty, but cleared her head considerably and her stomach began to settle down. The parking lot was full of people milling around, smoking and waiting to be called to their tables.

Beyond the shell-paved lot, the narrow road circled around a modest quay and fish processing plant on the bay side of the point, where in season dozens of fishermen worked the waters out beyond the marsh. Most brought their catch to be weighed and packaged for sale in the local markets. The wharf teemed with twenty or more cats in all sizes and colors hanging out around the seawall. They chewed fish heads or begged for tidbits from the restaurant. Margaret usually longed to pet them, but they were such a scrofulous lot Alice wouldn't allow it.

It was just at dusk, and the sky was picture-postcard red even in the wintry light; the Gulf was placidly beautiful with a rose-silver sheen. Too bad her camera wasn't handy – it would have made a gorgeous timed-release shot. A chorus of meows met her as she walked across the narrow strip of asphalt toward the line of low docks where both pleasure and working boats were tied.

"Sorry guys, didn't bring you a thing this time," she said. They clustered around her feet, not ready to give up. A few other people were out on the seawall taking in the sunset, and a boy with a dirty face and scruffy clothes ran past her up the road after a dog clenching a candy bar in its teeth. It made her laugh; she was sure Margaret would never let Dawg get that close to a chocolate bar. Which made her think sadly of Nik again although she'd been fairy successful at blocking him out of her thoughts the last few days. She was about to turn back to the restaurant, her head totally cleared, when one of the men on the quay spoke to her.

"Evening," he rasped.

Her heart stopped. She knew that voice because she heard it in her head every time she wrote his dialogue. Beside him lounged his cruel lieutenants Brown and Lathe – she recognized their clothing and knew their faces as they stood shoulder to shoulder facing her. They looked for all the world like flesh and blood people from the physical world; yet their eyes were not quite right. She saw them as black holes with tiny flickering red lights, like coals burning: soulless, and totally dangerous.

Alice swallowed a scream and fled over oyster shells and potholes back to the restaurant, expecting cold hands around her neck or a hunting knife in her back at any moment. She made it to the parking lot untouched and gasping, slowed to a walk as she approached the line outside the restaurant, and then shouldered her way back inside the front door. Sliding into the booth seat beside Margaret, she wheezed for breath.

Margaret was instantly on the alert. "What is it?"

"Them ..." she whispered. "Those three main ones, from the book."

"Where?" Margaret looked out the window into the gathering gloom and beyond to the red sunset fading at the horizon.

"Docks," Alice said, getting herself under control. "I know it wasn't my imagination because he spoke to me, in a real voice that I heard with real ears."

"What did it sound like?" Margaret's eyes had gone wide and dark. At one time Alice would have read that look as total panic, but now she knew better. "Was the dog around anywhere?"

"I ... I didn't notice, I just turned and ran." They sat for a silent moment, surrounded by restaurant noise and the din of relaxed, sociable voices talking about nothing more compelling than seafood and football scores.

"Let's go home," said Margaret. "Fast."

Alice nodded and grabbed the check. After paying, they moved out of the crowded foyer onto the steps and down onto the sandy path. It was quite dark, the last rays of the sun extinguished in a lowering cloudbank that was moving in from the southwest. Distant thunder boomed, and a long straight spike of lightning lit the water for a few seconds. Alice hung back by the door, shivering in the frosty air and scanning the parking lot for shadowy shapes. Not seeing the three she was looking for, she nearly jumped out of her skin when an icy hand took hold of hers.

"Raine! Good god, you startled me," she gasped.

Raine's eyes searched Alice's face, clearly aware that something was up. "Tim and I tried to get your attention, but you obviously didn't see us. Hi, Margaret, how's it going?"

"Okay."

"That's good." Raine was partly smiling, but Alice could tell she wasn't convinced. "You look a little wild-eyed, Alice, to be truthful. Everything all right?"

"I ... just thought I'd lost my car keys, but I found them. We're headed home right now."

Tim pushed his way through the crowd around the front door and joined them. "Hey, Alice. You girls out on your own tonight?"

"Right." She managed a reasonably sociable smile, but inside she was screaming.

Tim draped his arm around Raine. "Tell Nik to stop by when he has time; I've got some fungi I was hoping he could ID for me – found a bunch of it in the leaves near some rotten logs. Looks like pieces of Styrofoam."

Alice blinked. "Right. I'll tell him."

Raine was watching her closely, not smiling.

"Did Sesshomaru come home?" asked Margaret.

"No, not yet." Raine's expression softened. "We've looked all around the yard and nearby woods–"

"Raine's had me out with a flashlight every night, but it's pretty clear we're not going to find him after all this time. I made a possible rabid animal report to the sheriff's office, but nobody's come out yet to check."

"You don't know a rabid animal got him," said Raine. "That's just a guess."

"Yeah, but what else would you suggest?" He looked from Raine to Margaret to Alice.

Alice got her car door key in hand. "Say, would you guys mind walking with us to the car? It's near the back of the parking lot, and without Nik I don't like walking back there in the dark."

"No problem," smiled Tim. "Lead the way."

Alice headed down the path to the road, aware that Raine was watching the way both she and Margaret scanned the shadows and jumped whenever lightning lit up the sky.

They got to her car without incident, and Alice slid into the driver's seat with relief. Margaret buckled her seat belt and locked the passenger door in one motion.

Raine leaned down and searched Alice's face, concern and confusion in her eyes. "Call me sometime, okay?"

"I will."

"I mean it."

Raine's smooth, porcelain-doll looks were deceiving; she was tough underneath, as Alice well knew. She'd survived divorce and the death of a child, as well as caring for an aged Alzheimer's-ravaged parent who'd finally expired in her arms. Her marriage to Tim, a widower, was fairly recent, but as far as Alice could tell, they seemed perfectly suited to each other. Each had paid their dues with someone else.

"I will, really." Alice cranked the car.

"If you don't, I'll call you," said Raine and waved, stepping away from the car.

Alice backed out of the lot and onto the road. A light rain was beginning to fall, and she turned on the wipers.

"See any sign of ... them?"

"No." Margaret sat alert, her face pressed to the passenger door window.

Alice cast her own sidelong glances as they pulled away from the parking lot, but it was too dark to see anything distinctly. Then suddenly Margaret jerked around in the seat, looking behind them as the car began to pick up speed.

"There! Mom, there he is – my Indian!"

Alice stepped on the gas.

Margaret turned around, discovery and fear in her eyes. "They're standing by the side of the road back there, and one of them is the same guy I saw in the woods."

"How ... how can you be sure?"

"Same clothes, same face, everything– it was him! I knew there was something wrong with that guy in the woods; he didn't look dead, but he didn't act alive either. If that's what's-his-name from your book, then we can both see him!"

"What're you saying? That he's some kind of zombie? "

"I mean he's from the other side, from some other reality. You wrote about him and he came."

Alice was shaking her head. "How could I do that? How could anyone do that? So what do we do ... burn the manuscript to get rid of him?"

"You could try that, yeah."

Alice had been facetious, but Margaret obviously was not. The idea of all her research and hard work at the computer documenting the individual stories of all the characters she'd come to know going into the fireplace was unbearable.

"I don't think we need to go that far," she said. "Maybe we need to make sure he's not just a tramp or a stalker of some kind, which is bad enough. There could still be a rational explanation."

Margaret slumped down in the seat. "He won't go away, then. Just like I know that Quinkan thing won't go away just because I want it to. You have to know how to undo it."

Alice was speeding along the main coastal highway heading toward the parkway and home, the nighttime trees and occasional houses and trailers flowing past in the rain. Ribbons of lightning streaked and forked across the sky in front of them as the storm moved in. They drove in silence for the next fifteen minutes, listening to the tires swishing along the highway and the rhythmical thump of the windshield wipers.

As they neared the Camp Apalachee entrance, Alice suddenly jerked the wheel and careened off onto the steep shoulder of the rain-soaked road. Half a dozen horses galloped madly across the highway behind and in front of the car, leaped the camp rail fence, and crashed into the woods near the springs.

"God, did you see that?" she yelled.

"Somebody let the camp horses loose!" Margaret said, shocked. "We should go back and tell the director."

"I'm not turning around."

"Okay, but we should call the camp when we get home."

"Fine, you do that." Alice's hands held the wheel in a death grip.

"Mom?" Margaret was looking at her. "The horses could be hurt – a car might run into 'em if they aren't rounded up."

"Did you get a good look at them?"

"No, you swerved and they were all around us and then jumped the fence. It happened too fast."

"Well, I did."

Instantly she saw in her mind's eye the horses that had been closest to her, wild-eyed and foam-flecked. They had carried riders on their bare backs who whipped their shining flanks and dug their ribs with long spurs. But worst of all, one of the riders had turned its head to look at her. It swung a noose made of rough hemp and grinned in passing; it had been none other than Jeral Maunder. How she knew this was beside the point. As Margaret had said earlier regarding her "Indian," she just knew.

Alice pulled the car up under the house and shut off the engine.

"Wait here and I'll turn on the light." She got out and went to one of the house pilings where the switch was and flipped the floodlights on. Margaret got out and hurried to catch up with her. Together they climbed the stairs, and Alice unlocked the front door. The house was cozy inside.

"I'm glad we left the heater on," she said, shrugging off her coat and shaking rain out of her hair. Margaret hurried to the hallway and hunched over the flow of heat coming up through the grate.

Alice went to the kitchen and nuked a half cup of coffee she'd abandoned when they'd decided to go out for supper. She wondered where the cat was; usually he'd beat them up the stairs to get to the heater or the food dish first. Sipping the coffee, she checked in the bedrooms and bathroom, where he sometimes napped among the towels in the linen closet.

"What are you looking for?" Margaret asked.

"Just wondering if Figaro was back here."

She tried to sound noncommittal. Out in the living room, she checked the couch and easy chair. Going to the kitchen, she noticed the crunchies in his dish hadn't been touched, which meant he hadn't been in since they took off for dinner. She went out on the deck and looked around. The rain was slacking off, although she could still hear distant thunder booming out over the Gulf. Shivering, she turned back toward the warmth inside when she saw what she had been dreading.

She went back in, slid the glass door shut behind her, and stood staring at the floor.

"What's wrong, Mom?" Margaret was the kitchen making hot chocolate.

Alice gulped. "Figaro's dead."

"... no, NO! Not my Figs ...." Tears were streaming over her cheeks.

Alice took a breath. "It looks like some dogs got him. You can see where he clawed around the cat door trying to get in ... I forgot it was still blocked up." She tried to banish the image of his final terror-stricken seconds and dug her knuckles into her eyes. "I'll wrap him in something. You don't need to go out there."

"Yes, I do."

Margaret slid the door open and stepped outside in her stocking feet, Alice following. Figaro lay on his side under the porch swing, his head crooked at an impossible angle. Dried blood stained the corner of his mouth and his amber eyes were half-lidded. His tail was brown where he'd shit himself. Tears stung Alice's eyes as she put her arms around Margaret and held her close, her frosty breath mingled with damp red curls.

"I'm sorry. It's a nasty sight."

And then she couldn't speak; sobs were wrenching her throat apart. Poor sweet kitty, if they hadn't tried to keep out that stupid possum he could have escaped. She imagined him running up the stairs for safety only to find no escape from whatever hunted him down. She and Margaret cried together. Finally she pushed the door open and went in.

"Come inside," she said, shaking. "I'll take care of him."

Margaret ran for her room and shut the door. Alice lay down on the couch, hurting inside. Why was everything going to hell? She had never felt so alone, not even the first night in the house after Whit moved out. She dreaded having to wrap Figaro in a plastic bag and dig a hole out in the woods somewhere as soon as it was light, making sure it was deep enough that he wouldn't get dug up by scavengers. She was certainly physically capable of doing the job, but emotionally it was nearly impossible to face.

She needed help, but those who had offered – Eve, and now Raine – were not who she wanted to get it from. Well, nothing ventured, she decided, and picked up the phone. If he wasn't home, she would leave a message. She would make no mention of the restaurant episode, of course, but news of Figaro's death would certainly get his attention.

CHAPTER 25

THE FOLLOWING morning, they buried Figaro under a large dogwood tree that flowered with hopeful abundance every spring in the front yard. Alice held her face expressionless as a mask, her mouth set, while Margaret lit a stick of lemongrass, stuck it in the newly turned earth, and said what was in her heart. Alice was fine until she heard something about Figaro's friends Tux and Sesshomaru waiting for him at the Rainbow Bridge, then she gave up trying to be stoic. This was her longtime feline companion that had been murdered, slaughtered by some force she did not understand, and anger was beginning to replace fear. As she was to discover, it was a turning point.

"I'm going into town to see Nik," she said as they walked back to the house. "Do you want to stay or come with me?"

"I'll come. What're you gonna tell him?"

"That something is killing our neighborhood pets, and we don't feel safe. I'll tell him that Tim called the authorities, but they haven't done much about it. I won't tell him about what we saw before we got home last night, unless he asks directly about unexplained events. I might stop by Eve's house, too, on the way home."

"Cool, I can play *Ragnarok* on Ethan's Play Station."

They piled into Alice's car and were in town by noon, so Alice headed first to one of their favorite in-town cafés for lunch. By 1:30 they pulled up in front of the three-story yellow brick apartment complex where she assumed Nik still held a lease. Its black wrought iron railings along the external landings and staircases had been designed to give the building a New Orleans patina, but to Alice it looked like a slightly seedy motel. Because mostly graduate students and single working people lived there, no children's scooters or other toys littered the landings and tiny grass patches around the ground floor apartments.

On the second floor Alice rang the bell for number 214 and waited. He could be sleeping late, given that this was Saturday, so Alice rang again and then knocked. When he still did not answer, she rummaged around in her purse, pulled out a pen and notepad, and wrote, "Figaro was killed last night. Please come back. We miss you." Unsure how to close – should she write "Love" and scare him away for certain, or simply sign her name, which might sound too cold – she finally just wrote "A. & M." and hoped he would fill in whatever intended meaning those initials might carry. She slid the note under his door.

She went back downstairs where Margaret waited in the car and called him on her cell phone. No answer, so she could only assume he had gone out early. With a little luck, he would discover the note before they got home in the afternoon, and perhaps would call or even decide to join them before dark. Punching in another number, she waited while it rang and rang.

"Hey," she said, when Eve finally answered. "Want some company?"

Eve sounded genuinely pleased. "Sure, are you in town? Is Margaret with you? Great, come on over. Dan's in Atlanta for a few days, and the boys are bouncing off the walls. I'll put on some coffee and we can hang out while the kids wear each other down."

It was past 4:30 when Eve refilled Alice's cup and shuffled back to the kitchen in fuzzy gray bunny slippers. Skin-tight faded jeans and an oversized sweatshirt so large on her slender frame that it was probably Dan's completed her weekend uniform. Alice admired her from across the room – even in bunny slippers she looked great. Some people were lucky that way. Sounds of the kids laughing and shouting filtered back to them from the game room.

"Why don't you just take a week or two off ... go visit your mother or something?" said Eve. She sank back into the couch cushions and propped her feet up on a black teak coffee table.

"I can't do that, I've already used a big chunk of vacation time. But even if I hadn't, the Dreamtime showing has generated an ungodly amount of traffic and media coverage – a lot of people have been calling and writing for details. Everybody wants to know if the thing's cursed. I tell them why don't they come see for themselves. And then this other job blew in–"

"Oh right, you told me there was a shipwreck salvage."

"–and there's no way I can leave all that up to somebody else." Alice sipped at her cup; somehow Eve's coffee was better than hers, too.

She didn't see Eve much anymore, but that old conflict of enjoying her company and envying her perfections hadn't completely disappeared. It was through Eve that she'd come to know Whit, Eve's older brother, and after she'd married him, she hung out with Eve a lot, even though Alice's imagined frump factor worked overtime when they were together. The effect was still there, she decided, but not nearly as strong as it had once been. Maybe it meant she was becoming more comfortable with herself.

"I have to be on the job, at least through the next two months. The Aboriginals won't be gone until the end of March, and we've only started cataloging the treasure, and then it has to be cleaned and treated for division between the State and the salvors."

Shrieks and screams from the game room interrupted her, and Eve darted away to see what mayhem the kids had inflicted on each other.

Alice stretched her legs out and put her feet, warm in their wool socks, on the coffee table over a copy of some hunk 'n fitness magazine. The cover displayed a crop-topped honey with oily muscles slithering up the quadriceps of Mr. Cosmos. Alice winced; never in a million years could she ever have a body like that. Eve spent time in the gym with a personal trainer several times a week, she'd told Alice, and believed she had never been in better shape. The day she bench-pressed over seventy-five pounds, which wasn't bad considering she only weighed a hundred and fifteen, had instantly caused three other weightlifters, one of them male, to hit on her with offers of dinner and a night on the town.

"No problem," Eve said, returning. "Just typical video-game adrenaline."

"That's good."

"So where were we?"

"Work stress, or maybe life stress." Alice weighed how much of an ally Eve could be, considering her own lifestyle. But she never doubted Eve's genuine affection for her, even without Whit.

Eve looked at her candidly. "Why don't you just say what's bothering you?"

Alice pulled her feet up under her and crossed her arms. "It's not that easy. The exhibit is getting to me, on top of what I told you about Figaro."

"And Nik moving out."

"Yeah, that too. I did get a bite on my book proposal, but I'm thinking about getting rid of the whole thing."

"Why?"

Alice shook her head. "You wouldn't believe me."

"Try me." Eve sat up straight, her expression attentive.

"I'm think I'm starting to see people from the book, in real life."

Eve didn't say a word, so Alice continued. "I thought I saw the main character here, at your New Year's Eve party, although I talked myself out of it after we got home. I was sick with a fever and took some cold medicine that could have clouded my judgment. I thought that was the end of it, but I saw him again last night, on the wharf at the Roost."

Eve's eyes widened. "Did he talk to you?"

"Just a greeting – 'Evening,' he said."

"Does anyone else see them besides you?"

"Well, Margaret saw the three people that I saw on the seawall, but I can't prove who they really were, although I know."

"That doesn't sound good."

"I know. So what do I do, check myself into the psych ward of the hospital?"

"Maybe not that, but you should get some kind of help. I wonder if living alone out in the woods like that hasn't made you a little paranoid, if you don't mind the suggestion."

"No, I don't mind. I am definitely feeling paranoid – I hear sounds in the exhibit that nobody else hears, I see people that my logic centers tell me can't exist, my lover moves out, and my cat is killed. Yes, you could say I am feeling paranoid." Alice realized her voice was rising so she shut up. It was embarrassing, being that confessional, but she was desperate.

"I could give you the name and number of a psychologist I see sometimes when I need stress relief ... she might be able to help."

"You think I need a shrink."

"Who doesn't? We live in stressful times, impossible demands are put on us every day, and it's a wonder more people don't see and hear things that upset them."

Alice sighed. "Sure, give me the number."

Eve popped up from the couch. "Just a sec, I'll get her card." Alice watched her go down the hall toward Dan's private office. Making an appointment for Prozac or whatever drug was currently in fashion wasn't appealing, but might be her only solution unless she and Margaret could come up with something better. Eve came back and handed her a tasteful beige card with small print, which Alice tucked into her purse without reading.

"Want a refill?"

"No, I'd better not." Alice checked her watch. "It'll be close to dark by the time we get home." And Nik might call, she thought.

239

"I'm really sorry about Figaro." Eve was a cat person and understood.

Alice smiled. "He was a great cat, the best. I know Margaret took it pretty hard, but she doesn't say much. I don't think we'll get another one anytime soon."

"Certainly not until you find the cat-killer," Eve said.

"One of our neighbors contacted the sheriff's office, so maybe they can find out what's going on," Alice replied, "although I'm not getting my hopes up."

She pulled on her boots and collected her purse and car keys. "Let's go see how hard it'll be to break up the video game tournament so we can get on the road."

"Well, you guys be careful going home. Call me if you need to. You could even stay here for a while, if you don't feel safe out there. I'm sure Dan wouldn't mind."

Alice wasn't so convinced, but that didn't matter. Moving in with the Lees wasn't an option as far as she was concerned.

"Thanks for the offer," she managed, and went to the game room to collect Margaret.

It was overcast and quite dark by the time they pulled up under the house.

"Mom, I don't wanna go up the stairs in the dark."

Alice mentally cursed herself for a fool at having left in such a hurry that they'd not turned on any lights downstairs for their return. The moon was new, so there was no natural lighting from the cloud-shrouded night sky.

"I'll go turn on the flood lights, and then we can go up."

Buttoning her coat up around her neck, Alice got out in the freezing dark and felt her way over to the piling with the switch, and then relaxed a bit as a bright circle of light filled the yard. The entire front clearing and a good way down the drive showed in stark relief, but most of the house staircase up to the deck was shrouded in shadow, the floodlights aimed away from it.

She fumbled for the house key on her key ring. Fourteen steps to the top. One of these days she was going to get a switch installed that would turn on the front door light from the step at the bottom. In fact, she resolved to take care of it tomorrow – this was absolutely the last time she was taking the steps up in the dark. Alice studied the ascent. Muscles twitching, she set her foot on the bottom step and heard a low growl. She froze.

Holding her breath, she tried not to move, imagining what it would be like if she were turned to stone. There were scratching noises above her, and then she saw the darker shape at the top of the stairs, a huge rough-furred canine with bared fangs and ruby eyes. White-hot adrenalin flashed through her body.

"Margaret, stay in the car."

"What?" She was opening the door.

"Stay in the car!"

Alice cut her eyes toward the base of the steps, searching for a weapon, and spotted a hand-sized chunk of concrete left from when the piling foundations had been poured, but it was too far away to reach. She made a move toward it, and the growl started again, louder. The beast was coming down the steps, which creaked under its weight.

"Get away!" Alice shouted, knowing the mere sound of her voice wouldn't scare the thing off. In fact, she wasn't sure if it was a dog at all ... it seemed too big, easily the size of a small pony, with massive shoulders. Ears laid back, it stalked with ponderous, purposeful footfalls down the stairs, one taloned foot at a time. Talons? Those weren't proper dog feet – what the hell was it?

The creature snarled and gnarred with a horrible gagging sound from deep at the back of its throat that made Alice weak at the knees. She was trembling violently from both cold and fright, barely able to keep from fainting. She was a prey animal transfixed by the approaching predator. Bumping against the stair railing, it descended, yellowed fangs revealed in a mock smile; then it stopped midway, as if sizing her up. Without warning it launched itself at her throat. The thick quilting of her coat collar deflected its bite as she jerked back, and steely teeth sank into her shoulder with a nauseating crunch.

She screamed and fell under its weight, her face crushed against its foul-smelling hide of coarse bristles. Her shoulder was losing all sensation as the thing locked its jaws and shook her like a rabbit. Despair filled her mind with the primeval terror of flesh doomed to feed other flesh, of helpless blood spilled in sacrifice for the appeasement of unknown gods. Slipping into shock, a portion of her mind detached itself and dispassionately remembered watching a film about a woman being mauled by a bear. The only thing that had saved her was rolling on her stomach and playing dead. Alice turned her face toward the dirt and went limp, letting her arms flail like a toy losing its stuffing as the beast gave her another violent shake. Blood pounded in her head, her left arm flopping like a dead thing.

The jaws clamped tighter, and Alice screamed in mindless response like a hare uttering its death cry just before the kill. Then, inexplicably, it let go. The head went up, questing, attending, but still growling deep in its throat. In a red haze of pain, Alice heard its guttural snarls form into hideous words: "... rarrr ... harrrh, pleass lettt meee ...."

It muttered to itself and began pacing back and forth beside her, its horrid mouth still drool-slick and gaping. At one point, it said in a clear, human voice, "Where is the other one, the young one?" Then it lapsed back into snarling bestial half-words. While it was thus occupied, Alice twitched and jerked in shudders where it had dropped her at the foot of the stairs, her face lying against the jagged hunk of concrete. Her good hand closed around the rock, but it was a hopeless involuntary gesture; she knew she didn't have the strength to throw it.

The devil-dog clumped back to her and put its muzzle down to her ear, hot wet breath steaming her cheek. Keeping her eyes tightly shut, she felt rather than saw its crimson-lit gaze glide over her. It pawed once at her torn sleeve with talon-like claws and said distinctly, "Not allowowowed to kill the channel arrrarr, but otherrrs I will rrrr." With that, it leaped over her body, crashed heavily in the underbrush and dry leaves like a maddened elephant, and pounded off in the direction of the pond.

Alice lay near the bottom step, shivering and barely conscious, until all sounds of the beast's passage through the woods had disappeared. Banging sounds thudded somewhere nearby, and she forced her eyes open. It was Margaret knocking on the window of the car door, mouthing something to her. She raised her face, and the window rolled down.

"Mom? Is it gone?" Her voice had a hysterical edge.

With her good arm, Alice pushed herself to a sitting posture and made a mental inventory of bones and muscles, amazed to find herself alive.

"Yes, I think it ran away. God only knows why." Then relief flooded through her pummeled body as she saw truck headlights coming along the drive. "There's Nik. Get out and go upstairs as fast as you can. You'll have to use the upstairs key," she panted, "I don't know where mine ended up."

Margaret got out of the car and came to where Alice half lay, half crouched on the ground.

"Mom, there's blood ...." Margaret's eyes were tearing up.

"Get inside! Nik's here, everything's under control – just go on!"

Margaret needed no further urging and fairly flew up the steps.

Alice collapsed against the house piling and waited for Nik to park. He got out of the truck and stood still for a moment, trying to take everything in, then he was on the ground beside her, lifting her head with strong, careful hands. Dawg ran around the yard, his fur bristled, growling and barking in loud challenging yelps.

"Easy, don't move yourself, let me do it." Carefully he got her onto her back and gingerly straightened her limbs. "Don't move your head," he said. She knew he was afraid she'd broken her neck or back, but the pain was all in her shoulder.

He went to his truck and called 911, having to repeat directions to the house several times with controlled fury. Coming back to her, he scanned the line of trees.

"What did this?" he said, wiping blood from her face with a corner of his shirttail.

"Big dog ...." she said, at a loss for any better description. "Bigger than a Great Dane, thicker, heavier. I think it knocked me out for second when it jumped on me. My head hit a rock or something. It was trying to get me by the neck, but just missed." She couldn't bring herself to tell him about the red flame-lit eyes.

He brushed hair out of her face, and she could see blood on his fingers. "You might have a concussion," he said. "Just lie still until the paramedics get here. The dispatcher said it might take twenty minutes for them to find the house."

He got up and went back to the truck. She could hear him rummaging around in it, and in a moment he returned with a sleeping bag and his backpack. He unrolled the sleeping bag and tucked it around her, and sat down on the ground beside her. Opening the backpack, he pulled out his pistol and checked the chamber for bullets.

"Is Margaret safe?"

"Y-yes, she ran upstairs as soon as you got here." She was shaking violently.

"That's good." He was staring down at her with those blue Nordic eyes, fingering the shredded wool sleeve around her shoulder, his face paler than usual. Finally he said, "My god, Alice, *jag förstår inte*, what the hell's going on?"

"I tried to tell you. You weren't interested," she breathed.

The wail of the approaching ambulance cut her off, and they waited in silence as it wound its way around the driveway and into the front yard. A sheriff's car followed it.

While paramedics removed Alice's coat to set her dislocated shoulder and stitched the gash on the back of her head, Nik tried to deal with the deputy, who seemed inclined to think at first that he might have a domestic abuse case instead of a wild dog attack. It was only when he spoke with Alice and got a description of her injuries, which thankfully did not include her neck or spine, that he changed his tune. Nik glowered in the background as Alice helped the deputy fill out his report.

The driver of the ambulance approached her with a form and a pen. He was frowning.

"Miz Waterston, I strongly recommend that you go to the hospital and get started on a rabies series. Since there wasn't any actual puncture wounds, I can't make you go, but you'll need to sign this waiver that says you're refusin' the shots. An attack like you got, even without findin' the animal in question, is pretty serious. Rabies is always fatal, once it sets in."

Alice took the pen in her good hand. "Where do I sign?"

"You're certain you don't want to go into Citrus Park to the hospital?" the deputy asked.

"Yes," she insisted. "My doctor's been called, and I'll check with him on Monday. Nothing's broken, so I'm going to stay here. I'll go right to bed."

"Well, suit yourself," said the deputy, looking at her like she was a fool. "I'll send somebody out in the morning to go look for that dog. You really ought to go get yourself a rabies series."

"Right," she said, knowing there was no way in hell she was going to do that.

Once everyone was gone and Alice put to bed with a sedative, Nik sat at the kitchen table with Margaret, reading the list of Assumptions and Unexplained Events. A large bowl of popcorn was slowly dwindling between them, with Dawg getting an occasional bite.

"I don't know how to accept any of this, even if there were rational explanations for everything," he said slowly. "I can't believe in the supernatural. I would have to have a personality transplant to do it."

Margaret made a sideways smile. "Yeah, my grandma's the same way."

"But what I *can* do, in real-world terms, is make sure you and your mom are physically safe. I'm going to call some hiking friends of mine, and we'll scour these woods. If there's anything to find, we'll get it. And I'll get that upstairs porch light switch installed so you won't have to go up the stairs in the dark."

"That would be super." Margaret smiled and sipped her chocolate.

"You're pretty calm, considering what just happened," he said.

"Not really... I'm scared as hell, but I know what's going on," she said bluntly. "I just have to figure out what we need to do. There's a reason it's here, the demon-dog, so we have to figure out what it wants and how to make it go away."

"I'll shoot the *djäveln* if I see it," said Nik.

Margaret knew he meant it, but she also assumed it wouldn't make any damn difference if what she'd seen shaking her mother like a dead rabbit was really Gaiya the Devil Dog or a Quinkan wearing that disguise. What she needed was the proper shamanic spell for protection and banishing, and she was privately hatching a plan to find it.

CHAPTER 26

ALICE WENT to the doctor on Monday, got her shoulder and collarbone x-rayed (a hairline fracture, but not worth splinting), signed another form refusing rabies treatment with the promise that she would take the series of shots if the beast that attacked her were found and proved rabid, assuming she wasn't dead by then, got a prescription for a good painkiller, and went to bed for the rest of the day.

She was up and about on Tuesday, and back at work by Wednesday with an arsenal of evasive explanations for what had happened to her.

Nik was back and committed to staying with them, although he refused to discuss the possibility of the paranormal. Alice was content to leave things at that – it was enough comfort just to have him there. They had even gotten a break from the cold, with Monday and Tuesday sunny and cool, and no sign of the freezing rain of the week before.

On Wednesday, however, her first day back in the office, gray clouds filled the sky at the tail end of a cold wet afternoon. The view from Alice's office window was particularly dreary; cold seeped in through the glass while she watched the clouds pile up. The forecast was for rain off and on throughout the afternoon, with no promise of a letup through the remainder of the week. It was a good day to be inside with the heat turned up. Her shoulder was stiff and mottled with four hideous bruises where the creature's jaws had gripped her but not punctured the skin thanks to the thickness of her overcoat. All she wanted to do was sit and stare out the window, watching the rain come down. And think.

As promised, sheriff's deputies had come out to the house on Monday and walked the property. They came up with nothing, of course; it was a disappointment, but not a surprise. Hiding in the back of her mind was the secret hope that if the beast were killed, Harrow and his cohorts might disappear as well. The idea was completely irrational, but it kept her pulse steady.

In fact, things had been quiet for the last two days. No apparitions, no threats, no dreams. She had kept away from the Dreamtime exhibit and concentrated on working through the treasure trove in the vault. Sorting through the gold jewelry was an indescribable thrill, not just to admire the beauty of the pieces, but also to imagine the lords and ladies who might have worn them. A braided gold band set with a single large fractured emerald slipped onto her ring finger in a perfect fit – she'd held it out admiringly.

"You want that one? It's yours," Jessie had joked. Didn't she wish. Putting the ring on had also given her an uneasy feeling, sensing what the drowned woman whose finger had worn it must have felt when the ship went down ... it was too traumatic to think about. The *Marquesa* had carried passengers as well as crew, many of whom had taken articles of great value and beauty to the bottom with them. She took the ring off and made a mental note to never do that again.

Interestingly, Jessie expressed a similar unease at handling items such as the navigator's astrolabe or an ornate dueling pistol that had the owner's initials worked into the handle. He showed her how it incorporated the wheel-lock mechanism of flint and steel that ignited the powder charge, and they speculated about the person who'd carried such a firearm.

It was hard work sorting and cataloging each piece among the thousands of items in the vault, but the time spent in Jessie's company made the hours flow like water over a millrace as they talked and theorized about the fate of the *Marquesa*. He laughed easily, and her mood lifted just by virtue of concentrating on something other than her own worries. She told him an edited version of her wild dog attack story, and he was suitably impressed.

"How many stitches?" he asked.

She showed him the back of her skull where it had connected with the chunk of concrete. "Looks painful. Here, are you comfortable enough? You just call out the numbers, and I'll do all the moving around." She basked in his sympathy.

Earlier that week while she was recuperating at home, the people at National Geographic had called Shelton and proposed a television special on the discovery and salvage of the Spanish treasure ship. The Florida papers were full of treasure news, and reporters were catching gold fever. She felt nervous at the prospect of taking part in the video sequences to be shot at the museum, but it was all in the line of duty. The publicity wasn't going to hurt the Hardison Museum one bit; in fact, it might even make them famous when added to the publicity from the notorious *Land of Legends* exhibit.

She was planning to work with Jessie that afternoon, plotting a strategy for the logistics of the "Marquesa campaign" as they were now calling it. She pictured them squeezed into his rat's nest of an office.

As if summoned, her phone rang.

"Ready whenever you are," he said. "Randy's made rubbings of the best coin faces and bar IDs, and Cheryl's just about finished typing the final inventory list. Victor's got contact sheets for us to look at, and we need to figure out what we want to say on TV. All systems are go."

"I'll close up and be right there."

She was feeling pretty good now, thanks to the painkiller she'd swallowed about an hour ago, and realized with some surprise that she had been able to focus on something else without obsessing over rotting churches, lunatic preachers, and the hound of the Baskervilles. This was just the diversion she needed to pull herself together.

It was a smidge after five when she got down to the bottom floor, and the lab doors were already locked, so she had to knock. Jessie let her in.

"Hey. I told Cheryl not to lock up when she left, but I see she did anyway. C'mon."

She followed him back to his office.

"Lots to do," he said, snapping his fingers and fairly twitching with constrained energy. "Pull up a chair."

She was amazed to see that he had cleared away some of the debris to make room for another chair and that she could actually see the surface of his desk on the side where he was working. The layers of papers and journals had been shoved to the side against the wall, and his prized replica fifteenth-century French crossbow was perched on top, weighting the pile in place.

"Hey, I've never seen these before." Alice pointed to his curio cabinet that held a row of tiny animals carved in amber hiding behind a litter of chert scrapers and spear points.

"Yeah, neat, aren't they? I just found them when I uncovered the desk."

"You idiot, nobody else in this building loses valuable artifacts just because they leave their desk buried for years."

He laughed with self-conscious humor and shrugged. "I can't change the way I am. Besides, you and Faye wouldn't have anybody to laugh about if I cleaned up my act."

"How do you know what we laugh about?" she teased.

"I have my ways. You're not the only one who lurks in the *Trinidad*'s captain's quarters." He smiled maliciously.

"Don't be ridiculous." She was giggling.

"Don't worry, I won't reveal your secrets. But look here ... the *Marquesa* is going to make us all rich and famous."

He had a legal pad full of notes taken from Shelton's phone conversation with the NatGeo production staff, plus some ideas of his own. She scooted her chair up beside him, and winced, having forgotten for a few glad moments about her injured shoulder.

"Hey, let me get that." He pulled the chair a bit closer, so that their knees were nearly touching. She leaned an elbow on the corner of the desk, trying to find a comfortable position.

"The special's tentatively called *Lost and Found: The Marquesa Saga*. What do you think?"

"It's catchy – I like it. Their idea?"

"Of course. You don't think anybody down here came up with something that slick, do you?"

"Not a chance." They were laughing together again, and his hand brushed hers as he reached for Victor's contact sheets.

More small talk and conspiratorial laughter passed between them. She was aware of little sparks of excitement leaping along her nerves; the room looked surreal, with heightened sharpness and color. The atmosphere felt charged, and thunder boomed outside. Home and everything it contained was a world away from Jessie's smile and sea-green eyes.

They looked at vault photos, especially the close-ups of the jewelry, and made a list of where in the lab the sound bites could best be shot and who would say what. They were in synch, working together smoothly – it was liberating, and she had forgotten all about time and the awful things she'd been going through.

Rumbles outside reminded her occasionally that she was probably going to have a soggy drive home and should get on the road, but she didn't want to pull away from this small oasis of well-being. He made a joke about the less-than-charitable motives of the Deep Six treasure hunters, and they laughed together, their shoulders touching as Alice leaned her elbows on the desk. Far away in somebody else's reality, it seemed, lightning stroked the sky, but here there was only Jessie and his impish laughter.

Shifting her weight off her elbows, she winced and caught her breath at the pain in her shoulder. Jessie caught her by the hand.

"Hey, steady there. You okay?"

She turned to look at him. His face was just inches away from hers, and then suddenly she was leaning in toward him and felt his mouth on hers. A piece of her mind watched her audacity with shocked surprise.

Fleetingly she felt the tip of his tongue, but it didn't enter her mouth. She ended the kiss and leaned away. Had he kissed her back? She couldn't tell. He looked up at the door, then back at her, smiling slightly.

"I had a feeling that might happen," he said. His hand lay clasped in hers, not retreating but not really holding. "But I don't think it's a good idea," he said softly.

Her skin felt icy, her capillaries constricting, but she managed to say reasonably, "Okay."

"Is it?" he asked, looking at her directly, catching her glance before it could slide away.

"It's okay," she said again, nodding and marveling at her control.

She unclasped his fingers and slid her hand along his forearm as she sat back in her chair. Alice folded her arms over her chest and put both feet firmly on the floor.

He cleared his throat and said, "It's just that ... I'm not interested in anything outside my work. My career doesn't leave room for this kind of thing."

Alice listened and nodded, but felt as if the features of her face were sliding out of place, so she tried forcing them into an understanding expression. An uncomfortable tightness constricted the back of her throat, but she knew she could not cry in front of him. Instead she said, "Sure, I understand." Her mind was racing: playing back the sensations of the kiss, reading her body temperature that veered uncontrollably from freezing to sweating, and only half attending to his words.

He was saying, "I'm sorry if I may have led you into a misunderstanding, it wasn't intentional. What I mean is, I enjoy your company, but ...." His voice trailed off, which was just as well. She didn't want to hear what the rest of the sentence would have been.

She stood up awkwardly and gathered up the notes they'd worked on. "Well ... um, what do you think we should do now?"

"Nothing."

She felt her breath leaking out slowly. Did he mean their work together or something else?

"All right," she answered. Backing away from the desk, she scraped her chair out of the way and headed for the door.

"See you tomorrow," she finished lamely.

"Take care," he said and smiled, tipping his chair back against the file cabinet behind him.

Her legs felt like water as she went down the hall and out the back door of the museum. It was dusk, and the streetlights were beginning to come on, shining in small pools of watery haze that surrounded each solitary eye on its metal stalk.

Alice stood beside her car, stuck. Her mind was scrambling over itself, retreating from and returning to the dreadful moment of the kiss in a frantic loop. She felt paralyzed. No matter how hard she wished, the moment couldn't be taken back. She would give anything to become a fleck of space dust right about now. Numbly, she unlocked her car and got in. It would be a long unpleasant drive home unless she could get her mind on something else. And, of course, the "something else" demanding to be thought about was Nik.

CHAPTER 27

SEVEN FIFTEEN. Alice raced down the highway through Whiteoak. The trip home became an endless vanishing point of two-lane blacktops with an occasional watery blur of headlights swimming past, an effect not entirely caused by rain on the windshield.

It wasn't so much the rejection that stung, although that was bad enough. It was the knowledge that she'd stepped over a line her common sense had been trying to steer her away from ever since she'd first been introduced to Jessie Birch. She'd been married then, but even so, his good looks and slightly roguish attitude had invaded her primal brain and made a home there. She'd fantasized about him, which she imagined most of the other women around him did as well, but she'd made herself keep it in check while she and Whit were trying to work things out.

Once Whit was gone and she was manless, it had been difficult to keep Jessie out of her head. Nik had come along somewhat out of left field, and his effect on her had been much more gradual, cumulative in an unassuming way. They were an instant intellectual match, but she hadn't warmed to him physically until months after she'd met him. And now, one unguarded moment had messed up her relationships with both men. Or so it seemed in her current state of confusion. At the moment, she wished she could just die.

"Not," she said hastily, remembering what had met her on the stairs in the dark.

She took the curves of the driveway too fast, clipping a few bushes with the sloping nose of the car, and roared up into her parking bay under the house. Shutting the engine off, she sat biting her lip, her pulse racing. Nik's truck was in the bay beside hers, so she knew he was home. He hadn't turned on the floodlights, but the new porch light shone weakly through the mist of rain at the top of the landing.

Sitting quietly in the dark, unable to mobilize, Alice wondered how she could have completely misread the situation with Jessie. Hadn't he flirted with her in dozens of teasing, suggestive ways? It seemed impossible that their compatibility and personal attraction could have been all a one-sided fantasy, and yet he'd said it as plainly as possible – he wasn't interested. She was furious that she had let herself become so vulnerable. This was a reckless thing she'd let happen, revealing herself emotionally naked, so to speak.

"Shit," she said, glaring out the car window at the dark wall of rain.

The scene with Jessie continued to play itself in her brain, making her want to step out of her skin and temporarily be someone else. Having to face him again as a colleague and pretend this momentary humiliation had never occurred was going to take some emotional gymnastics. A few tears leaked out, but that was it. No relief this night.

Blinking, she opened the door and a flicker of movement snagged her peripheral vision.

"Oh no, please not now," she whispered.

Suddenly her teeth were on edge as a high keening rose above the murmur of the rain. Another flicker along the tree line beyond Figaro's dogwood was gone by the time she trained her eyes on the spot. Cold fear replaced all thoughts of Jessie. She had an image of herself stranded in a lifeboat cut loose, drifting away from the channel marker into dark waters where terrible things waited for her, things she only barely understood but felt strangely responsible for.

The rain was increasing, and lightning split the sky with a crash of thunder that sent her into a protective crouch with eyes shut tight. An image floated across her inner vision, vaguely eel-shaped in form, pale with reddish streaks, black holes where eyes should be, and no mouth. She opened her eyes. The creature was there above the treetops, barely visible through the driving downpour. Alice jumped in fright, bit her lower lip, and tasted blood. Wind sang in her ears, mixed with the sound of water rushing somewhere, a hollow booming cataract of water pouring relentlessly ... canyon noises. Other eels crowded in behind the first, hovering and rippling in undulations riding the storm gusts; their ghostly faces pulsed with a corona of lightning streaks that flared with each boom of thunder. Suddenly, she straightened up and walked out into the front yard, ignoring the downpour. She knew what they were.

Touch us, the thought came into her mind like a pop of light that exploded and dissipated in an instant. The contact didn't come as words, or even pictures, just an instant sense of knowing. It made perfect sense, it was the thing to do. *Reach,* sang the pops of light, *make the bridge.* Strange words came to her lips.

"These are men's mysteries ... I cannot." The light motes popped in her mind, carbonating her blood. *Reach, make the bridge.*

"I am not a strong culture woman, I don't have the Law. I cannot ...." she whispered to the rippling forms.

The Wandjina spirits filled the clearing, towering over her like pillars of primordial smoke, transparent yet somehow holding shape. Her hands stretched forward, fingers fanned open, to the figure directly in front of her. Slowly her fingertips brushed air and met heat. A shock of electricity exploded down both arms and held her trembling, unable to move. Alien consciousnesses invaded in a rush, exploring, momentarily possessing every atom in her body. She screamed silently as inhuman thoughts flooded her synapses, her body shuddering with searing pain and joy, stimulated beyond endurance. Too much, her stunned brain was screaming, turn it off! And just as suddenly, the contact was broken.

Her legs crumpled, and she lay in the puddles filling the yard. The image in her mind was that of being held under a faucet turned full blast so that gushing light energy flooded into her mouth, filled her body, and leaked out in gushing streams from every pore. Her ears were ringing to the point of deafness, and she wondered if she would ever hear again. As if in answer, a long growling howl rose on the wind. One final pop of light, distinct against a background babble of singing, chanting voices, came as a complete statement, *the cursed one returns.* Then with a bone-shuddering thunderclap they were gone, and all was silent. The rain was slackening, and, in fact, was now no more than a drizzle.

Alice got to her knees, trembling. Electricity still flickered along her arms, down her spine, and over her skin; she could have stayed there forever, unmoving, an attuned receiver longing for yet dreading the next broadcast. Sharp howlings and snarlings issued from the direction of the pond, breaking the spell. Behind her, the door slammed and Nik came down the stairs, his high-beam camper's flashlight stabbing at the shadows around the house pilings. Dawg was right behind him, barking in a continuous stream of ear-piercing yarks.

Alice stood up, shivering and drenched. The luminous shadows were gone, but the atmosphere felt thick; she couldn't get enough oxygen, and there was a funny tang to the air, like ozone.

"Alice?" Nik came out into the yard, and she could see that he held the pistol in his other hand. "I heard the howling. You'd better get upstairs," he said, looking at her with concern.

"Nik, wait—"

"Just stay inside." He pushed her toward the stairs and headed off in the direction of the pond trail.

"Wait! You don't know what you're doing!"

But he was already into the trees, Dawg at his heels. Alice turned and raced up the stairs. Inside, Margaret was huddled on the couch with a blanket up to her chin.

"I've got something to tell you," Alice said, breathless. She sat down beside Margaret, heedless of her soaked clothing.

"I saw them. I ... touched them."

"Which them?" Margaret whispered.

"Wandjinas. They came on the storm ... maybe they were the storm, or caused it. Doesn't matter, they've gone now. But I don't think they mean to harm us ... it felt like they were looking for something, or someone. They called to me ... told me to make a bridge, whatever that is."

Margaret sat up straight. "You talked to 'em?"

"Sort of. Not in words, just an instant knowing, in my head. I can't explain it."

Margaret was now very excited. "Well it's obvious – they were after the Quinkan!"

Alice's mind was churning. "Maybe ...."

A pistol shot cracked and was followed by several more.

"Nik," she breathed.

"He can't kill it that way," said Margaret.

Alice put her good arm around her daughter and drew her close. She was too drained and frightened to get up and change her clothes, or even to kick off her sodden shoes. What if Nik didn't return? How would she defend the two of them against the unknown?

She wasn't sure what she had done to trigger this nightmare, but she now had no doubt that Cadjer Harrow and his minions weren't going to disappear just because she wanted them to. She hadn't an inkling of what it would take to make them go, but her experience with the Wandjinas now had her convinced of one thing: it was all of a piece. All those things she and Margaret had written down on their list of unexplainables were connected.

The front door burst open, and Nik came in, white-faced.

"Did you get it?" she asked, knowing the question was foolish.

"I don't know ... I shot something ...." He put his gun on the bookcase and shut and locked the door.

Dazed, he came toward them, and Alice moved over so that all three of them were squeezed together on the couch.

"Didja see it?" Margaret asked.

"I saw something," he said, unable to put a name to a thing that didn't exist in his reality.

Alice took his hand, glad of its solidity.

"I followed the noises to the swamp ... and just like you described it, a huge black dog of some sort was down there. Dawg charged it, but it caught him by the scruff and tossed him aside. I cornered it at the edge of the pond. I put the gun up, and the *djävla* thing leaped right for me." He sat silent, reliving the moment.

"What happened?" Alice prompted.

"I pulled the trigger, hit it, got in two more shots, and then there was no body. I'm telling you, I felt the damn thing's paws hit my chest, and then it wasn't there."

"I believe you."

He was shaking his head, unable to come to terms with the evidence of his senses. "I shot something, but what?"

"I told you," said Margaret. "We've all seen it now. We're a team."

He looked at her, the expression on his face more upsetting than the tale he'd just told. It was the face of a man staring through an open door into the land of nightmare where normal rules didn't apply. "Tell me again."

Margaret repeated the legend of Gaiya the Devil Dingo, and all she had gleaned about Quinkan spirits from the Internet. Then she turned to Alice. "You need to tell him your part of the story, too."

"Agreed. Although I've changed my mind about some of it."

"You were standing out in the middle of the yard in the pouring rain," he said. "What was that all about?"

"I saw ... a vision. Or maybe they were real – who the hell knows what the difference is anymore? I saw Wandjina spirits, first just one, then a bunch of them up above the trees in the rain, and then they came down and filled the clearing in front of the house." Alice could hardly believe she was saying this with a straight face.

"You're not talking about a hallucination, are you?" Nik sat slumped over, completely out of his depth.

"I know what I experienced, and it was not what I would call hallucinating, in the clinical sense of the word. I do think," she continued, choosing her words carefully, "that our physical reality is the tip of the iceberg. I am coming to believe that there's an unseen reality beyond our five senses and that sometimes, like now, the two can bleed into each other. These beings, entities, are as real as we are, but they don't exist in our plane, if that makes any sense."

Nik rubbed his temples. "It makes no sense, but keep going – I'm still listening."

"That fact that we can perceive them at all is shocking. It's something people with special abilities – shamans or wise women or holy men or psychics, whatever – can do, but most people shut it out and never let themselves get to a place where they can ... hear the broadcast. That's the best way I can describe it. I've been hearing it for months now, but wouldn't admit it."

"Who's broadcasting?" he asked. "And please don't tell me it's aliens."

Alice allowed herself a small laugh. "What's on the other side of our reality? Anything that's strange could be called 'alien.' But no, I wasn't thinking of little grays in spaceships. I meant a consciousness from the non-physical realm, wherever that is."

"The Ancestor Spirits of the Dreamtime," said Margaret.

Nik was starting to get his wits back. "Well, you're not an Aboriginal, Margaret, and neither is your mom. How come this devil-dog is stalking you?"

"All I know," said Alice," is that this all started when the Aboriginal art exhibit rolled into town. I've checked back through reviews and news stories of the *Land of Legends* show in all the places it's been before here, and nothing the least bit strange or questionable has been reported. Not one thing. So why here? What's the connection?"

"We got three links," Margaret said. She ticked them off on her fingers. "The Quinkan that comes out of my closet, the exhibit that brought the Wandjinas, and Mom's book."

"I'm not following," said Nik. "Unless you've changed it completely, I thought the book was about local history, not Australia."

"It's the Quinkan that ties everything together," said Margaret. "The main guy in Mom's book, that man I thought was an Indian in the woods, has a big black dog. We've all seen it, and Mom and I saw the man, too."

"But what's the connection?" he persisted.

Margaret's expression narrowed, her eyes black. "I think that preacher from the book has got a Quinkan, or it's got him."

"A ghost dog," said Nik. Alice could tell from his expression that he thought the idea ridiculous, but he wasn't laughing. "I don't know ... maybe I was too keyed up, and it jumped over my head or something."

"Don't try to explain it away."

"But I can't accept the supernatural as an explanation. I just can't." He massaged his temples as if trying to rub out the image that threatened to unhinge everything he believed about the known world.

Alice realized that her shoulder was killing her, and the pinched muscles along her neck and back were cranking into a major headache.

"All right then, don't believe," she snapped, and got up, shucking off her damp jacket and kicking her shoes out into the living room floor. "Maybe in the daylight somebody will find the damn thing lying dead in the woods. But I doubt it. I assume Dawg is okay?"

"I felt him for broken bones, but he seems all right. He limped home behind me. He went into the laundry room and curled up on his bed."

"Smart dog."

She left them sitting there and went to the bathroom to brush her teeth and gulp her remaining painkillers. All she wanted to do at the moment was crawl under the covers and sleep for a month.

Nik followed her to bed, and they lay in the dark listening to each other breathe. At last he rolled over, and his breathing became deeper and more regular. Typically, Nik slept like the dead, with his chest barely rising and no sound at all, not even a tiny snore. At first it had unnerved her, but now she was thankful for it. Alice continued to stare at the square of the window, nearly invisible at first but turning gray as the hours inched toward daylight. She was unbelievably fatigued and her head ached; finally she began to yawn.

Running through a plowed field, her heels dug in and kicked grit up the back of her legs. It was too dangerous out in the open, she had to find cover. Men on horseback, she could hear them coming ... there was nowhere to hide. She spotted the dark shape of an abandoned tobacco barn at the far end of the field and ran like the wind, barely slipping inside the sagging barn door in time. She hit the floor, lying motionless and out of breath in the shadows as the unseen menace passed outside. Her breath came in violent, trembling gasps, but at least she was safe.

Suddenly, heavy hollow steps behind her shook the floorboards. It took forever, as if seconds had stretched into centuries, to turn and look up into the burning eyes and sulfurous breath of Cadjer Harrow, mere inches away. Somewhere an iron bell clanged, and his face became a snarling animal with canines the size of a T-Rex rack.

She struggled to wake, trying with all her will to shriek, to bring someone to her rescue. She could feel the scream in her throat as cold hands felt for her windpipe. The screech was escaping anyway, climbing, turning into a keening chant. A summoning? Winds with the force of a typhoon blew over the landscape, taking off the barn roof and sucking everything up into a funnel that roared and crushed all in its vortex like the greatest black hole of all time. Her final fleeting dreamscape image on the event horizon was of a cold, luminous presence regarding her with eyes that were deep wells of starlit space. She could dive into those eyes and be lost forever.

CHAPTER 28

A WEEK later, Alice woke before the clock radio alarm went off and lay in bed thinking. Things had been deceptively quiet since Nik's attempt to kill the demon-dog, but every nerve in her body remained on guard, waiting. They were all on edge, but a veneer of normalcy had settled back over their daily lives as they got up and went to school and to work.

She groaned and rolled out of bed. Six-fifteen and still midnight dark outside on a miserable Wednesday. The sun wouldn't be up until she was halfway to work an hour from now. The house was so cold the windows were frosted. Tiptoeing down the hall to the bathroom, Alice wondered if she would ever be warm again. She hit the light switch and gasped in pain, momentarily blinded by white light over the sink. Sitting down on the closed toilet seat and shading her eyes, she waited for her throbbing retinas to recover. Fumbling for the bathroom heater switch, she flipped it on and shut the door, huddling in front of its red electric glow.

Bad dreams had continued to ruin her sleep since the middle of last week when Nik shot at the dog that wasn't there (the dog that *talked* itself out of trying to kill her), and she felt foggy and lumpish. The specific images from the dreams faded as soon as she woke up, but the anxious, vulnerable feeling they generated remained. The devil-dog's body was nowhere to be found, of course, but it hadn't showed up alive either. She didn't know if that was a good thing or a bad thing, but Nik had convinced himself that he'd scared it off.

The one bright spot in the gray succession of days had come from an unexpected source. Raine called on Sunday, as she'd threatened to do if she didn't hear from Alice pronto after their chance meeting at Pelican's Roost. Nik was asleep on the couch when the call came, so Alice had taken the phone into the study and shut the door. Looking at him there had made her sad; normally Figaro would have been spread out over his stomach in a blanket of yellow tabby fur.

She talked with Raine about superficial things first, skirting the darker issues of killed cats and phantom hounds from hell. Alice didn't have the energy to go into the details of the Camper's Legend book, as she still called it, although she'd referred to it as *Massalina County Mystery* in her book proposals. But they did talk about Margaret's dreams and her own personal list of unexplainables. Raine's response had been guarded, but not disbelieving.

"When you open certain doors, things come through," she'd said.

"But how can we tell when we've opened a door?" Alice had countered. "Some kind of psychic security alarm should go off. And how do we even do it in the first place? That's what I want to know."

"Some people are more 'open' than others," said Raine. "Do you consider yourself a psychic person, Alice?"

"No, not really. I mean, I play around with visualizations and things like that ... but do I channel spirits or have precognitive dreams? I don't think so." She had hesitated before continuing. "But I think Margaret does."

"How does she feel about it? Has she tried to develop these abilities?" Raine had asked.

"We've talked about it some, especially recently. She's convinced the animal thing that keeps showing up in her dreams is a Quinkan spirit from the Australian Dreamtime. I don't know what to think. Could something like that be real, and if it is, why did it latch onto her?"

"Have you seen it, too?"

"No, it only comes to her. But ...."

"But what?"

"I just realized ... if the thing that attacked me is what Margaret says it is, then I have seen it."

There was silence on the phone.

"Raine?"

"I'm listening."

"Well, that's not all. Promise you won't laugh at me ... I think I've seen the Wandjinas. Or something I imagined looked like them. Or nothing. I don't know! I don't know shit anymore."

Surprisingly, Raine's response had been reasonable, comforting even. "Alice, here's what I think you should do. You need to consult an expert—"

"Sorry, Eve already tried to get me to see a shrink. No thanks."

"That's not the kind of expert I had in mind," Raine said evenly. "You need an Aboriginal elder, a wise woman or senior man of high standing."

"Yeah, fine. Know any I can call up?" She immediately regretted having said that, but what other response was there?

"E-mail," said Raine. "You told me Margaret found the info on Quinkans online. Maybe you can do the same to find a clan elder or an Aboriginal scholar who knows what to do. Aren't there any Australian cultural centers with websites? I'd start there."

Alice had sat with the phone in her hand and a look on her face Raine would have appreciated. The advice was so obvious she couldn't believe it. She'd gone to get Margaret, who talked to Raine for at least twenty minutes about psychics, shamans, and the world of the "other." When they got off the phone, Margaret had immediately gone online and begun the search for a guide. In the space of an hour they'd found and sent messages to half a dozen potential experts. So they'd thrown their cry for help into the great cyber-ocean and now were just waiting for someone to find it and send a reply. But in her heart of hearts, Alice didn't expect anything useful to come of it.

A knock on the bathroom door nearly stopped her heart.

"Are you okay? You been in there a long time." It was Margaret.

Alice stood up and opened the door. "Nothing's wrong. Just sitting here thinking, and trying to get warm. You want in?"

"Yeah." Margaret crowded into the small bathroom beside her and crouched down in front of the heater.

"I could just go light the hall heater," Alice said, not moving. "But that would be too easy."

They laughed and leaned against each other for warmth. In the comfort of their bodies held close against the cold, there was the illusion of well-being. It was much better than getting dressed and going to the museum.

At work, Alice had been plodding along in a fog that vacillated between near panic and self-pity. Jessie had communicated and conducted business with her as if nothing had happened between them, but he seemed to keep her at arm's length, taking care not to rub shoulders with her in the elevator or sit beside her at the administrator's meeting. She could only assume it was deliberate.

She didn't expect today would be any better. Both Jessie and Nik had been in her dreams, mixed up with frightening images that lingered on the edge of waking but refused to come with her into the daylight.

She seemed to be losing control, even over ordinary things around her. On Monday her car had refused to crank when she was ready to leave for work, and Nik had jumpstarted it from his truck battery in the freezing predawn air. The engine took its own sweet time sputtering to life, and she was half an hour late to work by the time she dropped Margaret off at school and got out on the highway. Margaret typically rode the bus to and from school, but not now. Alice didn't want her standing out by the roadside in the early morning half-dark waiting for the bus to come, and she likewise didn't want her to come home by herself to an empty house with who knew what lurking in the yard.

"Don't forget to get off the bus with Judy. I already cleared it with her mother. I'll pick you up from her house when I get home."

"Okay."

Alice turned off the electric heater and gave Margaret a squeeze. "Time to get dressed."

She opened the door and went out into the darkened hallway. "Jesus H. Buddha, I hate getting up in the dark. I need a job that lets me work at home."

"Yeah, then you could home-school me, and I wouldn't have to get up either."

"You wish."

Alice wished, as she sat in her office later that morning drinking coffee that was too strong, that she knew how to smoke. People chain-smoked when they were miserable – it emphasized their silent suffering and somehow made it glamorous. It was odd that she both wanted and didn't want anyone to notice how depressed she felt.

"Hey, did you know you only got one light working in your ceiling? It's damn dark in here," said Hannah. She slouched against the doorframe, craning her neck to look up at Alice's office lights.

It was true. All the fluorescent rectangles were dark except one, and it had a subliminal flicker that played with her peripheral vision.

"I know. It's been like that since the holidays. I keep forgetting to let maintenance know."

"How could you forget? You can't see in here."

"It's not that bad."

"It's okay, if you like working in a cave. I saw Jessie in the lobby, and he asked me if your *Marquesa* write-up was ready yet."

"It's not."

Alice felt inertia settling around her shoulders. Maybe the report would never get finished. She nursed the desire to disassociate herself from everything that had to do with the museum. And worse, she was having trouble getting her stalled novel out of her head, although she had no intention of working on it ever again. It seemed appropriate, though. Her mood was as black as the plot.

"You want some advice?" Hannah was still there.

"No."

"He can hurt you and not even notice."

"Who?"

Hannah shrugged and tried without success to cross her arms over her generous breasts. "Nobody, I guess."

"I'll see what I can do to get that report finished. I've done all the research. I just need to pull it together." She got up and refilled her cup. "Want some?"

Hannah studied the toes of her boots. Whatever she was thinking stayed hidden. "Nope, I'll be in the break room if you need me. Come have a doughnut."

"Thanks, I might do that."

Hannah went away, and the office was quiet again. What to do? She'd already checked her e-mail a dozen times, but there was no response from anyone. She got up and forwarded her phone to the museum store. Faye was always willing to have somebody distract her from working.

She got off the elevator and walked out into the carpeted lobby with its gray plush furniture. Nobody ever sat on it that she could tell, but it looked impressive. Endowed by a private foundation and with generous public support, the Hardison could afford such amenities.

At a glance, the souvenir shop appeared empty, but Alice pushed the door open anyway, and then went no further – the voices she heard from the back of the store stopped her cold.

"Here's your watch, careless," said Faye. "You left it in the bathroom."

"And what were you doing in the men's bathroom?" Jessie's voice had a throaty edge to it Alice had never heard before.

"Gene found it and asked me who it belonged to. You want it?" Alice leaned forward just enough to see them standing beside the rack of T-rex T-shirts that came in ten sizes and as many colors. Faye held the watch up to him. He didn't take it from her, but instead just held out his wrist. Alice felt her throat constrict as Faye took hold of his arm. She turned his hand over and pushed up the sleeve of his old university sweatshirt. Then she buckled the watch in place.

Alice was hardly breathing. She wanted to get the hell out of there, but kept watching. He put his hand on the shelf beside Faye's shoulder and leaned close to tell her something that made her smile with a sly, flirty expression. Even with her shoes off she was tall enough to look him directly in the eyes, maybe even a little taller. She said something back and ducked under his arm. He turned to follow her, smiling. That was enough. Alice came to life and fled across the lobby and down the main gallery ramp before they came out.

The ancient Australians towered around her in silent witness to her humiliation. Jessie was interested in Faye! How stupid of her to imagine he would even spare a moment's attention on a divorced woman with a half-grown kid. Where were her brains? Dropped off a cliff with her self-respect.

She went into the exhibit and stalked through the maze of art and artifacts, ending up in front of the Wandjina panel, staring up into the sightless eyes of the ghostly figures. Had they really come to her in the rain? It was unthinkable, but she remembered quite well what she had seen and heard, and felt. There was no way to forget the momentary shockwave that passed between them when she reached out her hand.

"Why?" she said aloud, looking up at them. On the opposite wall, the Quinkans waited. Walking toward the pool of light in front of the Split Rock mural, she stepped over the velvet rope that separated visitors from the exhibit. A quick look around assured her that she had the room to herself. Alice took a deep breath and, reaching over her head, pressed her palms against its smooth surface, fitting her fingers to the black stenciled shapes of forty-thousand-year-old hands. Breathless, she waited, vaguely aware of the sacrilege this act represented. She was uninitiated, not a wise woman, not part of a clan, not even the right ethnicity. Not even a believer, she might have said a month ago, but now this last attribute no longer applied.

Within seconds, the room was filled with subterranean rumbling, as of boulders rolling and crashing in the swell of an avalanche. The room swayed and the panels swung dizzily from their ceiling chains, the brass pedestals with their velvet ropes falling and clattering against each other as Alice steadied herself for the electrical shock she expected to experience again. Instead, a tremendous booming thunderclap exploded between her ears, knocking her sprawling across the floor and into the ropes. She recognized the familiar taste of ozone on the air; rolling over, she stared up into the fathomless gaze of the Lightning Man.

The room went black. Was she dead? Then gradually the lights flickered and returned, revealing the marble tiles of the gallery floor where she lay face down. Alice crouched like an animal, completely deafened and shaking as if naked in a snowbank. She felt her face with her hand; it seemed solid enough. She wasn't sure what had just happened, but one thing seemed apparent – the powers weren't hers to command.

The lights came back on, but dimmer. Getting to her feet, Alice realized with horror that in her fright or whatever had just happened, several metal rope stands had fallen over, causing a three-foot artifact pedestal to topple as well. Carefully she put it upright and replaced the wooden dingo sculpture that had sat on it. Nothing appeared to be damaged, but it was such a close call her knees were trembling. Her injured shoulder was in agony.

Alice went quickly back to her office without meeting anyone, which was damned lucky because she felt like a bullet in the chamber ready to go off. This was edge city ... better be careful. She started to sit down at her desk, but there was a message taped to her chair. It was from Shelton, requesting her to stop by his office as soon as it was convenient. Alice stared at the note, written in Pilar's hand. How could he already know what happened in the gallery? Was she about to be fired for negligence? That wasn't logical – she shook her head to get the cobwebs out. It must be something else.

Shelton's office was at the opposite end of the long hallway from hers, and this afternoon it seemed dim, as if the power were heading toward a brownout. What were the odds, she wondered, that all the fluorescent tubes in the building could blow out at the same time? No less likely than anything else she had just seen.

"Alice. Please come in." She closed the door softly behind her. Not that Pilar in the outer office didn't already know everything there was to know about how the museum was run, but if this was going to be bad news, at least it was going to be delivered in private.

Passing up the chair across from Shelton's desk, she chose one beside his park-view window and sat down. Rain swirled and beat against the glass, and she could see it pooling around the curb in the street below.

Shelton cleared his throat. "I just wanted to ask how you've been. I know you had an injury recently."

He waited, as if she should be able to read his mind and know how to respond appropriately. She smiled and said nothing.

"I just wondered if you felt fully recovered."

"I guess so," she answered. "Why?"

"You just seem ... worn down, a little on edge perhaps?"

Alice blinked. He must be referring to her snappish contribution to Monday's shipwreck strategy meeting.

"I just wanted to suggest," he continued, "that you take the rest of the week off, if you need to. The *Marquesa*'s not going anywhere. We have plenty of time to get things in order, and the *Land of Legends* exhibit is doing fine."

She nodded. So he didn't know she'd knocked a piece of it over.

"Well, that's all I wanted to say. Just take care of yourself."

"That's very considerate of you," she said, and then added, "A few days off might help. I'll think about it."

"I hope you will. You're valuable to the museum, and I want you to be happy here."

"So do I," she said. Was he reading her mind? Time to get out. She smiled and backed out of his office, escaping into the empty hallway.

She thought about going back down to check on the gallery, just in case it looked amiss. The elevator door hissed open when she pressed DOWN, revealing a darkened cage. Either something was definitely wrong with the electricity or she was manifesting some cloud of misery that followed her throughout the building. She hated elevators, but this was testing her limit. Fighting panic, she got in and punched MAIN, praying for a safe flight as the lights flickered on the way down and her stomach did acrobatics. Finally the car thumped to a stop with no harm done. She got off and rubbed at the knotted muscles across the back of her neck.

"Hey, Madam Curator." Victor lounged near the entrance, hands in his pockets and an unpleasant grin on his rat's face. "Good thing you weren't in there when the power went out."

"What?"

"The storm. Blew out all the lights for a few seconds. We're running on generator power right now.

"Really."

"Yeah, didn't you hear the thunder? Lightning must have hit a transformer close by. It shook the whole building."

Alice walked across the lobby and looked out into the street. The main fury of the storm seemed to have passed, but it was still raining steadily, with water pouring down the street and foaming in whirlpools around the storm drain at the corner. It was a good thing she'd decided to pick Margaret up at Judy's. If she'd had to walk the length of the driveway to the house she would have gotten soaked. In fact, if it rained like this tomorrow and Friday, the last thing Alice wanted to do was be out in it.

She ducked into the receptionist's office.

"Mind if I use your phone for a minute?" she asked the intern behind the desk. She dialed the extension and waited, biting her lip.

"Shelton? This is Alice. You know that leave time we were talking about? I've decided to take it."

CHAPTER 29

THE RAIN had slowed to a light drizzle, but still Alice found the drive out of town slowed by traffic making its way around flooded intersections. Conditions weren't much better until she'd reached Magnolia Parkway. She pulled up into the sandy yard in front of Judy's house and honked. Margaret waved from the porch and came running through ankle-deep puddles. She pounced into the passenger seat.

"Can we stop somewhere? I'm starving!"

"Like where?"

"Anywhere. I'll die if I have to ride home on an empty stomach."

Alice was annoyed – now that she'd officially gotten the next two days off, she couldn't wait to get home.

"How about the fast food place on 87? It's not that far," Margaret said.

"Actually, that's several miles out of the way."

"Pleeeze?"

"If that's what you really want. But you owe me."

Margaret flashed her a quick grin. "Thanks, Mom."

Alice sighed and aimed the car toward State Road 87 and its waiting burger joint.

Margaret inhaled her cheeseburger, chocolate shake, and fries and added their containers to the garbage bag overflowing in the back seat. Trash had been accumulating for days through Alice's indifference, and now it threatened to turn her beautiful car into a redneck jalopy.

"Satisfied?" Alice asked. "Can we go home now?"

"Um hm." Margaret was licking her lips.

Alice watched with dismay as she kicked off her wet shoes and pulled her feet up underneath her. Surrounded by rancid French fry and wet tennis shoe smells, Alice flew down the highway and turned at the church crossroads, tires squealing momentarily on the rain-slick asphalt. The skies had cleared for a brief stretch of the trip, but now the clouds were bunching up and starting to sprinkle again. They were just passing the county roadside dump site when Alice suddenly put on brakes and began to back up.

"Mom, what are you doing?"

Margaret turned around in the seat and looked out the back window. Alice was aiming the car across the road to the sandy margin in front of the dump.

"I'm gonna shovel out this garbage pit of a car."

She opened the door and got out. The smell surrounding the dump was incredible, somewhere between three-day-old dead armadillos and overripe bananas. A squadron of flies zoomed through the open car door and bumped back and forth against the back windows in furious confusion. She grabbed a fistload of trash and kicked the door shut. The boxcar designated for household garbage was situated at the bottom of a shallow, sloping trench, but even so the container's sides were too high to pitch the stuff into. Instead, she tossed it down toward the open pit underneath the rusting floor of the boxcar and started back for another load when a sharp whining near the top of the trash heap made her stop. She listened intently but couldn't hear it again. Sometimes heartless people abandoned kittens and puppies at the dump; she would have done anything to try to save them. But there were no yippings and mewings, now that she was paying attention. In fact, nothing was stirring up and down the long empty stretch of road. Not even a passing car. She went around to Margaret's side and opened the door.

"Hand me the rest of that shit, will you?"

"Hurry, Mom, my nose is getting jungle rot."

"I'm hurrying," she snapped, and a few more flies sailed through the open door.

Carrying the last of the trash in both hands, she picked her way over the tin can lids and rain-soaked diseased carpeting to the edge of the dump site, tossing the paper bags up and barely over the side of the boxcar. Then she stood for a minute in the drizzle, just listening.

It was so quiet. A hawk cried overhead and soared across the open dump to a sheltering stand of pines a hundred yards down the road. With no cars in sight, the only sounds were the faraway swish of pines with the rain in their branches. Behind the dump, a fallow peanut field stretched for a flat mile or two away from the road, abutting the pines on its southern boundary. Beyond the trees and around a bend in the road, she knew, was the mechanic's garage and just beyond that the intersection with the parkway that went past Black Creek Ferry Road. They were almost home.

Across the road from the car were dense trees and an abandoned shack overgrown by kudzu vines. Nothing moved. She had been sort of holding her breath and breathing in shallow gulps, trying not to inhale the fetid air, but finally had to refill her lungs and instantly noticed an acrid tang that rode the breeze, lancing through the rancid garbage smell: ozone ... electrical discharge ... lightning. Her skin prickled. She hurried back to the car and got in, locking the door.

"Lock, please," she said to Margaret, pointing to the passenger door and trying to keep her voice level. She forced the key into the ignition with trembling fingers and cranked. The engine turned sluggishly but didn't fire. Alice began to sweat. She put one foot on the brake pedal, pressed the accelerator flat to the floorboard with the other, and tried again. The starter ground as before, more slowly this time. She tried a third time, pumping the gas pedal.

"Don't do this to me," she muttered in a fury. Margaret watched her, silent and frightened. She concentrated all her energies on the stubborn car, but the gas wasn't igniting and the starter was turning the crankshaft ever more slowly, running the battery down.

"Mom ...."

Alice's look silenced her. Trying to stay calm and think clearly, Alice remembered the car had done this same act last week and had to be jump-started. She was obviously going to have to get help. She dug her cell phone out of her purse and punched it on. When the low-bat light began flashing, she barely heard Margaret's whispered "uh oh," because she was busy mentally kicking herself. She'd known the phone needed charging, but it kept getting pushed out of her mind by other things. Now, because of her stupidity and carelessness, they were in a potentially dangerous situation.

"Sweetie, listen. This is very important." Alice put her hand on Margaret's shoulder. The girl felt like a bundle of sticks, she was so slightly built; the idea of leaving her in the car alone was unthinkable, yet that's exactly what she was about to do.

"Somehow I have to call a wrecker, or Nik, if I can get him, so ... I'll just run down to the store at the corner and get help."

"I want to go with you."

"No, now listen—"

"I won't stay here by myself."

"It's safer if you stay here with the doors locked. It's starting to rain

271

again and I need to run really fast, so I can't worry about you falling behind."

"I can keep up."

"No, you'll start wheezing, and I can't stop and wait for you to catch up."

Margaret's mouth was settling into a pout, but Alice could tell she had given in.

"I'll run fast – it won't take me five minutes to get there." She was feeling around behind her seat for her athletic shoes, left in the car from her last trip to the gym in town, which seemed light years ago now.

Margaret watched in silence as Alice put them on. Her fingers were trembling so badly she wasted several minutes trying to get the laces tied. The sun was just above the tree line, so she'd have to hurry.

"Promise me you won't move a muscle until I get back."

"Okay."

Margaret's voice was barely audible. Alice could tell from her face that she was terrified at the idea, but would comply. Alice put her hand on the door handle, and tears stung at the corners of her eyes. Margaret was the world's best kid. Alice vowed to make it up to her somehow if they could just get through this.

"Try the car again, Mom, just to see," Margaret pleaded. She was scrunched down in the seat, making herself tiny.

"All right. Just once more."

Alice pressed the brake, turned the key, and all they got was a slow whump-whump as the battery lost its charge. Alice opened the door and got out.

"Just stay inside and keep the doors locked."

She judged the distance to Coastal Small Engine Repair at maybe less than a mile. Jogging with Nik down their dirt road in mock competition, they could easily do eight-minute miles. This was no different, and right now she had every reason to burn it. Cold rain was falling lightly, plastering her thin jacket and slacks to her body, but she ignored the discomfort.

She began running along the sandy margin of the road, watching her feet to avoid tripping over discarded bottles and small gullies where runoff had undermined the pavement. She concentrated on her breathing, in-out, in-out, and was passing into the shadows alongside the pines when she heard the faint rhythm of something else pacing her off to the left. She ran faster, and was gasping for breath now, the cold air scraping her lungs raw. What did that sound remind her of?

It was paralleling her course, and then she knew – she'd heard it in the museum vault. Horses galloping, a distant rumble of hooves like a foxhunt still some length down the course but gaining on the prey every second. Running full out, Alice leaped a roll of rusted fencing wire lying across her path and nearly went down. Sheer momentum kept her from falling, and she pounded on, spotting the garage just up ahead. With its weathered walls and brick chimney poking up from the tin roof, it more closely resembled a turn-of-the-century schoolhouse than a mechanic's shop. It had obviously been other things before the engine repair folks moved in.

Stumbling into the sandy yard in front of the garage, she saw a couple of old cars and a herd of motorcycles crowded together in the tiny parking lot, blocking access to the door. Alice flopped down on the top step and nearly doubled over, gasping for air. She was dripping wet and couldn't have run another step.

Margaret crawled into the back seat and hunched down, her eyes barely level with the window. She could still see the sky, but the road was invisible. Except for the noxious sight of the dump on her left, the scene could have been peaceful, beautiful even, with pine boughs washed deeply green and thin streaks of sunlight silhouetting the massive clouds on her right.

She sat very still, her mind focused. She was building a wall of light around her mother, enclosing her in an orb of protection from which she could operate and find a way to get them both home safely. She concentrated totally on this image, blocking out any fear or negative thoughts that might intrude and taint the image of her intent. Her breathing was so slow and light that she felt herself slipping into a state of mind that wasn't sleep but wasn't quite awake either. She even ceased to be aware of the flies bumping against the windows.

"That won't do any good, you know."

The Quinkan was in the seat beside her, in the form of a frilled lizard. Its long tongue flicked out and struck two flies in one blindingly fast slap. Licking its lips, it crawled up onto the headrest of the driver's seat and cocked its head at Margaret.

"You're not listening. I said it wouldn't do any good, all that white light stuff. Waste of time." Its tongue flicked out and tasted her cheek.

Margaret jumped and pressed herself against the seat, as far away as she could get from the fanged mouth and glittering reptilian eyes. Somewhere in the back of her brain was the thought that lizards shouldn't have teeth like that, but she supposed a Quinkan could look anyway it wanted to.

"I really would like to eat you now," it said, its thin tail lashing the upholstery. It clung to the headrest with clawed feet, pulsing red and dark muddy brown. "I'm very tired of this game," it hissed, "and think I should just like to collect you and be gone. If not for him, I should have had you long ago." Its body grew a couple of inches in length and leaned in toward Margaret, its mouth agape. It hopped onto her lap.

The sprint in the damp and cold had done Alice in. She was wheezing badly, but since her inhaler was locked in the car with her purse, she'd just have to endure it. Spare change and car keys clacked around in the zippered pocket of her jacket, but that was all she'd carried with her. It didn't matter, she just needed to get someone on the phone, maybe even Raine or Tim, and then this mess would get sorted out. She stood up, climbed the plank steps to the narrow porch, and pushed the door open. It was warm inside. She looked around for someone to ask if there was a phone she could use, only something wasn't right. There was a black pot-bellied wood stove in the way. Several men were backed up to it, hands hooked in their galluses, cheeks packed with tobacco. They regarded her as if she were an intruder from another galaxy.

"I need to use the phone," she said, looking around. The back wall was covered in farm implements from a past era: tribbles, froes, hand reapers, crosscut saws. It was like looking at the Hardison's pioneer exhibit shown last Fourth of July. She had stopped in here a year or so ago to have Whit's old riding mower repaired, and it hadn't looked like this at all. How could they have made such radical changes in the place? Instead of the racks of newspapers she remembered up front, a round iron-strapped barrel filled with oats occupied the space. A huge coil of rope lay on the counter next to a steel cashbox, no electronic register in sight.

"What you wantin'?" A man stepped from behind the counter.

By his attitude, he seemed to be in charge, but he was not the person she knew to be the owner of the garage. A twining snake design incised into the coal black skin of his face twitched as he approached. He stood a good foot taller than anyone else in the room. Staring at him, Alice suddenly knew who this was, and the realization made her light-headed. She tried to croak some response, but it was strangled by her labored breathing. Heart thudding against the walls of her chest, she ran to the door and found the way blocked by a figure clothed in the somber garb of a church deacon. Lathe.

"Get out of my way!" she shouted, forcing the sound out of her aching lungs, and fought to get past him. He took hold of her jacket, trapping her between his body and the frame of the door. He looked at her with an expression that suggested things no sane person would contemplate.

"What manner of woman is this who dresses like a man?" he said to the others, who moved in closer. She realized that all the members of Harrow's inner circle, referred to as the Hand in his hellish notebook, were present and accounted for. All that was missing was Harrow himself. Alice struggled to free herself from his grip, and just when she had decided to aim a swift knee at his trouser bulge, inexplicably he opened the door and tossed her outside.

"I yield, she's yours. I was just havin' a little sport," he said to no one she could see.

His laughter boomed at her back as she leaped down the steps and then tripped over an object lying at the bottom in the mud. It was a body.

Alice felt like the ground was tilting, she was sliding, and there was such an awful ringing in her ears, sounding the alarm that too much blood had suddenly drained from her brain. She stared in shock at the crumpled form, a thin young black girl in a faded gunnysack dress with bloodstains across the hem. With horrified fascination, Alice reached out and turned the cold face up to the fading light ... and screamed. The face was that of Belinda Rider.

"Timara! Help, Timara!" Margaret yelped, scrambling into the front seat, away from the scythlike claws of the Quinkan.

"You shut up!" it hissed.

"TimaraTimaraTimara!!" Margaret shrieked, her eyes never leaving the Quinkan's face.

She watched in terror as its reptile grin began to morph into a pointed canine snout. Its body swelled out into a round bloated little piggish creature with tiny stick legs, the hair ridge along its back stiff and brindled in color. It landed with a plop into the driver's seat. Its eyes were deep blood red, like little twinkling garnets.

"Stop that!" it barked. It was growing, changing before her eyes into Gaiya, the devil-dog.

A sudden movement outside the car, just at the edge of its sloping hood, distracted the Quinkan for a moment. Margaret caught a glimpse of it as well; it seemed to her that the merest of shadows passed outside the driver's door. Without hesitation, she unlocked the passenger side and leaped out, slamming the door on the dingo's snarling snout. For a fraction of a second, a shape like a tall, impossibly thin child's stick drawing appeared in front of her, but when she blinked it was gone. The car, however, was filled with the most frightful yowls and screeches. The dingo shape was rolling around, thrashing and lashing about with its talons in all directions, rending the seat and lunging against the windshield. Margaret gasped as hoof beats thundered past in a whirlwind, and then just as suddenly, she was completely alone in a silent stillpoint where nothing moved and there was no sound. The trees and fields faded, the car was no more, and she stood naked in the dancing light of flames leaping into the night sky somewhere, sometime, far away.

In blind terror, Alice stumbled back over the body of Belinda Rider and fell to her knees. Where were the cars and motorcycles? The sandy ground in front of the shop was empty, with nothing but a hitching post in front of the steps. Lurching to her feet, she ran back out to the road just in time to see riders coming out of the trees about halfway between the building and the pine grove. They slowed to a trot and the lead rider seemed to sit taller in the saddle, as if searching for something. They crossed the road and came at a trot toward the shop, the riders still questing as for an unseen quarry. Then the leader waved his arm in an arc and they sprinted forward, responding to a single unspoken command. There was no place to hide; she couldn't go back inside and couldn't stay where she was, out in the open.

Darting into a thicket of yaupon and smilax on the far side of the building, she couldn't tell if they had actually seen her or not, but she crouched down in the thorny foliage like a hare, heart banging against her ribs, and not moving a muscle. A feeling of déjà vu coursed through her, and she remembered – this was how she'd felt in the dream, hiding in the old tobacco barn while an unseen menace searched for her outside. Only here she was in the flesh, in what seemed reality but wasn't, in fear for her life.

The horses cantered up to the storefront, splashing through deep puddles. She could see their muddy hooves dancing around as they converged on the spot. The riders dismounted and clumped up the steps into the building, slamming the wooden door after them.

Alice held her breath and waited while the riderless horses continued to mill around in the mud. Knowing she must run now, she bolted from the underbrush, scrambling for heart-stopping seconds in loose rocks underfoot and spooking the horses further. She could see up close how wild they were, with whites of their eyes showing, nostrils flaring, ears laid flat against their sweating necks. Their tangled tails and manes were matted with burrs and twigs, as if they'd been ridden through hell and back. A tremendous roan stallion reared and screamed, snorting and pawing frost from the air.

But Alice was already yards down the road when a coarse voice yelled out the door at the animal. Her lungs were bursting as she made it back to the car in the fastest sprint she had ever done. Digging frantically in her pocket for the keys and finally wrenching the door open, she threw herself into the driver's seat and felt her heart stop. The car was empty, and the upholstery shredded. She sat stunned and breathless, completely done in.

Slowly the passenger door opened and Margaret got into the car, sitting down slowly with a careful placement of arms and legs, clasping her hands together in her lap.

"Sorry about the seat," she said simply. "I didn't know they would fight it out in the car."

"Who?"

"The Quinkans, the Imjim and the Timara. The one that's been after me is an Imjim, the bad kind, and when it was suddenly here in the car with me, I just somehow started calling for the other kind, the good Quinkan. And it came."

"Where are they now?" Alice was shaking, but amazingly, she could see that Margaret appeared as calm as if they were discussing plans for dinner.

"I stood outside the car while they were thrashing around and then they disappeared when the hoof beats came through."

Alice felt lightheaded. "Did you see them ... the horsemen?"

Margaret shook her head. "Just heard sounds of horses galloping, and the wind started blowing, bending the trees, and then everything was gone." She stared at Alice with wide black eyes. "I went somewhere else. I met somebody, or, I was somebody. She sent the Timara. But I don't think the Imjim is gone for good. I think it will take something more powerful than another Quinkan to banish it."

Alice swallowed back tears. Her immediate urge was to let go of everything and crush her child to her chest in relief, but that could come later, once they were safely at home. She put the key in the ignition and cranked the car. It came to life smoothly, as if it had never balked or failed to serve.

"Did you call anybody?" Margaret asked. The grocery store episode flooded back, and once again Alice felt fear clenching her gut.

"No," she said. "But I'll tell you about it after we get home."

Pulling onto the blacktop, she gunned the car straight down the road, intending to plow through whatever obstacles might be waiting at the corner. But when the garage flew by, there were no horses or riders or hitching posts. A few old cars and lawnmowers were rusting in the weeds beside the building, and all the motorcycles were gone from the tiny paved parking area. The shop appeared closed; the lights weren't on inside, although it was nearly dark.

Alice eased her foot off the gas and braked for the turn, unanswerable questions crowding her head. How could she have hallucinated the entire episode that had just taken place? She wasn't that far gone, she hoped. She could have invented the feeling of danger at the dump or the sounds of pursuit through the pine grove, but damn it, those horses in front of the shop seemed real enough, and she couldn't explain away the interior of the garage and the people who spoke to her. Worse, though, was the dead girl. She had tripped over the body. Whatever it was, it had been horribly physical for that moment.

Alice cut a quick glance at Margaret. "Are you feeling all right?"

"Yeah. But I need to think about something."

They rode the rest of the way home in silence.

CHAPTER 30

NIK SET his tea to brew and stoked the fire until flames spiraled up the flue, shedding a cascade of bright sparks. Deeply disturbed, he neatly restacked the printed pages Alice had left him to read. He didn't know if it was any good from a literary standpoint since fiction was not his usual reading fare, but some things in the plot were a cause for concern. It didn't bother him that Alice had created those images and put them on paper – what chilled him was the fact that she thought the characters, especially the guy who appeared to be the main villain, were real and possibly stalking her.

"What you do you think, fella, are we being haunted?" He sat on the floor beside Dawg, who had been allowed inside to recuperate on a fireside pallet improvised from an old bedspread. Dawg's limp had not gone away since the fight in the woods, and the bite marks on his neck were beginning to look bad, so Nik had taken him to the vet for an x-ray and a rabies shot. As it turned out, he had a broken toe and infected punctures, so they returned home with antibiotics and a warning to keep him inside for the next few days.

Nik sat staring into the fire, trying to put his thoughts in order. He would have liked to call his father in Stockholm, but didn't know what he would say once he got him on the line. The old man was technology phobic and not available by e-mail, so that option was out. His father was a Lutheran minister and the chief reason Nik had adopted an atheist's outlook early in life. Nevertheless, their relationship was cordial, and Nik relied on him occasionally for advice. His parents knew he was involved with a nice professional woman with a child from an ex-marriage, but that was all. He didn't confide in them much, which was just as well. What he was thinking at the moment would only upset them.

He was feeling resentful and a little selfish. Alice had seemed like the perfect fit for a lot of reasons, and Margaret was no impediment to their relationship; in fact, he liked her and enjoyed interacting with her, so it irked him that this supernatural element had come suddenly into their lives and screwed everything. He thought he loved Alice, but what was he to make of her conviction that they had been invaded by the paranormal? And indeed, what was he to make of that little episode down by the pond? He replayed in his mind for the hundredth time every detail of the event, from the abnormal size of the beast, to the reddish light that flamed up in its eyes as it charged him, to the weight of it on his chest, to its evaporation into … nothingness. How could matter unmake itself before his very eyes, matter that was solid enough to leave lasting injuries on his real dog? What would his father call such a thing – a devil? Was the Aboriginal Dreamtime terminology Margaret used any less accurate than a Christian label? For once, he was philosophically over his head.

He had tried to rationalize the experience in M-space terms, assuming that if there were parallel universes whose rippling membranes got close enough to touch and create clumps of matter spawning what some people still called the Big Bang, who was to say it couldn't also allow realities from the converging universes to bleed into each other, like particles streaming through a tear in the fabric? Physicists didn't understand how cosmic membranes interacted and whether they were the answer to the ever-elusive theory of everything, but it was one of the better working models they had. With a little mental shoving, he could twist it around to apply to his current dilemma, but he didn't feel satisfied with it.

One thing he was clear about, however: two people he cared about deeply were in physical danger of some kind. Alice's shoulder injury was pretty damned real. He would try to protect them in any way possible, even if it meant putting himself in danger … that much he was sure of. As for the rest, he would just have to see.

He was glad Alice had called him earlier in the day with the news that she was taking Thursday and Friday off. That was good; he thought all along that she had gone back to work too soon after the dog attack. At least somebody at the museum had the good sense to send her home.

Dawg raised his head and gave a questioning whuff.

Nik got to his feet. "Just stay put; it's only the ladies returning, I think."

He turned on the porch light and went to meet them on the landing. Alice appeared somber but quite happy to see him and put her arms around him as soon as she reached the doorway. He did the same, carefully avoiding squeezing her shoulders too hard. Margaret quickly disappeared into her room and shut the door.

"You know what I want?" Alice said, pulling him inside.

Her face was so drawn and pale, Nik's guard went up.

"I want to heat up a huge frozen pizza, eat it in front of the TV with the dumbest sitcom playing, and then curl up on the couch with a fire in the fireplace and my lover in my arms like a normal person. Is that too much to ask?"

Nik laughed, relieved. "I think all of that can be accommodated. Sit down on the couch; I'll take care of the rest. Ah, I hope you don't mind about Dawg. The vet said he should stay inside because of his toe and bites. They washed him, so he shouldn't smell too bad."

Alice laughed out loud. "Dawg's a hero. He can stay, no matter what he smells like." Nik mentally scored himself a victory and went to the kitchen to prepare supper.

Alice got the quiet, normal evening at home with her makeshift family that she had asked for. In fact, Nik turned out to be much better at playing chef than she had imagined, and he surprised them with pizza supreme, salad with sunflower seeds, and a white wine Uncle Hal had tucked into the box of gifts Alice brought home from Christmas in Gull Harbor. Margaret gave him a thumbs-up and went back to her room, to study, she said.

Nik settled down on the couch with the comforter over his feet and the newspaper in his lap. Alice cleaned up the kitchen and stood for a moment, just looking at him. He belonged there, no doubt. She went over to the couch and picked up the comforter.

"Mind if I join you?"

Nik smiled and tossed the paper onto the floor. He said nothing, but opened his arms to her. She burrowed into his surrounding warmth under the comforter and leaned her head back, offering her mouth to him. He kissed her back, and ran his tongue along her ear, whispering, "*Vill du ha sex?*" Soon they were both wriggling out of their jeans on the narrow couch, panting like a couple of teenagers covertly getting it on under the covers while the parents slept in the next room. Nik was solid and real, a delicious taste of physicality – no spooks, no phantom voices, no demon dogs. He was, in fact, just what she needed. Before long they were both dozing, along with Dawg who snored louder than any human.

Around midnight, Alice yawned and slipped out from under the comforter. She leaned down and kissed Nik's sleeping face, careful not to wake him. Dawg opened one eye as she pulled on her clothes and tiptoed past him; he thumped his tail a few times, but didn't get up. She went and stood in front of the hall heater, warming her backside and yawning, when she noticed the study door was shut, with a light showing under it. It was late for Margaret to still be up, so she tapped on the door, and then went in. Margaret's eyes were glued to the monitor, reading an e-mail message.

"You should be in bed," said Alice. "I know we haven't talked about this afternoon, but I'm too sleepy to do it now."

"Look, somebody wrote us back."

"No shit! Which one?" Alice was incredulous. She had not expected anyone to respond to such an outrageous request from a total stranger across the ocean.

"Daniel Lamprie, the guy from Queensland who wrote all the travel books."

"So, he took us seriously."

"Looks that way." Margaret was smiling, her face animated and engaged. Quite different from the detached state she had been in earlier.

Alice stretched out on the day bed. "Go ahead and read it to me," she said.

Margaret leaned in toward the monitor and began to read.

"Dear Margaret Sullivan: I have read your message with interest and no, I do not think you sound like a crazy person. I do indeed believe you could have experienced what you describe. The Aborigines believe that children are still strongly surrounded by the spirit world from which they came and would not find it strange at all for you to be able to see spirit beings. The Quinkan spirits are not to be taken lightly, and I can tell you from my own experience of traveling among the Aboriginal peoples of this world that what most people think of as reality is an illusion kept in place for their own protection. As to why a Quinkan spirit would attach itself to you, let me ask you this. Do you have an Aboriginal connection of some kind, that is to say, are any of your relatives of Aboriginal descent? If you are not sure, then I suggest you may want to research your genealogy for information. The Australian Institute of Aboriginal Studies has a website that could help you do that. As to how to banish a Quinkan, I'm not sure that's possible, but of course I am not a clan elder and do not have knowledge about such things. It's said that an Imjim can be thwarted by the Timara, so perhaps that's something you should pursue. In any case, best of luck to you.

Regards, Daniel Lamprie."

She turned to Alice. "So that *was* a Timara that fought the Imjim in the car! And somebody sent it to me." Margaret's eyes were shining with excitement.

Alice chewed over this latest development. Someone from the Internet had thrown them a lifeline of sorts, but now what?

"Do you think Grandma would tell us anything about your dad?"

Alice made a face. "Doubtful. She's never told me anything useful. But you're her golden child, so you might have better luck than me. All I know is, they got married and went off to Australia. She said he caught a fever that was running through an outback station they visited and died there. She came back to the States alone. Well, not quite alone – she was pregnant with me."

"Poor Grandma," said Margaret, "That's really awful. She lost her husband and got left alone in a foreign country. That's really sad."

"Yeah, it explains a lot about her," said Alice, thinking that wasn't the half of what was wrong with Suzanne. "From what I've dragged out of Uncle Hal, Ned Waterston – Neddy as he was called – was an artist drifter she met somehow in Miami and married without telling the family or even introducing him to anyone. She doesn't even have any photos of him. I always had the impression when I was growing up that he was some kind of blot on the family pedigree."

"Wow," said Margaret. "I didn't know our family was so weird."

"Thanks a lot."

"No, I mean it's cool. Maybe he was psychic and maybe it runs in the family after all. That would explain me, wouldn't it?"

Alice was reluctant to go down that road, but it seemed unavoidable at this point. "What exactly about you would it explain?"

"Raine thinks I have psychic abilities. She says it sounds like I'm open, you know, third eye and all that, or even a channel. I think so too, 'cause I sure channeled somebody when the Quinkans started fighting. If only I knew how to do it on purpose instead of by accident."

"Tell me about that," Alice said, her skin prickling.

"When the Imjim jumped me, I just yelled out 'Timara,' which is what the good Quinkans are called. I didn't even think, I just yelled it out."

"And that brought something else?"

"Yeah, this shadow thing that looked like a twelve-foot walking-stick insect. It was shiny reddish-black and so thin that when it turned sideways I couldn't see it. I only saw it for a second, but the bad Quinkan had a fit when it showed up. Then ..." she paused, remembering. "Then, everything around me just kind of faded out, and I was somebody else, or in their head. A girl, older than me, but younger than you. She knew I was there, and she showed me a picture she had painted on a piece of wood. It was a stick figure like the good Quinkan. So I know she sent it. But I don't know who she was."

"Sounds like a guardian of some kind," said Alice.

"I wish."

They lapsed into silence, each buried in her own thoughts. Alice reflected that a guardian was exactly what they needed, but it was still hard to believe you could just ask for one and have it show up.

Margaret yawned and stretched. "Should I write the guy back?"

"Yes, definitely. He took us seriously, so we should extend the same courtesy."

"I could tell him about the Timara coming to my rescue. Maybe he would know if that's good enough to make the Imjim go away or if we need to do something else."

Alice nodded. She was wishing she had a guardian that would make Cadjer Harrow go away and his hellhound with him. And then she realized what a dunce she had been.

"Cadjer Harrow was a half-breed," she said, thinking out loud. "But maybe not half Red Indian like everyone assumed. No, what if he was something else ... one of those clippings said he was, what, newly arrived from foreign lands or something like that. What if the foreign part was Aboriginal? That could explain why we see him with a Quinkan disguised as a dog following him around. So, the question is—"

"—what kind of evil magic or sorcery was he into?" Margaret was visibly excited.

"But would a human be powerful enough to control a Quinkan?"

"Maybe it controlled him. Maybe he was cursed or something."

This was sounding right, Alice could feel in her gut that it fit. She was starting to replay parts of her book in her head, making puzzle pieces match up. If he had been a witch doctor of some kind, that might explain why the current Reverend Rider was so hot to destroy his little book. And what if it held Aboriginal images of sorcery or whatever passed for black magic in their belief system?" The thought was exploding her brain.

"Write Mr. Lamprie back and ask him if he knows of any sorcery images that might be used to curse somebody or work some kind of magic that would bind a spirit to someone."

Margaret began typing as fast as Alice could think. "Ask him, too, if he's ever seen a black hand stencil, as opposed to the usual red or white ones, and if he has, what he thinks it means."

The keys clattered and then Margaret hit SEND and sat back, a satisfied half-smile on her face. "Now what?" she said.

Alice shrugged. "We wait and see. But right now you need to go to bed, you have school tomorrow. I, however, can sleep as late as I want to," she said, yawning hugely, " and I intend to enjoy every second of it."

After Margaret was settled in bed and kissed good night, Alice turned out the light and went back out to the couch. Nik had not moved a muscle from where she'd left him, nor had Dawg. It was mildly humorous to her that she would need to wake him up in order for him to go to bed.

She slid the glass door open and stepped out onto the deck, feeling strangely calm. The rain was gone, and the air was frosty but not wet. Looking up at the sky, she could see the star field cold and crystalline above her, diamonds on velvet. The sense of peace she was currently feeling could only be ascribed to the fact that a stranger, someone completely external to her own life, had acknowledged what she and Margaret were going through and had even led them to that "Eureka!" moment when she'd seen a glimpse of the larger pattern she'd been sensing all along. It was no guarantee of safety, but there was the illusion of it. Like Margaret, she had reached a stillpoint, a moment of suspension between the cosmic inhale and the great exhale. She could only hope that when the latter arrived, it wouldn't blow them all away.

CHAPTER 31

NIK GOT dressed as quietly as possible. Alice was sleeping soundly, and he knew how much she needed to rest and recuperate. Margaret was already up and ready for school, sitting in the breakfast nook last time he checked, just waiting until the absolute last minute when she would need to meet the bus. He had a two-hour seminar starting at 7:30 and was already running late, but he'd agreed to wait with her at the end of the driveway until the bus came. She was hand-feeding her toaster waffle to Dawg, which Nik supposed was all right. He felt like hell about Figaro and could imagine how much Margaret missed him, so he didn't mind if she wanted to spoil his mutt by sharing her breakfast.

Just before leaving, he looked in on Alice one last time. Light from the hallway spilled into the bedroom and heightened the shadows, making her face look gaunt and a bit skull-like. It hadn't really come home to him until now that she was thinner. She was always complaining about needing to lose a few pounds, but this was more than a few. He had even realized that her clothes fit more loosely, which in itself was noteworthy because he rarely noticed what people wore or how they looked in their clothing. He was worried, but it was not in his nature to interfere in other people's business, so he was reluctant to say something to her. But now that she made it clear he had been incorporated into the household, he debated whether he should voice what he was thinking.

He knew she and Margaret had sat up late into the night doing something in the study, but she wasn't talking and he wasn't going to pry. Discussing people's secrets and private anxieties even when they were willingly shared was uncomfortable ground for him, but he felt an urgency to make some kind of suggestion to her about her physical well being. Her face was pale against the pillow as she slept deeply without dreaming, her mouth a little open the way Margaret sometimes looked when she fell asleep on the couch, oblivious to the television blaring away.

He thought about the night when he'd come back late from the pub. He never intended to be gone that long, but Stuart and the rest of the departmental crew were hard to get away from once a round of beers had been ordered. When he'd come through the door, she'd given him a shock. Her appearance was alarming, haggard and hollow-eyed, and he understood then that her fears were wearing her down. Their discussion after the dog episode did nothing to calm those apprehensions. It crossed his mind that the beast really could have been rabid, and she might be in the first stages of the disease. For the first time in their relationship, Nik felt cold fear. He had no idea what he would do if she contracted a life-threatening illness and died.

He pulled the comforter up around her neck, turned off the hallway light, and went back out to Margaret.

"Let's go, eh? Your mom will kill me if you miss the bus."

"No prob." She was letting Dawg lick syrup off her fingers.

Nik hurried down the steps and got in the truck, cranking and hauling it into gear in one practiced motion. He waited with the engine running while Margaret gathered her books and came down the stairs. She clambered into the passenger seat, and Nik backed out into the front yard. He could just see sunlight creeping over the trees and spilling down into the clearing with the promise of a fair day. His stomach growled. He hadn't eaten anything, but that could wait until he got to town. The long drive to the university from Alice's house served him well, because it gave him time to think, an exercise he was fond of under any circumstances, and he had more than enough to mull over these days. He wondered whose brain he could pick about membrane-theory, and if he could find out, without it seeming too blatant, how it might relate to the paranormal.

When Alice finally rolled over and opened her eyes, it was nearly ten o'clock. Chilled sunlight filled the bedroom, but Nik had pulled the comforter up around her so only her ears and nose were icy. It was almost too hot under the pile of covers, but it felt good, too. Once she finally got up, she was going to stoke the fireplace to a roar and make the house toasty warm so she could move around comfortably. She would probably have to go out and gather fallen branches near the edge of the woods, but was willing to do it if it was the only way to get a decent fire going.

She intended to spend the day reading back through everything she'd written about Cadjer Harrow and revisit every scrap of evidence on him in the library file. Now that it seemed she'd stumbled onto the truth of what he was, she needed time to figure out how she had set him in motion in her reality and, more specifically, how he might be counteracted. She needed time to reason things through, to organize and analyze, using the methods she was best at. Yesterday she had been nearly hysterical with fear, but now she just felt determined. Because of Raine's advice and Daniel Lamprie's e-mail message, there seemed to be some hope for a possible course of action. She and Margaret were no longer alone in this, and once she'd finally allowed herself to believe the unbelievable, a plausible solution was taking shape in her mind. She just needed time alone to try to fully understand what she had done, in order to undo it.

She pushed the blankets aside and sat up, the cobwebs in her head clearing away. Because safety-minded Nik had turned the gas heater off when he left, the house was an igloo again; it couldn't be over thirty degrees inside. She pulled on sweatpants, a T-shirt and a turtleneck sweater, plus a large sweatshirt over that. Adding heavy wool socks and her old hiking boots, she felt reasonably ready to face the day.

In the kitchen she found an empty plate on the floor beside Margaret's chair and assumed Dawg had gotten his share. Once coffee was brewing, she went to the fireplace and discovered the firebox already stacked with wood and kindling ready to light. Bless Nik. He was instantly forgiven for turning off the heater. Crumpling a page of newsprint and wedging it underneath the kindling, she lit a long kitchen match, held it to the newsprint, and watched with satisfaction as it caught the edge of the paper and filled the firebox with curling yellow and orange flames. In just a few minutes, she could feel the heat on her face.

She crouched, staring into the fire and absorbing its warmth, watching the satisfying randomness of the flames curling over and through the wood and paper. She heard the timer go off on the coffeemaker and pulled out of her reverie, feeling somewhat at ease. With a steaming cup, Alice went back to the study, turned on the computer, and then collected her book manuscript pages and pulled the library folder off the bookshelf. With the manuscript printout in her lap, she sat on the carpet and read it page by page, underlining anything that felt important to her plan. Now that she had a completely different perspective on the events of the story, certain things such as the name of Harrow's inner circle – The Hand – held a different significance. She wrote, "hand stencils/black hands/black magic?" in the margin. She also circled the name of the church and double-underlined the words "Heavenly Powers." There were clues everywhere, if only she could figure out how they fit together.

Next she read through all the notes she had made after her talk with Raine last Sunday night. "Thoughts are things," she had written, "not just ideas, but physical electrically charged units of energy that directly affect matter around us." It struck her as a fundamental truth when she'd written it down; this morning it still had the feel of authenticity and was now helping to chart her course of action.

Raine had also left a little book in her mailbox, titled *Thought Forms*, with a note to look at a certain page. It said in black and white what she'd subconsciously felt all along and what Margaret had tried to suggest. The passage on creative writing summed it up neatly ... that once created, the thought form developed something of self or personal desire and was therefore capable of volition and action, that it could in turn affect those who were physically alive and stir up their feelings. "Such a form can be seen by others," the author asserted. He went on to explain that the thought form was an image formed within the mental body of its creator and afterwards externalized, a phenomenon "equally true when exercising the imagination." The rest of the page Raine had underlined in red: Alice turned to it now and read it again:

> The novelist in the same way builds images of his characters in mental matter, and by the exercise of his will moves these puppets from one position or grouping to another, so that the plot of his story is literally acted out before him. It is hard for us to understand that these mental images actually exist.
>
> Some novelists have been dimly aware of such a process, and have testified that their characters when once created developed a will of their own, and insisted on carrying the plot of the story along lines quite different from those originally intended by the author.

Reading those paragraphs again gave her goose bumps; it was the best description of her own writing experience she could have imagined. She wasn't so sure Harrow would like being referred to as a thought form, but what else was he?

Raine had given her more supporting evidence from a book Alice remembered reading as a college freshman when it was making the rounds among those "in the know." On her note pad she had written, "page 72, *Seth Speaks*: coordination points act as channels through which energy flows, forming invisible paths from one reality to another." What had seemed like gobbledygook years ago now seemed to be the only explanation for what was going on. Alice was holding her breath; this was just too close to home. She read on: "Mental images, accompanied by strong emotion, are blueprints upon which corresponding physical objects, events, or conditions will occur. The intensity of a feeling, thought, or mental image is the important element in physical manifestation." Alice instantly thought of the cheek-marking scene in her own novel that she'd experienced as real the moment she'd put the words on paper.

Touching her cheek, she emptied the library folder and reread every piece of evidence it contained, knowing now that it had been collected and given to the library by Cecil Rider. She was just getting up to stretch and stoke the fire when she realized with a shock that she had not seen Harrow's notebook in the folder. She looked again to be sure, but it was not there. Her mouth went dry, and she raked through her memory of the last several weeks to figure out the last time she could positively remember seeing it. That turned out to be the disastrous meeting with Rev. Cecil, when she'd pulled it out of her purse and deceitfully handed it to him, and he'd dropped it like a hot coal on his study floor. She had then grabbed it before he could toss it into his own fireplace. But where had it gone after that? She remembered hurrying out to the car in a state of confusion, throwing everything she was carrying into the back seat and driving away.

From there, she could not picture whether it got brought upstairs with the rest of her stuff or not. She did clearly remember removing the book from the folder and taking it to the interview in her purse, but she had no memory at all of putting it back in the folder. It was possible that it could have just been lying around in the back seat for two weeks with all her other garbage ... she broke into a sweat. What if it had been thrown out by mistake at the dump? Had Harrow sensed it, and come to get it with his mounted escort? Or worse, had one of the Quinkans taken it when they fought in the car? Her hands were shaking as she tried to make notes. This was a terrible lapse on her part, and might prove their undoing if she couldn't find the stupid thing. She knew it contained rituals and notes of things he had tried and what the results had been. It was not only a record of accounts and daily business, as she had first assumed – she knew now that it was a working sorcerer's spell book.

Maybe it had fallen on the ground around the dump when she was throwing stuff into the boxcar. There was no way she was getting out at the dump site again, but she could just cruise slowly past and look out the window to see if it lay on the ground somewhere. That was only a day ago, it might still be there. Doggedly, she pulled all her research materials out again and was searching around and behind the bookshelf when she heard the phone ring. She was too engrossed in looking for the missing notebook to run and catch the call, but when her answer message beeped and no one left a message after the tone, she was curious.

Going to look, she saw that there were three messages already in the queue. Checking for calls was usually the first thing she did after getting home from work, but they had all been so distracted, no one had checked for the past day or so. She punched the PLAY button and got the first message, from Raine, telling her to look in the mailbox for the book on thought forms. She erased it and played the next one.

"Hey, Margrits! You never did call me back. Do you wanna trade CDs or not? Call me, 'kay? Okay! Bye!" She saved Judy's message, and played the last one.

With dread, she recognized the voice at once.

"Miss Waterston? This is Cecil Rider. It's ... very unfortunate that I've missed you. Please call me at my office as soon as you find this message. Good-bye, and please don't fail to return this call."

Alice ran to her purse and scrabbled through its contents until she found the scrap of paper with the number for St. Christopher's. She dialed the number and held her breath as it rang and rang. After eight rings, she got the church's recorded message.

"Reverend Rider," she said, leaving her own message in this game of phone tag, "this is Alice Waterston. I'm returning your call. Sorry I didn't find it earlier, but I was busy. If I don't hear back from you this morning, I may drop by the church to see if you're in. Thanks."

Now to the business in hand. She refilled her cup and went back to the computer. If her writer's imagination had made Harrow and his evil crew a reality, it would just have to unmake them in turn. Opening the chapter containing the scene with Belinda's rape and murder, she rewrote it so that the girl's pleas melted Harrow's cold heart and he agreed to stop persecuting her mother. That was much better. She saved the file and opened the initiation chapter. She erased the entire ritual and wrote a scene in which Harrow blessed the service attendees and wished them all a prosperous New Year. In the same manner, she went through each file, changing the dark parts to bland, innocuous harmless events.

Then she created a new chapter, which she titled "Epilogue," and quickly sketched a different climax to the story wherein Harrow would renounce the so-called Body of initiates and give up his evil ways. Then he would die of natural causes and his sorrowing congregation would erect a tombstone for him years later. Not as riveting as her original ending, but a lot safer. She pecked away at the keyboard for nearly an hour and finally pushed back from the desk, drained but satisfied. She saved the file, copied the entire book folder onto a CD, and then erased everything having to do with the book or its research off the hard drive. Harrow's literary life now existed nowhere except on a small disc of plastic.

She went to the kitchen and called the church again, with no luck. She hung up, irritated. It was eleven-thirty on a Thursday morning – weren't people supposed to be in their offices? Nothing to do but try again later, or go by there when she went to look for the book.

Now for the second part of her plan. She stoked up the fire to a roaring blaze, sat down on the living room floor, adjusted a cushion behind her back, and leaned against the couch. She stared into the fireplace until she felt calm, then closing her eyes, she brought Harrow into her mind's eye as clearly as possible. It wasn't hard; he lurked in her inner vision all the time these days. She visualized him becoming paler, then transparent, and finally evaporating away completely into a swirl of molecules, then atoms, then nothing. Then she repeated the procedure for each of the other characters in the book, and as an added precaution she surrounded her house and property with a high wall of blinding white sunlight and a pair of Timara sentinels standing guard at the driveway entrance. That should do it. Her head ached with the effort, but she hoped it would be successful.

Working on her fifth cup of coffee, she settled into Whit's old recliner and played back in her mind all the changes made in the manuscript. Then she sat up – damn it all, she'd forgotten to write in a part where Belinda's mother recovered with no ill effects. It could be added to the former rape chapter easily enough. She went back to the computer, put in the CD, and clicked on the file for Chapter 8. Suddenly the system froze, and she found herself staring at the blue screen of death. There was nothing to do but power off and reboot. Clicking on Chapter 8 again, it opened this time, but she could see immediately that it was a larger byte size, the size of her original version. She checked her other changes, and saw that they too had reverted to the original version. Had she somehow copied the wrong set of files onto the CD? Fuming, she decided to check the new Epilogue chapter, but couldn't find it in the list of chapter titles. She cursed the computer for its stupidity and tried again. What had she done? There was no new Epilogue chapter at all. Where had she saved it? A quick search for the file name gave her a confounding message: FILE NOT FOUND. She clearly remembered saving each file and copying the entire folder to the CD, but all that work had disappeared somehow. Alice was dumbfounded.

Then she realized something else. Like an idiot she had forgotten to print out a copy of the newly revised chapters. She always ran off a copy on the printer when each chapter was finished, but not this time. At least with a hard copy she could have retyped all her changes back in. But the rewrite was lost, and the house was freezing again.

The fire had sunk to a smokey smolder, all Nik's diligently gathered wood burned to embers. It was surprising to her that she had endured the cold for nearly an hour without turning up the heat; she had become so single-minded in devising her plan that she hadn't even noticed the temperature drop. When she went to check on the hall heater, she saw the pilot light had gone out. She got the kitchen matches and relit the gas, huddling over its blue flame and shivering in uncontrollable spasms, as much from fury as cold. The lost files were an impossible frustration.

Alice sat back down at the computer, grinding her teeth, and quickly rewrote the Epilogue chapter and saved it. She toyed momentarily with the notion of erasing the entire manuscript and all her research notes off the CD, but couldn't bring herself to do it – too much hard work and creative sweat had been invested in it. She decided to just let the rest of the manuscript sit for the moment, until she felt like facing the complete rewrite again. She was about to power off, but on impulse checked the CD directory again, just to see what was there. The chapter headings scrolled by and her hand froze on the mouse. Once again, her Epilogue chapter had completely disappeared from the directory.

In a red rage, she turned away from the screen and shouted, "Stop this! Whoever you are, stop!" She was shaking. "I'll fight you! GODDAMN YOU, I'll make you all disappear!" she screamed, coughing, her throat raw.

Dawg came quietly up to the study door, his claws tick-ticking on the bare floor. His tail was down and his head ducked as he looked up at her.

"Oh honey, I don't mean you. Come here." She bent down and rubbed under his chin and up around his ears. The effect was immediate, and his tail began to thump. "Sorry, I got a little carried away. You're a sweet old mutt, and I love you." She hugged his drooly face and got up. What was she doing, yelling like that? It was extremely out of character. Increasingly her emotions had been cresting to the surface, to the point that she couldn't stop them, nor did she even want to.

Cold as a tomb in here, she thought. Paranoid, she suppressed that image at once. If indeed thoughts were things, she had to patrol her imagination with watchdog vigilance because if it had opened some kind of etheric door through which wicked men could materialize, there was no telling what her heightened fear and anger could pump undeserved life into. The answer was obvious: she knew at once what that raw mental energy had fueled, and so did Margaret. Alice pulled a mask over her emotions. It took every scrap of concentration she could manage.

She went to the bedroom and got another sweater, then pulled on her repaired overcoat, found two unmatched gloves, and grabbed the car keys. She checked Dawg's water and food, then locked the house and went downstairs. Settling resolutely into the tattered driver's seat of her car, she pulled slowly out of the yard and drove a steady 45 all the way to the dump. Slowing as it came into view, she coasted up onto the sand and gravel beside the site and sat with the car idling. There was debris scattered all over the dump site, but nothing that looked like a notebook. So be it. She stepped on the gas and headed in the direction of the church.

Considering what she planned to do, she felt remarkably calm. Her hands were stiff with cold, and there was a kind of subterranean shivering going on at the neuron level throughout her body, but she had no intention of turning around. She did not consider herself a particularly brave person, and for most of her life had avoided conflict and confrontation whenever possible, but she felt changed somehow. She was tired of being timid little Alice, never making a scene and rarely doing anything that would be considered out of the ordinary. And oddly, for the moment, she did not feel afraid.

Reaching the parking lot of St. Christopher's, she pulled up in front of the pastor's office and got out. No cars in the lot but hers. She tried the office door and found it locked. Where the hell was he? She needed an ally, and he was the only one suitable. She required his knowledge, those carefully saved and hidden facts he refused to share, and now he seemed to have deserted her.

She got back in the car, pulled onto the road, and drove the mile and a half back down to the old mother church. Resolute, she parked the car beside it and got out. Still too angry to be afraid, Alice climbed the rotting steps, stopping only long enough to note the newly applied spatter-painted black handprint on the weathered siding, and set her feet on the dusty boards of the church floor. Her ears had begun a subliminal ringing, but she ignored that, too, and walked to the very center of the building, where she stood, waiting.

The din in her ears was swelling, and it wasn't bells as she had thought, but deep voices chanting, rising and falling like waves crashing on boulders. The sound was all around, yet the empty shell of the church held not a mouse, not a spider, but still the voices sang an unintelligible litany that pleaded for audience with the Great Ones whose names rolled like thunder in her head. She'd heard those names before ... Ngalyod, Tjabuinji and Jagtjadbulla, Namarrkun ... names echoing across the void like the summoning of the gods. Alice knew who owned those names – the Rainbow Serpent, the Lightning Brothers, and the great Ancestor Lightning Man with his host of Wandjina spirits.

The slightest of movements from the shadows brought all her senses into focus. She was ready. Then Cadjer Harrow moved out of the darkened corner of the staircase that led up to the ruined bell tower. Startled in spite of her resolve, Alice backtracked a few steps, and he stalked her across the boards. At his heels trotted his familiar, the giant soot-black dingo, as hideous as on their first encounter except that it glared at her with one flickering red eye – the other was blind, shot out, she assumed, by Nik's pistol.

"I don't believe in you," she said, standing her ground. "I made you up – you're not real, you don't belong in this world."

The beast nodded its shaggy head in acknowledgment. "Your pitiful worrrld is just as unreal to meeeh," it snarled, in that horrible guttural dog-voice she remembered with revulsion. "I am hrrh here hrrh not willingly arrrh."

Harrow only laughed softly, his actual voice snapping in her ear, exactly as she'd imagined it many times.

"Which of you is the master?" she said to him. "The beast follows you around, but I don't believe he is subservient to you, am I right?"

He crossed the space between them in an eye blink, and pushed her back against the wall, pinning her with his forearm against her throat. She coughed, and gasped for breath.

The dog began a high-pitched whinnying that was probably laughter but sounded to Alice like a hyena being throttled. Before her horrified eyes, it slowly morphed into a shape somewhat like an immense pot-bellied pig, then a reptile that was vaguely salamander shaped and about the size of a Komodo dragon. It flicked a forked tongue over rows of needle-sharp teeth as its mottled skin pulsed dark muddy red. She was seeing Margaret's adversary in the flesh, and that knowledge confirmed what she had prepared herself to face: it would probably take something more powerful than benevolent Quinkan spirits to send it back where it came from.

"The currrsed one doess not command me, yehttt we are bound to each othrrr," it said in its saliva-choked growl. Long threads of drool slipped from its mouth and fell, smoking, onto the wooden floor. A hole was etched in the board where it pooled. Alice retched and felt weak in the knees.

The creature continued to shift its shape, shrinking down to the size of a gecko. Before she could draw breath again, it had scampered across the boards, climbed Harrow's black surcoat up to his shoulder, and perched blinking at her with garnet eyes.

"And happily or not, we are both bound to you," said Harrow. He laughed in harsh, hoarse barks that pierced Alice's eardrums. "Because you aren't done yet, are you?"

"Done ... with what?"

"There's a bit more to my story that you haven't told."

"I'm not going to—"

"But we insissst," hissed the lizard.

"I'm not doing it," she said. "Whatever you've got planned, I won't help."

A piece of her mind couldn't believe what she had just said. She was having a testy argument with an apparition instead of groveling on the floor in blind terror.

"You're going to finish it – the way I want it done."

His fist encircled her throat and held her, chin angled up toward his mahogany face that held those eyes, coal black with no irises. His other hand slipped inside her coat, down her chest, and stopped at the waistband of her sweatpants. She saw through eyes blurred with panic that two more figures approached out of the gloom. No, please ... her resolve was slipping, maybe she didn't have the strength to confront him after all. With fingers of ice he gripped her injured shoulder and shook her the way a dog worries a rat it wants to terrorize, but not necessarily kill. Then he pulled her tightly against him.

She could feel him stiffening against her thigh. Her mind went blank with terror, and Harrow began to laugh with malicious acknowledgment.

"You are a temptation, my dear, but the Aborigines have a serious taboo against incest, you know. But then again, since I am an outcast, why should I be concerned over the fate of my immortal soul, such as it is ... but I do thank you for bringing me back."

"I didn't—" she whispered.

"Stupid woman. Of course you did, or perhaps I should say, you and the lovely Margaret did. She clearly has more power than you."

"Leave her out of this."

"Too late. I've met your lovely daughter, as you know, although she didn't have much to say."

Alice tried to turn her face away from those eyes. "Margaret has nothing to do with any of this."

"On the contrary, she has everything to do with it."

Alice looked at him blankly.

"You don't know, do you?" His laughter filled his barrel chest and exploded in a prolonged guffaw that wouldn't stop. "You don't *know*. You don't know what you are. This is exquisite."

Alice was shaking violently. "I know what *you* are – that's enough."

"More than enough," the Quinkan chirped.

"I'll finish your story," she said, "but not the way you want."

"Be my guest, Miss Waterston, or whatever you call yourself. Please do be my guest. I shall be greatly entertained." Brown and Lathe whispered to each other from the shadows.

"Repulsive humans," croaked the Quinkan, who leapt from Harrow to the floor, and with a violent shudder resumed its dingo shape. It spoke clearly this time, in the voice of a young man with a vaguely Southern accent.

"Like myself, my lusty companion here isn't allowed to follow his instincts with you," it rasped, "which would be to satisfy himself and then kill you, but that's only because we still need you for the link." Its distorted face tried a hideous smile, the fur around its neck bristling.

Alice heard her voice as if from a distance, as if someone else had spoken. Surely she wouldn't have the courage to ask such a question herself.

"How are we linked?"

She looked into the soulless eyes of Harrow, his breath close enough to make frost on her neck. Impossibly, the serpent carved into his cheek coiled and uncoiled under his weathered skin.

The demon-dingo laugh-yelped, its jaws gaping wide, revealing fresh blood clotting around its teeth and tongue. What had it recently killed or eaten? Alice's brain was shutting down; she found it difficult to remember where she was and what her purpose had been in coming there. Cascading in and out of her hearing was a cacophony of sound: deep chanting voices and shrieking hurricane winds punctuated by booming thunder. She imagined two separate forces fighting to gain entry, each staking some claim on her fear-paralyzed mind and body.

The bare shell of the church was disappearing, or maybe she was blacking out. Suddenly an image of the pulpit appeared, with the initiates of the Body lined along the aisles of the church, candles blazing in their hands, illuminating their faces under the cowls of their robes. They chanted the names of power: Kurangara, Barrginj, Namarrkun, Namandjoik. Behind the pulpit, she now saw, hung an immense canvas shimmering with ghostly images set against geometric circles and spirals. The stylized Ancestor spirits were painted with eyes and noses prominent but with no mouths; they floated against a gray background, their slender tubular bodies decorated with vertical red stripes and radiating coronas of yellow and white. Beneath them were conjoined male and female figures, copulating with arms and legs outstretched, and below them rows of geometrical shapes and emblems encircled by a gigantic serpent.

A shred of her logical brain complained that Australian Dreamtime sorcery had no place in a turn-of-the-century rural church; combining of these two things was what happened in nightmare, where disparate elements of the exotic and the familiar appeared together in baffling lunatic scenarios. There was no mistaking the subject of the canvas: the fifteen-foot Rainbow Serpent coiled around and among the figures of the Wandjina, with supersized renderings of the Lightning Man and what she now recognized as malevolent Quinkan figures.

"Why? What is this for?" The voice she heard was distant, light years away – it might have been her own.

"Power, of course. Why else does one engage in sorcery?"

Which voice had answered she couldn't tell. It boomed in her ears and seemed to shake the walls of the church. "I believe you have something that belonged to me when I was alive. I shall have need of it again."

"I have nothing of yours," she lied.

"I know that our mutual friend the priest does not have it, although it was left in his keeping. Do you think perhaps it was fate that he hid it where you would find it?"

Harrow began to laugh in booming, hollow yawps, blotting out all sounds except his doglike yelps and the incessant high screaming whine that had grown so familiar she was beginning not to notice it. He tossed her away like a dead mouse, then came and stood over her with his black mud-caked boots. Touching his fingers to his open mouth, he showed his teeth, streaked in red. Had he fed on something unspeakable as well, or perhaps he and the Quinkan had merged?

He knelt beside her, just as she'd seen in her dream where she'd hidden in the tobacco barn. Suddenly his face contorted into a black smear and long knobby fingers tore her clothes away from her torso, exposing the white flesh of her breasts and stomach. She twisted frantically in the creature's grip, kicking and flailing away from the talons that raked her chest and sought her soft midsection. She was screaming her throat raw, thrashing like a maddened animal caught in a hunter's trap.

Its talons pricked her skin, but then the hand was yanked away.

"Nononono," it gibbered, rolling over on top of Alice, pinning her to the floor. Its features, so close to her own, were morphing, shifting back into Harrow's. His black eyes paralyzed her, and she felt that breathless deep-space freezing in her chest that she'd experienced when the first Wandjina panel had been unveiled. With a vicious shake, Harrow released her and stood up.

"I'm being interfered with, but I'll visit you again soon, and we'll conclude this business," he said, and then stepped back, his snarling laughter and that of his deputies rebounding off the walls, as well as the inside of her head. She could hear his heavy-heeled boots ascending the bell tower stairs, and as she dared one last look, he vanished in a spiral of dust motes where sunlight from a high window hit the staircase.

Alice crumpled to the dusty floor in a rag heap as the church went silent. Twitching in jerks and spasms, she lay alone in its shadows.

CHAPTER 32

ALICE SAT up, dazed. Wind whispered through the pines in the grove, rising and falling with soft reassurance that the natural world outside was perfectly normal. The flooring creaked and she froze, but it was just the sound of age and dry rot settling into the hundred-year-old timbers.

Stiff and sore, Alice got slowly to her feet, wondering how long she had been lying there. Her hands and clothes were filthy from where she'd hit the floor and rolled in the dust and dirt, and the area around her throat where Harrow's grip had threatened to choke off her breath was too painful to touch. She could only assume the bruise marks must be appalling. There was a bloody scrape between her breasts where the Quinkan's claws had sliced through four layers of her clothing. But she had no broken bones, and most surprising, she was still alive.

Pulling her coat over her chest, Alice cast fearful glances at the dark corners around the deserted staircase and the back doorway. Were they really gone? Listening for any hint of sound beyond her own wheezing breath, she scanned the empty room from wall to wall. There was nothing to see, only a bare shell of heavy planking with no hint or sign of anything out of the ordinary. It was just an old wooden structure slowly falling apart, its iron nails tugging at their holes, termites gnawing along their tunnels in the flooring, worms boring into the woodwork of windows and doors. It was so quiet she could almost hear them chewing. To the ordinary eye, it was an abandoned eyesore by the side of the road, but to her it was a terrifying gateway to somewhere else.

She looked at her watch and could barely read the time through the crystal, which was cracked in a sunburst of jagged lines. That must have happened when she hit the floor, and now that she noticed it, her left elbow ached and her hip on that side was sore, probably also badly bruised. It was just after three o'clock. Dazed and shaken, she walked unsteadily to the door and eased herself down the steps with care; it wouldn't take much to punch through the rotted boards, and the last thing she needed was another fall. The handprint was still on the outside wall, but now it seemed terribly faded, as if it had been there for decades, if not centuries. Outside, the landscape was gilded with afternoon sunlight, but to the north, a dark blue sky shading toward cobalt signified massing thunderheads. To the south, the sky was clear and bright turquoise. She took a deep breath and felt a little better; the air was crisp and clean, and her head was beginning to clear.

What she needed most was a safe place to pull herself together and rethink her strategy, but home was out. Harrow might be waiting. The church office down at the crossroads was a possibility, but when she drove back down to it, it still appeared to be closed. Just to be sure, she hobbled up to the annex and knocked on the office door. There was no answer, so she got in the car and drove slowly down the deserted county road toward the parkway. There was a gas station with a small diner and grocery store a couple of miles beyond the entrance to Black Creek Ferry Road where she might collect her thoughts and make some calls. As she drove, she watched the lowering sky in the distance as it deepened to indigo. It was building up to a real monster of a storm over Citrus Park.

Shifting her weight painfully in the seat as she turned onto the parkway heading toward Magnolia, she considered the possibility that there were pulled muscles in her left hip and thigh. Her body was trembling with both cold and shock, and even though the car heater was turned up full blast, she couldn't feel it. Her neck and face were especially numb where Harrow's icy fingers and frozen breath had touched her. If her visualizations hadn't dimmed him in the least, and her computer was somehow prevented from erasing the words that had brought him to life, what was left?

Caught up in her thoughts, she almost overshot the driveway into Jubel's One-Stop before she realized where she was. Stomping the brakes and wheeling sharply into the parking lot, Alice pulled up not far from the single generic gas pump. Suddenly, exhaustion overtook her, and she sat like a zombie in the seat, her head slumped forward and her eyes shut, her brain spinning like a helpless gerbil in a wheel while her body refused to move. She couldn't get Harrow's empty black eyes out of her head. In a way, they were as bad as those of the Quinkan, who was every bit as horrible as Margaret had described it, or worse.

It was clear now that her two separate problems, her book and the exhibit weirdness, were one and the same. The Quinkan had said it – they were "bonded" in some way. She hadn't been able to see it before, but now, having confronted Harrow and the Quinkan together, the larger whole was beginning to come into focus. She remembered what she'd read as background research for the exhibit before it arrived. For the Aborigines, the many centuries of rock paintings represented not only places sacred to their culture, but active embodiments of their Dreamtime Ancestor spirits, the lords of thunder and lightning, fire and flood, life and death.

The Wandjina, for example, were believed to be both very sacred and potentially dangerous, since they governed the cycles of nature that fed and watered the land and the creatures that lived on it. They were also guardians of the Law, which was the code of behavior that governed human existence and was handed down to the Aboriginal peoples through their senior men and women of power after the Dreamtime creation events. It was well known that these spirits could visit retribution upon clans and individuals for breaking ancestral law. The continued repainting of the Wandjina images by chosen ones from the family groups who had inherited that responsibility was essential to keep the power vibrant and connected to the people. It was also said that retouching the paintings could release the power of the spirit residing in the image.

Alice racked her brains to figure out how this knowledge could explain the situation she found herself in. She knew that the exhibit itself had been put together with great care to obtain agreement from all Aboriginal clans and artists involved with the images presented in the show. As far as she knew, no taboos had been violated. But somehow, there was a bridge between the Dreamtime entities of thunder and lightning and the manifestation of Harrow and his inner circle. Just how that was possible, or how she had triggered it, was beyond her imagination.

Her thoughts spun around that single unanswerable question: he needed her to keep the link, but how had it been made in the first place? Raine would tell her that her writing had caused energy to flow along some psychic pathway that linked their separate realities, but that didn't explain the Quinkan's relentless harassment of Margaret. It had been invading her dreams for several years. Fear gripped her in the gut as she remembered what Harrow had said about Margaret. Perhaps Margaret was the primary link, and Alice had just fed it by finding the library folder and writing down the words that made Harrow live on the page. He wanted the ending written his own way, which meant her words did have some influence over him. But what did he want that was different?

The facts around which she'd planned the climax of her book were slim. In 1899, Harrow led the persecution of the luckless Indian that ended in the man's lynching. Before that date there were a multitude of entries in his notebook documenting what seemed to be the growth of a cult, under his leadership. The height of its power and seeming hold over the surrounding community of Snake Bite, which she'd renamed Little Shiloh in her manuscript, crested a year or so before the lynching. The notebook listed a number of initiated brethren from 1896 to 1899, increasing by a dozen or so each year and totaling thirty-five at his last entry. She recalled there were also pages listing names of those who had refused or been denied initiation. Those unfortunates had lines drawn through their names. She wondered if they had been physically eliminated as well. It had given her the idea that she'd written into her story, that those not worthy were burned to a cinder in the initiation circle, and she suspected now that there was more than a grain of truth in that horrific image.

Further cause for speculation was Harrow's obituary; it gave the date of death, February 21, 1900, while not naming the cause. But again, there were clues to be found. The tombstone inscription said he had been "laid low." Alice suspected this was what he wanted to change – he wanted her to undo, to "unwrite," whatever justice had been dealt him, as he laughingly said, when he was alive.

If that were true, she needed to destroy every instance of her book that had brought him to life, every scrap of paper, every computer file, every photo of the place where he'd done his wicked business. To accomplish that, she needed to get home at once. It was also clear that she couldn't go pick up Margaret at school because there was no telling what might happen when she got back to the house. A confrontation was coming, and at this point she wasn't betting on who would survive.

Pulling herself together, Alice felt around in her purse for her cell phone, but couldn't find it. Then she remembered where it was ... on the kitchen counter where she'd left it after putting it on the charger. She was too drained to even get angry with herself; it was just one more thing that was working at cross-purposes. It meant she would have to go inside the store and ask to use the phone. Looking in the rear-view mirror, she checked her face and neck. Bruised, as she expected, with startling dark red and purple blotches spreading out in a hand-shaped pattern. In fact, with her torn clothing, she looked like a classic spouse abuse case. Alice slumped in the seat, tired beyond belief. Harrow had marked her, but there was nothing she could do about it at the moment, so she ran a comb through her tangles, got out, pulled her coat tightly across her blood-stained chest, and went inside the store, determined to stare down anybody who looked at her sideways.

The place was tiny, and the aisles so crowded together that two people couldn't walk down them side by side. The area in front of the cashier's counter was equally cramped, and the counter itself was crammed with so many racks of candy and cigarettes and jars of bubble gum that there was scarcely room to place purchases or money. A middle-aged woman with pink curlers in her hair sat in a lawn chair behind the counter. Barely visible behind the stacked jars and racks, she was watching a soap opera on a small black and white television set squeezed onto the far end of the counter.

Distant thunder rumbled, and the lights dimmed.

"Could I use the phone, please?"

"Pay phone's outside by the door," said the woman.

"Um, you don't have one in here I could use?"

The woman shook her head. Exasperated, Alice went outside without another word. The pay phone was in a half-booth bolted to the side of the wall. Looking through her purse, she found dollars, but no change other than pennies. She went inside again.

"I need change for a dollar." She shoved it across the counter.

The windows of the store were steamy, and it was greenhouse warm inside, but Alice couldn't feel it. She hoped the urgency in her voice would push the woman up out of her lawn chair and over to the cash register.

"Okay, how you want it broke?"

"Uh ... four quarters."

While Alice fretted, the woman took the dollar and with excruciating slowness opened the cash drawer, lifted the money clamp and slid the bill into its proper slot, smoothed out the stack before lowering the clamp, and then sorted through all the loose change until she found the right pieces. Unbelievably, Alice could see that every denomination appeared dumped at random into all the coin slots. Finally the proprietress counted out four quarters and laid them one at a time on the counter between the jars of Tootsie-Roll miniatures and Slim Jim pickles. Alice was embarrassed at the way her fingers trembled when she picked up the money.

"Freezing out there, ain't it," stated the woman affably. She chewed with vigor at something Alice hoped was gum.

"Sure is. Thanks." She turned to go.

"That was some storm we had day before yestiddy. Lanny Sturgeon ...

you know, that writer from the Magnolia paper, he does the sport fishing column, and he said it was the darndest–"

"Right. I'm kind of in a hurry," She pushed the door open.

"–said he sure didn't know why we been having such a wet winter this year–" The door slammed on the rest.

Alice ran out to the phone and felt a few cold drops spatter her face. Damn! She was going to have to make her calls in the rain. The northern sky was black with thunderheads, and a sudden white streak split the cloudbank, discharging with a bone-rattling crash.

She searched her purse for the phone number at St. Christopher, but the piece of paper was lost. Resigned, she dragged out the heavy phone book chained to the ledge under the phone, found the number, pushed in the first coin, and pressed the buttons. Cecil Rider answered on the first ring.

"Yes?" His voice was tentative. Even so, it sounded soothing, comforting. Alice knew she would give anything right now to be sitting in his cozy office, listening to him telling her things were okay, that she would be all right.

"Reverend?"

"Yes."

"This is Alice Waterston. I'm the–"

"I know who you are." The voice had lost its softness and some of its restraint. "What I really want to know is what you are. Are you one of them?"

"Sir, I don't–"

"I know you've waked things up in the old church again, because I've seen him. I want to understand how you've done it, and why."

Alice tried to think where to begin or how to explain what she'd been going through since November, but her mind wouldn't function clearly enough to find a good starting point.

Cecil Rider finally said, "This is a monstrous thing you've done."

"I know."

"I have myself mostly to blame, for keeping those things. An old man's foolish sentimentality, and see what it has cost us."

"Please believe me, it wasn't something I planned. I mean, what I planned had nothing to do with any of this." Alice stopped. It was too complicated.

"Help me," she said, finally. "You wouldn't before, but now you'll have to because I don't know what to do."

She waited, and so did he. Closer rumblings and more drops. Anxious and hurting, she cleared her throat.

Finally he said, "Antoine Rider was my father ... you may have seen his sermons in the folder. His sister, my aunt, was murdered by that demon whose book you carry."

There it was, out in the open. But now that his link to the players in the drama was confirmed for her, Alice had no idea how that knowledge was going to help her.

"My father, Antoine, was eight years old when his sister was raped and murdered by fiends who called themselves a church, but were not. They were a blasphemy – an abomination." His voice bit into his words. Alice felt like a worm.

"Like the one whose name you spoke so carelessly, I too am a custodian of sorts," he continued. He seemed to have made up his mind to deliver his story whether she responded or not. "I had hoped to bury the dead – and the undead. When I had stones set up over the remains of Joseph, that poor Indian man, as well as the other we were referring to, I meant it to mark the end of that piece of history. I thought that enough years were gone by that people wouldn't remember. And I could let go of all those pieces of paper I had been saving since my father died." He paused, and then said, "I was a fool."

"No, you were a saint. I'm the fool," Alice said and truly meant it. "Reverend Rider, I have to ask ... how did he die?"

She heard him sigh into the receiver. "I assume you mean the black one, since you obviously know how poor Joseph met his end. My father told me that an arm of fire shot through the church one night in the middle of an initiation and burned him like a hog on a spit. My father, a very brave and very terrified youngster, was spying on them, hiding on the tower stairs when it happened."

"What do *you* think happened?" Alice's throat was so sore it came out as a kind of croak, hardly like a human voice at all.

She was damp and cold, and shivering. Rain was starting to fall in a thin mist, but it would only be a matter of minutes before it got worse.

"Miss Waterston, I would like to think it was an act of God. Or at the very least, a lucky fluke of nature."

Raindrops were splattering on the plastic phone cubicle and were beginning to soak through her coat. She had to hurry the rest out of him. Lightning snapped through the cloudbank, and Alice counted one one-thousand, two one-thousand, three one-thousand. Thunder boomed on cue and drowned out the old man's voice. Pretty close, she thought, maybe only a few miles away.

"My father believed," the reverend continued, "that this false preacher, if indeed he could be called human, wasn't strong enough to command those he had called up. Perhaps they consumed him and sent his soul to some appropriate place."

"Reverend Rider, did your father believe that Harrow was possessed by something? Did anyone ever mention a huge black dog with him?"

Cecil Rider spoke slowly, weighing his words carefully. "I don't believe the first minister of that church was a man of God. And I believe he got the end he deserved. As to his familiar, it was not seen again after his demise, according to those who lived through those times."

"Was it killed?"

"I have no knowledge of that. Sorry."

"Was there ... a painting hung in the church, like on a sheet or a wall-sized piece of canvas?"

"Yes."

Alice was shaking to the point of dropping the receiver. It was freaking her out that what she had thought to be her own twisted inventions were being confirmed as true. As she'd feared all along, but not wanted to acknowledge, she'd somehow been tapping into real events and simply describing them as they'd unfolded.

"My father said the people tore it down to cover his remains. It became the shroud in which he was buried. My father claimed that thing was terrible to look at, that the images on it moved and could put those who looked at it too long under a spell. Only the Indian Joseph – who was simple, you understand – could handle it without being affected. Some even said he painted some of the images. I wouldn't know."

"I believe they were right, on both counts."

Rain lashed at Alice's face and ran down her collar. She was trembling like a palsy victim. "I've g-got to hang up. P-please forgive me, for everything."

She hung up without waiting for a reply. There probably wasn't much more he could have told her anyway; she knew the rest. Sleet stung her face with tiny needles while lightning popped in the woods nearby, catching a tree on fire and sending a short-lived column of white smoke up into the torrent. The air reeked of ozone. Soaked through all her layers of shirts and sweaters, Alice jammed another quarter into the phone. It took five agonizing rings to connect.

"Zoology Department," said the graduate assistant on duty.

"Is Nik Thorens there? And hurry, please." She was standing in water, muscles chilled and clamped into a spasm that was part cold and part raw terror.

"Please hold."

"No, wait–" The line went quiet. "Shit."

Alice clamped her teeth on a sneeze and gasped for air. Her bronchial tree was constricting, cutting off oxygen and making her light-headed. She wondered if she would suffocate before someone could find Nik and take her off hold.

"I'm sorry, there's no one in the lab right now."

"Well goddammit, tell him his girlfriend called to tell him goodbye, in case he never sees her again. And that he should pick up her daughter at school. ASAP." She slammed the receiver down and shoved in another quarter. Lightning crackled and the dial tone clicked off, then came back. Death by electrocution, that would probably be it. She punched in the number as if in a trance.

"Sorry we missed your call. Please leave us a message. Bye now."

Her own cheery voice grated over the phone, followed by a beep, followed by nothing. Not that she really expected anyone to answer, she just wanted to confirm that Margaret hadn't taken the bus home and was there by herself.

Alice slogged around to her car and got in. She sat for a minute or two, dripping puddles onto the floorboard. The dirt road to her house would be a quagmire by now, but she had to go. With the mindless resolve of a slug she started the car and drove at a crawl through the storm until she reached Black Creek Ferry Road, which was rapidly turning into a river of mud. Her low-slung car, so smooth on the highway, spun and fishtailed into the rain-filled ruts, sliding sideways every few yards. She gunned the engine, forcing it through the trenches left by other cars, knowing that if she slowed and allowed the wheels to sink, they would bury up to hubcaps and never move again.

It took ten minutes of concentrated hell to travel the one mile to her driveway. Small branches and debris had fallen across the track, but she crunched over them and ignored a larger twig that got caught up under the front axel and skrokkked repeatedly against the wheel well. Parking at the base of the stairs, she sat with the headlights shining on the front steps and patio, listening to the slapping wipers. Although barely mid-afternoon, the sky was so dark that streetlights were probably coming on outside the museum in town. Alice felt a brief flash of Wandjina faces in her mind. Well, let them come, she thought.

There was nothing suspicious on the stairs, just sheets of rain cascading off the edge of the roof onto the deck, an icy waterfall for her to stand under while she tried to unlock the door with fumbling hands. Alice leaped out of the car and ran upstairs, heedless of the rain-slippery steps. She could hear Dawg barking at the top of his lungs and wondered how long he'd been at it. She got the door open and lunged inside, knowing she was going to die of pneumonia, but not before carrying out her last-ditch plan. Before she could stop him, Dawg darted between her legs and was down the stairs at a sloshing gallop.

"No! Dawg, come back! You stupid ...."

She went out onto the landing but couldn't see which way he'd gone. Hellfire, she wasn't going after him. And then she stopped, oblivious to the rain pummeling her face. There were figures in the yard, at the edge of the trees. Harrow had gathered the members of the Hand about him. If he intended to recover the notebook, though, he would be sorely disappointed. Maybe he could somehow force her to rewrite his death, but there was no way she could tell him where his lost book of spells had gone. If there was any justice, it had found its way into the dumpster and would soon be incinerated. She ran back inside and locked the door.

Thunder crashed with an accompanying white flash that filled the room with blinding light for a split second. Alice squeaked and said a mental plea to whomever that there would be enough time. The house was beginning to creak as wind tore at its corners and chimney flue. Alice wadded up the last two days' newspapers and tossed them into the fireplace. Then she grabbed a can of charcoal lighter from under the sink where it had been sitting for several years unused and doused the papers in large squirts – possibly the most dangerous way she knew to start a fire, but she was out of time.

Wind was shrieking, windows rattling out of their casements. The elements had gone insane and raged wild across the helpless landscape. Thunder and lightning smashed around the house, as the lords of flood and fire met together overhead. Their minions howled across the treetops, and the front door burst open with enough force to shatter the quarterpanes as it slammed against the wall. Rain blew in, wetting the floor halfway to the fireplace. Alice ran into the study and snatched up the box of CDs that held her last saved version of the novel plus the original story outline of the Camper's Legend and all her research notes. On the way out, she gathered up the library folder and the neatly stacked pages of the manuscript she'd let Nik read, which was her only clean copy of the chapters that had been sent out to publishers. All of it went into the fireplace on top of the lighter-soaked newsprint. Then she struck a handful of kitchen matches into a plume of flame that engulfed her fingers. Yelping in pain, she threw the torch onto the folder, manuscript pages, and spilled CDs. She pumped more fuel onto the pile, and it ignited with a roar, so that soon vile-smelling flames and smoke were billowing up the chimney. She grabbed the poker and moved the pile of pages around, making sure the fire consumed all of it and feeding it with spurts from the can. The CDs quickly became a melted lump of plastic.

Still clutching the poker, Alice went out onto the deck and looked at the gale raging overhead. She could hear them, the Wandjina voices, and at the bottom of the stairs she saw him, looking up at her with his flat black eyes. The wind tore at his hair and long coat, and he fought to keep his footing.

"I'll have the book now," he called over the continuous rolling thunder.

"I don't know where it is. Threaten me all you want, but it won't help you find it."

"Lies!" he shouted and started up the stairs. Behind her she heard a poisonous yelping and turned to see the one-eyed dingo, perched on the deck railing like a gargoyle.

"When the cursed one has what he wants, then I shall indeed feast on you and your obnoxious offspring," it snarled.

Alice felt her knees giving way. She dropped the poker and half fell, half sat into a crouch, soaked to her skin. She watched Harrow with paralyzed fascination as he took another step toward her. But then he looked sharply to the right and up into the trees at the edge of the clearing. They were parting, bending aside as if something impossibly massive waded through them. The look of dismay on his face told her this was something unaccounted for, a new peril she couldn't imagine. He continued to stare upward at nothing, but then she gradually began to see the outline of a monstrous two-legged shape walking toward them through the trees. Partly transparent, its torso towered above the whipping branches, its massive thighs like pillars of light from another world. The storm blew around and through it, and streamers of electricity flowed from its head, forming a corona of blazing tendrils.

The figure stepped into the clearing and leaned slowly down toward them, ants on a tiny strip of wood far below. Its outline was chalk white, and its face held black holes where eyes would have been and no mouth. She could see right through its body, or into it, rather. Geometric crisscrossings of arteries snaked up and down its limbs, spiky backbone, skeletal hands and feet, and exaggerated genitalia. She was looking into a living X-ray.

"Namarrkun," she whispered, although she couldn't hear the word; she merely felt the sound leave her lips.

Distorted voices rode the storm and clanged in her head, and somewhere above it a single howl pierced the torrent. Alice squeezed her eyelids tight against the pain it sent through her body. The Lightning Man bent down and slowly stretched out an arm toward Harrow. Sparks shot out from the Ancestor's joints in bright flashes as it angled down over the cowering figure. In a brighter explosion that sent Alice's retinas into recoil, it engulfed Harrow in its fist and snuffed out his existence not unlike the way she'd once seen Nik wet his fingers and pinch out a candle flame. A grating, scraping wail that skewered her teeth to their roots passed through her as deadly cold enveloped her body. Consciousness was slipping away.

She crouched by the doorway and bowed her head to her knees, waiting for the end. The familiar whining screech of that first day in the museum filled her ears and gradually formed into ideas that she understood in her mind rather than heard as intelligible words. The voice of Namarrkun said, "*Iamcomenow, thatoneisnomore* ...." The words whistled away on the shrieking wind. All about him the Wandjina danced and rippled in moiré patterns of rain and flickering light, singing their siren song of wind and sky and stars.

CHAPTER 33

NAMARRKUN BENT close to Alice, as if sniffing her scent. She instinctively put up her hand in front of her face, and saw with terror that she was bathed in a haze of spiraling light like tiny particles or dust motes siphoning off into the greater gravitational field of the Ancestor. Her molecules and atoms were being sucked into the deep well of stars behind his eyes. She was too shocked to even think how to pull away.

Then for the briefest of instants, she saw and felt the solid core of Namarrkun: cold beyond measuring, with bronze, iridescent skin stretched taught over a humanoid frame, impossibly thin yet strong as steel or titanium. The face showed high cheekbones and a stern brow, with no mouth – what need was there for a mouth when its thoughts were directly imprinted into the particles that made up the physical body? The Ancestor was man and not-man; a Sky God that in the Dreamtime had materialized itself into densely packed strands of energy and shown matter how to make a man, then moved on, leaving its imprint on the universe.

The howls in her ears were fading. Her eardrums must have burst, so that she would be deaf forever, if she lived to worry about such things. Her hands were becoming paler, slightly luminescent, and she realized with another shock that she could see the huge enigmatic face of Namarrkun through them. Looking into its eye sockets, Alice could feel her physical identity slipping away, losing its focus as a human creature and returning to the web of dark matter that held the cosmos in place. The face of the Ancestor filled her field of vision, and the approaching eye socket became a whirlpool of spinning bright sparks into which she fell headlong, as the world she knew ceased to be.

She was enveloped in a texture that she could only describe as velvet darkness, with sparks of light all about her, moving in random spurts and sprints, yet with focused trajectories that spoke of purpose. When she tried to see them clearly, they dashed out of direct sight, and hung in her peripheral vision so that she knew they were there but could not look directly at them. It occurred to her that they might experience her in the same way, as a random spot of consciousness in the greater unformed space-time fabric that moved in waves, rippling and shimmering with potency that might have been tangible if she'd had a body with which to register its dimensions.

The velvet dark gave neither warmth nor chill, but she felt suspended, or more precisely, supported, within it. She stretched her being-ness out a little way from her point of origin like an amoeba and felt another presence, which immediately linked with her. Suddenly she was aware of many others so linked, of legions beyond count that together formed the velvet dark. She laughed, yet had no mouth. Her laughter was golden yellow and shot out from her in spikes of light. She thought purple and a line of musical notes hung in front of her although she had no eyes to see them. She sang the notes and the scent of flowers washed over her although there was no body with which to smell or feel. She was simply a point of awareness, and as such she was aware of everything.

A vast ball of fire burned with reverberating bass notes off to her right, and beyond it another. In a spiraling ring they formed a pattern of unbearable sweetness, a sharp spiciness redolent of orange and cinnamon and something unknown to her but exquisitely scented. Fountains of fire erupted in plumes from the spheres, and she felt them both as a shower of melody and a delicious tickling, although she had no body.

She held consciousness with the others and kept the burning spheres in place, in their great spiraling ring of light and sound. She became aware of other spirals held by other layers of beings above and below her, some compact and some so wide she could not sense the end of their reach. She began to hum, and realized others had joined the song, or perhaps she had joined theirs. Together they hummed and sang as the colors played over the visions that she perceived with no eyes. She was not corporeal – there was no need to define how she and the others like her saw what they heard and tasted what they felt. They were being, essence, and their purpose was holding, touching, humming, keeping things in place.

Occasionally there would come a sensation that had been alarming at first, but became pleasurable once she got used to it. It was a feeling of being extruded, momentarily sucked gently toward something and then released, like a fleck of foam on the outgoing tide. She had no real sense of time against which to measure whether the intervals were regular or how long in between. In fact, she forgot about them each time until they arrived again.

Then somewhere within the closest ring of spheres there came a sound not connected to the rest. It rolled beneath them as a bass note sustained by a cosmic pipe organ, a long, low hollow note that rose and fell like vibrations in a plucked string. It boomed in her non-ears and saturated her photons. Without thought, she dropped out of the web and down into that soundstream, feeling it wash over and through her consciousness as if through a sieve. There was a smell less diffuse, a sharp tang of something that was other than the fabric into which she had been woven. She tasted it in sweet shades of coral and deep scarlet, of white and yellow and black. It was condensed. She decided to go there, and the crushing cold of deep space engulfed her for what might have been heartstopping seconds, if she had possessed a physical heart.

She stood in her own body on the edge of a cliff, surf pounding a rocky shoreline below. The water glittered with diamond sparkles of light, and constellations shone beneath the waves. Behind her, tongues of flame from a bonfire leapt high in the night sky. Turning, she saw a grouping of figures tall and still as a grove of trees at the edge of the firelight. One of them detached itself from the group and came toward her. It was shrinking in size and gradually assuming the form of an Aboriginal woman.

"Where....?" Alice's thought flowed out of her like spilled water.

"Sky Home," came the answer, a flash of color in her mind.

"Who....?"

The woman fixed her with bright eyes of liquid gold. Her bronze hair floated out from her head in curling waves of energy, her darker skin reflecting starlight and firelight. From her outstretched hand, tendrils of color streamed and coiled around her wrist. She touched Alice's forehead.

"Hold fast. Settle the business. Return the *tjuringa*. Be who you are." The Ancestor's instructions popped in her mind in bright splashes of red and yellow.

Then just as suddenly, the woman's hand pushed quickly against Alice's head, and she fell backward into the shining sea below.

"Hey, what's that in the driveway?" Nik could hear fear in the shrill pitch of Margaret's voice.

He slammed on the brakes and the truck skidded to a lurching stop, barely missing the leaping shape in front of them. He got out, ignoring the driving rain, and heard the incessant hoarse barking.

"Dawg? Hey, fellow, it's me ... Dawg, c'mon ...." He reached his hand out. Dawg came forward, eyes bugged and ears flat, growling deep in his throat. Then he leaped at Nik and landed full in his arms, wagging and wriggling as he recognized his master. Nik carried Dawg back to the truck and dumped him in the seat beside Margaret.

"He seems okay. Let's go find your mom."

Margaret nodded, hugging Dawg's wet neck but not smiling. Nik recognized that look, the set of the mouth, eyes slightly squinted. He'd seen it on Alice when she was steeling herself to do something she didn't want to do. He would have liked to say something encouraging, but frankly he feared the worst. He wasn't good with platitudes, having been raised to speak plainly and truthfully regarding all aspects of his life. He'd turned that mindset toward science as a teenager, and generally avoided situations where he would be called upon to mouth insincere assurances and just tell people what they wanted to hear. So he was unable to reassure Margaret that her mother was probably just fine, because he didn't believe it himself.

The message delivered to him by the switchboard assistant didn't make a whole lot of sense, but he got the part about needing to pick up Margaret because something unforeseen had happened. He wasn't well equipped to imagine what that might be, but after the hour he'd just spent talking with Stuart about metaphysics and colliding universes, he was almost willing to admit there some kind of danger that was out of his realm of experience.

As they came around the final driveway curve, he could see with a sinking heart that Alice's car was parked in the middle of the yard with its lights on and driver's door open. There was no normal circumstance under which she would leave her car like that. Margaret's silent shocked expression mirrored what he was thinking – they might already be too late.

Margaret bolted from the truck and raced up the stairs, Dawg at her heels. Nik went to Alice's car, dreading what he might find, but a quick look inside revealed nothing. He turned off the headlights and closed the door, even though the interior was soaked. She was going to have to get that seat reupholstered, and probably the carpet replaced. He stood for a moment longer, listening to the trees dripping water. He knew something terrible had happened, but was unable to imagine what it could have been. Taking a deep breath, he turned his steps toward the house and went up the stairs.

The living room was a wreck, and a burnt-plastic stench hung in the air as smoke still curled out of the fireplace. Footsteps running up the stairs brought Alice back from the warm dark place where her mind had taken refuge.

"Namark...." She was surprised to hear her own voice, and a little disappointed that it produced no colors rippling across her mind.

Her muscles cramped as she tried to move and become reaccustomed to wearing a body – to her heightened senses, physicality was vastly overrated. She was lying on her left side just inside the door, curled into a tight ball. Raising her head, she opened her eyes to slits; it was still light outside and getting lighter now that the storm had passed. Rainwater dripped from the eaves.

"Mom!" Margaret's hands were on her face, touching her cheek. Touching, holding, supporting. "Mom, say something. What happened?" She was on the floor beside Alice, rubbing her mother's hands and icy fingers.

A figure stepped over the threshold, pushing the broken front door out of the way. Alice put up her hand for protection, but was too weak to hold it in place. Holding ... a piece of her was still holding. Holding the spheres in place.

She squinted up at Nik, picking his way over the debris scattered about the room where the storm had blown through it. She saw him kneel beside her along with the small person he called Margaret. Then they were together, holding. She tried to sit up and fell against his chest.

"Easy, you don't need to move," he said.

She shut her eyes again and felt him hoist her up with Margaret's help, and they eased her onto the couch. He was saying something. She might decide to listen, but it was so tempting to just fall asleep. She could sleep for years.

"I tried to hurry, I ... Herre Gud, Alice! Jesus, what did this?" She could feel his hands trembling as he touched her neck and bare chest. His voice sounded like flowers. She could sleep now.

"Mom ... I'm here. It's me." Ah, that was the other one, the spicy scent that had drawn her back – the taste of orchids and water lilies.

Nik was holding her gently, as if she were a sick child, supporting but careful not to squeeze. "That message you left scared the hell out of me," he said. "I picked up Margaret, and we came straight here."

She looked up at him and managed a smile, at least it felt like a smile. "I had the hell scared out of me too, so we're even."

It was a ridiculous thing to say, and she felt laughter bordering dangerously on hysteria bubbling up, making her hiccup.

"Careful, don't choke yourself," he said, raising her head and shoulders up a bit.

Alice smiled again. That was the person she knew as Nik, the voice of reason. She was beginning to appreciate how much that voice meant to her. A delicious calm began to spread over her aching shoulders and back, and she relaxed against him, feeling his warmth. She was sinking again, into enveloping blackness, noting that she had survived somehow, for what that was worth.

"Mom ... please be okay ...."

There was that exotic sweetness again, like a taste or a smell, connected to the voice – in the velvet dark she had understood, but now it was slipping away with her memory of where she had gone. Gone. He was gone, too, the cursed one – her head was empty of him. She was so tired.

"Just let her sleep here while we clean this place up. Jeez, look at the door. Watch out for all that glass."

"Dawg, get out of the way, don't step on the glass. Hey, look in the fireplace."

She could hear them talking, but couldn't follow the thread of their conversation. She had changed, no doubt. But how to explain when she didn't understand it herself? Maybe she could get it back, somehow, but the most important thing was this: she had survived.

FEBRUARY-MARCH

CHAPTER 34

"WELL, HELLO, stranger!"

Gene came out of the museum's documents library on the third floor and spotted her. He shifted his empty cup to his other hand and put out his arm to engulf her in a welcome-back hug. Alice allowed him a brief, friendly squeeze.

"Hi, Gene." Of course he'd be the first one she would run into after a month's leave of absence.

"You look super," he said, his eyes traveling up and down.

Nik's mother would have been pleased; the new silk suit was her gift to Alice during their brief stay in Stockholm after the foray.

"Thanks. Three weeks in Norway and Sweden ... what's not to love?" She would be paying for it for months to come, but the trip had been worth every *krone*.

"Bet it was cold, huh?"

"Not too bad. I used to really hate being cold, but now it doesn't bother me so much."

"Did ya eat any funny mushrooms at that toadstool convention?"

"Sorry, Gene, no, we did not. Just boring morels in wine sauce with roast duck ... things like that." She sucked her stomach in at the thought of those extra pounds added to her overseas baggage.

He followed her as she walked down the hall toward her office. Strange, in some ways it felt like she had never been away, and yet at a fundamental level she was not the same person. Time would have to tell how this fact was going to affect what she did from here on out.

"By the way, I've been using your coffee pot while you were gone."

She'd assumed that. "No problem. That's why I left the door unlocked." Not true, Shelton had asked if she minded letting his intern use her desk for a couple of weeks, since there was no empty office space available.

"And Hannah used your computer a few times, said she was cataloging photos of the shipwreck haul."

Damn. Was she going to have to reestablish her territory all over again? She could see that the door to her office was already open. Gene followed her inside.

"Too bad you missed the Deep Six outfit when they came to divide up the spoils with the State."

"Well, after I get settled back in you can tell me all the gory details."

She balanced her purse, briefcase, and newspaper with her old skill, elbowing the light switch on. Blinking in the white brightness, she noted that maintenance had replaced all the fluorescent tubes. She had expected a fine layer of dust over everything, but clearly her office had been Grand Central Station while she was away. Even her struggling *anthurium* was still alive in its pot on the windowsill. She assumed that was Hannah's work – she was a plant person.

The wing chair was piled high with journals, newsletters, thick manila envelopes probably holding conference proceedings or exhibit announcements, and other assorted company mail. A stack of pink message slips was weighted down by one of the geodes from her bookshelf. Without reading any of it she could tell she would be nonstop busy for days. A small arrangement of spring flowers sat in the middle of a cleared space on her desk. The florist-supplied card read, "Welcome back, not a day too soon. Shelton." A nice, thoughtful gesture. Typical.

"Well, catch ya later," said Gene. Alice nodded, but didn't look up, knowing it would encourage him to stay. "Want me to close the door?"

At that, she did look up. "Yes, thanks." She was surprised, and gave him a direct smile.

Once he was gone, she picked up the pile of mail and plopped it onto her desk. It was then that she realized her desk chair had been replaced with something roomier and more padded. Alice smiled again and wondered if this was another ploy to make her feel welcomed back, or just the evidence of someone using her office who couldn't stand her old basic swivel chair. No matter, the new chair felt comfy and she was keeping it.

Sticking out of the jumble of mail, a gray envelope with the maroon *Libris* emblem caught her eye ... uh oh. She ripped it open and read the polite request for the complete manuscript of "Massalina County Mystery." For a second she couldn't process what that was, and then remembered it as the temporary title she'd given her novel in her query letters. The letter was the editor who'd responded to her back in January. He'd circulated her sample chapters among the senior editors and there was interest, so when could she please supply the whole thing?

She booted up her computer and began composing a reply letter in her mind. So sorry, a house fire has rendered the book inaccessible ... then she suddenly spotted the rolled-up poster leaning against her desk. She smoothed the poster out flat and was swept away with its bold design. The image was an artist's rendering of the *Marquesa* plunging through a black storm-churned ocean, sails in tatters and sailors clinging to the rigging. Broad white lettering across the top proclaimed, "LOST AND FOUND: The Marquesa Saga." Near the bottom of the poster, a sidebar detailed the date, time, and channel listing of the special to be presented on TV by the National Geographic Society in the spring. Well, well. She had missed the TV commentary sequences they'd shot at the Hardison, which was just as well; she hadn't been looking all that photogenic back then.

Clipped to the corner was a note in Jessie's impatient scrawl, a brief noncommittal message about the promo materials and a suggestion that she drop by the lab when she got back. Alice sat quietly holding the note and probing her feelings on that score. Was anything left? There was a twinge, faint and deeply buried. Fine. Let it stay that way. Nik needed no competition, Nik had no competition.

She turned back to the computer and considered her reply to Assistant Editor Edmundson. So sorry, the completed manuscript was lost overboard during her recent cruise through the fjords of Norway, and she doubted whether it could be reconstructed in her lifetime. How would *Libris* like to consider a field guide to Gulf Coast mushrooms instead, complete with professional-quality illustrations and photographs? She could assure him that some of the photos were truly breathtaking in color saturation and clarity of detail ....

As soon as her reply letter was signed, folded, and neatly tucked into an envelope, Alice tossed it into her OUT basket and headed for the door. There was one other thing that had to be done, now, before she found something else to distract her attention.

In the main gallery, the *Land of Legends* exhibit was coming down, and she could hear the voices of the museum crew issuing orders for disassembly long before she came through the gallery entrance. How different it looked when she got there. All the lights were on and the place was a hive of packers, technicians, and union people from the trucking company. Most of the panels were already crated and packing material littered the floor.

Two panels were still in place, so she quietly made her way around hand-trucks and four-wheeled dollies to look one last time into the eyes of Namarrkun. She stepped over a roll of foam packing and stood within feet of the panel. The rain god held his hammers upraised, his companion spirits grouped around him. She brushed the panel with the tips of her fingers and felt ... nothing. It was almost a disappointment, now that she understood why Namarrkun and the Wandjinas had come alive in the world for those few brief weeks. Harrow was gone, and probably she would never know exactly what he had done to become cursed by the Dreamtime Ancestors, but obviously they were not his to control.

She walked over to the Split Rock panel and looked up at the hand stencils. They were red and white, as the slides had shown, and black hand prints were nowhere to be seen. Had she, in the extremity of her fright, imagined changes that had seemed so real at the time? Did it even matter now? She decided it didn't, and left the gallery, walking up the ramp and turning toward the museum store.

Faye sat in her usual spot on a high stool at the cashier's counter, chin in hand, watching out through the glass walls of the shop. Waving to her, Alice pushed open the door and went in. Faye hopped off the stool and met her with open arms.

"Wow, look at you! Did you have a great time?" She gave Alice a crunching hug and stepped back. "I want to hear everything. I bet Margaret hated being left behind. I know I would."

Alice laughed. "Yeah, she put up a bit of a fight about it, but with school and the expense, it just wasn't practical. She didn't mind staying in town with my sister-in-law too much. I brought you a little something." Alice reached in her pocket and handed Faye a small box.

Faye opened the lid and then sucked in her breath, holding the box up to the light. Nestled in a bed of cotton fluff was a heavy sterling silver pendant of a Thor's hammer on an equally sturdy silver chain.

"I got that from the shop at the Nordic Museum in Stockholm."

"Alice, this is gorgeous. I don't know what to say."

"Got myself one, too. I'm thinking of adopting Thor as my patron saint," she said, only half kidding.

"Liked it there, did you?"

"Loved it. I could live there. Norway was great, too, we had a great time in Trondheim, where the conference and foray were held, but I felt really at home in Stockholm."

"You met Nik's family, I guess?"

"Oh yeah. His dad's a Lutheran minister, very proper and reserved with a great orator's voice. His mom is a little more relaxed, but still kind of quiet. Really nice people. His youngest sister's a lark. Took me shopping, and we spent a lot of time going to all the museums in the area. Yeah, I could live there."

"I thought you hated the cold. You must have gone through a transformation while you were there."

Alice laughed out loud. That was, more or less, an excellent statement of how she felt. "I believe I did."

On this her first day back at work, Alice had driven into Citrus Park along the route through Whiteoak, but now she and Margaret were headed home down State Road 87, which would take them past the camp and the two churches.

"Did you sense anything?" Margaret asked when Alice told her about the exhibit's end.

"No, there was nothing. The connection's broken. I even put my hands on the panels, but they're gone. Not that I'm complaining."

"I know. I didn't see the Quinkan either, not in my dreams or anything, the whole time you and Nik were in Norway. I think it really is gone. I hope."

Alice relaxed into the driver's seat. First thing tomorrow she had an appointment to drop her car off at the trim shop in Magnolia and have the upholstery and carpeting replaced. Then it would be like new, and all traces of their ordeal would be erased. The events of this past winter seemed far away now, even imaginary, yet she had been avoiding the county road and its landmarks for the four days since she'd returned from overseas. Today was the first time she'd gotten the nerve to drive past it.

"Mom, look." Margaret sat bolt upright, craning her neck.

Alice looked toward the clearing in the pines. It was more than a month since she'd been trapped in the old church by Harrow and the Quinkan, and she wondered if she was ready for the sight of it again. But it wasn't what she'd expected to see.

The belfry had fallen and collapsed a part of the roof. One wall was caved in, and a long flatbed truck backed up to the entrance held most of the two-by-fours salvaged from the framing. Several men in their shirtsleeves, members of St. Christopher's congregation, she supposed, worked at dismantling the weathered siding and tossed termite-riddled scraps onto a trash heap near the truck.

"What do you think happened?"

Alice glanced again at the remains, receding in the rearview mirror.

"Died of old age, like everybody should. There was really no reason to leave it standing. Nobody was using it anymore."

Alice settled back and watched the road. It was almost warm enough to roll the windows down, and she noted with pleasure that the redbud trees scattered through the woods were starting to put out sprays of tiny pink flowers. The dogwoods wouldn't be far behind.

That evening, after supper, she sat on the steps with Margaret, listening to the frog chorus coming from the pond. It was a beautiful spring night, and in the moonlight she could see that Figaro's dogwood tree was just beginning to bud out.

"I missed you guys," Margaret said, leaning against her.

"Same here. Next trip, you go with us."

They sat for a while, just listening to the woods. Finally Margaret broke the silence.

"I've been thinking ...."

"Yeah?"

"If what's-his-face was really cursed, then the Wandjinas musta been after him for a long time if they only caught him here."

"Maybe he went where they couldn't reach him until I helped him come back. You can bet I won't do that again."

"For sure."

"Not that I think he could come back. I wish you could have seen how that looked when Namarrkun got him ... snuffed out, just like that." She pinched her thumb and index finger together.

"Awesome."

"In a sense, I think the Wandjina were like the Furies, following him across time and space, for whatever taboo kind of thing he must have done. Because that's what it looks like to me, that there was a transgression of Aboriginal Law that had to be punished. And when those two things – the exhibit and my novel – intersected, they all came through. Hey," she nudged Margaret. "Forget about all that. It's just good to be home."

Music came drifting through the open door, and Margaret jumped to her feet.

"Nik's watching *Spirited Away* again. Hey, don't start without me," she called, the screen door banging behind her.

Alice stood up and went down the steps to empty out her car before taking it to the body shop in the morning. She collected her umbrella, music CDs, the new car phone charger Nik had bought her, and all the books and trash from the floorboards. Taking one last look, she felt around the driver's seat for any change that might have fallen down between the seat and the transmission console. There were a couple of quarters, a ballpoint pen, and something else. Something with corners. She got down on her knees and looked under the seat and saw something wedged up under the frame. She aimed her flashlight at it just to make sure, but there could be no doubt, no matter how much she wished to the contrary. The missing notebook had been found.

Alice stood up, pondering what to do. She knew what Cecil Rider would say: burn it now to a pile of ashes. But a part of her hungered to read it through carefully in the light of what she now knew about Harrow and the entities that had pursued him. One thing she knew without question, she couldn't leave it under the seat for the upholstery guys to find.

She walked out into the yard and looked up at the night sky. The bright dusting of stars along the Milky Way was clearly visible, so close she almost thought she could hear the ceaseless humming holding it in place. She stared unblinking at the sky, then sighed. If she was hoping to be struck with a sudden message from the velvet dark that would tell her what to do, it was not forthcoming.

Turning back to the car, she tried to remember how she had tasted a bit of that knowledge during her fleeting immersion in the world membrane. And there was something else. It lay at the edge of her mind like a faint whiff of perfume from a night-blooming primrose. She had understood something that seemed radically important at the time, but now it was gone.

Perhaps one day she would be allowed to recall what it was.

ABOUT THE AUTHOR

M.A.C. Petty has been fascinated with the Dreamtime tales of the Australian Aborigines for decades. She has an enduring interest in and passion for modern Aboriginal art, which features prominently in much of her writing. Now, she brings together all the mystery and compelling imagery of the Dreamtime traditions into her first novel, *Thin Line Between*, Book 1 of the four-book series, *The Wandjina Quartet*.